She d

with

She tried to ignore N   rate on the task at hand.

She knew how strong he was, how firm his muscles were. It was the first thing she'd noticed earlier when she'd been pressed against him beneath the stairs. She'd felt his arm tighten and tense beneath her hand as she'd pinched him to end his unwanted kiss. It mattered not that it had been a most pleasant kiss. More than pleasant, it had been world-tilting. Still, it was completely unwarranted and unwanted.

"Why were you here tonight?" she asked. His gaze slowly rose to meet hers, and the full impact of his clear blue eyes nearly stole her breath away.

"Perhaps I came for that kiss," he said, his mouth tilting in a smile.

PRAISE FOR

SEDUCE ME

"Robyn DeHart's vibrant characters sweep the reader into a clever and sensual romp that is not to be missed."

—Julia London, *New York Times*
bestselling author of *The Book of Scandal*

*Please turn this page for more
acclaim for Robyn DeHart...*

Also by Robyn DeHart

Seduce Me

Desire Me

Robyn DeHart

FOREVER

NEW YORK   BOSTON

Copyright © 2010 by Robyn DeHart
Excerpt from *Treasure Me* copyright © 2010 by Robyn DeHart
All rights reserved. Except as permitted under the U.S. Copyright Act of 1976, no part of this publication may be reproduced, distributed, or transmitted in any form or by any means, or stored in a database or retrieval system, without the prior written permission of the publisher.

Cover design by Alan Ayers
Hand lettering by Kate Forrester
Book design by Giorgetta Bell McRee

Forever
Hachette Book Group
237 Park Avenue
New York, NY 10017
Visit our website at www.HachetteBookGroup.com.

Forever is an imprint of Grand Central Publishing. The Forever name and logo is a trademark of Hachette Book Group, Inc.

Printed in the United States of America

First Printing: June 2010

10 9 8 7 6 5 4 3 2 1

To Kathleen Woodiwiss, Amanda Quick, Teresa Medeiros, and Johanna Lindsey, you are the reason I started writing historical romance, and what an amazing ride this is. Thank you for the wonderful stories.

And to Paul for more reasons than I can count, but mostly because you always think I'm beautiful even when I'm neck deep in a deadline and I haven't put on real clothes in days. And for always saying, "You can do this." I love you, baby.

Acknowledgments

Most good books are a collaboration of sorts, so I would be remiss if I did not thank several people. To my critique/ brainstorming partners Emily and Hattie, I honestly don't know what I'd do without y'all. You're always there when I need to bounce around some ideas. I hear the beach calling. To my husband, Paul, who has always been a great supporter and fan of my work, you had some great ideas for this book. Thanks for sharing your brilliance. My amazing editors, Amy and Alex, who patiently hold my hand while offering feedback I so desperately need. You push me to be the writer I need to be. A huge thank you to Claire Brown and the rest of the GCP art department—y'all are unbelievable and so talented it's ridiculous. Thank you for creating such beautiful covers for me and my characters. And last, but certainly not least, my wonderfully charming agent, Christina Hogrebe, who has talked me down off more bridges than I can count. You are a gem and I love working with you. Thanks for everything.

Desire Me

Prologue

~~~~

On the coast of Cornwall, 1873

Maxwell Barrett lit his lantern, then moved into the damp cave. Behind him, he could hear the waves beating against the rock that surrounded the opening of the cavern. He didn't have much time. It was that reason alone that drove him forward at this swift pace. Otherwise he would have meandered, investigating every nook and cranny he could reach. But he only had two hours before the tide rose to once again cover the entrance to the cave.

Two hours before he would drown.

Unless he had miscalculated, and then perhaps he had even less time. Either way, he needed to get in there and find the map, then get the hell to dry land.

The cave appeared and disappeared with the tides, which was why it had taken him nearly four months to locate the blasted area, and still it remained to be seen whether he'd find what he had sought for the past two years.

Beneath his boots, the uneven rocks—slick with moss and water—made his journey all the more harrowing. He'd slipped several times already, but he held firm to his lantern and kept moving forward. He knew he was right about this cave, he could feel it.

Today he would find the map of Atlantis.

He skidded across a wet stone, his weight shifted, and he fell hard upon one knee. The rock sliced through his wool trousers, biting into his flesh. Fortunately, he managed to avoid shattering the lantern. Max got to his feet and inhaled sharply.

He could do this. Hell, when he was fifteen, he'd found a long-forgotten buried treasure of a pirate queen. He was seventeen now. He propelled himself forward, careful where he stepped. Still, it was Atlantis...finding the one and only map to the lost continent would certainly prove that Plato's writings were fact and not fiction. If he did that, his parents would truly notice. Everyone would have to take notice.

Long stalactites reached down to him like ancient fingers. Max bent and twisted to avoid impaling himself, but he kept moving forward. Always forward. Still he could hear the waves behind him, like an hourglass reminding him he had a finite amount of time.

The deeper he traveled, the more constricted the air became. He sucked in a breath; his nose filled with the chalky scent that could only be found in earth's little crevices. His heart beat wildly.

The tunnel before him split. The walls of the cave pulled in and formed two paths. One was big enough for him to continue walking, though crouched over; the other was not even large enough for a small child to pass through. The choice was made for him. The Atlanteans who had ventured here before him to hide the map certainly would have used the larger passage.

Still he hesitated.

The stalactites were a reminder that flowing water could grow rocks as well as break them down. He hoped time had not changed the constant flowing water and narrowed the correct path, thus forcing him in the wrong direction.

Only one way to find out. Max felt along the rock wall with one hand, and with the other, he held the lantern in front of him, though the pitiful amount of light made the exercise seem almost worthless. Beneath his fingers, the stone was cool and wet. Something slithered under his palm, and he jerked back his hand.

Again the area narrowed, so much that, in order to continue, he had to turn sideways. Drowning would certainly be a most dreadful way to perish, but drowning in this constricted channel would be even worse. He picked up his pace, unable to run, but moving quickly through the stone passage. The rock at his back brushed through his hair as he moved, and the stones in front of him would skin his nose if he wasn't careful.

The darkness ahead of him grew thicker and blacker as he hiked farther into the cave. Finally the crevice he'd been moving through opened back up. He took a step, but found only air beneath his boot. His balance shifted, and he leaned forward, nearly falling, but he was able to grab the cavern wall to his right to steady himself.

He found himself standing on the ledge of an underground lake. He held the lantern out and bent over to peer into the pool. It was difficult to see, but the water must be several feet below him, and while it was not a fall that would likely result in death, he'd prefer not to test the fates.

The ledge encircled the water, and he could tell that the area to his right was far narrower than the one to his left. So Max moved to the left and followed the rim around. The opening he'd climbed through was the only break in the cavern's wall around the lake, at least as far as he could see.

According to his research, this cave should lead him to where the Atlanteans had hidden their map. Everything he'd read indicated it would be sealed, dry in the midst of water. Max looked up, trying his best to scan the ceiling of the cavern. It seemed highly improbable that someone had climbed to the top, because the walls were slick with moisture. And there didn't appear to be any legitimate hiding places above to stash anything.

Dim lantern light glanced off the walls, enough for him to see the shape of his own hand, but not much more. So it was possible more lay ahead of him. He kept moving.

The ledge narrowed. Nearly his entire boot hung off the edge; only a small sliver of his heel remained supported. He pressed his back against the cavern wall and slid himself across the small ridge. Suddenly the glow from his lantern revealed a large chunk of quartz, creating an eerie bluish light.

It was here, in this angle and in that lapis glow, that his lantern reflected off something in the center of the lake. A wooden pedestal jutted out from the water, and sitting atop it was some sort of container.

His heart quickened. That had to be it. The map was hidden in there. He was seconds away from slipping his feet off the ledge to jump into the lake when he noticed something moving in the water. He slid over to his right to position himself on a sturdier section of the ledge, and he once again bent forward with his lantern in hand.

There in the water drifted a decaying body. Nearly down to the bones, the corpse wore clothes that were shredded and hung like an ill-fitted suit. It swayed back and forth in a macabre dance of death. Through the abdomen of the man was a wooden spike. Then Max noticed several other similar spikes of different sizes and heights scattered around the wooden pedestal.

If Max had jumped, or fallen, into the water, that could be him now, skewered on a pole, waiting to bleed to death.

He stood up straight. "Interesting."

Without a bridge from this ledge, how was he supposed to get to the map without skewering himself on the spikes? He looked around, scanning his surroundings for any material he might be able to use. Nothing.

The sound of water falling drew his attention to the crevice he'd crawled out of. Water spilled out of it, draining into the lake below. He watched as the dead body continued to undulate in the dark liquid.

Therein lay Max's answer. The only way to get to that pedestal without impaling himself was to allow the lake to fill up until it reached the platform. Waiting that long, though, would significantly decrease his odds of getting back out of the cave alive.

There didn't appear to be another way. It came down to two choices: walk away from the map and therefore any proof of the lost continent, or risk his life in hopes of creating fact out of fiction. He inhaled slowly and straightened his shoulders. If there was one truth about Maxwell Barrett—it was that he was relentless in his search.

He would get that map today or he would die trying.

Max had left his pocket watch on the shore when he swam to the cave's opening so he had no true measure of time. However, nearly two feet of empty space stretched from the top of the water to the pedestal. So he guessed it would take close to thirty minutes for the lake to fill. He was a strong swimmer. He would have enough time, and he would make it out of here alive.

No spikes pierced the water immediately below him. Slowly he lowered himself from the ledge into the pool, the cold ocean water chilling him instantly. He trod water trying, in vain, to acclimate himself to the frigid water. Just a little more depth in the pool, and he could make his move.

He ignored the temperature and swam toward the pedestal. Water was now pouring over the ledge more rapidly. The surge of water pulled the dead man into the murky depths, but he bubbled back to the surface after a moment. A handful of spikes still breached the surface, but the water had swallowed most of them. He did his best to navigate around them. He accidentally kicked one with the tip of his boot, then swam right into another one. A sharp tip scraped across his shin, tearing through his trousers and cutting his leg. Age had done nothing to dull the danger of the wooden spikes.

With considerable concentration, he made his way to the center pole that held up the wooden platform. There was enough water in the pool now that he could heave himself up to reach the pedestal. Gazing down upon his treasure at last, shivering slightly in the cold, he held his breath, not quite believing his eyes. Upon closer inspection, Max could see that the container in the center was a glass tube. He tried to pry it off, twist it, pull it—anything to remove it from its resting place—but it would not budge.

He'd come too far to give up now. With a swift movement, he slammed his fist into the side of the glass, and it shattered. He retrieved the leather package, tucked it inside his shirt, and then jumped into the water, ignoring the cuts on his hand. He came within an inch of hitting another spike. There was no time to be relieved, though; the water surged around him and soon the path he'd taken here would be completely submerged.

Quickly he climbed back onto the ledge and made his way back to the thin crevice he'd followed to the pool. The elevated water hit him just below his waist as he slid back the way he'd come, though this time with no lantern to guide him. He'd left it behind when he'd jumped into the pool, and there'd been no time to retrieve it.

Water lapped at his belt. Panic pulled at him with bony fingers of dread. He pushed the fear aside and moved forward, but his pace was sluggish as he fought against the water's current. Eventually, though, he made it out of the tight crevice and back into the main part of the cave, just as the water reached his shoulders.

A wave crashed against the opening to the cave, and a moment later, as water surged in past him, he nearly lost his footing. He sucked in a huge breath as the water surrounded and consumed him.

Max swam.

Against the current and with the waves slamming into him, he swam with every ounce of strength he had. His lungs burned and screamed for air as he fought the water. Salt stung his eyes as he searched for light at the surface.

Finally he breached the surface and gasped for breath.

Yes, he could have given up and let death take him in that cave, but then he'd be as nameless as the corpse back in that lake. Finding this map would put his name on the lips of everyone in England.

He allowed the waves to rock into him as he floated and concentrated on breathing. A minute later, he was swimming again; this time to the rocks that climbed up to the shoreline above.

The cliff bit into his hand as he struggled up to the land. His damp clothes weighed him down, and the exertion from the swim had wearied his legs, but still he kept pulling himself upward. Ten minutes or so later, he stood at the top, his breathing labored and his heart pounding. He was exhausted, but exhilarated as well. He might very well have just changed history.

The package tucked in his shirt was coated with some waxy material that Max assumed made it water-resistant. He reached inside and pulled out the folded material, then slowly, reverently, opened it.

It was beautiful—unlike any map he'd ever seen—the rings of Atlantis, alternating water and land. Hand drawn and hand colored, the water channels seemed as if they'd be wet to the touch, and the mountain ridges sharp beneath his finger. Poseidon's palace shone brightly from the center ring of land.

Max folded the map back and slipped it into the pouch at his side. He had done it. He had proven the existence of the lost continent of Atlantis.

Chapter One

London, January 1888

Spencer Cole turned the pistol over in his hand, the gleaming metal shimmering beneath the moonlight. Tonight could go one of two ways, and he was prepared for either. He tucked the gun into the waistband of his trousers. A carriage rumbled down the street, so he pressed himself against the outer wall of the townhome.

The cloying sweet smell of jasmine permeated the air. Damn garden was full of the stuff. He hated jasmine. With one finger, he plucked a delicate white bloom, dropped it to the dirt, and ground it beneath his boot.

His greatcoat hugged his shoulders and helped to keep him shrouded in the near darkness. Earlier he'd changed clothes and removed his bright white shirt in favor of something darker—a muddy brown to better blend with the night.

He considered the task at hand. This officer had been more challenging to find. Initially Spencer had been told the man was in Africa, so Spencer had decided to wait until the officer returned to London. Then two weeks ago, he had intercepted a message that stated otherwise. If the note was to be believed, the man sat upstairs now.

The first target had lived alone and was known for drinking, on duty or off. He'd been loud and boisterous and disliked by plenty. Spencer had not even bothered offering him a choice. Killing him had been easy. Too easy. He'd been passed out from too much drink, and it had taken nothing more than a lit match to the curtains for the entire townhome to go up in flames. Worthless bastard.

Spencer had been unable to leave a message with that body. He'd allowed his temper to get the better of him, letting his own personal bias distract him from his task. But it was crucial that people knew of his purpose, his destiny.

So with the second, he'd been more precise and taken more time. First he'd offered the man a deal; a chance to be a part of something important. The fool had declined. Spencer had used a blade then, slicing the man from ear to ear until his blood had poured out and his head had nearly been severed. It had been exceptionally messy. Without a fire, he'd been able to leave his first message with specific instructions to print said message in the *Times*. Spencer had no way of knowing whether the guardians he sought read any of London's newspapers, but Londoners did. And printing such notes would breed their fear. Spencer loved that. Certainly Scotland Yard was on alert now, and the townspeople would follow shortly.

Which led him to number three. Spencer eyed the lit

window above his head. This officer had a family, a mistress, and too many friends to count. And many accommodations from her majesty. The officer had much to lose. Perhaps all of those reasons would persuade him to accept Spencer's generous offer. If not...

Spencer spat.

After discovering this man was in fact in London, Spencer had begun to track his movements, watching him as a hunter studies his prey. He'd done the same with all of the officers he was targeting.

Spending two weeks in this sweet-smelling garden, watching and waiting, had seriously tried Spencer's patience. But tonight was the night. Tonight the target was alone. His wife and two daughters had gone out to the theater followed by a late-night ball and would be gone for hours yet. Inside the house, the older man sat, unaware of his part in a much bigger plan.

There were far more officers available than Spencer needed, so he'd carefully chosen his targets. Seven lives to signify the seven rings of Atlantis. They would fall by his hand or join him and fall from grace. Either way, they would begin the prophecy, leading his army. He looked down at the ring on his right hand, the one that led him directly to the elixir. This was his destiny, and it mattered not who got hurt in the process. A prophecy older than anything here in London, this was bigger than even he.

A clock somewhere in the distance chimed the eleventh hour. It was time.

He made his way to the French doors that led from the garden into a parlor. With considerable force, he was able to break the lock and open the door. The room was dark and uninhabited, but enough light from the hall scattered onto the floor, preventing him from walking into any of the furniture. The ripe scent of furniture polish tickled his nose.

He knew that General Lancer's study occupied the first floor, so he crept out of the parlor and down the hall. A scullery maid stepped into the hall, and her eyes widened as she saw him. She opened her mouth to scream just as he grabbed her by the throat. He pulled her close to him. Her large brown eyes teared up as she stared at him.

"Do not scream," he said. "If you scream, I'll be forced to kill you. Understand?"

She nodded fervently.

Of course, he would kill her regardless. However, he preferred to do so quietly as to not alert his true target to his presence. Quickly he withdrew the knife he kept secured to his boot and shoved the blade into her throat. Her scream was caught as the knife went through, and the hissing sound of air oozed from the wound. She fell to the floor in a crumpled heap, her brown gaze frozen with fear.

She'd given him no option. It was better for him to make his way through the house undetected.

Step by step, he crept through the hallway, peering into the rooms flanking the corridor. He nearly walked in on a couple of servants pressed up against a large buffet in a darkened dining room, but their muted sounds of passion covered the slight squeak of the door.

Finally he found the correct room. A soft glow filtered beneath the doorjamb, and as he pushed the door open, he came face to face with the man he sought.

The older man sat behind his desk, white shirt open, no cravat, with books and journals piled on the desktop.

"Who the devil are you?" he asked. He came to his feet.

"It matters not who I am," Spencer said evenly. "Sit down."

"I will do no such thing." His hair, though white, was still full and wavy, and his eyes still sparked with intelligence. "Wait a moment"—those eyes narrowed—"I do know you. What do you want?"

Spencer could not deny the slight thrill that shot through him. He reveled in being recognized. But that was not his purpose tonight. He deliberately slowed his breathing.

"I have a proposition for you," he said evenly.

The man's nostrils flared. "Did she send you?"

"A great war is coming," Spencer said, ignoring the man's question. "England is not prepared."

"We have the greatest military in the world," the man sputtered. Deep lines creased his already wrinkled forehead. "You have some nerve."

He wouldn't be one of the select, Spencer could see that, but he had a duty to fulfill. Slowly, he withdrew the tiny vial. "I have the solution here. One tiny drop and you would become cleverer, stronger, more alert. The best general you could be." Spencer nearly rolled his eyes. Were it up to him, he would simply dispose of all of them and start fresh with men of his own choosing. But his specific instructions were to invite them to join his cause first, and should they decline, only then could he kill them.

"I don't know what you're trying to imply, but I can assure you, I take great offense. I am already the best general I can be or most any other man could be." He braced both arms on his desk. "I think it is time you should leave. Tomorrow I shall send up a report of this event. Intruding into my home, insulting me, and then offering me some sort of magical potion that is probably nothing more than opium. I won't have it," he growled.

Spencer allowed the man to rant; in truth he found the whole display rather entertaining. Especially in light of what was shortly to come.

"If that is the case, then I'm afraid your skills are no longer needed," he told him. With one swift movement, he withdrew the pistol from his waistband. "I believe I told you to sit down."

Resignation showed clearly in the target's face, and he slowly lowered himself into his chair. Despite the years the general had spent in the upper reaches of the military, his battle instincts had not dulled. He had the sense to know when he faced a superior opponent.

"I have plenty of money," Lancer said. "And I can have my wife's jewels brought down to you. Whatever you want, I can provide." He held out his hand. "Here, I accept your offer. I'll take the vial."

Briefly Spencer considered the general's offer. His military skills could prove useful, but it was too late now. The man's loyalty would always be in question. Pity.

"If only it were that simple," Spencer told the man. "I'm certain I could use a man of your stature and skills. But you should have accepted my offer when you had the chance." He swiped a decorative cushion from the chair behind him, then walked to the desk and aimed the gun directly at the man. "But it was not to be."

"All I have to do is call, and I'll have a room full of men coming to my aid," Lancer warned, though the deep swallow suggested more fear than threat.

If that were true, the man would already have called for assistance. Spencer stepped around the desk to stand behind the man. He slid the pistol against the thick, white hair. "Go ahead." Spencer shrugged. "Call for help if you must, but then I will be forced to kill them as well. I would prefer not to do that."

"Did she send you?" His voice wavered. Then he shook his head as if answering his own question. "Surely not."

Enough playing. As much as he enjoyed the torment for his own personal enjoyment, he had a task to accomplish. "No more talking," he whispered. Then he placed the cushion between the pistol and the man's temple and pulled the trigger.

Only four more to go.

Sabine Tobias turned over in bed and stared at the dark ceiling above her. She hadn't been sleeping well since they moved to London seven months before. After living in a country village for the first twenty-four years of her life, she hadn't yet grown accustomed to the sounds of the city. Tonight she would have sworn she'd heard something or rather someone rustling down below her window. Inhaling, she held her breath and attuned her ears, listening. There, she heard it again. Perhaps merely the wind, or an alley cat, but there was definitely a noise.

Her ears seemed to pick up every stray sound. It was probably nothing, but what if it was more? A thief, perhaps. Or a murderer? Sweat beaded down the center of her back. Her stomach roiled with nerves.

She swung her legs to the floor and padded out of her tiny room and into the hallway. There she nearly ran into her eldest aunt, Lydia.

"Did you hear it, too?" the older woman asked.

"I did," Sabine whispered.

"I think someone is outside." Lydia held her candle out

in front of her as she walked to the staircase, her pale yellow nightdress billowing behind her.

They hadn't even gotten halfway down the stairs before her other two aunts left their rooms, and together they all crept to the first floor to investigate. Lydia stopped at the base of the stairs.

"The noise," Lydia whispered. "It's inside now."

Sabine's heart seized with panic. Slowly the four of them tiptoed into the storeroom at the back of their little shop. There, sitting at a small table, was a man. It was an intruder!

"I'm sorry to wake you," the man said, his voice wispy and full of breath.

"Madigan?" Lydia asked. She rushed forward.

Relief washed over Sabine so quickly she nearly fell over. At least her aunts knew this intruder.

" 'Tis me," he said.

"You scared the devil out of us," Agnes said. Her fading red hair hung loose in a braid down her back. It flipped over her shoulder as she chastised the man.

He shook his head, then coughed. "I don't have much time. I've come to warn the child."

Lydia placed her candle on the table, then lowered herself into the chair next to him. "Calliope," she said to her youngest sister. "Let us get some more light in here."

Soft light spread through the room as Sabine helped Calliope light the wall sconces. They hadn't yet been able to afford the new electric lights, but the old lamps shone brightly.

Madigan, as Lydia had called him, crouched in the wooden chair, looking pale and in pain. At the first complete sight of him, Sabine's aunts gasped.

"What has happened to you?" Agnes asked, moving closer to him.

Calliope withdrew a bottle of homemade liquor from behind a cabinet and poured him a glass. "You don't look well, old friend."

All three of her aunts knew this man and yet she had never seen him, nor heard them speak of him. And she had lived with them her entire life. Even when her parents were alive, her aunts had always been there. Sabine knew he was not from their village, of that she was certain. Nor had she seen him here in London, and they had been here with their little shop for nearly a year.

He drank the whiskey, then nodded toward Sabine. "Come here, all of you."

It was on her tongue to give him a tart reply, because she did not know this man, but Lydia shook her head. "Sabine, now is not the time," she said.

Sabine nodded, then drew closer and sat in the chair Lydia had abandoned. Agnes sat next to her, and Calliope hovered with her bottle of whiskey.

Madigan was a tall man and nearly as broad. His thick, dark curly hair and full beard covered much of his face, but could not disguise his kind brown eyes.

"I have much to tell you in very little time," he said in a gravelly voice, then coughed again. He winced in pain.

"May I get you anything?" Sabine asked. "We are healers of sorts. Calliope"—she turned to her aunt—"could you fetch my kit? It's right behind you on that shelf."

He reached a hand out and stilled Calliope. "There is nothing any of you can do to help me." He took a ragged breath. "I came to warn the guardian."

Sabine's stomach twisted. They had never, not once, revealed the identity of the guardian outside their village.

She eyed her aunts, trying to gauge their reaction, but their expressions revealed nothing. She turned back to the man.

"There are three of us," he said. He shifted in his seat and his face contorted with another wave of internal pain. He fell into a coughing fit.

"Us," he had said. So this was one of the other guardians. She, of course, knew of the existence of the other two guardians, the Seer and the Sage. But as each of the three guardians lived separately in their own villages, she had never met either of them. They kept to their own, as it were. She knew only that they were both men.

Historically all of the guardians had been men. Until her mother, then Agnes. And her aunts believed Sabine would be next. Though Sabine knew that would not be the case. If she were meant to be guardian, she would have been selected when her mother died. She used to argue that point with her aunts, but her protests had fallen on deaf ears, so now she didn't bother.

It had been a shock to all of her people when her mother had been born. Every Atlantean family up until then had always had at least one male child. Never before had an Atlantean fathered a female first and then three subsequent females. So when Sabine's grandfather had passed, the people had no choice but to accept her mother as the first female guardian. And the ancient ceremony had confirmed that choice. They had all believed she would fail, and when she did, they had mocked her name.

"But very soon," Madigan continued once his coughing eased, "only two will remain." He placed a warm hand on Sabine's shoulder. "The prophecy has begun," he said.

"Phinneas warned us months ago," Agnes said quietly.

Madigan nodded. "Yes, Phinneas saw the signs sometime last year. Warning signs, but this—" He looked up at them, his eyes filled with such sorrow. "It has started. The Chosen One has arrived."

"Are you certain?" Calliope asked.

Sabine knew that Agnes had received a warning, but she'd never known from whom. This must mean Phinneas was the Seer, which meant Madigan was the Sage. The warning was why they had moved here to London, why they had opened this little shop in Piccadilly.

"The prophecy," Sabine repeated. She'd been warned of the prophecy her entire life. What Atlantean hadn't heard tell of it? Though none had ever seen it, at least none that she knew. Perhaps this Phinneas knew the specifics, though everyone knew that the prophecy had been torn from the Seer's book.

All Sabine knew was there would be a battle and the guardians would protect the elixir from the Chosen One.

Agnes was in danger.

Fear took root in Sabine's stomach. She took a steadying breath. She refused to get distracted by anxiety. She would not make the same mistakes her mother had. Sabine had every intention of redeeming her family name by preventing the prophecy from being fulfilled.

When she and her aunts had received that warning those months ago, they'd developed a plan.

"We've prepared ourselves as best we could," she spoke up. "'Tis why we moved to London. We are on alert, but certainly we should not live in fear." She said it aloud to remind herself, to squelch the remnants of fear tingling inside her.

Madigan smiled. "She is a brave one."

"Yes," Agnes agreed.

"Tell me about this scheme of yours, child," Madigan said.

"Since we know very little of the prophecy," Sabine began, "it has been challenging to prepare. But we know the Chosen One will rise and attempt to steal the elixir, thus destroying the guardians." Sabine sat forward. "And, of course, we know the dangers of misusing the elixir."

Sabine paused while Madigan nearly collapsed in a coughing fit. He took a large gulp of whiskey, then nodded for her to continue.

"Are you certain there is nothing we can offer you?" Sabine asked. "Surely you must know that Agnes is the Healer." Perhaps he did not trust their abilities. No doubt word had spread about what had happened to Sabine's father. It had taken years before anyone in her village had trusted the Healer again.

"No, please continue," he said.

"We know that the Chosen One has a way to detect our presence, somehow sensing those who have used the elixir. So as a precaution, I came up with a way for us to hide in plain sight," Sabine said. "Obviously, we can do nothing to hide ourselves or the fact that we're exposed to the elixir. But we can change those around us. We're selling the elixir," Sabine said.

Madigan straightened as best he could; a deep frown creased his brow. "Have you gone mad? That's an invitation for danger," Madigan said, then turned to her aunts. "How could you let her do this? You'll lead him right to your door."

"We are not fools," Sabine said. She reached over to Calliope, who handed her one of the glass jars. "It is no different than the healing concoctions, and we are very careful with the measurements." She set it on the table in front of him.

" 'Tobias Miracle Crème for the Face,' " Madigan read. "Are you quite serious?"

She said nothing more, but sat quietly while he thought on what she'd told him. So far her aunts had said nothing. This had been her idea, a plan to protect Agnes. They had thought long and hard before agreeing and setting the plan in motion. Now, several months later, their products were successful, and the elixir was slowly being spread across London.

He uncorked the lid, then held the jar of crème to his nose and inhaled. With the tip of one finger, he withdrew a small amount and rubbed it onto his arm. "It absorbs into their skin," he muttered. His brown gaze lifted to meet hers. "So to him, we all look the same."

She nodded. "We also have other products. In fact, we've become somewhat of a sensation in the last few weeks. Society, it would seem, has taken notice."

"How much elixir do you use in each jar?" Madigan asked.

"One single drop," Agnes said.

"I suppose the women in town are loving how well it dispels their wrinkles," Madigan said.

"Precisely," Agnes said. "The more they use it, the more it throws him off our scent, so to speak."

Madigan was quiet for a few moments, then he nodded. "That's brilliant. I had wondered why you'd relocated to London. It's rather unorthodox for guardians to abandon their village."

"For their protection," Sabine said. She'd known it was a risk to move Agnes away from their people, but it would have been an even greater risk to stay. They'd made arrangements for their people to come and retrieve the healing ointments and tonics and bring them back to the village.

"Madigan, I don't understand how you know the

prophecy has begun. Have you spoken with Phinneas recently?" Agnes asked. "He has not mentioned it in his letters."

"No, not in the last month or two," he said.

Lydia stepped forward. "Did you find the map?"

Generations of their people had searched for the map of Atlantis, as it was the only remaining place to find the prophecy in its entirety. But their hunts had been futile.

"Not precisely found it, but I have located it," Madigan said, then he coughed, a chest-rattling, body-racking cough that resulted in his wiping blood from his mouth.

"Madigan, why have you not taken some of your elixir to clear your lungs?" Sabine asked. "Or allowed Agnes to assist you; she's a wonderful healer."

"I told you, it is far too late for me." He shook his head and was quiet for a moment before he spoke again. "I couldn't stop him. He hit me over the head, knocked me out. He took it."

"The elixir?" Lydia said.

Madigan simply nodded.

"How long have you been without it?" Agnes asked.

"More than a day," he said. Then shook his head. "I don't know how long I was out, so I'm really not certain how long. I was so careful." He gripped Agnes's hand. "I'm so sorry."

"It has begun then," Calliope said.

That was why Madigan looked so ill. If a guardian lost his elixir and did not recover it within two days' time, he would perish. She had seen it happen before with her own mother. It was a mystical connection that even Sabine did not understand, but there were some facts that you simply did not question.

"Give him some of your elixir," Sabine suggested.

He shook his head. "Elixir won't work for me now, at least none but my own. Besides, she needs her own." He met Sabine's eyes. "She's the important one." His breathing was labored and raspy. "I used my time getting here to warn you. Phinneas can look after himself. Though I did send him a message to warn him."

"What do we need to do?" Sabine asked. Whatever it took, she would do it to ensure Agnes and the rest of her aunts were safe. She would not lose anyone else. Madigan had used precious time to come and warn them instead of pursuing his own elixir. She owed him her gratitude.

"You need the entire prophecy," Madigan said. "You must have it to have any hope of destroying the Chosen One."

"The map," Sabine said. "You said you located it."

He coughed again, took another sip of the whiskey, then released a weary breath. "A man, an Englishman, found it many years ago. He still has it now."

"Phinneas's vision was right," Agnes said. "He said a great one would find the map and lead the way to our salvation."

Madigan reached into his coat and withdrew a folded piece of parchment. "I've given you his name and address. Unfortunately that is all the information I have on him." He placed his hand over Sabine's. "It is imperative that you get that prophecy. Without the map, you have no hope of surviving the Chosen One."

Sabine made no move to unfold the paper once he'd placed it in her hand. He'd given her this task. He was trusting her to retrieve the one thing her people had sought for years. She kept her eyes on the man in front of her. He was a few breaths away from dying.

"How long have you known about this?" she asked. "About the man who has possession of our map?"

"Not long. Initially I only knew it was an Englishman. It took me awhile to uncover his identity," Madigan said.

"Will he sell it to us?" she asked.

"No. I already tried that a couple of months ago," Madigan said. He grabbed her hand. "You can do this. We must have the prophecy."

Sabine swallowed.

He eyed her aunts. "We have no other choice."

Madigan had died that night in their storeroom, a most painful and terrible death. As a girl, Sabine had watched her mother die and now another guardian had perished. She would do whatever was necessary to keep Agnes safe.

So she did what any lady in need would do. She hid in a darkened carriage outside the gentleman's home and waited for him to go out for the evening. She knew he planned to go out, as he'd readied a carriage for himself an hour earlier.

Madigan's note had not given her much information about the Englishman in question, one Maxwell Barrett, Marquess of Lindberg. She knew where he lived and she knew that he had in his possession the legendary map of Atlantis. Madigan had been studying Mr. Barrett for a couple of months, but as it turned out the man was rather mysterious.

Madigan had said the man would not entertain bids to purchase the map, which left her with two choices—she could break into the man's home and, in effect, steal the map. Technically she could make an argument that the map belonged to her and her people, yet she doubted that she would make much headway with the authorities should she get pinched.

Or she could try to persuade him to allow her a peek. The latter seemed infinitely preferable to a small prison cell. One could not protect the world from a prophesied disaster if one were trapped in prison. But if tonight's efforts proved to be a complete failure, then she would certainly reconsider the theft. A woman had to do what a woman had to do.

He was a member of London's illustrious Society; certainly that meant he was a reasonable fellow. She simply needed to make the gentleman's acquaintance. Tonight seemed as good a night as any, plus she didn't appear to have the luxury of time on her hands. If the ancient prophecy had already begun, then the hourglass had been turned, and the grains of sand were swiftly falling around her. Without the prophecy in its entirety, Madigan was right, they were basically fighting blindfolded.

If she were to persuade a man to do her bidding, she knew there were certain distractions she could use to her advantage. One was beauty. Though she had never been particularly comfortable playing the role of seductress, she had done her best to dress the part tonight. She'd donned a gown the English would deem appropriately attractive, an ivory gown sewn of the most luxurious of silks. It fit her perfectly, which in itself was remarkable considering she'd purchased it from the display in the shop's window. The cap sleeves edged with delicate lace revealed her upper arms. Then from fingertip to elbow, she wore matching satin gloves. The gown's plunging neckline lifted and squeezed her breasts until they were practically bursting through the material.

She'd also had Calliope do her hair up in light wispy curls that barely brushed her shoulders, just hinting at their softness. She very much looked the part of a proper English lady. She fidgeted with the necklace hanging around her neck. To others, it would appear to be a simple gold chain, but hanging from the necklace, and hidden beneath the bodice of her gown, was a crystal vial with a small amount of elixir. Agnes had given it to her months ago and instructed her to keep it with her always.

From her vantage point, she saw a man in a greatcoat, the black wool stretched across his broad shoulders. He put on a top hat as he stepped off the last stair and into the waiting coach. Then it rolled out of the driveway. She instructed her driver to follow.

She hadn't yet figured out how she would sneak into the ball or soiree, or wherever he was going, without a proper invitation. Perhaps her lovely dress and a well-placed smile would grant her admission. She kept her eye on the carriage so she did not lose her man. But her driver stayed close. She wished she'd seen his face, though, as it seemed unlikely she would recognize him in a crowd. All men of wealth wore similar coats and hats.

It took less than twenty minutes for them to pull up outside a three-story redbrick building. The man walked up to the black door and entered. Sabine noted there were no identifying markers indicating the type of establishment, though she assumed from the neighborhood that this was a business and not a residence.

The street was quiet as she stepped down from her rig. Nerves fluttered wildly in her abdomen, and she pressed a gloved hand against her stomach to calm herself. Now was not the time for her to feel anxious.

She had a job to do; it was plain and simple. With a

pinch of her cheeks and a tight nibble at her lips to pinken them, she made her way to the door. She would mill about, watch for a while, then find the gentleman in question. The heavy door opened, and Sabine found herself standing in a smoke-filled gaming establishment.

She nearly scoffed. The most prized artifact of Atlantis was in the hands of a gambler. She had half a mind to be utterly incensed, but perhaps this could work to her favor. With that thought, she went in search of the marquess.

Chapter Two

❦

Max picked up his hand and glanced at the cards, a lousy combination that on its own would win nothing. It was why he loved this American game—for the bluffing. Even with a mediocre hand of cards, he could win.

His table mates were a motley crew, and he had very little difficulty deciphering when they held good hands or when they knew they would lose. Two of the older gentlemen had made excuses and left the table when the betting had increased. Now only four remained. A grizzled man with a full shock of white hair and a voice deep and cracked. A young man, perhaps one could even consider him still a boy, as not even a hint of whiskers appeared on his chin. And the Earl of Chilton sat across from Max, a fine opponent when he wasn't drinking. Tonight, though, the man had had one too many sips.

The fourth player was, by far, the most interesting. A woman, dressed in a cream-colored confection with a plunging neckline that left very little to his well-developed imagination. She was the kind of woman one expected to see across a candlelit ballroom surrounded by suitors, not in a smoke-filled gaming hell surrounded by drunken fools. With her lustrous, mahogany-colored hair and her warm caramel eyes, she was nothing short of stunning. Though her darker complexion led him to believe she wasn't originally from England, she had no accent to give him a hint of her homeland.

Though he'd never seen her before, she certainly looked like a refined lady, but he wasn't completely convinced. While she had the mannerisms down and the look just right, something was different about her. And he knew he had never seen her before, as she was not the sort of woman a man forgot.

Initially Max had found her distracting, but after losing to her two hands in a row, he'd straightened his seat and kept his eyes off her tempting cleavage.

Though she had won more hands than most of the men at the table that night, she was not an accomplished player. However, she proved, at times, difficult to read, almost as if she were an actress slipping into a role, and while in character, she became charming, flirtatious, and daring. But every now and then a veil would slip over her eyes, and Max would catch a glimpse of insecurity. He had yet to decide whether that was from the cards she held or something else.

"I raise," she said, her voice a warm, fluid honey. She arched a perfect eyebrow in his direction. "My lord," she said.

Max glanced around the table. He knew from Chilton's smug expression that the man had a good hand. The old man had already laid down his hand, as had the young one. But what cards did the pretty miss hold?

"Such a temptress," Max said, never taking his eyes

off her as he dropped his coins into the betting pool. "I'll call your wager."

Chilton's brow furrowed, and he grumbled something incoherent, then backed out of the game. Evidently his hand, as good as it may have been, did not give the inebriated man enough confidence.

They had another quick round of betting before the dealer called for their hands, and Max flipped over his cards. Two pair to her three of a kind.

"The lady wins," the man said.

With delicate gloved fingers, she scooped the coins in her direction, then stacked them neatly.

Chilton stood. "Enough of this foolish game for me." He eyed the lady at the table, then looked at Max. "You've got a lovely playmate tonight, Lindberg. I believe I'll retire for the evening," he said as he slipped away, though Max spotted him finding a new chair at a different game four tables over.

Max collected his new hand and eyed the cards. As if they had been dealt by a deity, Max looked down on four kings.

Again the other two gentlemen folded, leaving the hand down to Max and the lady, the mysterious and lovely woman with the caramel-colored eyes. This time, though, he could not lose. He had a brilliant hand.

She picked up a few coins, then paused over the center pot, glancing at her cards before slowly raising her gaze to his. "A different wager, perhaps."

Intrigued, Max nodded. "What did you have in mind?" Immediately his mind conjured images of all the sinful acts he could do to her body upon this very table. It would take hours for him to explore every delectable curve. He'd start at that sweet spot directly below her ear along the column of her neck. Then he'd work his way down.

"Your map, Maxwell Barrett. I only want the map." Her words came out slow and deliberate.

Ah, she knew who he was, and she knew about his map.

It was no great secret that he hid away. Still, he'd never broadcast it across Society. What would have been the point? It was popular to go in hunt of treasure or artifacts, but there was no scientific proof of the existence of Atlantis.

He'd once thought the map would be the ultimate proof, but no one except the men of Solomon's had paid much attention to his discovery. So now the relic simply hung on his wall. Why the interest now? And how had she known?

Women talked, he knew that. And he'd had more than his fair share of women. And on occasion, he'd had one of them bent over his desk, though he wouldn't have guessed many would give much thought to an old map. It would be quite the knock to his pride that one of those women might have noticed any element of his decor when he'd assumed they were more pleasantly engaged. The idea nearly made him chuckle.

It was on his tongue to inquire how she'd heard of his map, but more important was why she wanted it. "What does a beautiful woman such as yourself want with a dusty old map?" he asked.

She smiled, and it transformed her face from merely lovely into something much more. Her sheer beauty was like a kick in the gut.

She tugged on one of her satin gloves. "Perhaps I'm a scholar. Like yourself," she said with a delicately arched eyebrow.

"I'm an adventurer, not a scholar." If she legitimately

knew anything about him, she'd know that. "And you don't look any more like a scholar than I do."

Her shoulders shifted so subtly, one could hardly consider the movement a shrug. "Then perhaps I'm merely curious. Do you accept the wager or not?" she asked.

Max looked back at his cards, then slowly slid his gaze up to her. "Tell me your name."

She nodded. "Sabine Tobias," she said.

Somehow in the midst of their exchange, a crowd had developed around their table. Low whispers flitted around as well as the occasional jab directed at Max. If Max wasn't mistaken, a side wager had been established on who was going to win their hand. That was the one thing you could be certain of in Rand's Gaming, people were always looking for a wager.

"Well, Miss Tobias." Max leaned forward and leveled his gaze on her tawny eyes. "What do I get if I win?"

"The pleasure of winning," she said with a faint smile.

Max shook his head. "I'm not certain that's enough. How about a kiss?"

The crowd around them cheered. Shock broke through her careful façade, and her eyes widened, but she quickly recovered. "I don't believe I was offering any kisses," she said. "How about if you simply get to keep your dusty old map," she added, tossing his words back at him.

Perhaps she knew more about him than she'd let on, or perhaps she knew more about the map than the average collector. He'd held on to that map for years despite several high-priced offers from other parties and one attempted theft. The map hadn't been the conclusive proof he'd once believed it would be. His quest for Atlantis stretched across his adulthood and still he had not found it. But he was getting close. He could feel it.

Miss Tobias sat quietly, but her pulse ticked impatiently in that sweet spot beneath her ear.

"I believe you have a bet," he said. "You win this hand, and I will give you my map."

She paused a moment, trying to gauge his meaning. "You know to which map I'm referring," she said.

"I believe I do."

"Then we have a deal."

"But if you lose," he said slowly, "I get that kiss."

She opened her mouth to protest, but after a breath, she said nothing and merely nodded.

"The wager has been set, now let us see your hands," the dealer said.

Silence surrounded them, and it was as if they were playing alone in his parlor. Miss Tobias flipped her cards, one by one, revealing three sevens and two queens.

"A full house," the dealer said.

A slow, satisfied smile spread across the lady's face, a cat with her bowl of cream.

The pleasure of her smile was so enticing, so seductive, he was almost sorry he was going to win. Almost.

First Max turned the two, the one card in his hand that didn't matter, then just as she'd done, he slowly turned each card over.

"Four of a kind wins," the dealer said.

The smile evaporated from Miss Tobias's face.

"Nicely done," she said tightly. She came to her feet.

"I believe we will cash out for the night," Max told the dealer.

Once they had stepped away from the table, Max put his hand on the lady's elbow to direct her to a private room.

"What do you think you are doing?" she asked tartly. She pulled her arm free and eyed the door behind him.

He leaned against the door and allowed himself to take in the full length of her. She was taller than he would have guessed, though by no means would he consider her a tall woman. But he did imagine that her legs were shapely and long. From his vantage point at the table he'd been able to see her voluptuous breasts, but he'd not been able to enjoy her narrow waist and full hips. She had the kind of body women envied. Whereas other women spent fortunes on all manner of contraptions to perfect their shapes, it did not appear that Miss Tobias had so much as a corset on beneath that glorious dress. She, it would seem, was perfect all on her own.

"You lost the hand," he said.

Her lips pursed. "I realize that."

"Which means I won."

She swallowed and again his eye was drawn to that tender flesh behind her jaw line. "You're enjoying this, aren't you?" she asked. Her right foot tapped a random rhythm on the wooden floor.

He smiled. "Most definitely." He shoved off the door-jamb and walked toward her. "Tell me, Miss Tobias, what part should I not be enjoying? That a beautiful woman shows up at my favorite club to pursue me?"

She held up her hand. "Not to pursue you, only your map," she corrected.

"Perhaps, but instead of asking to purchase my map, you chose to negotiate a wager." He took her hand and examined the satin-encased fingers. "I do appreciate a brazen lady."

"There is nothing brazen about my behavior." She

withdrew her hand. "My lord, I see no reason to drag this on all evening. I realize you find this entire scenario vastly entertaining, but I do not have time to amuse you any longer. I agreed to a kiss. Now I shall give you one, then be on my way."

"Indeed?"

Without another word, she braced both gloved hands on either side of his face and leaned up to him. Her soft lips brushed seductively across his, but instead of giving him a quick peck, then retreating, she lingered. Her warm breath mingled with his own, and he wanted to pull her closer, kiss her deeper, but she moved back before he had the chance.

"Now then, I do believe our business is complete," she said.

"That was a lovely kiss," he told her, "but it wasn't exactly what I had in mind." He pulled her to him, her lush body pressing against his own, then he dipped his head to her neck. "This spot," he murmured. "I've been looking at it all night." He tasted her, the flesh as tender as he'd imagined. Her nails bit through his jacket and into his arms. "Perfect." Then he let her go.

She eyed him thoughtfully, but said nothing. It would seem there were ways to make the lady speechless.

"I do believe we'll be seeing each other again," he said.

She said nothing, but merely turned on her heel and left the room.

Sabine Tobias. Why would someone be that desperate for an antiquity? There had to be a reason, and chances were, it would be a good one. It shouldn't take too much investigation to uncover who she was and what she wanted with his map.

* * *

The following day, Sabine Tobias grabbed a handful of glass jars and headed out to her storefront. She wouldn't say that last night had been a complete disaster, though certainly not a success either. But she knew for certain the man in question had possession of the map. And she knew where he lived. Oddly enough she also knew what it felt like for him to lave warm kisses on her neck. Everything about him had been unexpected.

Since the night before, she'd spent entirely too much time reliving that one moment, and not enough on devising a new plan. So far a trip to his home seemed to be her best option. But she'd need help from her aunts to ensure that she didn't get caught.

Sabine should have been bone-weary from her unexpectedly late evening, but instead her mind was surprisingly active. She constantly relived every breath from the night before, wondering what, if anything, she could have done differently.

"We open in ten minutes," Lydia said as she rushed from the back room.

Word was certainly getting out as of late, because their business had nearly tripled in the last few weeks. Evidently someone in London—someone important—had decided Tobias Miracle Crème was highly in fashion. She and her aunts were making the facial crème as fast as they could and still they sold out each day.

Her aunt Calliope came out right behind her with an armload of her own. "Sabine, you came in so late last night," she whispered. "I tried to stay awake, but..." Lydia passed by and Calliope stopped talking. She smiled sweetly at her eldest sister.

After they were once again alone, Calliope continued, "I thought maybe you'd gotten yourself into trouble."

"No need to be so secretive. Lydia knows where I was," Sabine said as she placed the jars on the shelf.

Calliope's pale blue eyes shone. "How did it go with the map? Did you see it?"

Sabine plucked the jars from her aunt's arms and started stacking them neatly into the fabric-lined baskets they used for display. "No." She frowned at her aunt as she pulled a stray thread out of Calliope's wispy grayish-blonde hair. "I followed him. And I ended up not at a ball as I'd thought, but in a gaming hell." She filled Calliope in on the rest of the details, their wager, everything except for the kiss.

"You lost?"

"I did." She put a hand on Calliope's arm. "But I'll think of something. I've got one idea already. I know Lydia will not approve, but I believe I might simply have to break into his house. Madigan entrusted me with this task, and I do not want to let him or Agnes down."

"I'm opening the doors, ladies," Lydia said as she swept past them, then made her way behind the curtain.

Lydia had assumed the role of the eldest in the family when Sabine's mother had passed. She fussed over each of them, and Sabine loved her for it. While the shop was open, though, she stayed in the back tending the books and packaging orders. She had never gotten used to their living among the English.

Sabine glanced behind her aunts to assure they were alone. "But it will require assistance from each of you."

Punctuated by the sound of tiny bells, a tall and well-dressed gentleman entered the shop.

"We'll talk more about my plan this evening," Sabine whispered.

The man wore a hat that partially hid his face, something Sabine knew was considered rude in polite Society. A true gentleman would have removed his hat once inside the shop. Other customers, all women, also entered the shop and began to mill about. It was how it had been for the past few weeks. They'd open their doors, and the people would come almost immediately, and often they'd be sold out of the facial crème three hours after opening.

The man immediately walked over to the nearest shelf and grabbed one of the jars for a closer inspection. His tall frame seemed even more so in her small and delicate shop, and his dark suit stood out against the pale fabrics of linen and tulle they used in their shelf displays. This was a lady's place, and he looked very much a man as he pawed at her wares. His large hands dwarfed the delicate jars of crème.

Then he removed his top hat, and steely blue eyes met her gaze. *Maxwell Barrett.*

"Miss Tobias," he said with a rakish grin.

"You found me," she uttered foolishly. Of course, she had given him her name. Normally that might not have yielded a successful search. London was a densely populated city, but the mention of the name Tobias to nearly any woman in Society would have brought him to her door. Perhaps the marquess was married—a fact she had not considered last night when she'd kissed him.

"It would appear so."

Not precisely a blond—though his hair wasn't dark enough to be considered brunette—he was about as attractive as men were allowed to be. Yet there was nothing pretty about him. With a chiseled jaw and deep-set eyes, his features were undeniably masculine. She was unable to do anything but stand there and stare at him. Away from the smoky confines of the gaming hell, she was able to fully appreciate his features. Last night, she'd recognized he was handsome, but here in the light of day... She mentally shook herself and moved away from him to stand behind the counter.

He followed her, as did Calliope, her eyes bright and full of curiosity.

"What do you want?" Sabine asked, her voice lowered to a whisper to avoid disturbing her other customers.

He chuckled, then met the gaze of her aunt. "The lady interrupts my game of poker last evening, completely distracts me, then makes a wild wager, and she wants to know why I would want to speak with her." He leaned against the counter and flashed a brilliant smile at Calliope. "Would you not be the least bit curious?"

"I would indeed, my lord," Calliope said in agreement.

Sabine leveled her gaze on her aunt. "You are not helping." She pushed her with one finger. "Will you put the rest of the stock out? And keep Agnes and Lydia in the back."

Calliope smiled at them both, then disappeared behind the curtain.

"You own this establishment?" he asked. He glanced at the rest of the storefront, then back at her.

"I do." Well, she and her aunts did together.

"Beauty aids and hair tonic." He picked up a jar, eyed it, then set it down. "Interesting."

Calliope came back around the curtain, an armful of jars balanced precariously. "Carry on," she said as she passed. "Don't mind me none."

"Are you going to tell me why you want my map?"

He offered a smile, one so piercing she feared her knees might buckle.

"Oh, for pity's sake," she muttered. She squared her shoulders. "I don't believe I owe you an explanation." Her voice came out with more bravado than she felt.

"You think not?"

"I do. My lord," she added, forcing herself to be polite. Her throat was dry as she licked her lips.

"You may call me Max." He pulled her hand to him and placed a kiss on the top of her wrist.

Sabine momentarily got caught in the blue trance of his gaze, then jerked her hand back. "I don't believe I shall call you anything. Is there something else I can assist you with?" She wanted him out of her shop. Though she did need his map, discussing the map or anything else related to Atlantis was far too dangerous with other customers about.

She supposed she could simply ask him if she could see it, but at what cost? Last night, with a simple wager, he'd requested a kiss. What more would he require for a look at the map? Not to mention she could easily tell from this conversation that he was a curious sort. He would have questions. Questions she could not answer.

Besides, the more she thought about her plan, the more certain she was that tonight she would sneak into his house. "Perhaps you need some hair tonic? Our products have been known to invigorate new growth."

Smiling at her again, he said, "Trust me. I'm quite vigorous."

She stepped away from the counter. "Then I suppose that shall be all."

He grabbed her arm and stilled her. His rich azure eyes met hers and did not waver. Was this to be some sort of

contest? She always had a difficult time walking away
from a challenge. Fair enough, she met his stare and did
not move. She could outlast him. The corners of his lips
tipped in a smile.

Before either of them could speak again, the tiny bells
rang through the shop. Sabine looked away. Customers
were a priority over her silly pride.

A woman entered and hadn't even closed the door
behind her before speaking. "Well, well, well, the Marquess of Lindberg. I certainly hadn't expected to see you,"
the woman purred as she stepped forward, her kohl-lined
eyes roaming boldly over the marquess. Her lips were
painted with red rouge, drawing attention to their fullness.
She was a tall woman. Unlike most women of height, she
was not lithe or overly thin, but lush and curvaceous, soft
and round in all the appropriate places. No doubt a much-
admired creature among the men of London.

He turned at the sound of her voice. "Cassandra, you
know there is no need for such formalities."

She sauntered forward, then held her hand out to him.
As he leaned over it, she positively glowed. "Max, it's
been far too long."

"Has it?" he said playfully. "Whatever are you doing
here?"

"Surely you know," she said. "Tobias's is fast becoming
the most sought-after beauty product in all of London."

For the time being, it appeared that Sabine and the
marquess were finished with their brief confrontation.
The interlude wouldn't last long, though. Eventually this
woman would leave the shop, and the marquess would
continue his questions. She might not know him, but
Sabine could tell that Max Barrett was not a man who
gave up all that easily.

"May I help you with anything today?" Sabine asked. Intentionally she faced the woman, putting her back to the marquess. "We have many products designed for the modern woman; which did you have in mind?"

Cassandra turned her icy gaze to Sabine. "The Tobias Miracle Crème is the *only* item I require," she said, then she shifted her attention back to Max.

Sabine ignored the woman's superior tone. "How many jars would you like?"

"If it's as good as I've heard, I should probably start with several." Cassandra touched her pale blonde locks and smiled coolly. "You've been selling out, yes?"

"Every day for several weeks." Sabine couldn't help noticing how the marquess appeared rather amused, standing there with his smug smile as he looked from one woman to the other.

"Three will be good then." The woman held up three long fingers, but never once met Sabine's eyes.

"Whatever are you doing in here?" Cassandra asked Max. "Buying a gift for a new love?" She ran a finger down the marquess's arm.

Sabine went about packaging the three jars, all the while watching their exchange.

"A friend's wife, actually," he said.

Sabine was amazed at how easily the lie slipped off his tongue. She'd have to remember that in her future dealings with him. Not that she planned on having any.

"It's her birthday," he added with a smile.

"Lovely," Cassandra said. "How very considerate of you."

Now at least Sabine knew that the man was not married. It mattered not, though she supposed it was nice to know she hadn't kissed a married man.

"Madam," Sabine said as she held out the bag with the three jars.

Cassandra sauntered over to the counter and counted out her money, then instead of putting it in Sabine's outstretched hand, she dropped it onto the countertop. As she turned to leave, she paused and leaned in close to Max's ear and whispered something. With a saucy smile, she made her way out of the shop's door.

He turned to face Sabine once again, and there on his left cheek was the perfect imprint of the woman's red lips.

Sabine chuckled.

"What?"

"Nothing." She shook her head. Let him walk around London with rouge on his cheek. "Friend of yours?"

He paused and then recognition lit his eyes. "Ah, Cassandra, she was a"—he paused—"friend. I suppose you could call her that."

Clearly they had been more than merely friends at some point. For reasons she did not want to consider, her amusement went sour in her stomach. He could have all the *friends* in the world, and with his dashing good looks, probably did.

As Sabine crossed in front of him to one of the display shelves, he placed a hand on her shoulder. Suddenly it was as if all the air in the room had been removed. His warm fingers held tightly to her sensitive skin, and she knew he could feel her pulse racing beneath his touch.

She pulled free. "Sir, I do not know you and would prefer you not handle me in such a manner."

A few customers shot them questioning looks.

"I do wish you'd leave," she whispered.

He chuckled. "Not before you tell me why you were after my map."

With less grace than she would have liked, she stepped away from him. "There is nothing to tell. I have a fondness for maps. You could say I'm a collector. I heard you had a rare one in your possession." She shrugged and hoped she looked casual. "'Tis all."

His eyebrows quirked. "You would have me believe you are merely a simple shopkeeper with an interest in an extraordinary map?"

She *was* nothing but a simple shopkeeper. That he thought her more both thrilled and saddened her. "Yes, indeed, quite simple."

Tonight while he was out, no doubt losing more of his fortune in frivolous games, she would sneak into his house and take what was rightfully hers.

"And you just happened to learn about my map?"

"Purely by luck," she lied.

He eyed her suspiciously, clearly not believing her poor attempt at deception.

"Pardon me, ma'am," a woman said. "I have a question about these products."

"I'll be right with you," Sabine said, then turned her attention back to Max. "I have customers to attend to. If you'll excuse me." Sabine stepped away and gave the woman her attention, but she remained oh-so-aware of Max's presence. When she glanced back to where he'd been standing, he was gone. He'd vanished with a stealth she found unsettling.

The customer, who realized Sabine was no longer listening to her, cleared her throat loudly. "Is something wrong, miss?" the woman asked when Sabine turned back to her.

"No, it was nothing." Sabine forced a smile.

Max was a distraction she could not afford. She could only hope that's all he was, for she had the feeling he would be a most formidable foe.

Cassandra St. James climbed into her carriage with a smile on her face. She opened one jar and inhaled the rich herbal scent. There were definite hints of rosemary and jasmine, perhaps lavender, but she was unsure. With the end of one polish-tipped finger, she scooped a bit of the crème and smeared it across her cheek. The luxurious crème slid over her skin, absorbing immediately.

She had heard the gossip around town about the new beauty crème and had noticed a marked difference in several of her friends' complexions. But this could be even better than she'd hoped. This could be what she'd been searching for—the fountain of youth, jarred, and on sale in the heart of London.

What other reason would Maxwell Barrett have for being in such a shop? He would never purchase such a personal gift for another man's wife. No, his presence there could mean only one thing.

Atlantis: that mythical land that he had once told her had been the home to the fountain of youth. Somehow that Tobias woman had made the ultimate discovery, and Cassandra would definitely uncover whatever beauty secret the woman hid.

She was an odd woman, dressing in a boring, ill-fitted gown of gray wool. Yet somehow, instead of making the woman appear drab and dull, the steel-colored dress had contrasted nicely with her darker complexion. Her dress, though, was not what interested Cassandra.

She had to find a way to get into that shop to see what

ingredients that woman was hiding. If she had found the Atlantis secret to eternal beauty, Cassandra wanted it for herself.

Tonight she would send Johns and his men to see what they could find.

Chapter Three

·~∙≺~≻∙~·

What was the lovely Sabine Tobias hiding?

She was a woman of mystery. Last night at the poker game, she'd been a temptress. Her dress had been daring with its plunging neckline. Yet today when he'd gone into her shop, she'd been dressed plainly, though her thick chestnut locks had been unbound, draped around her shoulders. Rather inappropriate for a young woman, though Max found it utterly appealing.

If she wouldn't be forthcoming with him about why she wanted his map, he'd find out on his own. There were other ways to uncover such information. But for the time being, he had decided a little covert investigation of his own was the appropriate choice.

Which was why he was currently hiding in the darkened alleyway behind Miss Tobias's shop. He withdrew a tool from his pocket and slid the sharp point into the keyhole of the shop's back door. A few moments of maneuvering the piece, and he heard the lock give way. He pushed open the door, and it moved without a sound.

The room was dark and quiet and clearly served as a storeroom. He stood still for a moment, allowing his eyes to grow accustomed to the darkness. Fortunately, the two windows against the back wall allowed enough light to give adequate visibility.

It was a tidy space, sparsely furnished. A large shelf lined the far wall and various ingredients and empty jars crowded the surface. Herbs tied in bunches were hung to dry above the windows. Ahead of him was the curtained doorway to the front of the store, and on either side of that doorway were some cupboards. To his left was a stairwell. His preliminary research indicated it would lead up to the living quarters above, where Sabine and her aunts had resided for the past seven months. It was not an uncommon practice among merchants.

Max moved farther into the room. He wasn't even certain what he searched for specifically. But Sabine Tobias must know something about Atlantis. Why else would she be so secretive about her desire for his map?

He knew there were other people, besides himself, who sought the lost land. Some searched for treasure, as it was said that Poseidon had built the entire central palace out of gold. Some searched for ancient texts with secrets to medical cures, because Atlanteans were rumored to have achieved advancements in all areas of science. Still others sought the fountain of youth or healing waters that were rumored to flow through the canals in Atlantis.

Max, though, wanted it all. He wanted to find the actual city. Just as Pompeii had been lost beneath mounds of ash, so he believed Atlantis survived beneath the waters of the Atlantic Ocean. He was not foolish enough to believe it would have remained unscathed. Water erosion certainly would have altered much of the rumored land. But something existed below the surface, and he intended to find it.

He couldn't resist pursuing the possibility that there was a new clue, especially not when it came wrapped in the tantalizing package that was Miss Tobias.

He crept forward to better examine the items on the shelves. Along with dried herbs and oils, he found lanolin and glycerin and all other manner of ingredients. A basket of ribbons sat next to the empty jars.

What was the crème Cassandra had purchased? Some fashion of smoothing crème. And Sabine wanted his map. She, too, sought treasure, though of a different sort. She was after the fountain of youth; that had to be why she'd come in search of him.

He continued sifting through the shelves, but there were no secret texts or books or anything that would hint at what Sabine might know of the map.

Thus far his search had been futile. He should probably turn and leave. Chances were if Sabine had something to hide, she kept it upstairs in the living quarters, and he couldn't risk sneaking up there. But he'd never been able to walk away from a worthy puzzle, and it would seem that Sabine Tobias might be the most interesting mystery he'd come across in a long while.

He took steps toward the front of the shop. Perhaps there would be something hidden in those cupboards. The floor creaked beneath his weight. He stilled. There was yet another noise.

The doorknob jiggled from behind him. Someone else was trying to get in. Perhaps Miss Tobias returning home late from another game of chance? Quickly Max moved to the other side of the stairwell and hid in the narrow cubby beneath.

The door jerked open, and two men lumbered in. Max could hear a third voice outside the door. Three men, one outside to keep watch. Sabine Tobias's shop was certainly gaining in popularity. What a pity he hadn't thought to bring along a couple of thugs himself. Max withdrew farther into the shadows.

If he hadn't been certain before that Sabine Tobias was hiding something, now it seemed quite evident. From beneath the stairwell, Max couldn't see much of what the men were doing, but he could make out a few words of their hurried whispers. They didn't sound educated, and they didn't seem to know specifically what they were searching for. They'd obviously been hired to break into the shop. In Max's experience, "employees" of that nature were highly unreliable. They took no personal interest in their assignments and generally proved to be rather unmotivated. Not to mention a bit dim. No doubt their search would not be thorough.

Max settled his back against the wall, prepared to simply wait them out. However, when the stairs above him shifted slightly, Max moved to the edge of the cubby to get a better glimpse. Delicate, pale ankles attached to feminine bare feet crept down the steps.

Bloody hell! Miss Tobias. Did the woman have no sense at all? What was she doing sneaking down to investigate? Surely she did not intend to fight off would-be thieves in nothing more than her nightrail.

He craned his neck, looking for the thugs in the unlit storeroom. Thank goodness, they were busy rifling through the cupboards. He positioned himself, and once the lady came within reach, he clamped a hand across her mouth and pulled her into his hiding place. Her muffled protests were punctuated by those delicate feet kicking into his shins. He stifled a groan of his own.

He turned her around to face him, careful not to uncover her mouth. Sabine Tobias stared up at him, her eyes wide and angry. He frowned at her, then leaned close to her ear.

"Kick me again, love, and I'll let the wastrels get you," he warned in a whisper.

Her lovely, expressive face tensed.

He nodded to the noise around the corner from them, then pulled them farther into the darkness beneath the stairs, thankful that the thugs were making enough noise to cover the sounds of his own struggle with the little minx. Idiots to think they wouldn't be discovered, making all that racket.

He put one finger up to his lips. "Shhh." Once she nodded, he removed his hand from her mouth. But he made no move to release her. She had enough fire in her to do something foolish in the name of bravery. If she let on to their hiding place, she could get them both hurt. He'd taken on two men in a fight before, but three was asking a bit much. So he held her firmly against him.

While he wasn't visually able to enjoy Sabine's flimsy nightgown, pressing her this close against him left little to his imagination. She was plump where a woman should be, rounded hips, lush breasts, soft bottom. He tightened his grip on her narrow waist, enjoying the feel of her soft curves. She smelled of fresh herbs and warm bread and felt just as delicious. He inhaled slowly.

One of the men ran into a shelf and a glass fell to the floor, shattering. Sabine sucked in a harsh breath and nearly said something.

Far be it from Max to miss an opportunity. So with that

thought, he threaded his other hand into the back of her lustrous hair and pulled her face to his. A moment later, he tasted her just as he'd done the night before. This time, though, her soft lips opened, probably more from shock than desire, but an invitation was an invitation.

He deepened the kiss, slipping his tongue between her gently parted lips. She tasted of chocolate and cinnamon. He'd intended only to kiss and quiet her, but the feel of her made desire surge through his legs and into his groin.

Her hand slowly slid up his arm. He cupped her bottom and pulled her closer, pressing her to him. Then she pinched the skin at his bicep. It was not enough pain to cause much damage, but he did jerk back from her.

She glared up at him, then opened her mouth to say something.

But before she could, the man at the door stuck his head in. "Hurry."

If the man had looked a little to his left, he would have been able to see the white of Sabine's nightgown billowing out from beneath the stairs. Max grabbed the fabric and cinched it by her hip. No doubt her lovely leg was nearly completely revealed, but at least her nightgown was no longer waving surrender from beneath the stairs.

"We go upstairs," another of the men said in a harsh whisper. "We haven't found nothing yet." He started up the staircase.

A choked sound squeaked from Sabine's throat. Her eyes widened with fear, and her mouth formed two silent words, "My aunts."

Bloody hell! Looked as if he was going to have to take a chance with those odds after all.

Max grabbed both of Sabine's arms and switched their places. "Stay," he whispered. Then he crept out from his hiding place and grabbed the leg of the man on the lower stair. Max pulled sharply. The thin man fell onto the stairs, hitting his head on the hard wood. The other man turned and ran back down the stairs, heading straight for Max.

It took one solid blow to the man's nose to bring him down. Blood sprayed as the bone and cartilage shifted.

"You broke my nose," he howled. "You son of a bitch."

"Watch out," Sabine cried.

But it wasn't enough warning for the punch to Max's left kidney. Pain radiated up his back and down his hip. He groaned, but shook it off and turned to meet his assailant. Another punch headed his way, but he was able to duck and slam himself into the man, knocking the thug off his feet.

By this time, the noise had awakened the other household occupants, and ladies' voices came from the rooms overhead.

"What the devil is going on?" one asked.

"Sabine?" another said.

The first man Max had struck was now attempting to get to his feet, but Max was able to hit him on the head, and he sank back to the floor. The one with the bloody nose struck Max on the jaw, rocking him backward. Max would be lucky if the punch only resulted in a blackened eye and didn't also bruise the entire side of his face.

The other man made a direct line toward Sabine.

Three older women came rushing down the stairs, their nightrails flowing behind them. They all carried makeshift weapons: a fire poker, a heavy candelabra, and a small, jeweled pistol.

Excellent. He was getting the shit beat out of him, and Sabine was about to be rescued by the fairy godmother brigade.

Max took another hard blow to his shoulder before he managed to grab the third man and slam his head against the doorframe.

A shot rang out. "Get out!" the woman shrieked. "Out, out, out!"

The three thieves wasted no time in scrambling out the door.

"You, too," she said to Max.

But Max did not move. Instead he simply stared at his chest, where a bloodstain grew across his coat.

"Lydia, you shot him!" Sabine said.

Chapter Four

———❦❦———

D amnation," Agnes said.

"Oh, no," Calliope said.

Panic seized Sabine. Her mind stumbled over several scenarios in which Max bled to death on their floor. But then she caught sight of his crooked smile. Damned man was too stubborn to die of a piddling gunshot wound.

She took several steadying breaths. Agnes was here; she would ensure all was well.

"Let's get him upstairs," Sabine said. She braced herself against him, wrapping her arm around his waist. "Don't get any foolish ideas," she warned, remembering their heated kiss under the stairs. She herself tried to ignore his taut abdomen and firm back.

He chuckled but allowed her to lead him up the wooden staircase.

They stepped into the small kitchen, and she helped lower him into one of the chairs. She was painfully aware of how confined the space felt with his large masculine form there. Her aunts immediately went about gathering the items they needed: a small bowl of water, tweezers, a clean rag, and some makeshift bandages. For a moment, she was back in the kitchen in their cottage in Essex preparing to care for one of the villagers who'd had an accident with a hoe or who had gotten into a brawl after imbibing too much whiskey. There everything had been peaceful, but here in London, life moved at a much quicker pace. Though she had always considered herself a calm person, the bustle kept her on edge.

But they weren't in Essex, and this man was not one of their own. He did not know of their ways or of their capabilities. And she would risk much in sharing them, but his complexion had paled, and his coat was heavy with his blood loss. They had no choice; they certainly couldn't risk his bleeding to death or developing a life-threatening infection.

"Don't forget the salve," Sabine said.

"Truly?" Lydia asked. Her three aunts exchanged looks.

"Yes," Agnes said. "We will need the salve."

Lydia would not question Agnes. As the guardian, she was the Healer, and the elixir would be used as she deemed necessary. They would never have even paused to consider its use on a villager. But this stranger would notice when his wound healed twice as fast as it ought.

While Agnes gave further instructions, Sabine pulled Max's coat off his shoulders and down his arms.

Blood stained his white shirt, coloring a large section of his chest beneath his right shoulder.

"Damn," he swore.

Calliope stepped forward with a glass of deep-red liquor. "Here, this should help with the pain."

"A lady after my own heart." He raised the glass in a toast, then winced. "Thank you." He downed it in one gulp.

He tried with one hand to unbutton his shirt, but he took too long, so Sabine swatted his fingers out of the way. "Here," she said. Her deft fingers worked the buttons swiftly, though she would have sworn she'd felt them shaking ever so slightly. There would be no reason for that, though. On more than one occasion, she'd helped Agnes tend to men's wounds. She pulled the shirt the rest of the way off and exposed his wound.

It was caked in blood, and she could not see enough of the actual bullet hole to gauge the true damage. Blond hair covered his torso, but in the wound area, it had matted. Without warning, she ran the wet rag against the wound. Rivulets of blood and water dripped down his arm.

"That stings," he growled.

Sabine had to clean the wound. Perhaps in her determination to ignore his fine form, her ministrations were rougher than she'd intended. "Don't act like a child," she warned. "Besides, it's not that deep." She caught Agnes's eyes as she obviously lied to Max.

Agnes nodded almost imperceptibly.

Sabine hoped he wouldn't notice that it was, in fact, quite deep. The best thing for all of them was to convince him the injury hadn't been that bad to begin with, and then he might not be so curious when it healed quickly. They needed to patch him up and send him on his way before he became suspicious of their ways. Now that the Chosen One was searching for Agnes, they all had to be extremely vigilant.

A cold chill shivered down Sabine's neck. What if *this man* was the Chosen One? Her hand stopped midstroke, and she met Max's eyes—clear blue and lined with real pain. No, Madigan would have known if Max was the Chosen One. He had their map, and he considered himself a scholar, though he'd referred to himself as an adventurer. And hadn't Agnes said that Phinneas had once had a vision about a "great one" discovering their map? She relaxed a bit.

"Little more than a grazing," she added.

Lydia's eyes rounded, and Calliope opened her mouth to argue, but Agnes shook her head. "Calliope, pour the marquess some more of your fine whiskey."

He sat taller. "Wasn't the first time I got shot," Max ground out. "Probably won't be the last."

Lydia poked a scar on his back. "Shot in the back, I see. Perhaps you shouldn't invade people's homes in the middle of the night."

"Lydia," Calliope chided as she handed Max the whiskey.

"Who were those men?" Sabine asked as she continued to wash his wound.

"I don't know. Thugs hired to find something would be my guess." He winced. "They were digging through all your belongings, then headed upstairs to continue their search." His blue eyes locked onto hers. "Care to share what you're hiding?" he asked.

"I don't know what you're talking about. We have absolutely nothing to hide." She turned back to the basin and poured clean water into the bowl. "They obviously had mistaken our shop for someone else's."

"Then why were they intent on going upstairs?" he asked.

"Perhaps they planned on ravishing us," Calliope said with great drama.

Sabine pressed near his wound until he grimaced. "The bullet seems to still be lodged in your chest," she said.

"I thought you said it was a grazing," he gritted through his teeth.

"My mistake," she said with a shrug.

"Let me remove the bullet. You can prepare the ointment, Sabine." Agnes stepped forward. "But first you tell me who you are." She leveled her gaze on him.

He nodded once. "Maxwell Barrett, Marquess of Lindberg."

"And precisely what were you doing in our shop?" she continued.

He met Sabine's glance. "I just happened by and saw the intruders. Perhaps I was merely in the right place at the right time."

Sabine made no move to correct him. "Our hero," she said tightly. She watched as her aunt gathered the tools she needed and then approached the table.

"I am Agnes," her aunt said as she sat in the chair next to him and scooted it forward. "These are my sisters: Lydia, whom you probably have realized is the one who shot you. And Calliope, my youngest sister, the one responsible for that foul liquid you're consuming at a rather alarming rate. And this is our niece Sabine, but it appears that the two of you have already met." She paused and met his gaze. "I'm afraid this is going to hurt."

"Splendid," he said dryly. "And up until now this evening had been so pleasant."

Sabine watched Agnes use the tweezers to pull the bullet out of the marquess's chest. His jaw tensed and ticked, but he made no sound. Of course, he'd had three glasses of Calliope's homemade whiskey, so he wasn't feeling much of anything.

While Lydia finished cleaning the wound, Sabine turned away from them to ready the salve. She scooped out a small amount into a shallow dish, then stirred it to loosen the compound. She had assisted her mother this way when she'd treated villagers. But that was a long time ago, back before everything had changed for Sabine.

His wound was worse than she'd expected, and one of her aunts had caused it. All they needed was for him to turn them in to the police, and attract all kinds of attention from the newspapers. Not a great way to hide.

Of course, he had broken into their shop. The story he'd told her aunts was convenient and prevented her from having to answer any of their questions. But she'd need to be left alone with him to inquire further about the truth.

He'd been here to ferret around just as those other men had been. Was he their accomplice? That seemed unlikely considering the fight they'd gotten into.

"He's going to need stitches," Agnes said. "Lydia, fetch my sewing basket."

"Why—" Lydia started to argue, but Agnes held up her hand to stop Lydia.

"In case it might have escaped your attention, you shot him. And it appears as if the marquess has saved our lives tonight from those three villains," Agnes said. "Now go and get the basket."

Lydia made no additional protests, but she glared at her sister. "I think we should kick you to the curb as we did the other thieves," she said to Max before she went to grab the basket. "Damned English," she muttered as she traipsed down the hall.

Sabine stepped forward. "Agnes," she said, placing a hand on her aunt's shoulder, "I believe I can manage the

situation from here. The three of you should return to bed."
She nodded firmly to show her resolve. "You need your
rest."

"Are you certain?" Agnes asked.

Sabine merely nodded. Though Sabine wasn't the
Healer, she had been trained as one. Her mother had
died and the guardianship had been passed to Agnes, not
Sabine. It had taken her a couple of years to find confidence amid the doubtful gazes of the villagers who sat
waiting for her failure. She gave her aunt a reassuring
smile. "I'll patch him up and then the marquess will be
on his way, isn't that right?" Sabine nudged his knee.

"Yes, of course," he muttered.

"All will be well, I promise," she said. Her three aunts
stood huddled in the kitchen, merely staring at him.

"I'd thank you for the hospitality," Max said, his deep
voice rumbling through their small kitchen, "but I wouldn't
need such ministrations if I hadn't been shot. But a pleasure to meet all of you." He then gave them a cocky grin.

Sabine could see humor etched around his eyes, and
the knot in her stomach began to dissolve. His smiles
seemed to simultaneously calm and disarm her.

Once her aunts had finally left them alone in the kitchen,
she busied herself with the task at hand, determined not to
allow it to bother her that she was alone with him. It was
of no consequence. She'd been alone with plenty of men.
True, none were as handsome as the marquess.

She knotted the thread and sterilized the needle over
the candle's flame. Meanwhile, she tried to ignore Max's
muscular chest and concentrate on the task at hand. Men
without their shirts were not new to her. Back in Essex,
men often worked in the fields without shirts. The men in
her village were strong and healthy, but they had darker

complexions, with black hair covering their stomachs. In contrast, Max was much fairer than the men in her culture, and his dark blond hair spread across his chest. A lighter sprinkling down his torso narrowed to a tight line that disappeared into his waistband.

She knew how strong he was and how firm his muscles were. Earlier when she'd been pressed against him beneath the stairs, it was the first thing she'd noticed. She'd felt his arm tighten and tense beneath her hand as she'd pinched him to end his unwanted kiss. It mattered not that it had been a most pleasant kiss. More than pleasant, it had been world-tilting. Still it was completely unwarranted and unwanted. She did not have time to dally with this handsome man nor any other. Her focus was on assisting her aunts and especially keeping Agnes safe.

She didn't dare admit that she had, just this evening, journeyed to his home to sneak inside. Sabine and her aunts had sat in a carriage outside his townhome for nearly two hours waiting for the man to leave for the evening.

Lydia had fallen asleep due to boredom. Agnes had become rather cranky, and Calliope had wanted to go forward with the plan and break in despite the marquess's still being at home. But he'd never readied a carriage for himself, never called for a horse or a rig. And the lights in that downstairs corner room had never dimmed, even after other rooms had gone dark. Had that been his study? Perhaps where he kept the map?

In the end, they'd left, returned to their shop, and gone to bed.

And now he was here, doing a little burglary of his own.

"Why were you here tonight?" she asked. The needle pierced his skin, and he sucked in a sharp breath. She made her touch more gentle. There was no need to take her frustration out on his tender flesh. She tried to keep her attention on the stitching.

His gaze slowly rose to meet hers, and the full impact of his clear blue eyes nearly stole her breath away.

"Perhaps I came for another kiss," he said, his mouth tilting in a smile.

She quickly looked away, instead concentrating on his wound. Suddenly being kind and gentle seemed less important; being quick became her goal. He grimaced as she pulled the needle through his flesh. "Well, if that was the case, I believe you came for naught."

"Indeed?"

"The kiss was uninspired at best." She would not allow him to see how truly distracting she found him. "In my estimation, it hardly warranted a special trip, especially in the middle of the night. We both would have found a decent night's sleep more rewarding."

He winced again, whether from her insult or the stitches, she couldn't be certain. Nor did she care, she reminded herself. And it especially didn't matter that she was lying. He need not know that the kiss had shot tingles through her body from her scalp to her toenails. That even still, as she sat here before him, she could taste him, still feel his warmth pressed against her.

"What do you know of my map?" he asked, and this time his voice had taken on a darker tone.

She ignored her churning stomach. It would be best if she kept her nerves to herself. Not only that, but she needed to keep her eagerness at bay. They had to have that map. The lives of her people and family depended on it.

"Someone told me you have in your possession the

only map of the legendary continent of Atlantis." She made another stitch.

Again his eyes met hers. "And who is this someone?" He gave her no time to answer as he continued. "Miss Tobias, it is not widely known that I own that map. Though certainly in some circles…" He trailed off. "I would have assumed that most map collectors would be more concerned with countries that are widely accepted as fact rather than a mythical continent."

She paused over the next stitch to allow her hands to cease shaking. Damn him but he rattled her. It was no great secret that many did not believe in the existence of her homeland, but she had not considered that detail in her lie. He had a good point. A typical map collector would not bother with Atlantis. Real collectors valued detailed maps whose accuracy could be compared with real places. But she couldn't change her story now.

"I don't recall who told me." She hoped she sounded casual. She added a short laugh to enforce the point. "And I collect maps from all over. Fact or fiction. I could not speak to what other collectors might deem appropriate. It's not a scholarly pursuit with me. I told you, I merely find them attractive."

"Might I see your collection? I have a great affinity for maps as well," he said.

The needle slipped, and she accidentally jabbed him. "Sorry. I'm afraid I don't keep them here. This isn't our primary residence."

"Of course," he said. He sat quietly for a moment before he spoke again. "Generally those maps worth collecting do not come at a cheap rate."

"Surely you are not suggesting that I don't appear wealthy enough to be a legitimate map collector," she said. "That would be horribly rude and quite presumptuous."

"Of course not. I could never be that crass."

"Ah, such charm," she said as she pulled the thread through. "I bet that sort of thing works well for you. Most of the time," she added with a little bite to her tone.

"Most of the time," he agreed.

"Perhaps you shouldn't make such assumptions. Things are not always as they appear," she said.

He said nothing, merely sat quietly with that seductive grin of his.

She finished the last stitch and tied off the thread. "There you go." She paused and looked up at him. She once again found herself trapped by his soul-stirring eyes.

She looked away after a moment and tried to recover herself. "You need some salve," she muttered. Gently she smeared a generous amount of the thick ointment over the stitches and the surrounding area. "This will help it heal."

"Thank you," he murmured.

"Regardless of why you were here tonight," she said, "I do appreciate your assistance."

"You need to be careful. Someone is after you, Sabine, and though you won't tell me, I suspect you know why. If you don't have the good sense to let me help, then at least seek assistance from someone." This time she saw no playfulness in his eyes, no teasing.

His advice was sound; she could not deny that. But she had no one she could ask for help. "We can protect ourselves."

"Four women living alone should always be cautious," he said.

She busied herself by cleaning up the supplies. "We are cautious." She had no one but her aunts. "We are perfectly safe here," she insisted, despite the blatant evidence to the contrary.

"Yes," he agreed wryly. "Your aunt's shooting accuracy not withstanding."

He stood then and tugged his shirt on. He cringed as he stretched out his arm to slide on the bloodstained coat. But she made no move to touch him again.

Together they walked down the staircase in silence, then he turned to her and said, "Another kiss for my trouble?"

"I think not," she said, though the invitation and his wicked grin sped up her heart.

"Pity." He bent and pressed his warm mouth over her hand.

Sabine shut and locked the door behind him, then turned for the staircase and nearly walked right into Calliope and her other two aunts, who weren't far behind.

She jumped. "Good heavens, you frightened me. What are you all doing sneaking around?"

"We weren't sneaking," Agnes said.

"We came to assist you," Calliope said.

"Assist me with what, precisely?" Sabine asked as they all made their way upstairs.

None of them answered.

"Did you check the amphora?" Sabine asked.

"Yes, it is right where I left it," Agnes said.

And immediately she felt the fool for even asking. Of course Agnes had taken proper measures to ensure the safety of the elixir.

"He's the one with the map," Lydia said, her arms crossed over her chest. "The one Madigan told you about?"

"Yes," Sabine said. They all followed her into her room. She sat on her bed, hoping they'd get the hint that she was ready to sleep. She didn't want to fend off their questions.

"Younger and more handsome than I'd have thought," Agnes said.

"Indeed." Lydia nodded, her lips pursed.

Calliope nodded enthusiastically.

"I hadn't noticed," Sabine said.

"And I suppose you didn't notice how firm his body looked," Agnes said.

"Agnes, truly!" Lydia chided.

"What?" Agnes tossed her arms up. "I'm old, not blind."

Sabine ignored them both.

"He came into the shop this morning," Calliope said. She eyed her sisters with a wide grin.

Sabine shot her a warning look.

"And you didn't tell us," Agnes asked. She tsked her tongue. "Keeping secrets from your aunts."

Sabine knew Agnes was teasing her. She'd been the very same aunt who had encouraged Sabine to have a part of her life she kept to herself. Still, Lydia was standing right there, and she would expect an answer. "There was no need to," Sabine said.

"What did he want?" Lydia asked.

"He wanted to know why I wanted his map." Sabine shrugged. "How I'd found out about it. Questions any person would have if a woman showed up out of nowhere offering you a wager for your prized possession."

"What did you tell him?" Agnes asked.

Sabine took a deep breath. "I lied. I told him I was a collector."

"He doesn't believe you," Calliope said with a shake of her head.

"That I realize," Sabine said.

"And we still need that map," Lydia said. "Desperately," she added.

"I'll think of something." Sabine eyed her aunts. She had to. And she wanted to accomplish the task without too much of their assistance. They needed to be able to rely on her.

"And what of the other men?" Agnes asked. "What did they want?"

Sabine ran a brush through her hair. "I don't know."

"They had to be after the elixir," Agnes said.

Lydia shook her head. "It is too soon for the Chosen One to have found us. We are too well hidden. Madigan even agreed. And he took extra precautions to make certain he wasn't followed here."

Madigan. He had risked his life to warn them about the prophecy, to tell Sabine where to find the map, and thus far, she had failed in retrieving it. Sabine set the brush down.

"Perhaps it was nothing more than a robbery," Calliope offered. "Yes, I'm certain that's what this was. Stores get robbed all the time."

"Still, they could have been after the elixir," Lydia said.

"Something doesn't fit. Why were there three of them? It's the Chosen One, not the chosen three." Sabine shook her head. "I heard them, and they weren't looking for anything in particular. They were common thugs, nothing more. I cannot believe the Chosen One would send bumblers to do such an important job."

Atlanteans were warned of the Chosen One, since he was the most powerful enemy of her people—cunning and clever, with ways to detect the presence of elixir. Would a person like that make such a mistake? She didn't think so.

They were quiet for a moment as if considering her words, then Lydia took a few steps forward. "Was the use of the elixir necessary tonight?"

"I did what I had to do. You saw his wound. It was deep, the bullet was lodged, and I worried about infection," Sabine said.

"Yes, but he is an Englishman," Lydia said.

Sabine stood from her bed to create distance between her and her eldest aunt. She opened her mouth to answer, but before she could, Agnes spoke. "I am the Healer. It was my choice."

Lydia took a deep breath and nodded, but said nothing more.

Sabine had to get her hands on the prophecy, sooner rather than later. Tomorrow she would pay Maxwell Barrett a visit.

Chapter Five

~~~~~~~~~~~~~~~~~~~~~~~~~

Tonight's kill would be simple. His plan was so clever he still couldn't believe how easy it had been to set up. Spencer waited in dense woods, just outside London, perched on a black horse. Luring his prey had taken some creativity. He had to be careful.

No one investigating these murders could link them to him. Not yet. So he hadn't been able to send notes or invitations. No, he'd made his requests in person. But in the end, his hard work would pay off. Because of his brilliance, he would get two with one clean swipe.

The *Times* had not printed his last two letters, warning the guardians the time had come and their end was near. Perhaps this would get their attention. Though somehow he doubted it. The English were ridiculously arrogant, foolishly believing nothing and no one could cause their country significant harm. Hell, he could send a letter detailing his entire plan, and they would never believe anyone could be capable of such a feat.

He didn't plan on giving these two gentlemen the

choice of joining him. Two generals killed at once would guarantee the authorities took notice. After he took care of the men tonight, he would be leaving for Cornwall. It had taken him a while, but he had finally located the next guardian.

For the completion of the prophecy, he required all three amphoras of elixir. As legend had it, the person who had all three amphoras of elixir became immortal.

Horses' hooves sounded off in the distance, and his own mount stomped in response. He ran his hand down the mare's neck to calm her. Slowly he slid from the saddle, then tied her loosely to a tree. He retrieved a halved apple from his pack and held it out to her. Her whiskers tickled his palm as she took the treat.

The frigid night breeze bit into the exposed flesh on his ears and face. He would have been far warmer enclosed in his carriage, but he couldn't afford to have another witness. Already he had the other driver to be concerned about. Now carriage wheels rumbled closer and closer to his hiding place.

He made his way to the middle of the road and withdrew his pistol. Aiming it straight at the approaching carriage, he held his stance. Though the dark of night was beginning to settle, light from the horizon still illuminated enough of the sky for him to see the surprised and fearful expression of the driver. The man made an effort to swerve, but at the last minute, he pulled the reins, and the horses skidded to a stop inches from Spencer. The steeds stomped restlessly.

He'd made a mistake at the last killing with that servant girl. Having extra bodies for the authorities would only sully his message. He could not afford to indulge himself so carelessly again.

With purposeful steps, he made his way to the driver, never lowering his gun. "Run," he told him. And the driver made no delay in doing precisely that.

"What the devil..." One of the men from the interior opened the door and sputtered when he saw the gun aimed at him. It was Clyde, the adjutant-general, which made him the most senior officer in her majesty's army, though many remained perplexed by how the man made it that far.

And Spencer knew precisely who would take his place—a fine gentleman already sympathetic to Spencer's cause. "Good evening, gentlemen," he said calmly.

"Cole," Clyde said in surprise. Then the man chuckled. "Quite a jest"—he nudged the man next to him—"pretending to rob our coach." He motioned to the pistol in Spencer's hand.

Clyde, of course, was the easy prey, always up for a night of drinking and prurient entertainment.

The other man, Mercer, found no humor in the situation. Naturally more suspicious, he had been harder to tempt onto this deserted country road. Clyde had achieved his position through the connections of his powerful family, but Mercer had clawed his way to the top through cunning and ambition. "I thought we were meeting you at the Hog's Hair Inn."

Spencer shrugged. "Change of plans."

"What do you want?" Mercer asked.

"What's going on?" Clyde asked.

Mercer's shrewd eyes narrowed. He had quite the reputation for being a brilliant strategist. He put his hand to his belt.

"There's no need to go for your weapon," Spencer told

him as he raised his own gun. "There isn't time. I can assure you I'm a perfect marksman."

"Our money," Clyde said as realization struck him. "You can have our money."

"I'm afraid money is not what I'm after." Mercer pulled out his own pistol, but Spencer was faster. He fired a shot straight into the man's heart. Then he shot the older man in the head.

Clyde's expression froze into a look of permanent surprise, and Mercer clasped a hand to his chest, struggling to get off a single shot as his heart pumped the last of his blood from his body.

"And you make five."

"Son of a bitch!" Max cursed loudly as he pulled off his shirt. He tossed it into the newly lit fire warming his bedchamber. The flames roared as they engulfed the linen. He stood in front of the mirror looking at the gunshot wound just below his shoulder. The stitches were even and small; she'd done a good job, he'd give her that. The wound, though, was an angry red mark and hurt like the devil. He'd be fortunate if it didn't leave one hell of a nasty scar.

But tonight had been futile.

Except for the kiss. She'd been surprisingly passionate. Yet full of pluck and fire. Precisely the sort of combination he found irresistible in women. He'd been tempted by their interlude at the gaming hell, but now he knew how Sabine Tobias felt in his arms. Under normal circumstances, he would pursue her, yet she seemed utterly unmoved by his charms. Of course, this wasn't surprising given that he had broken into her home.

He had not gone there for a kiss, though, while it was a worthwhile diversion. And he certainly hadn't gone there to offer protection to her or her aunts. Protecting people had never been his forte. Information was what he'd been after, and still he knew nothing about her connection to his map. She refused to admit knowing anything significant about it, but he knew she was lying. Most collectors preferred more legitimate ways to obtain items of their interest. Once or twice over the years, he'd been contacted by solicitors representing such individuals, but he'd never even considered selling the map.

Earlier that evening, his security guard had alerted him to the presence of a waiting carriage with four women inside. It had been hidden well, but with a clear view of his front door. They'd waited for a couple of hours, then had given up and left.

Her underhanded approach led him to only one conclusion. There was more to the charming Miss Tobias than met the eye. The late-night visitors to her shop only backed up that theory. Unfortunately for Miss Tobias, he was a man who enjoyed a challenge. And he fully intended to find out exactly what she was hiding.

Sabine wanted that map, and when she came to retrieve it, he'd be here waiting.

"Say it again. Slowly this time," Cassandra said through gritted teeth.

"We didn't find nothing," Beaver said, scratching at his scruffy chin. His dirt-encrusted fingernails made Cassandra shudder. Filthy beast.

"Nothing," Cassandra repeated. She strolled through her parlor, running her fingertips over the furniture as she passed. "Nothing." She sized up the three men and offered them a smile that was more snarl than anything. "How is it that you found nothing?"

Johns stepped forward, holding his stocking cap against his abdomen. "Miss, we searched the entire residence."

Five years her junior, Johns was a perfect male specimen, as if his muscular frame had been chiseled first in marble. And his face rivaled that of Adonis. His sheer size was normally enough to frighten anyone away from him, but Cassandra knew he was not quick to violence, and she could persuade him to do almost anything. He was her most trusted employee and, though it galled her, most frequent lover.

"We didn't really know what we was looking for," Johns continued.

"Anything that resembled the healing waters." It was what she'd told them she was after, a simple lie for simple minds. No one could know about the fountain of youth. "Or notes or a recipe for their products." She stepped around the parlor furniture to where the three men stood before the hearth. Eyeing them closely, she took her time to make them nervous. "Tell me, did you talk to any of the women, give them any indication what you were looking for?"

"No," Beaver said, his head shaking back and forth in confirmation. "We ran when they started shooting at us. There was a man, too. Broke my nose."

She steepled her red-painted nails beneath her chin. "A man lives with them?"

"I don't think so," Johns said. "I didn't see him, but I think they was shooting at him, too."

"Interesting," she said. She stepped over to the third one, enjoying the fact that she stood a head taller than the scrawny man. "What about you, Platt? What do you have to say for yourself?"

The man simply stood there.

"You know, Miss, he don't talk," Beaver offered.

"So you keep telling me," she said, never taking her eyes off Platt. "But it's always been my experience that if you kick a dog hard enough, he'll always yelp." She winked at Johns before walking away.

Once she'd reached her gold brocade settee, she sank into the luxurious fabric. "Now then, gentlemen," she said tightly. "What is it that you're going to do to make this little foible up to me? You know how I loathe disappointment."

The three men looked blankly at one another, presumably hoping that one of them would have a brilliant idea. Which, of course, she was not expecting. She decided how things were done around here, and they knew that, but that didn't prevent her from taunting them.

"I prefer to think I'm a generous employer. I should think among the three of you, you might come up with one entire brain and find one worthwhile idea."

"We looked all through the storeroom," Beaver said. "We tried to get upstairs to search, but that's when the man jumped out at us."

She needed to find out who this man was. Perhaps he knew of the fountain, too. Perhaps she had competition.

Cassandra was on the right track. She knew that much. Max had provided her with the confirmation that this Tobias woman was where Cassandra should be looking. She had something to do with Atlantis or Max wouldn't be sniffing around the woman's shop.

She held up one of the jars she'd purchased. Something in this crème made women look younger. She'd already experienced it herself. But using crème wouldn't keep her forever young, Cassandra knew that. She needed the fountain itself.

"Leave," she commanded her men. "I will devise a new plan. In the meantime, stay out of trouble, and I'll send for you when I need you."

They all turned to go, and she caught sight of Johns's broad shoulders. "Johns, not you. There is something else I need you to attend to."

Chapter Six

Max had just swallowed his first sip of brandy in an attempt to dull the pain when a knock came on his bedchamber door.

"A gentleman to see you," his butler said.

Max frowned. "At this hour?"

"He is with the Metropolitan Police, my lord. He's waiting in your study."

Son of a bitch. He'd barely gotten home, and they'd already sent the police calling on him. They'd shot him; he would have thought that enough retribution for breaking into their shop. Not bothering to put on another shirt or shoes, Max made his way downstairs to his study, and upon entering, he found Justin Salinger standing in the doorway. Justin was a fellow member of the exclusive legend hunter's club, Solomon's. Max relaxed a little, knowing he wouldn't have to come up with some story to explain his presence at their shop.

"I need your help," Justin said.

"It's bloody late, Salinger. Help with what?" Max

asked. Normally Max was more hospitable, but the gunshot wound irritated the hell out of him. He knew Justin, but not well. The man was new to Solomon's, so they had only met on a few occasions. Max came around his desk and motioned for Justin to have a seat opposite him. "Brandy?"

"No. My apologies about the time," Justin said with a smile as he noted Max's appearance. "It's for an investigation, actually."

"Here on official business with the Yard, then?" He flopped into the chair adjacent to the inspector. Perhaps Justin really was here to arrest him. "That little minx. Did they report me right after I left?"

"Report you?" Justin shook his head. "No, I'm here about a murder," Justin said. "Five of them, actually."

"Well, then, if you're not here to haul me off to prison, I think I'll have a brandy. Are you sure you don't want one?"

Justin smiled. "You've convinced me. Brandy would be good."

Max relaxed a little and poured them each a drink. He handed one to Justin.

"I have to ask"—he pointed to Max's stitches—"what happened?"

Max shrugged as he returned to his chair. "I got shot tonight."

"The little minx?" Justin asked, repeating Max's earlier words.

"Not exactly, but close enough. I haven't decided yet if she's going to be worth all the trouble she will no doubt cause."

"But you're going to wait her out." Justin smiled.

"Something like that." Max took a swig. He still didn't

know what the hell any of this had to do with him, but at least the inspector wasn't here to bring him in. "Five connected murders?" Max asked.

"I believe so. Someone's after the crown." He took a sip of his drink, then balanced the glass on his knee.

Max frowned. "What are you talking about, Justin?"

"The generals that have recently died. Have you seen anything about that?"

Max nodded. "In the papers. They did say there were a couple of suicides," Max said. "Something about a mistake in a mission in Africa."

"The first death was initially believed to be a suicide or even merely an accident. But the bodies have continued to mount, and we're now considering that first one a homicide. Five generals in a shockingly short amount of time. Last night, General Lancer was found in his study with an apparent gunshot to the head."

Max leaned forward. "It does seem unlikely the first isn't connected to these others," he said.

"General Reasoner was the one killed in the fire. We assume now he was our first. Then General Carrington had his throat slit, and Lancer was shot in the head," Justin said.

"What of the other two?" Max asked.

Justin leaned back and wiped a hand over his face. "Killed tonight in a carriage just outside London. Mercer and Clyde. They were together, presumably heading to a meeting of some sort, though it's unknown whom the two of them would be meeting together. Under normal circumstances, an army officer would not meet with one from the navy. And it was well known that they didn't care for each other." Justin shook his head. "Makes no sense. They were ambushed. The driver is missing. We're still trying to find him, but..."

"Perhaps the driver shot them and then stole their valuables," Max said.

Justin exhaled slowly and then came to his feet. "It was the first thing we checked. Both men had substantial amounts of money on them and were still wearing their jewelry."

"Those two men together." Max whistled. "The highest-ranking military officer and a naval officer."

"I know. We know with certainty that their deaths are connected to the other three. We found a damned note." Justin leaned forward, bracing his arms on Max's desk. "*Not* written by either victim." He pinched the bridge of his nose. "I really shouldn't discuss these matters with a civilian, but I need your expertise."

He pulled the parchment out of his pocket and dropped it onto Max's desk. As Max reached for the note, Justin slammed his own hand down onto it. "If you tell anyone I showed these to you, I'll shoot you."

"Get in line," Max said with a chuckle.

"The other letter didn't make much sense. We suspect there might have been one with Carrington, but perhaps his wife took it. She found the body. We've sent an officer over to discuss the matter with her."

Justin handed Max the note across the desk. Max unfolded the parchment, then scanned the florid lines.

"Bastard wants us to print this in the *Times*," Justin said. "The language is so peculiar. 'Seven rings of Atlantis,'" Justin quoted. "What the hell does that have to do with our military?"

Max looked up from the letter. "This is why you came to me?" Max asked.

"Yes. Everyone at the Yard thinks the killer is delusional or something. I figured if anyone knew anything it would be you."

Max linked his fingers and rested his hands atop his abdomen. "Seven rings of Atlantis," Max repeated.

"That's familiar to you," Justin said with a broad smile. "I knew it would be."

"Yes, I recognize it." Max nodded slowly. "But I don't know why anyone would use it."

"What is it?" Justin asked.

Max pointed over his shoulder to the map framed on the wall. "It's from the map. It took me years to locate all the inscriptions and to complete the necessary research to make some sense of it. It's the ancient prophecy woven through the map's illustrations that predicted the destruction of Atlantis."

"That does not help me, Max. I can't go back to the Yard and tell them it's a prophecy."

"*Was* a prophecy," Max corrected.

"That's beside the point."

Max shook his head. "Clearly someone has a message they want to get out. You said they want you to print it in the newspaper. What would be the point of that?"

"I'm guessing that stems solely from arrogance," Justin said. "But it does appear to be an actual message to someone."

"I might know who to ask." No one had inquired about his map in years, and suddenly it happened twice in two days. Max didn't believe in coincidences. He looked down at the note again and pointed to the top. "This is addressed to the 'guardian.' I've never come across mention of that in any of my research."

"I suspect it to be her majesty. Which brings me to yet

another favor. I want to see if she has heard anything and to perhaps warn her that it might be time to increase her security. For herself and for her officers."

Max raised his eyebrows.

"I need to get in to see the queen, and there's nothing about my status that will get me an audience with her," Justin explained. "Third sons who work for the Metropolitan Police are not too high on the list when it comes to the monarchy."

"I haven't seen her majesty in quite a while, but she always seemed rather fond of me," Max said with a grin.

"Thank you." Justin sighed heavily. "Now tell me about this prophecy."

"Take a look for yourself," Max said.

"Is it true you found it when you were only seventeen?"

"Yes," Max said.

Justin accepted the invitation and came around the desk to stand in front of the large, framed map. "This is quite a masterpiece."

It took up nearly a quarter of the wall. The hand coloring had not faded over the years so it remained as vibrant and beautiful as the day Max had discovered it. He never tired of looking at it. It only fueled his desire to one day see the sunken land for himself.

"Yes," Max agreed.

After several moments of staring at the map, Justin leaned back. "Where is the prophecy?"

"You have to look closely," Max said. "Follow the water rings, then that grove of trees." He pointed. "The prophecy is embedded in the images of the map."

Justin stared back at the map. "Oh, here we go. Hidden symbols," he muttered. "Problem is, though, I don't read Greek."

"*The seven rings of Atlantis will fall by fire and steel, opening the path for the army of one. Empires will crumble and crowns will melt. The three will lose their blood unless the dove can bring salvation*," Max said. He'd memorized it years ago.

"What is the dove?" he asked.

"I've found no mention of that in my research either, though I have tried. Best I can figure out is it must have been some sort of weapon. Or perhaps a plan." Max shrugged. "Whatever it was, it didn't work. Atlantis was not saved, if the myth is to be believed at all. Though it seems unlikely anything would have saved them from the earthquake or volcanic eruption—or whatever happened that sank the island." Max released a heavy sigh.

"Frustrated?" Justin chuckled. "I've felt like that often in my Treasure Island research." He looked back at the map.

Justin had only recently been admitted to Solomon's. He'd just begun his search. So if Justin was disheartened about his quest for Treasure Island, well, Max could teach the man a thing or two about perseverance.

Max had been searching for Atlantis for the better part of his life. There were long stretches of time where it seemed he made no progress. Other times, it felt as if the proof he sought sat just out of reach. Just out of his sight. As if he might round the next corner and find it standing before him.

As frustrating as the endless search was, it was moments like that that kept Max going. Being a legend hunter took not merely skill, and intelligence, but perseverance as well. Max's instincts told him Justin possessed all three. If the intensity with which Justin focused on

Max's map was any indication. Justin stared at the map so long that Max expected him to say something more.

Max, on the other hand, had been a member of Solomon's for fifteen years. When he found the map of Atlantis at the age of seventeen, Solomon's had invited him to join. They had expected him to go on to do something amazing. He had expected the same thing.

Of course, he'd had his share of success aiding other members. Yet no matter how skilled he was at research and detection, proof that Atlantis had existed eluded him. The juicy grapes still dangled above the mouth of the starving Tantalus.

And yet, he knew with a bone-deep certainty that the proof was out there. Somewhere. There was nothing he wouldn't give to obtain it.

Justin began repeating the prophecy slowly, as if mulling over every word. Finally, he turned and said, "What if the prophecy isn't about the demise of Atlantis?"

"Impossible." Max shook his head. How many times, late at night, had he studied that map looking for hidden clues, then scoured through ancient texts for assistance? Naturally, he knew the words of the prophecy as well as he knew his own reflection. "What else could it be?"

"What I mean is, what if someone else *believed* it to be about something other than Atlantis?" Justin asked. His eyes held that spark of discovery. Bloody hell, what he was suggesting was certainly a possibility. That hint of a new clue was an irresistible lure to an adventurer like Max.

Grudgingly, Max rose to stand beside Justin. So this young pup thought he could discover something new in the map? Well, no one knew the map or the prophecy better than Max. Max stared at the prophecy, considering

Justin's words. If one *assumed* the prophecy wasn't about the destruction of Atlantis, then what would it be about?

"Something that hasn't yet happened," Max said aloud.

"Precisely. These rings"—Justin pointed to each on the map—"the seven rings of Atlantis, they were in place to protect the island nation, correct?"

"Yes, precisely. The alternating rings of land and water gave Atlantis great protection from warring nations." Max slanted a look at Justin. "And you said you thought the guardian referred to the queen. So who protects the queen? Who protects all of England?"

"The military," Justin answered grimly.

"Exactly," Max said.

"If I'm correct, then this murderer is following the prophecy, twisting it so that the seven rings represent seven generals."

Max's own enthusiasm dimmed a bit as he realized that the new discovery did not involve Atlantis.

"Five of whom are already dead," Justin said.

Max listened, but said nothing. This entire scenario seemed highly improbable.

"Who are the three that the prophecy refers to?" Justin traced a line of the prophecy through the glass.

"Justin, as far as I'm aware, very few people know anything about the existence of the prophecy. People have seen my map"—Max shook his head—"but I doubt they notice. It took me a long while to discover it."

"Perhaps it is printed elsewhere," Justin offered.

It was plausible, but none of Max's research had ever suggested that the prophecy was a warning about the future. Granted, he'd never found the exact wording of the prophecy printed anywhere else. Whether or not there was a connection, there were still lives in danger, and Justin was right, their queen needed to be warned.

"Who else would know about any of this?" Justin asked. "Any other Atlantis experts I could question?"

Sabine's lovely face appeared in Max's mind. She had arrived out of nowhere asking questions about the map. Did she have something to do with these murders? Max wanted to get answers from her before Justin had the chance. "I'll see what I can find out for you," he said.

Justin stepped back around the desk. "They'll be missing this out of the evidence room." He pocketed the note. "So I need to get it back. I should be going. My apologies for interrupting you so late this evening."

Max nodded.

"Let me know if you discover anything," Justin said.

"There is no time to delay with something such as this," Max said. "Tomorrow morning, we can try to see her majesty. Meet me at the palace."

Justin nodded. "Appreciate it."

Max continued staring at the map long after Justin had left. He would definitely have to pay Sabine another visit. Whether she was ready or not, it was time to share those secrets of hers.

Spencer looked up from his desk to stare at the girl. She was new, inexperienced and terrified. "What?"

She flinched. "There are two gentlemen here to see her majesty," the maid said.

"Who are they?" He stood and walked around his desk to lean on it. "You always need to know who they are before you come in here. I know you've been told that before."

Her chin quaked, but she did not cry. "Yes sir, Mr. Cole. It's an Inspector Salinger from Scotland Yard and the Marquess of Lindberg."

"Inspector Salinger." Cole thought on the name for a moment, but he did not recognize it. "That is not who we normally communicate with at the Yard." And the marquess. Interesting pair. Spencer knew little about the man other than that he was a member of that ridiculous club, Solomon's, foolish gentlemen who fancied themselves treasure hunters. But Spencer did know the marquess had the map of Atlantis. Once he had tried to break in and steal that map, but had failed. The security had been rather sophisticated. And he'd been young and foolish and inexperienced then. Everything was different now.

Had the inspector gone to the marquess as an Atlantis expert to consult on the case? "Show them in," he said.

The maid bobbed a sweet curtsy, then left the room. A moment later, the two men entered the waiting chamber. Just outside her majesty's offices, it was the closest one could be to the queen.

The inspector appeared to be of a similar age to Spencer, while the marquess had perhaps five years on them. Perhaps if he had been raised in a traditional fashion, they would have shared times at school. "Please sit," he offered. But the men made no move to take the offered chairs. "It's my understanding that you requested a visit with her majesty," he said.

"We did," the marquess said. "The inspector here"—he motioned to the other man—"has some official business to discuss with her."

"I am afraid that her majesty is not feeling well today." Spencer smiled. "Nothing to be alarmed by, though, I can assure you, but she asked that I take her meetings and then report back to her. What is it that I can assist you with today, gentlemen?"

The inspector eyed the marquess cautiously, but the marquess nodded, urging his friend to go forward.

"It would seem that someone is making sport of our military officers," the inspector said.

Ah, so that was why they were here. The Yard had finally paid attention. Had it been his note to the guardian that had made them take notice? Or perhaps this inspector was more clever than the rest. "Making sport?" Spencer asked, feigning ignorance.

"Killing them, sir. Five of them thus far." The inspector's concern clearly showed in his furrowed brow. "I thought it prudent to notify her majesty so that she might take the proper precautions. Alert the officers that they should be on guard," the inspector said. "Perhaps offer extra protection."

"You are certain these haven't been accidents? They are military men, after all," Spencer countered, merely for his own amusement. "I have heard of countless accidents on the field of battle and even in their own homes. Cleaning a gun, perhaps." Of course, he, as the Chosen One, would never try to convince them the killings hadn't been murders. Still, he couldn't resist toying with these two men, if only for a little while.

"No, we know for certain the deaths are connected," the marquess spoke up.

So the marquess had been brought in to assist with the investigation.

"There's more," the inspector said. "There is evidence at this last scene indicating that her majesty could be in danger. I wanted to warn her. Her security is of our upmost concern at the Yard."

"I can assure you, Inspector, that the security for Queen Victoria is quite thorough. But we will take your suggestion under advisement," Spencer said.

The inspector pulled a card out of the inside of his jacket and placed it on Spencer's desk. "If you could pass this along to her. Should she have any questions, I am at her service."

"Splendid." Spencer tucked the card into his own jacket. "I will be certain to tell her majesty of your visit and your concerns," Spencer said. "Rest assured that we will do whatever is necessary to protect our military officers. It would be devastating to our country to lose any more of them."

The men said their good-byes, then left. Spencer waited another moment, then lit a match and held it to the inspector's card. The flame ate at the paper, consuming the letters of the man's name, first in black then in ash. Victoria knew about the murders; she was kept informed. But there was no reason to notify her of this particular visit.

It was laughable that Scotland Yard had contacted the marquess for assistance—as if he were an expert on the subject of Atlantis. The man had found a map, but he was a treasure hunter, nothing more. All the same, perhaps it would behoove Spencer to investigate this marquess.

Unlike the bloody nobleman who was merely obsessed with the lost land, Spencer had Atlantis in his blood, beating within his heart. He was from a long line of great warriors, and it was past time for them to regain power and finish what his ancestors had started.

Max and Justin made their way into the main room of Solomon's. For a Friday afternoon, more people than usual filled the area. A familiar face smiled from the right-hand corner and waved the two of them over.

"Fielding," Max said as they approached the table. They shook hands.

Fielding folded up the newspaper he'd been reading and set it on the table.

It had only been a few months before that Fielding and his new bride had taken refuge at Max's house during a dangerous adventure, and now they were both members of the exclusive club. "Where's the wife?"

"Shopping." Fielding looked over at the door. "She was supposed to meet me half an hour ago. She's late, as usual."

"You know Justin Salinger, right?" Max asked.

"We've met once, I think," Justin said. The two of them joined Fielding at his table.

"Have you heard from the Raven?" Max asked Fielding.

Fielding leaned forward and tapped two fingers on the table. "The thing about my uncle is, he never makes his presence known until he either needs something or is setting a trap." Fielding smiled. "I don't suspect he'll hide forever, though. There's too much treasure out there waiting to be claimed."

Max nodded. "He's been causing problems for the men of Solomon's for years. More than likely we haven't seen the last of him."

"Of that, I have no doubt," Fielding said.

A moment later, two more gentlemen stepped inside. Max knew them all and waved.

Nick Callum and Graeme Langford sidled over to the table and took seats; Nick flipped his around and straddled it.

"It's a compulsion with you to be different," Graeme noted, pointing to Nick's chair.

Nick cursed Graeme in response.

"Children," Max chided, then laughed.

"How goes the Atlantis search?" Graeme asked.

Max shrugged. "New research of late, but I'm not certain it will lead to anything."

"He got shot," Justin added.

"Not the first time," Fielding said.

Max chuckled. "I forgot I told you that story."

"It was a woman that shot him," Justin teased.

"Who was it this time?" Fielding asked.

"What the devil, Salinger, if you tell all my bloody secrets, I'll tell yours," Max said. It was unlikely he'd share official police business, especially if her majesty was in danger, though any of that information would be safe here among these men.

Then Esme Grey came in, wife of Fielding and the only female member of Solomon's. Inviting a woman to join their infamous roster had never been an option until Esme. She and Fielding had been offered membership the previous summer after saving the crown jewels, not to mention Pandora's box. Max had wholeheartedly approved of the addition of the Greys to Solomon's.

"Hello, darling," she said as she swooped down to kiss Fielding's cheek.

Nick grabbed a chair for her from the next table.

"Thank you," she said, plopping herself down next to her husband.

"Did you spend all of our money?" Fielding asked.

She gave a dainty shrug. "Perhaps." Then she began digging into her shopping bag. "I know you will all be delighted to know I have purchased a new pair of gloves," she said, placing them on the table, "a new hat," again, it went onto the table, "and some fancy face crème." She set the jar down as well.

"I knew if we allowed a woman in our midst, she'd start bringing in fancy-smelling whatnots," Nick said with feigned annoyance.

"I'll have you know that none of this is for here, this is all for me," Esme said teasingly.

Max looked down at Esme's treasures. Normally he wouldn't have given much thought to anything a woman had bought. Shouldn't normally care about a lady's trinkets or toilet items. But just as he was about to look away, something caught his glance.

He snatched up the jar of crème for a better inspection.

"See there, you've already ruined Lindberg," Nick said.

Max shook his head, then he looked up at Esme. "Did you buy this at the little shop in Piccadilly Square?"

Her eyes widened. "Yes. A friend suggested it, said it's all the rage right now. It's supposed to remove unwanted lines from one's face." She smiled brightly. "Perhaps we'll use some on you right here." With her finger, she smoothed the skin between Fielding's brows.

He swatted her hand away. "Those lines make me look distinguished. Otherwise I'd be just as pretty as Nick here."

"Why do you ask?" Esme turned to Max.

"I had the opportunity to meet Miss Tobias recently," he said.

"Isn't she utterly charming? And so beautiful," Esme said.

"Charming and beautiful," Justin repeated. "You never mentioned that."

"So she's the lass who shot you?" Graeme asked.

"Not exactly," Max said.

"Honestly, Max, you must be more careful," Esme warned.

"I will endeavor to be so. Now if you would all excuse me, I'm going to see if Marcus is here." He stood.

"Research library," Fielding said. "He came in about an hour ago looking as stern and focused as ever."

Max nodded and left the table.

He didn't know Marcus Campbell well, only that he generally kept to himself, quiet and intently focused on his own particular research. That and he was building a unique machine that could be quite beneficial to Max.

As Fielding had said, Marcus stood behind a table in the research library poring over two large maps. He walked from one to the other, jotting notes in his notebook as he went.

"Marcus," Max said as he entered the room.

Marcus didn't acknowledge Max's presence initially; he simply continued writing in his book. When he finished, he looked up.

"Ah, Lindberg, it's you." Marcus looked back down at the maps.

Max took a seat. "How goes the submersible boat, Marcus?"

Marcus looked up from his map. "I told you that you may not borrow my design."

"Yes, you did. But you did not say whether or not I could actually borrow the boat." Max shrugged. "Once it's finished, of course."

"For this Atlantis escapade?" Marcus set his notebook down. "I would need proof."

"And more funding," Max noted. "I heard the Americans

are having another contest, awarding the winner two million dollars."

Marcus scoffed. "They want war machines with torpedoes. What I am building"—he jabbed his finger onto his notebook—"is for scientific exploration."

Max knew for certain that the plans for said machine were in that notebook—drawings, dimensions, and all of Marcus's well-developed research. "Precisely why I would like to use it," Max said, leaning forward. "I can assist with funding."

Marcus was quiet for several moments before he spoke again. "You bring me proof, and we'll talk," he finally said.

"Proof," Max repeated. "I'll be in touch, Marcus."

Without use of that submersible boat, Max would not be able to actually locate the lost continent. But to float above the sunken land, to get close enough to see the remnants of the buildings and the mountains, everything he'd seen illustrated in his map...That's what he needed to do. He had to find some kind of proof, something Marcus could use that would convince him Atlantis wasn't a lost cause.

Chapter Seven

$\sim\!\!\sim\!\!\sim$

Sabine sat quietly in the rented carriage. She took several deep breaths and waited for something to calm her rattled insides. Nothing did. She did not even know what had her so agitated. A healer should always check on her patients, and this man should be no different. Of course that wasn't her true purpose, and he'd know that. Max Barrett was no fool. He'd see through her guise. Still, she didn't know if he'd allow her to see the map otherwise.

She was out of time. Her nerves be damned; she had responsibilities. Without another thought, she opened the door and stepped down from the carriage onto the tree-lined street. Her gaze drifted down one side of the street and then the other. The houses were uniformly elegant and oversized. No doubt they were all as well appointed within as they were without. In the middle of all this ostentatious wealth sat the home of Maxwell Barrett. One of three residences, if Madigan's research had been correct. He might be ridiculously wealthy and powerful by Society's standards, but she would not allow this man to intimidate her. She was not without power herself, though hers was of a vastly different nature.

Dusk was settling as she climbed the stairs to the front entrance. The hazy blues and pinks of the sunset lit the horizon. She squared her shoulders, then slammed the large knocker against the black wooden door. The echoing sound seemed to mimic the pounding of her heart.

Before she knew it, she stood in the marquess's foyer while his butler went to fetch him. She tried her best not to ogle the entryway with its high, painted Venetian ceiling and shiny marble floor. It was nothing short of breathtaking, and if she'd had any doubts before, this entryway spoke volumes about the marquess's wealth.

One pat to her hair and then she smoothed her hand down the front of her bodice. Her new London attire was still a little unfamiliar to her, the way it molded to her body. She and her aunts had changed their dress when they'd moved here to better blend with the people. Her hand rose to her hair again, but she jerked it away. There was no need to preen for him, she reminded herself. It mattered not what he thought of her.

Still, as he entered the foyer, her heart leaped in her chest. The mere sight of him made her breath quicken and her pulse race. As much as she didn't want to admit it, she found herself utterly drawn to him.

"Miss Tobias." Max's sultry voice warmed her.

Annoyed, she brushed at her right sleeve, as if doing so would remove the effect his voice had on her.

It would do her no good to notice how handsome he looked in his starched white shirt and black coat. Nor the way his black trousers fit his long legs so well.

"I could make plenty of assumptions as to why you've come to visit me here at my home," he said. "But perhaps you want to merely tell me so I won't have to guess. It would go against the precedent we've set for our relationship, but let's be daring, shall we?"

Her cheeks warmed in response to his effort to disarm her, but she refused to be charmed by him. She was not here to flirt or be wooed. "I came to check on your injury. How are you feeling?"

"You came all the way down here to inquire about my well-being? I'm touched, truly." He flashed a knowing smile. "Well, if I must disrobe, we had best get out of the hall."

She followed him into what she assumed was his study. It was obviously a man's room, and the furnishings and fabrics stood out in dark blues and golds with rich woods. It smelled of brandy and tobacco and what she was coming to recognize as his scent. Hanging on the wall behind his desk was the map, huge and glorious. She longed to walk up to it and examine every tiny mark. The vibrant blues and greens of the alternating rings of water and land called to her, but she forced herself to look away.

"This is twice now you've gotten me to undress," he said as he finished unbuttoning his shirt.

"You are incorrigible," she said.

"Are you always so dedicated to your patients?" He shrugged out of the shirt and tossed it on the high-backed leather chair behind him.

She stepped up to him, ignoring his question, and touched near his injury. His skin was warm, but not feverish, and the stitches looked healthy, with the wound already beginning to close.

He moved his arm back and forth, then frowned. "It doesn't hurt. I don't think I noticed that all day." He shook his head. "It hasn't hurt all day. How is that even possible?"

She pretended to examine the wound further. "I told you it wasn't very deep."

"It hurt like the devil last night. Kept me up." He looked down at his chest and ran his hand over the affected area. "Yet today it's as if it were nothing more than a scratch." He eyed her suspiciously. "My last gunshot took more than a week to heal, and it was little more than a grazing."

"I gave you proper care. Those stitches are perfect," she pointed out. "And you are in good health, so it stands to reason that you would heal quickly."

"Not this quickly. What of that poultice you put in it? What's in that?"

She shrugged and stepped away from him. "Herbs and other ingredients. It's an old family recipe."

"You always have an answer," he said. It was quite evident he didn't believe her. He grabbed her shoulder. "But that's not why you really came here tonight." He paused for several beats, and she felt very much like the mouse cornered by the cat. "You want to see my map?"

"It's beautiful," she said, hoping she sounded casual.

"It is indeed a work of art."

But the rogue didn't so much as glance at the map as he spoke, instead choosing to stare boldly at her.

"The wager the other night, was I supposed to take that in stride? Not allow myself to become curious?" he asked.

"I told you everything you needed to know."

He leaned against his desk, stretching his legs out in front of him. "No, you told me the absolute minimum."

"You show up in my store demanding information." She jabbed him in the chest. "Break into my store presumably to steal something. You, you kiss me," she said indignantly, then added, "and now I'm supposed to simply answer your questions as if I'm to stand trial for something."

"I did not steal anything, nor had I planned to do so. And I only went to your shop because of that wager you made. I am glad you finally admit you know something," he said with a smile.

She opened her mouth, then promptly shut it. Damnation. Lydia had always warned her that her quick temper would get her into trouble.

"You are bloody stubborn, woman." He held up his arms in defeat. "You came here tonight to see my map. Now you've seen it." He motioned behind him.

But she needed more than a quick view, and he knew that. She said nothing, though. Instead she quickly tried to decide how much she could share with him, how much information she could divulge without putting herself or her aunts in more danger than they were already in. She glanced past his shoulder to the map.

"Answers are my price, Sabine," he said.

What had she expected? For him to simply step aside and allow her to inspect his prized possession without ever telling him why? As much as it galled her, she was going to have to tell him something. It was the only way to find the prophecy. She had no choice.

"How about this?" he continued. "You ask me anything you want to know, I'll answer. But then you must answer my questions."

She squared her shoulders and tilted her chin, then met his gaze. It was a decent bargain. She couldn't deny that she was curious. "Two questions; I'll answer two," she said.

"Fair enough." His lips tilted in a quick smile.

"Wait, I haven't decided if I'm curious enough about anything regarding you to make this bargain." She narrowed her eyes and stared at him. Of course she was curious, but she didn't want him to see her eagerness. Curiosity or not, she had to accept, but there was no reason to let him know of her desperation. She nodded.

She tried to decide the best questions to ask. Tried to wade past her own interest and instead focus on something that might assist her and her aunts. "Why do you have that map? What is your curiosity about Atlantis that led you to even search for it?"

"That's two questions," he teased, then he shrugged and answered. "I found that map many years ago after a childhood fascination with Atlantis. I've always had a curiosity about antiquities and myths, stories of lost treasure. The legend of Atlantis was my favorite. I suppose it simply stuck with me."

"But why the fascination?" she asked.

"Treasure," he said simply. "They say that Poseidon's palace was made entirely of gold."

She looked about the room—solid mahogany furniture, crystal decanters, fine leather-upholstered chairs. Even the way he dressed, despite his casual manner. The fabrics were all the best one could purchase. "You have plenty of wealth."

A smile slid into place, then he winked. "There is always room for more."

Questions asked and answered, yet she felt completely unsatisfied. She wondered now if she'd asked the right questions. Or if she should have agreed to three or even four. Perhaps she should have asked about why he had not followed his Society's rules and married and produced an heir. Why he had kissed her the other night—but then none of those answers would have given her any useful information.

Then it occurred to her that he was probably lying. The night they'd played cards, he'd readily walked away from a lucrative wager to instead request nothing more than a kiss. Chances were he didn't play at all to acquire wealth, but more for the sport of it. "Wealth," she scoffed, then crossed her arms over her chest for added effect. "You could have made up a more believable excuse. If you want me to be honest, you must be in return."

A muscle ticked ever so slightly in his jaw. "You are very perceptive, Sabine."

"I never gave you leave to use my given name," she said.

"I never have been good at minding my manners," he countered with an arched brow.

"Answer my question honestly," she urged.

"Very well. I went after that map to prove the existence of Atlantis."

"So you admit that you are a scholar?" she asked, unable to keep the surprise from her voice.

He chuckled, and the rich rumble was so authentic, so full of true humor, she fought the desire to smile in response. "Few would call me that. But I suppose there are less-fitting terms."

"And did you?" she asked.

"What?" he asked.

"Prove the existence of Atlantis?"

Again she saw the slight muscle tense in his jaw line. "To some perhaps. But not everyone." He pushed off his desk and crossed over to the chair where he'd earlier tossed his shirt. He slid his arms through the sleeves, but did not bother to rebutton it. Instead he left it gaping open. The resulting look was so sensual, so dashing, her mouth went dry. "There are those who still doubt, still believe the lost continent is nothing more than a piece of fiction penned by Plato."

"But the map?" She ventured another peek at the map. "That is not proof enough?"

He made his way to the chair behind his desk. "A map is merely a drawing. I've heard rumors that Lewis Carroll has drawn maps of his fictional worlds, but no one believes those figments of his imagination prove the existence of Wonderland." He said the words with such cavalier ease that she could not help but feel they hid great pain. Or perhaps she only imagined it because it fed her fascination with him.

"Indeed," she said. She'd never spent much time investigating what it was that the rest of the world believed of her culture. Up until the last year, she'd lived in a small coastal village surrounded by other descendants of Atlantis, still living in much the same way as their ancestors had so long ago. Pride swelled inside her to think that there were people out there who longed to know the truth of the Atlantean people.

"Satisfied?" he asked her, leaning forward and resting his elbows on his knees.

"For now."

He smiled broadly. "Now *I* ask the questions. Why are you after that map?" he asked. "The truth," he reminded her. "I know you're no map collector."

It seemed safer to stay broad, see what he would accept, what she could avoid telling him. So she started at the beginning. "My ancestors were from Atlantis," she began. "That map"—she pointed to emphasize—"is a family heirloom of sorts, and I only recently discovered it was here in London. With you." That was all complete truth.

He leaned back in his seat and steepled his hands over

his bare abdomen. In this position, his shoulders looked impossibly wide, his hands strong and firm resting against his tight stomach. As much as she wanted to deny it, she couldn't help wondering what his skin would feel like if she ran her fingers down his torso, not in a medical capacity, as she'd touched him before, but a lover's touch.

"You are a descendant?" he said. "From Atlantis?" There was nothing in either his tone or his expression that indicated how believable he found her story. Or if he'd decided she was utterly mad.

She nodded. "Yes. My aunts and I." She paused. "Well, we are not the only ones, obviously. In fact, the people who escaped Atlantis and fled here before Atlantis's Great War, well, they landed in several different ports along Britain's coastline. They then mingled with the culture here at the time and, while some of us still live together in small pockets, others have been living with the English for so long they are no longer even aware of their heritage."

She held her breath, waiting for him to laugh or toss her out. It was an admission she'd never made to anyone. Granted, she'd grown up among so many like her and her aunts, she hadn't had much opportunity. Still, it was not something they discussed in the open. Their heritage, while not a secret, was fairly well guarded.

His left eyebrow slowly rose. Max watched her face for several moments, saying nothing. Then he opened his mouth to finally speak, but he paused as if considering something before he began. "I believe I'll reserve my question until after you've examined my map." When she made no move to look, he swept his arms open. "Please, look as long as you'd like."

Excitement battered her insides as she made haste to

the map. She stood as close as she could without pressing her nose to it. The prophecy was here somewhere. She only had to locate it. There were no words along the border of the map, nor in any of the corners. Perhaps it was on the backside, but she couldn't very well take the thing off the wall and out of the frame. At least not yet.

She didn't know how long she stood there searching every inch. It was hard to focus on her search because she was so distracted by the details within the map: Poseidon's palace, military barracks, farms and cottages, and the three guardian temples. She forced herself to count each ring, her eyes moving along the circles searching for any words. But she found none. Then a symbol in one of the trees caught her attention. She looked closer.

"*The seven rings of Atlantis will fall by fire and steel, opening the path for the army of one.*" Max's voice came from behind her, but she stood utterly still, afraid if she moved, he'd stop. "*Empires will crumble and crowns will melt. The three will lose their blood unless the dove can bring salvation.*"

The words flowed over her like an ancient incantation, as if her very soul recognized them. She braced her arms on the cabinet below only to realize it was a large glass case enclosing a long spear. It was blackened and charred. She was just turning around to face Max when his arms splayed on either side of her, anchoring her in front of the map.

"Find what you were looking for?" he purred.

She looked up and met his gaze. His blue eyes were so clear, so beautiful, she nearly winced. Those were the kind of eyes that could pierce a soul, find hidden secrets and unveil them with little effort. For her, that meant nothing but danger.

"I don't know what you're talking about," she said stiffly. "I was merely admiring the map. It's really quite stunning. So unique."

He leaned closer to her, his eyes scanning her face. "Yes, beautiful," he said softly.

She ducked beneath his arms and moved away from him.

"You know about the prophecy. That's why you wanted the map," he said more to himself than her.

He'd said the word "prophecy," and her heart nearly stopped. Damn him, but he was making it nearly impossible for her to keep any secrets. She barely needed to say anything, and it was as if he could see inside her and pick out her very thoughts. Still she kept her mouth closed.

"You were quite serious before? About your family being descendants of Atlantis?"

"Yes, I was very serious."

"Then certainly you would already know of the prophecy." He leaned forward and pointed to the clump of trees she had discovered. "It's all there. Wound up in the map in various places." He identified another area in one of the water rings. Another below the palace.

She moved closer to the map, following his finger as it pointed out the inscriptions. Written in Greek, the words moved in and out of the images effortlessly. It was a wonder he had ever discovered them.

"It took me a very long time to find them all." He fell into his desk chair. "Why the interest in the prophecy? That's my second question."

She was silent for a moment, then sighed. "Of course we know about the prophecy. But this map is the only remaining place you can see the prophecy in its entirety." That was the complete truth, and it annoyed her how the knot in her stomach seemed to dissolve at her honesty. "It was also in an ancient text at one time, but the pages were stolen hundreds of years ago."

"And this is why you were after my map? To see the prophecy?"

She took a cleansing breath, closed her eyes, and nodded. "Yes."

"What do you know of the recent activities here in London?" he asked.

Activities? Could he possibly know about Madigan? Panic seized her heart. "Nothing," she said. She stepped around the desk.

"I think someone is trying to fulfill the prophecy," Max said.

She turned abruptly to face him, but she said nothing for fear of revealing too much. Instead she sank into a chair.

"There have been murders," he began.

"Madigan," she whispered. But then his words sank in. "You said murders. As in plural?"

"Five of our military leaders. With a promise for more. I'm guessing at least two, if we're going by the number in the prophecy," he said.

Military leaders, but that didn't include Madigan. She gathered a fistful of fabric from her skirt. "A promise?"

"He left a note. With the bodies." He shook his head. "Damn. I'm not supposed to even know this, but I was consulted by a friend from Scotland Yard because of my interest in Atlantis." He picked up a stray coin from his desk and rolled it between two fingers. "Does the term 'guardian' mean anything to you?" he asked.

Sabine knew her expression changed, and though she

quickly looked down, it seemed unlikely he wouldn't have noticed.

"It does." He leaned forward. "What does it mean, Sabine?"

"I can't," she said and shook her head for emphasis.

"Whoever this guardian is, he's in danger. Tell me what you know, and I can protect him."

"What do you mean, he's in danger?" she asked.

"The note left with the bodies was addressed to the guardian. It warned that the killer is getting close and that what he protects will soon be his."

Agnes and Phinneas were in danger. But she had known that. Now that she knew the prophecy, she needed the Seer's guidance to help decipher it. She needed Phinneas. She had to leave as soon as possible.

"Sabine, I can help. Trust me."

"The guardians guard the elixir," she said before she could reconsider. She eyed his face to see if she'd said too much.

"Elixir? What is that?" he asked. He flipped the coin in the air and caught it.

"No." She shook her head fervently. "I've said far too much already," she said. "You've asked your two questions."

"Can you tell me how many guardians there are?" he asked. "Scotland Yard is working on the case, and I'd like to be able to have the police protect them."

She met his eyes. "There were three. Though only two remain."

All his questions brought her doubts pouring down on top of her. Seeking the help of an outsider. She was violating one of the sacred rules of her people. A guardian would never have done this—further proof the selection of Agnes had been correct, and she did not deserve to be guardian. It was a significant risk to trust him, but he knew about the map and the prophecy, information she would need in order to protect Agnes.

She had to do what she felt was right, and at the moment, she needed this man's assistance. So for now, she had to trust herself, and to an extent, trust Maxwell Barrett.

Chapter Eight

Long after Sabine had left his study, Max stood staring at the map. He'd always assumed the inscription buried within the map had been a prophecy foretelling the destruction of Atlantis. But first Justin and now Sabine. It seemed rather impossible that this could be a coincidence. The murders, the letter to the guardian, and what of Sabine and her aunts' being descendants of Atlantis?

Perhaps the girl was mad. Caught up in a fantasy world she'd created after reading about Atlantis. But what if? That niggling feeling dug at him. What if she wasn't delusional? What if she was telling the truth, and not simply what she believed to be true, but the actual reality? If Sabine and her aunts were descendants of Atlantis, then that was his proof. Real flesh-and-bone people whose lineage flowed back to a land that no longer existed. Of course, there was no scientific measure to show their lineage.

"The guardians guard the elixir," she'd said. Elixir. It didn't jar any memories. So much about this prophecy didn't exist in any of his sources. Then again, in the past he'd focused on proving the existence of Atlantis. He'd paid less attention to Atlantean culture. He pulled a few books from the shelf and dropped them on his desk, including the newest from that odd American who claimed Atlantis was the birthplace of civilization. Max didn't consider the man a true scholar on the subject, but he needed information, and right now he'd take it from nearly anyone.

He opened another book, an ancient text written in Greek, and caught a glimpse of an illustration, a four-tiered fountain in the center of Poseidon's palace. Some legends claimed that it was the fountain of youth, a well-spring of immortal life. He'd never given much thought to that theory one way or another. Was this the elixir the guardians protected?

Again he stood and read the prophecy, even though those words were imprinted on his brain. He looked down and caught sight of the stitches on his all-but-healed gunshot wound. The pain had completely disappeared. She'd said it was an old family recipe. He just bet.

That ointment she'd used on him was nothing short of amazing. He glanced down at the illustration of the fountain. Fountain of youth...elixir.

"Son of a bitch." This probably meant that one of her aunts was a guardian. Which would certainly explain the thugs at their shop the other night.

He ran his hand over his stitches, marveling at his healing. That elixir could be the proof Marcus required for use of his submersible ship. Somehow Max needed to get his hands on it. Starting tomorrow, he would find a way to *borrow* some from her.

She certainly had said all the right words to pique his curiosity. From the wager to everything she'd told him tonight, he was utterly intrigued. Of course, it didn't hurt that she was quite likely the most beautiful woman he'd ever seen.

If someone were to design the perfect woman to distract him, wouldn't she be just like Sabine, though? Beautiful, aloof, full of mysteries and contradictions. And involved with Atlantis. She was almost too perfect.

In one swift movement, he reached over the glass case to the map and heaved the frame off the wall. It slipped from his hands as he was pulling it away and slid down. The corner of the frame struck the glass case, and it shattered. Glass fragments poured over his feet, and the noise echoed through the room.

His butler came running into the study. "My lord, are you all right?"

"Fine, I just broke the bloody case. Have another one commissioned next week to replace this one. We can't have this rusty old spear exposed where someone might hurt themselves." He grabbed the frame again and moved it over to his desk.

He looked up to find his butler still standing in the doorway, a frown furrowing his already wrinkled brow. The old man cleared his throat. "Yes, most certainly, my lord. Anything else?"

"No, that will be all."

He wasn't normally so clumsy. He was tired. Thoughts of the little minx had certainly troubled his sleep the previous night. However, he was a grown man and could certainly manage his desires. He was less prepared for having his intellectual pursuits stymied. When he encountered a puzzle, he solved it. When he needed answers, he got them.

Furthermore, people generally followed his orders.

Sabine did not. She did whatever she damn well wanted, regardless of the consequences.

In this instance, she'd insisted on returning to her shop, despite the obvious dangers. There was a killer on the loose, and unless Max was mistaken, the next target was one of Sabine's aunts. Therefore, the four women should obviously accept his protection until the danger had passed. It was only logical.

But were they here now, at his house, where they would be safe? No. They were not. They were at their shop, where unknown customers came and went throughout the day and countless bumbling thieves trespassed at night, and where their only defense was a single gun in the possession of a woman with poor aim.

The situation was intolerable. He removed the map from the frame and folded it into his bag. He eyed his mantel clock. It was late, but damned if he would get any sleep unless he took care of this tonight. When had he become so bloody protective? She hid secrets he wanted answers to; that was his only interest, he reminded himself. That, and he wouldn't mind getting her into his bed. He would have to go retrieve the women himself. If Sabine wouldn't see sense, then her aunts surely would.

Max didn't bother going to the front door of the shop, as the store had long since closed. Instead he went directly to the back. He knocked. A moment later, Sabine opened the door.

"You decided to knock tonight, how unusual," she said. She did not move from the doorway or invite him inside.

"Most amusing. Might I come in?" he asked.

"Very well." She stepped back then closed the door

behind him. "Let us sit down here then," Sabine said, eyeing the staircase. "I'd prefer not to worry my aunts with more talk of death and destruction." She pulled a chair out from the small table and motioned for him to take it. Then she proceeded to clean up the supplies that were scattered across the tabletop.

"With a murderer on the hunt for the guardians, don't you think you and your aunts would be safer at my townhome?" he asked. "What if this man comes after them here?"

She swung around to face him. "I never told you that one of my aunts was the guardian," she said.

"Do you deny that you are all in danger?"

But she said nothing, merely pursed her lips and looked away. She continued putting away her supplies, jars and ribbons and whatnots.

"I think it's foolish to risk it. It would be prudent for you and your aunts to come and stay at my house for the time being," he said.

Again she made no comment.

"It is quite evident that there is a killer after someone in this house; otherwise, you wouldn't have reacted in such a manner earlier when I mentioned the guardian. I can provide appropriate security," he said.

She released a heavy sigh. "We have a business to run. And we are not without skill to protect ourselves."

"Right, the candelabra, a most effective weapon," he said.

"He's right, Sabine," Agnes said as she came down the staircase. Her two sisters followed. "We cannot ignore the prophecy."

"It would be nice to feel more secure," Calliope said. "Especially with you leaving town."

Max sat forward. "Leaving? Where are you going?"

Sabine glared at her aunt. "To see an old friend. Nothing to concern yourself about."

He might have imagined it, but he could have sworn Calliope winked at him.

"What do you think about this, Lydia?" Sabine asked.

"We do not belong there." Lydia's voice was tight.

"Go stay in a fancy townhome full of servants and luxurious linens." Agnes sighed dramatically. "I can see how that might be taxing."

Max couldn't help himself and laughed heartily.

"We'll go gather our belongings," Agnes said. "All of us."

"I'll wait right here," Max said.

Sabine nodded, then left the room. Calliope waited until her other sisters had gone. "Tomorrow morning she's taking the train to Cornwall. She needs protection."

"Consider it done," Max said with a smile.

The following morning Sabine stood, waiting in line, at Victoria Station. She had snuck out of Max's townhome very early that morning to avoid detection. Currently, there was a family in front of her, a sweet couple and three young children. The smallest girl kept looking shyly at Sabine from behind a wooden doll. Sabine smiled and waved, which made the girl giggle and hide her face.

The family received their tickets and headed off in the direction of their platform. Sabine stepped up to the ticket counter.

"I need a ticket to Cornwall, please," she said. She counted out her money and placed it on the counter.

"Sorry, miss, but we're all sold out for that train today," the clerk told her.

"Sold out?" Sabine eyed the schedule. "How is that possible?"

"Yep, some bloke bought a whole train car." He shook his head. "Never seen that before."

"Splendid. Well, can you tell me when the next train leaves for that area?" She had to get to Phinneas, and soon. Of course she could hire a coach, but that would likely take two days' travel. The train would be so much faster because she wouldn't have to stop to change horses.

"Not until tomorrow. Sorry, miss." He shrugged his shoulders and gave her a sheepish smile. Dimples pierced his ruddy cheeks. "Oh, look there, that's the bloke who bought the car." He pointed a fat finger over her shoulder.

She turned and found none other than Maxwell Barrett leaning against a column. He smiled and waved.

She quickly gathered the coins she'd placed on the counter, scooping them up and dropping them into her purse. "Thank you," she muttered to the man. Then she made her way over to Max.

"Precisely what do you think you're doing?" She leaned closer and lowered her voice. "Are you following me?"

"I don't know what you're talking about. I had need to go to Cornwall, and I prefer to have my space."

"You knew damned well that I was going there today." She crossed her arms over her chest. "Well, you will have to share your space with me. And don't think to argue with me because I won't have it."

He held his arms up in defeat. "As you wish."

An attendant wearing a starched black uniform with matching hat met them on the platform.

"This way, my lord. We have your car waiting for you,"

he said. He led them down the arched corridor to an opulent car toward the front of the train.

Sabine stepped up into the car. The plush seats faced one another in groups of four. Wood paneling covered nearly every other surface save the windows. Luxury in motion, though at the moment the train idled at the station.

"If I can be of any further assistance," the man said. When Max shook his head, the man bowed and stepped back onto the platform.

"I did not realize one could purchase an entire train car for oneself," Sabine said as she sat on the velvet-cushioned seat.

"It's not customary," he said. He sat directly opposite her and smiled broadly.

But he had paid for it, and now for the next several hours, they'd be completely alone. She needed to do her best to stay on guard. He was charming and devilishly handsome, and she could not afford to slip and allow his wit and seductive glances to distract her. Especially not now. He might find all of this entertaining and amusing, but for her, for her family, this was about survival.

A few moments later, the train jerked into motion. Sabine held the armrests firmly to keep herself from jostling about. She watched out her window as the station, then the bustling London streets, chugged by.

"What else can you tell me about these guardians?" he asked.

She looked out the window, and the landscape passed by in a blur. Her stare became unfocused until she saw her own reflection in the glass. He knew she was withholding information from him, so there was no reason to deny it. "I can't tell you anything else," she said simply.

"So you know who they are?" he asked.

She nodded once.

"Her majesty? Is she a guardian?"

"Heavens no," she blurted out. The idea was ludicrous. "Queen Victoria is not Atlantean."

He nodded but said nothing more. They sat quietly for several moments, and Sabine relaxed a measure.

"You consider me an adversary," he said. He drummed his fingers on the wooden armrest. "That certainly creates an interesting dilemma."

"I don't consider you anything," she said abruptly. Not precisely true, since she considered him devilishly handsome and dangerously tempting.

"You certainly know how to wound a man's pride," he said. He stretched his well-sculpted legs out in front of him. Even though they were encased in his trousers, she could tell his thighs were muscular.

Her mouth went dry.

"Ordinarily women find me quite irresistible, I can assure you," he continued.

"Of that I have no doubt," she said tartly, then realized she might have given herself away.

"Indeed."

"Silly girls," she said, in an effort to disguise her slip. "To succumb to such obvious charm and good looks."

His lips twitched. "You prefer men who are less obviously handsome?"

She eyed him, trying to determine if he was toying with her or if he was completely serious. His sharp blue eyes revealed nothing.

"You seem to be quite immune to my charms," he continued.

The truth was she was not immune to his charms at all,

quite the contrary. She found herself utterly drawn to him. Shamelessly so. But she would be damned if she would let him know any of that.

Maxwell Barrett was used to getting his way with women. He was the sort of man who could make you forget what you were about to say, forget why you'd walked into a room, forget your own name. Precisely the sort of man she'd love to have an affair with, but there was something about Max that gave her pause. Could she indulge, and make certain her heart remained untouched? She knew Max was not a man who would easily fall in love. But neither did she.

"Your charms, as it were, have nothing to do with this journey," she said, then looked out the window.

He was only charming with the intent to disarm her. To try to manipulate the truth out of her. It was further proof that last night she'd been a fool to believe she could trust him.

A woman with a refreshment tray stepped into their car. "Begging your pardon, my lord, but here is the tray you requested." The woman placed the tray on the empty seat next to him, then left the car.

Max handed Sabine a glass of wine. "Would you care for some cheese or bread with that?" he asked her.

"Not now," she said.

"Your aunt sent me to protect you," he said.

"Calliope talks too much."

He leaned forward, bracing his elbows on his knees. His nearness allowed her a whiff of his scent. This morning, she found no hint of brandy or tobacco. Instead she inhaled sandalwood, masculinity, and pure seduction. Her nose twitched.

"Tell me about the elixir," he said.

His curiosity tugged at her. Atlanteans were raised to hold their country and their ways in great esteem, despite the loss of their actual land. To meet someone who had an interest in her people, well, it thrilled some small part of her. Surely most Atlanteans had shared a tale, a time or two. How else would the English and other people know of them?

She could be vague and give just enough to appease him without revealing anything dangerous. There was no need to tell him how a guardian's amphora never ran dry. A never-ending supply of elixir could tempt even the most noble of persons. And to make matters worse, she had already used some on him to heal his gunshot wound. He'd seen the powers at work. No, she would merely give him the basics, what he could find in a history book from Atlantis, if any of them had survived.

"It is said to be from the waters of Atlantis," she said.

He leaned back again, putting his legs out in front of him. They were so close that she could have reached down and brushed her fingertips across the top of his shin.

"What is it supposed to do?" he asked.

"It acts as an enhancer." She met his gaze, carefully selecting her words before she spoke. "For example, it would make Galileo more intelligent. And Oscar Wilde more"—she paused, searching for the right word—"eccentric. So I suppose for you, it would make you even more charming." She did nothing to hide the sarcasm from her voice.

"And likewise it would no doubt enhance your sharp wit." He nodded with a smile.

She laughed. She could not help herself.

"You should laugh more often," he said. "Life is intended to be enjoyed."

"Life isn't always amusing," she countered, then took a sip of her wine.

"Touché," he said.

She fingered the chain around her neck. The vial was hidden beneath her dress and rested safely against her body.

"So it's from the waters of Atlantis," he mumbled. "If it is an enhancer, then it would enhance youth and beauty as well, I suppose. Which is undoubtedly why some believe it to be the fountain of youth."

She sat forward. "Do people actually believe that?" she asked.

"There are tales."

She shook her head. That was ridiculous. Atlanteans aged just as any people would. "Though it might smooth someone's skin and add shine to someone's hair, it doesn't actually make people younger. It is not magic," she said defensively.

"But if it enhances—"

"Enhances what a person already possesses," she interrupted. "It does not create where something wasn't before, only makes existing traits stronger, bigger, more pronounced."

"One could argue that was a form of magic," he said.

"I would not," she said with a shrug.

"What of the healing capabilities?" he asked. Then his smile faded as he looked over her shoulder.

She turned, and through the glass in the door, she saw two men. One pointed and turned the door latch.

"Sabine, run!" Max said.

Spencer needed to get back to Cornwall. But damned if her majesty had not let him out of her sight. It had been one advisory meeting after another. He had more pressing matters to attend to, though he could not very well tell the queen that. To her and everyone around her, there was nothing more important.

That old man, Phinneas, had fooled him. When Spencer had arrived at the small cottage of the second guardian, he'd found a cabinet full of potions and tonics, so he'd naturally assumed it was the Healer he'd discovered. And he hadn't searched for anything but the elixir.

It had been a foolish mistake, one he probably wouldn't have made if he hadn't been rushed. But her highness required so much attention lately and he couldn't afford to raise her suspicions about his behavior.

After Spencer had returned to London, though, the words of the dying guardian had run through his mind again and again. Nonsensical words. Spoken like that of the Seer. Spencer had known that when it came time to take the Seer's elixir, he would also have to find the book—the book filled with all the visions and predictions of all the Seers. Spencer needed that book.

As soon as these buffoons were finished talking, he'd make his way back to Cornwall.

They were being followed. Or more precisely, Sabine was being followed. Max held firmly to Sabine's hand as they closed the door of their train car behind them. Standing precariously between one car and the next, they shifted from right to left as the train chugged down the tracks.

"Be careful when you cross," Max told her. The train curved to the right, and the coupler rocked in response. He stepped through the opened section and reached the other side. The men were now in their train car heading straight for the door at Sabine's back. "Sabine, hurry."

She looked back over her shoulder, then at Max. In one graceful movement, she leaped over the joint.

"Who are they?" she asked.

"The men from your shop."

Quickly, he opened the door of the next car, and they shuffled inside. It was another first-class car, much as their own had been, only this one was full of passengers.

"Pardon us," Max said as he dragged Sabine behind him.

Again they found themselves between two cars. The men were not far behind them.

"We need to find somewhere to hide," Sabine said. "Eventually we are going to run out of train."

"I realize," he said.

They found themselves in a dining car next. The rich aroma of shepherd's pie filled the air.

"A table, my lord?" a plump woman asked. She wiped her hands on her white apron, then motioned to an empty table. "This is one of our best," she said with a smile.

"Perhaps in a bit," he said.

The crisp breeze slapped his face as they once again stepped outside. He crossed the threshold, then held out his hand for Sabine. Her foot slipped. She nearly fell, but he was able to catch her and pull her close.

"I've got you," he said.

The door opened from the dining car. "Found you," one of the men said with a sneer.

Max punched the man, knocking him backward. He and Sabine tore into the door just ahead of them, and they found themselves in a luggage car. Trunks and cases surrounded them, making it difficult to maneuver.

"They're right behind us," Sabine said, her voice sharp with fear.

"I'm thinking." Max dragged a particularly large trunk in front of the door to block it. It wouldn't keep them out for long, but it might give them a head start. Fortunately this door was solid, with no window to allow the men to watch their every move.

"Max, in here," Sabine said.

He turned and found her motioning to an armoire. She opened the doors. Dresses in every color imaginable filled the space.

The car door shook as the men tried to break in.

"You get inside the armoire, behind the rest of those dresses," he told her. He handed her the pistol he kept tucked in the back of his trouser waistband. "Use this if you need to."

"Where are you going?"

"I'll be right there with you. First I need to send our friends looking elsewhere for us." He gave her a reassuring smile, and then he made his way to the opposite door. He opened it slightly to make it appear that they'd gone out that door and into the following car. Then he headed back for Sabine. He shoved trunks to block the path he took to prevent the men from seeing where they hid.

The door slid partially open. "There's something blocking it," one of the men yelled.

Max hurried to the armoire, stepped inside, and pulled the doors shut. Immediately the air around him warmed and everything went dark.

A hand grabbed his arm and tugged. He worked his way behind the lace-covered dresses to the back of the armoire where Sabine hid. She clutched his hand. They stood side by side, hidden amid satin and velvet and silk.

The men broke through the blocked door.

"We'll find them. They can't hide forever on this train," one man said.

Sabine held her breath. They both stood still.

The men moved through the luggage car, pushing trunks out of the way, presumably searching for a suitable hiding place for Max and Sabine. Max could see nothing; he could only hear Sabine's short breaths near his ear, feel her warmth as she huddled next to him. Her breast pressed against his arm, and he longed to turn her, hold her against him. Desire rippled through his legs.

The trunk outside the armoire shifted, scraping against the car floor. Max held firm to the armoire door. Gently, quietly, he pushed the bolt from the inside so that it slid silently into place. He just hoped he'd be able to pull it back and that they wouldn't be stuck in here until the owners came to claim their clothing.

Someone tugged on the door, and it clattered against the frame. "This is locked," the man said.

"They're not in here," another said. "Next car."

The door moved again, then stilled.

The outer door to the car slid open, then closed. It was too soon to leave the armoire, though. While Max didn't suspect those men were clever enough to set a trap, he didn't want to completely ignore the possibility.

"Are you all right?" he whispered close to Sabine's ear.

She nodded. "Hot," she murmured.

The air was tight, he couldn't argue with that. "Just a few more minutes."

"Then what?" she asked.

"I'll think of something."

Max didn't know how long they hid within the confines of the armoire. Sabine's breathing came in short spurts. The limited air was getting to both of them. He pulled at the latch, trying to unlock the cabinet, but the bolt would not move.

"What's the matter?" she asked.

"The lock is stuck."

"Are we locked inside here? For who knows how many more hours?" she asked.

"I'll get it unlocked."

"That's right, you do have a knack for picking locks, don't you?" she asked.

He would have sworn he'd heard humor in her voice. "I have, on occasion, had opportunity to unlatch a lock without a key." From his pocket, he withdrew a coin, then slid it up to the latch. It took some working, but he was able to slide the lock over.

Slowly, he opened one door. Cooler air moved around them, and he took a deep breath. He peeked around the door, but caught no sight of the men.

"I think we're safe. For now." He helped Sabine out of the armoire, then together they navigated the luggage car to go out the way they'd come in, then back through the dining car and the other cars until they had reached their own.

"We can't stay in here," Sabine said. "We still have several hours on the trip."

"This way." They went out the opposite end of their car and into the one in front of it. It was a car that had twelve compartments, including a sleeper. Max knocked on the wall next to the curtained area. The curtain moved, and a young man stepped forward.

"What?" he asked. Another boy, a few years younger, jumped down from the top cot.

"The car in front of this one is empty; I rented the

entire thing," Max said. "My companion here is not feeling well and wishes to lie down." He pulled two notes out of his coat pocket. "Could we switch with you? Of course, I'd pay you for any inconvenience."

The older boy smiled and turned back to look at his brother. They both nodded. He snatched the notes from Max's hand, and they grabbed their things and ran out without another word.

Max held the curtain open for Sabine, then closed it behind them once they were safely ensconced in the sleeping cabin.

"You think we'll be safe in here?" she asked. She sank onto one of the lower bunks, leaning forward so she didn't hit her head on the top.

"There are more people in this car," he said. "It's unlikely they will search for us here." Though he wasn't completely certain that was true, he wanted to give her some measure of comfort.

"They must have followed me here," she said. Then she looked up, her eyes wide with terror. "My aunts. What if more men returned to the shop? I know they're safe at your home, but what of work? I didn't even think..." Her voice faded as she dropped her head into her hands.

He sat next to her. "I asked some friends to keep watch while we were gone," he said. "Your aunts will be safe."

She looked over at him. "I don't know what to say."

"I believe the customary response is thank you."

But she said nothing. Instead she leaned forward and kissed him. More than likely, he shouldn't take advantage of the situation. She'd been through quite an ordeal. But he'd never been much of a gentleman, and damn, she felt good pressed against him. So he threaded his fingers through the back of her silky soft hair and pulled her closer. He deepened the kiss. She opened her mouth to him, and their tongues touched.

Lust forged through him.

He tugged her hair to lay her back on the cot. The coils groaned beneath their weight. Still they kissed, their lips melded together, their tongues intertwined. Her fingers dug into his arm, and she released small sounds of pleasure.

She drove him wild. Her touch, her taste, the feel of her beneath him.

He left her mouth and kissed the column of her throat, paying particular attention to that lovely spot he'd first noticed the night they met. Her pulse leaped beneath his tongue. She moaned again.

Today she wore a simple travel gown of brown wool. It did nothing to enhance her curves, but as soon as he touched her, the soft fabric left little between his body and hers. He slid his hand up her torso and cupped her breast. With no corset in the way, he could freely feel the softness. Her nipple beaded between his fingers.

Sabine arched toward his touch.

He kissed her again. Her hand slid up his back, pressing him farther onto her. She wanted him. He reached down and moved a hand up her leg, her skin smooth and soft beneath his palm.

His fingers traced behind her knee to the sensitive flesh of her thighs. Her teeth grabbed hold of his earlobe as his hand explored beneath her skirts. When he brushed lightly across the apex of her legs, she released a primal groan of desire. His own need poured through his veins and settled heavily in his groin.

Bloody hell, he wanted her.

He found his way up through the slit in her drawers.

Her flesh was hot and slick with her need, and she trembled when his fingers brushed against her. She continued to moan softly. He continued his exploration.

He slipped one finger inside her; slowly he began his rhythm. Her pleasure mounted as he moved his finger within her. He found the nub beneath her folds and stroked across it. Her mouth fell open, her eyes squeezed shut, and she arched toward him.

Closer and closer he brought her to the edge, then pulled back. She was fascinating to watch. Undoubtedly, she was the most passionate woman he'd ever touched, and he longed to be inside her. His own desire was becoming increasingly difficult to ignore. So he kissed her deeply, then leaned back as best he could to watch her climax.

His finger dipped in again as he flicked across her folds. She tightened around his finger as the pleasure shot through her. "Yes," she whispered. Her head pressed into the pillow behind her. "Yes."

Quickly he unfastened his trousers and guided himself into her before her climax subsided. She sucked in her breath and opened her eyes. He found himself lost in their amber depths as he pushed himself deeper into her. Oh, God, she felt good. Hot and tight and so slick.

Her climax started again, and her walls squeezed around his shaft as he increased the depth of his thrusts. And then as his own release rocked through his body, he released a primal moan and collapsed atop her.

Sabine listened to Max's even breathing as he lay next to her on the small cot. She could still feel the effects of their lovemaking on her body. Her flesh seemed to quiver every time she closed her eyes and remembered the sensations of their coupling.

She had thought she could indulge with Max. Have a brief affair, then go back to her life as it was before she'd met him. But this...His arm snaked around her waist and pulled her to him. She closed her eyes, loving the feel of his warm breath on her bare neck. Lying here with him only made her think of what it would be like to live like this every day. To wake up in the arms of a man you loved.

Of course, she didn't love Max. She barely knew him. Still, something powerful had happened between them today. Something she'd never experienced before. Perhaps she could pretend that Max wasn't the sort of man she could fall in love with. But hadn't today proven otherwise?

And what of the fact that he was English and she Atlantean? That mattered. Certainly some Atlanteans had left their villages and conformed to the English ways. But she was the daughter of a guardian; that should matter.

She needed to keep her wits about her, because she risked her heart as well as all her family's secrets.

Chapter Nine

Several hours later, they finally arrived in Cornwall. They had successfully hidden from the men for the remainder of the train ride. Max and Sabine exited the train with the throng of people from their car, hoping they'd blend in. So far they had not seen the men again.

Max hired a hackney to take them to the address Lydia had written down. The address Phinneas, the guardian, called home. Sometime during the night, when neither of them had been able to sleep, Sabine had explained that three ships had fled Atlantis during their Great War, each carrying a guardian. During the turmoil and confusion of the exodus, the ships had become separated. Each had landed in a different location in Great Britain. It had taken many generations for all of the Atlanteans to find one another, but once they did, the elders had kept communication open between the groups.

The carriage ride from the train station to Phinneas's house did not take long, because he lived close to town. The village was small, containing only a cobbler's shop, an inn and tavern, and a few cottages scattered about the hillsides.

Max kept waiting for Sabine to speak about what had happened on the train ride, but so far she made no mention of their interlude, which suited him. She was nothing more than a delectable diversion. He wouldn't lie; it had been amazing, and he would find a way to get her back into his bed.

The rig stopped, and Max wasted no time in getting down, then assisting Sabine. As they approached the small thatched-roof cottage, the hairs along his neck rose. The door, though closed, hung from one hinge. It was a cheery place with brightly colored flowers everywhere. Still, the aesthetics did nothing to stave off Max's wariness. Something was wrong.

They walked up the dirt path to the front door, and as he knocked, the door creaked open.

"Stay behind me," he said. He withdrew his pistol and led the way into the small cottage.

Phinneas's home had been ransacked. The chairs near the fireplace lay overturned, and the contents of the cupboards were now scattered about in broken pieces on the floor.

"Phinneas," Sabine called, her voice wavering.

No answer.

She took a shaky breath.

"We need to look around," Max said, trying to reassure her. "He might be out."

There was no sign of him downstairs, so together they climbed to the top floor. They found nothing more than a small bedroom with a bed, washbasin, and armoire. Phinneas lived a simple life, though it would seem a solitary one.

"He's not here," Sabine said. "Perhaps he received Madigan's letter and already made his escape."

Perhaps, but Max had his doubts. He led the way back downstairs and then out the back door to the garden area.

Again Sabine called to Phinneas, and again there was no answer.

They walked deeper into a garden filled with more flowering plants as well as vegetables. It was well tended, with a fence around the area.

Up ahead, sticking out from behind a large tree, were some worn boots, and they appeared to still be attached to a body. Max held his arm out to stop Sabine from walking farther. "Wait here." He moved closer to investigate.

Sabine ignored his instructions and followed closely behind him. Lying on the ground behind the tree was, in fact, a man. The body was contorted in an awkward position, as if in the last moments of life, his muscles had all simultaneously convulsed and he had collapsed in severe pain.

"He matches the description Agnes gave me," Sabine said.

She sucked in her breath. Max turned her away from the body. "I'm sorry, Sabine," he murmured. He held her shoulders tightly to keep her facing away from Phinneas's body.

"Two of them," she murmured. "Two guardians gone." She turned away from Max to again look at the body. "His face is frozen in the exact expression of pain that Madigan had." Her voice cracked. She swallowed and kept staring at the dead man's face. "Evidently when a guardian dies, it is most unpleasant."

Two guardians were dead. Which meant only one

remained. Someone was going to an awful lot of trouble to make it appear as if the prophecy had begun. Or perhaps there was someone out there mad enough to believe that he could bring about the prophecy himself.

"Poison," Max said. He saw no blood, no visible wounds on the body.

"No," Sabine said.

"This Madigan, you said he died shortly after he arrived at your house," Max said.

"He did. But not from any wound."

"That doesn't make any sense, Sabine," Max said. "Explain it to me."

She exhaled slowly. "The guardians are mystically connected to the elixir they protect. If that elixir is stolen or lost to them, they have a short window to retrieve it, and if they don't, they perish."

"Or the thief could have poisoned them," Max argued.

A deep frown settled on her brow. "Simply because you can't explain something does not mean it can't exist," Sabine said.

Well, she had him there. It wasn't completely out of the realm of oddities he'd seen in his lifetime. Hell, he'd seen Pandora's box. And he'd been chasing after a lost continent since he was a boy. He'd allow for possibilities like poison, but he shouldn't ignore the mystical.

"What is that?" she asked, pointing to the man's fist.

Something was caught in his hand. Max knelt on the cold earth and worked it from Phinneas's hand. "Paper," he said. He smoothed out the sheet. The penmanship was terrible, the note nearly illegible, but finally Max was able to determine what it said. " 'It has begun,' " he read aloud, then looked up at Sabine. "He must have spent his last moments writing this." Max shook his head. "None of this makes any sense. I always assumed the prophecy was about the fall of Atlantis."

"No, it's not." Sabine paced along the length of the fence. "It's a warning. The final bit of guidance from the elders of our culture. Their last attempt to protect us." She stopped and met his gaze. "And if I don't find a way to stop it, the Chosen One will find a way to destroy us all, Atlanteans and English alike."

It seemed unlikely to Max that one person could orchestrate the destruction of a modern civilization such as Great Britain's. But so far that one person had managed to murder five of England's most decorated and highest-ranked military officers. Max would be a fool if he underestimated that.

Sabine closed her eyes and repeated the words of the prophecy: "*The seven rings of Atlantis will fall by fire and steel, opening the path for the army of one. Empires will crumble and crowns will melt. The three will lose their blood unless the dove can bring salvation.*"

She was beautiful. Standing there with her eyes closed, speaking softly, she nearly stole his breath. He wished she'd wanted him to comfort her for more than a minute, though even having that thought gave him pause. He was not the comforting sort, having always preferred the lighter, more playful side of the ladies. Damned if he didn't need to focus more on the danger at hand than on whether he would be able to find his way up Sabine's skirt. Especially if such thoughts made him long to hold her as much as bed her.

"So the rings could represent the military leaders," she said.

"Or so whoever is killing them believes," Max countered. "I suppose the three would be the guardians."

She ran a hand over her throat. "The dove; I don't know what to make of that."

"You came here to get help from Phinneas. Perhaps you'll find some answers in his belongings," Max said.

"Yes," she said. "Good idea."

"You go ahead and get started without me. I'm going to bury Phinneas. I know it's not a proper burial, but we can't simply leave him here like this." He eyed the property around. "And calling the authorities would bring too many questions," Max said. "I think I saw a shovel leaning against the back of the cottage."

"Thank you, Max. I truly appreciate that."

He put his pistol in her hand. Her amber-colored eyes looked up at him. "Listen for anything and keep your eyes open. If anyone comes near you, shoot him. We can find out who he is later."

It had been nearly three hours since they'd found Phinneas. They'd missed the last train to London and instead had decided to stay the night in the small house and travel back tomorrow, allowing themselves more time to search the house. Max was upstairs in the sleeping quarters going through the man's bureau.

Admittedly, it was strange to rifle through the belongings of a man he'd never known. Part of Max relished it, loved the digging and the discovery. Even if the searching was between socks and in drawers rather than in dirt in a sacred place.

He kept his eyes open for anything that might have to do with Atlantis, prophecy or not. So far he'd found nothing but clothes that were threadbare and worn, books on ancient philosophy, but none that Max wasn't already familiar with, and a large collection of ribbons.

The ribbons themselves were ordinary, though varied in length and width and color, but Max found it strange that a man would collect them. These Atlanteans were a mysterious group. He thought of Sabine and how intriguing he found her. Was it simply her Atlantean heritage that had captured his interest? Or her stunning beauty? She appealed to him on a more primal level than any woman he'd ever known, matching him intellectually and passionately, and not only sharing his interest in Atlantis, but living it within her very blood.

He had one more corner of the room to look through, then he would join Sabine downstairs. She'd been digging around in the kitchen area, but so far she'd been fairly quiet, so Max had assumed she hadn't found anything of note.

Max tucked the bag of ribbons back into the drawer, then had second thoughts. He wondered what would possess a man to gather a simple item like ribbons into a large collection, but he supposed everyone had their own fascinations. Or perhaps they held more sentimental meaning. Sabine's aunts knew the man, perhaps they could shed some light on the collection. Max put the ribbons in his bag, then closed the drawer.

His shoes noisily tapped the wood-planked floor as he made his way to the remaining portion of the room. A small chest sat in the corner. On the top was a basin and water jug and below was a set of two drawers. Max touched the chest and it wobbled. He rocked it back and forth a few times, finally noticing the front right leg was shorter than the other three. He took a step back to kneel at the chest, and his foot hit a hollow sound. He stopped. He walked again and heard the same noise. He pounded his foot over the area. Definitely different from the rest of the floor.

Quickly, he knelt and tapped the boards with his knuckle. There was a noticeable difference in the sound over one board when compared to the surrounding boards. He ran his fingers along the edge of the board until he found a gap wide enough to wedge in his fingernail; there he pulled up and the board lifted.

It wasn't a large space, but the hollowed-out cubby was large enough to hide a cigar box. Max pulled it out, and there inside, he found a bundle of envelopes, all addressed to Phinneas. He quickly flipped through them, noting that they all shared the same penmanship and were all written in Greek, but none listed a sender's name. He tucked the letters in the same bag in which he'd placed the ribbons.

The cigar box lay empty on the floor, so he tried tucking it back into the cubby. But he could not make it fit. He reached his hand in and felt beneath the wooden planks. His fingers ran across something smooth. With considerable effort, he was able to pull out the item. It was a thick leather-bound book, written in a language he did not recognize.

He stowed the book, then replaced the loose floorboard. A cursory glance through the remaining two dresser drawers came up with nothing new.

He made his way downstairs to join Sabine. His feet had barely touched the bottom step before she asked, "Did you find anything?"

"Some old letters."

"None of them are recent?" she asked.

"I didn't look through all of them, but I don't think they are. They all appear to be from the same person. Phinneas had hidden them in a hollow floorboard."

It was well past dark outside. Sabine yawned, but tried to gracefully cover it with the back of her hand. Her hair had come loose from its confinement at her neck, and soft tendrils framed her face.

"I found clean linens upstairs in the bureau," he said.

She yawned again, then smiled. "Sleep sounds nice, but I don't know that I'd truly be able to rest."

"I also found a book," he said. "In a language I don't recognize."

"A book? That could be precisely what I need." She came toward him, and he pulled it out of the bag and handed it to her. Reverently, she ran a hand over the worn leather cover. "This is it. The Seer's book."

"The Seer?"

"The three guardians, the Sage, the Seer, and the Healer, each with a unique purpose. The Seer was the prophesier, and this book," she said, holding it out, "is where all his dreams and visions and predictions were written. Not just Phinneas, but those who came before him."

"We might be able to find out more about the map's prophecy in there," Max said.

"Only if Phinneas had recent visions about it. This is the book I was telling you about, the one that used to hold the prophecy."

"Then let's hope Phinneas had some good dreams lately," Max said. He leaned over her shoulder. "We might need to find a translator, though I don't know where, because I don't even know what that is. It looks a little like Greek, but every symbol is different."

Sabine smiled. "It's Atlantean."

"And you can read it?" he asked.

"Of course."

He looked around the kitchen. "Did you find anything down here?" he asked.

She shook her heard. "Nothing."

"You've had a long day, and you're clearly exhausted. Why don't you lie down?" When she started to shake her head in protest, he added, "You don't have to sleep, and you can use the time to look through the Seer's book."

She allowed him to lead her back up the stairs to the small bedchamber. He handed her the stack of clean linens, and then went about making a pallet on the floor for himself. The blanket that had been draped over the chair became a flat and rather sad-looking bed, but it would work for the night. And his coat, folded over several times, made a serviceable pillow.

After her bed for the evening was prepared, she sat on the edge looking around the room. "I wish I had known him," she said softly. "I feel as if he was a member of my family."

He said nothing. He had no words of comfort to offer, even if he wanted to. Which he didn't. The impulse he'd had to comfort her earlier had unsettled him. He could easily shock or amuse. He could seduce a woman with only a few words. But comfort? No, comfort was not for him. The urge to console her was too tender an emotion. Too delicate. And entirely too close to something deeper.

He couldn't risk letting her get too close. Couldn't allow her to touch that part of him he'd buried long ago. He knew all too well the pain of losing someone he loved.

He could seduce her. He knew she'd respond to his touch, and damned if he didn't want her. But touching her now could be mistaken as sympathy. No, he just needed to get some sleep.

With that thought, he peeled off his shirt and tossed it on the chair. Then he removed his stockings and boots. He lay on the pallet on the floor and was very aware of Sabine's breathing. Even as tired as he was, he was able to conjure an image of her beckoning him to the bed. *Damnation!*

He folded his arms behind his head and stared at the ceiling. His breathing and her paper rustling were the only sounds. He noted each page she read as the parchment brushed when she turned the pages. She said nothing, just continued to read.

After about an hour had passed, he rolled to his side. She sat cross-legged in the bed, the candle next to her nearly burned completely down. The book rested in her hands, and she mouthed silently as she read.

"You're about to lose that candle," he said.

She started at the sound of his voice. A quick glance at the candle, and then a smile played at her lips. "I suppose you're right."

"Anything yet?"

"Not yet." She set the book on the table next to the candle, then took a deep breath.

"Good night, Sabine," he said.

She pursed her lips and blew out the candle, shrouding the room in near darkness except for the moonlight casting shadows across the floor. He remained on his side watching her as she reached behind to unhook her dress. She slid out of the wool fabric, then sat on the bed again to remove her stockings. Though he couldn't see much detail, the outline of her leg as she rolled the stocking down was enough for him. The silhouette of her lush body fired lust through his blood. That simple image was far more erotic than the entire nude bodies of some of the other women he'd been with. His imagination could fill in the remaining details—her warm olive skin, the delicate curve of her calf down to her dainty ankle. Yes, he could imagine every last inch of her.

* * *

The moon peeked in through the worn curtains on the small window in Phinneas's bedroom. Sabine had been tired when Max found her in the kitchen, exhausted really, but with the discovery of Phinneas's book, sleep had evaded her. She'd read as much as she could, but could not make sense of much of it. And then there was the letter she'd found stuffed inside a cushion on the sofa downstairs.

Sabine listened for several moments before she moved. She wanted to make certain that Max was sleeping before she snuck back into the kitchen where she'd hidden it. It seemed Phinneas must have been working on the letter when he'd been interrupted. Perhaps by the killer. He'd hidden it, which led her to believe it might have sensitive information within, perhaps the identity of the third guardian. She wanted to be certain before she shared it with Max.

Her feet were bare, and she wore only her shift. Without the blanket covering her, the cool night air from the opened windows created gooseflesh wherever it touched.

She paused to allow the blackness around her to fade as her eyes adjusted. Max's even breathing from his pallet on the floor let her know he still slept. She stood over him a moment, unwisely admiring the way the cover drifted down to bare his chest. As softly as she could, she tiptoed past his sleeping form, then padded her way down the darkened stairs to the kitchen below. Once downstairs, she was able to light a candle, and the soft glow filled the tiny space.

When she'd first stumbled upon the letter, she'd nearly had the first half read when Max had come into the kitchen. So she'd shoved the parchment into a jug of flour for later. Now as she fished it out of the powder, she heard the stairs creak behind her. She stilled.

"What are you looking for?" Max asked, his voice darkly seductive in the candlelight.

Her heart felt as though it had fallen into her belly, and there it pounded in her gut. She took a quick breath as guilt pinched and prodded her. He had found that group of letters as well as Phinneas's book, and he had shared both with her.

No one was to know Agnes's identity as the guardian, and Sabine had already trusted Max with more information than she should have. But that secret she had to protect, and until she knew for certain it wasn't mentioned in the letter, she could not share it with him.

Before she turned to face him, she shook the flour from her hand, then tucked the letter inside the folds of her undergarment. "Nothing," she said.

When she met his glance, she could not miss the heat of his gaze as it traveled the length of her. She knew he was appraising her, seeing more of her curves. Wanting her. Sensations of his hands on her body, his mouth on hers, flooded her. She wanted him, too, but she knew now that when it came to Max, she was playing with fire.

However, his desire for her could provide the perfect distraction and give her a chance to escape without his discovering the letter. She sauntered over to him. She reminded herself of all that Agnes had taught her about men and their ways. They were easy to manipulate and manage if you used the right touch, the perfect tone. She'd seen that with Max during the card game. When she'd first sat down, he'd been so distracted by her presence that he'd lost more than one hand. With determination, she relaxed her shoulders and reminded herself of why she was here, of her duty to her family.

With one finger, she traced down his bare chest, something she'd longed to do since the night she'd tended his wound. She tried her best not to notice how firm and well muscled he was. But as his muscles tensed beneath her touch, she wanted nothing more than to splay both hands across his torso and feel every hard inch of him.

"I couldn't sleep, and I was merely looking to see if there was anything to eat." She smiled sheepishly. "I got hungry."

"And?" he asked, his eyes a steely blue from this close. "Did you find anything appetizing?"

She allowed her own glance to trail down to his waist. His abdomen was perfectly sculpted. Her mouth went dry. She looked up at his face. "Nothing."

"You're certain about that?" He stepped ever so close to her and dipped his head near her ear. His hot breath scattered chills over her flesh.

She was unable to tell if he was merely flirting in return or if he suspected something. So she did the only thing she could think of to deter him from further questioning. She kissed him.

His soft lips responded immediately as she leaned her body into his. She kissed him passionately, trying to convince him that this kiss had been her intention all along. That it was the only reason she threaded her fingers through the back of his hair. It was surprisingly soft; a sharp contrast to his solid and toned neck.

She did not enjoy his warm hands cupping her bare arms. Nor did she enjoy how molten his kiss was when he coaxed her mouth open and swept his tongue against her own. And she certainly did not enjoy the coils of pleasure that were springing from her abdomen and winding up around her to tease and tingle her breasts.

As their tongues molded to each other, desire surged through her body, peaking her nipples. She was losing control of the situation and herself. Kissing him was not the goal, only the means, she reminded herself. But her body did not want to listen. Her body wanted to wrap her legs around him and have him make love to her right up against this cupboard.

His lips trailed to her ear, then down her throat. He cupped her breast, and she arched into him.

Yes. She wanted this. She wanted him.

"You are exquisitely beautiful," he whispered against her hair.

She'd been flattered before, but coming from him, the words seemed to actually hit their mark, as if she were being told for the very first time that she was pretty.

But it wasn't the first time, and he was an experienced charmer merely toying with her. As much as that should have warned her to step away from him, she didn't move.

Then his kisses stopped, and he held a finger up to her lips to keep her from speaking. He snuffed out the candle, immediately shrouding them in darkness. It was then that she heard it—the noise that had caught Max's attention. Someone was at the front door.

Chapter Ten

Together they crept toward the back door. "Faster," Max whispered. They had nearly reached the door when she paused.

"The letters," she said. "They're still upstairs."

Max swore. Once again, he handed her his pistol. "Go outside and wait for me." With that, he tore up the staircase.

She slid out the back door, and he closed it behind her. He made his way up the stairs as quietly as possible and grabbed his bag where he'd already tucked the letters. He shoved the book inside, then swung the strap over his shoulder. There was no way to know who it was at the front door, but if it was the men from the train, Max knew they'd be armed, and he was outnumbered.

He heard the front door open while he was still upstairs. Now he was stuck, with no way out. The window on the second floor was far too narrow for a man his size. And to simply walk back down the stairs seemed foolish. Max looked around the room for a makeshift weapon.

The stairs creaked. Max grabbed the only thing he could find, the heavy candleholder from the bedside table. He hid next to the doorway and waited for the intruder to pass through. The shadow of a man entered the room, and Max slammed the heavy metal down upon the man's head. It clattered to the floor, and the man grunted in pain.

Max jumped down the short staircase and had barely hit the floor when the man crashed into him from behind. The room was dark so Max couldn't make out his features, but he knew that this man was taller and thinner than either of the men who had chased them on the train. Max rammed his fist into the man's back. A fist came down hard on Max's shoulder, nearly bringing him to his knees. But he recovered and ran headfirst into the man's gut, crashing him into the wall. The man's breath came out in a hard whoosh. Max hit him in the face, knocking him to the floor.

Escape time.

Max ran out the back door and grabbed Sabine by the hand. She screamed and tried to pull away from him.

"It's me," he said through his teeth.

She picked up her pace and together they ran. Max turned once to see whether the man followed, but there was no sign of him. Perhaps Max had hit him hard enough with that last blow to knock him out. On the other hand, he could have gone around to the front of the cottage to retrieve his horse or carriage to chase them.

So they didn't slow, they just ran.

Damned bastard nearly broke one of his ribs. Spencer shook his head as he came to his feet. He made it out the back door in time to see the man, along with a woman, run straight into the woods. For a fleeting moment, he could have sworn the man was Maxwell Barrett. He tore back through the house, then out the front door, and hopped on his horse to chase after them.

Chances were if the Seer's book had been here, it was gone now. The horse's hooves threw dirt up behind him as he galloped toward the woods. They were on foot, so there was no possible way they could outrun him. But half an hour later when he still hadn't found them, he was beginning to believe otherwise. Perhaps they'd had horses nearby. Or knew of hiding places in these darkened woods.

Spencer slowed his horse to a gentle gait and tried to listen to the noises around him. They were gone.

If that was the marquess he'd seen, then Spencer would have to find a way to retrieve that book. He already had all the information required to fulfill the prophecy, but he didn't want to run the risk of the remaining guardian's getting his hands on the book and possibly discovering a way to stop him.

After spending the night in a damp cave they'd stumbled upon in the woods, Max and Sabine made their way to the train station. Max had managed to steal some clothes for them from a clothesline, but they were still dirty and exhausted. He didn't bother trying to secure an entire train car for their return trip to London. The privacy was nice, but when you had men on your trail, it was better to blend in with the crowd. They sat across from each other in the dining car, a small table between them, sharing a meal. And they had begun to read over the letters they'd found in Phinneas's cottage, which as it turned out were mostly from Sabine's aunt Agnes.

"It still feels like a violation of her privacy," Sabine said.

"We can return them to her as soon as we get back to London. First, though, we should see if we can find any vital clues," Max said.

"They'd be more useful if we had the replies to these letters." Sabine took a sip of tea and looked out the window to her right.

Max read: "*I thought of you today, when we were making bread. Lydia tried a new recipe that included cinnamon and I know how you love the smell. The entire cottage smelled of the sweet herb and, for a moment, it felt as if you were there wrapping your arms around me. I will not speak of how I wish things were different, we know that cannot be. But you are in my every breath, every beat of my heart. All my love, Agnes.*'"

Max watched in silence as a few stray tears escaped Sabine's eyes. She continued to watch the scenery chug by outside their window.

"They were lovers," he said.

She shook her head. "I never knew."

"Why couldn't they be together?" Max asked.

"It is our way. The three guardians represent three separate peoples, similar to tribes." She met his eyes. "Phinneas is from the line of Seers whereas Agnes is from the line of Healers. There is no mixing. It simply isn't done," she said. "And Phinneas was a guardian. A union between them would have been forbidden."

"Is Agnes the third guardian?" Max asked.

Sabine chewed at her lip, then took a deep breath. "No, she is not. I am."

"You?" he asked.

She glanced around the train car before answering. "Yes."

"So then you must have come to London to find me and my map and to gain access to the prophecy?" Max asked.

"Not precisely, though we did need the prophecy. And we knew you had the map in your possession."

"But there still might be other information in that book that will help with the prophecy," Max said.

"Yes. I'm hoping Agnes can help decipher it, because she obviously knew Phinneas quite well."

They read silently for a few moments. "If not specifically for the map, why did you move to London?" he asked.

"To sell our products," she said simply.

Beauty products from a family of Atlanteans. A family where one member was a guardian, which meant they protected elixir from the fountain of Atlantis. He set the letter he was reading on the seat beside him. "Your products must be very good to cause such a stir in Society," he said. He was beginning to piece together the mystery surrounding Sabine, though admittedly he had not expected her to be the third guardian.

"I suppose," she agreed. "But you know it only takes getting something into the right hands and then everyone else has to have it."

"Not your typical jar of crème full of empty promises, though." He crossed his arms over his chest. "No, your products are authentic."

"What are you suggesting, Max?"

"The elixir. You're putting it in your crème."

She said nothing.

"Why, Sabine? Monetary gain?" he asked.

"Of course not." She frowned, clearly offended.

"If the elixir is as dangerous as you've suggested, why put it out there?"

"It was the only way. We did it for our protection." She chewed at her lip before continuing. "The Chosen One has ways of detecting those from Atlantis through the elixir."

Max thought for a moment before speaking. "So distributing it across London allows you to hide among the rest of us," Max finished for her.

She nodded.

"That's very clever," he said. He said nothing more for a while. She picked up Phinneas's book and flipped through it, narrowing her focus to one page, then slowly turning a page.

They sat in silence for nearly an hour while she read the book and he read the letters. So far, he hadn't found anything particularly useful in Agnes's letters, but he suspected that if they had Phinneas's responses, they might complete the puzzle. Some aspect of them seemed important to him, but he couldn't place his finger on it at the moment.

Mostly Agnes spoke of everyday life in their village, of missing Phinneas, and of the love that they shared. But every now and then, he'd come across one that felt as if Agnes was talking about something far more important than their vegetable garden or how one woman had had a particularly difficult birth. He folded the parchment back up, then set it aside.

Max watched Sabine read the book. She was hiding something, physically hiding something from him. He'd seen her conceal something behind her last night before she'd kissed him in the kitchen.

He could have accused her right then and there, but it

was far more interesting to watch her try to deceive him, particularly when her attempts at deception included hot kisses... Well, who was he to discourage her? She'd felt good pressed against him. Without her dress, he'd been one layer closer to touching her warm skin. On the earlier train ride, he'd touched her, but they had never removed their clothing.

A day later and he could still feel her mouth on his, her soft arms beneath his hands, her molten curves pressed to his body.

Thoughts like that would only cause the remainder of the train ride to be particularly uncomfortable, though, so he turned his thoughts to something else.

"I've been thinking," he said, "about this Chosen One. Scotland Yard is investigating the murders of our military officers. I think I've been looking at this entire thing the wrong way."

Sabine put the book down and leaned in. "How?"

"I thought what I needed to do—what we needed to do—was help them identify the killer. If we did that, we could protect the military and the last guardian"—he nodded to her—"and stop the prophecy. But I suspect that we should leave the detective work to the inspectors and instead focus our energy on something else entirely. What happens if the Chosen One finds the remaining guardian? What will happen to you?"

"He steals the elixir, the guardian dies, and the prophecy is completed. With the way events have unfolded thus far, I suspect he will try to use England's military to complete what the Atlantean army started so many years ago," Sabine said.

"Which was?" he asked.

"World domination. He will use the elixir to make your

military impossible to defeat. At least he will attempt to do so." She shook her head.

"Then instead of trying to discover the identity of the Chosen One, we should find the dove. The prophecy states it's the only way to stop him. He's already found the other two guardians. Despite your clever way to hide in plain sight, chances are he will eventually find your identity." He clasped his hands together. "So we need to be ready for him."

"With the dove," she provided. "The problem is, we don't exactly know what the dove is."

"Clearly they don't mean the actual bird," Max said.

She rolled her eyes. "Obviously not."

He took that moment to take the map out of his bag and spread it out on the table.

Sabine's breath caught. "I didn't know you had that with you," she whispered. She splayed her palm on the map as if trying to touch the actual island.

"I thought perhaps it would help the Seer with the prophecy if he could see it." Max shrugged. "But that didn't work so well."

She gave him a sweet smile. "It was a good thought. I have no doubt he would have loved to see it."

Max pointed to the inscription that mentioned the dove. "Perhaps it is a weapon of some kind. Which makes sense. If we are to do battle, we will definitely need a weapon."

She glanced down at the map and then back to his face. Something in her expression softened. She reached into her own bag and held out a folded piece of parchment.

"What is this?" he asked.

"I found it. In Phinneas's house," she said.

"This is what you were hiding," Max said.

She opened her mouth, then shut it with a heavy sigh. "I merely wanted a chance to read it first. Alone. I thought it might be something else." Then she shook her head. "Just read it."

He looked down. It was dated three days before and was from Phinneas to Madigan. " 'I believe I've located the dove, but have decided not to remove it from the current location. It appears safe enough and disturbing it might be even more dangerous.' " Max caught her glance. "He knew where the dove was?"

"Yes. It appears as though he might have deciphered that part of the prophecy."

Max kept reading, then flipped the parchment over. "The letter is unfinished."

"I think he was interrupted by the Chosen One and only had the time to hide the letter," Sabine said.

Max read it again, searching for a clue to the location, but found none. "Where is it?" he asked.

"I don't know. I was hoping he'd have something written in the book, but I haven't found it yet. I'll keep reading, though," she said.

But she did not open the book. Instead she stared at the map, soaking in every detail. It mattered not how awe-filled her eyes were or how lovingly she followed the lines of the map with the tip of her finger. He was on this quest, not primarily to help her, but to aid Justin and ultimately to find what he'd sought these many years. Atlantis was out there somewhere, beneath the surface, waiting to be discovered.

He cleared his throat. "This letter does not include you. Why would he notify only one guardian?"

"Perhaps he died before he had the chance."

*   *   *

Spencer had just returned to town when he'd been summoned to meet the queen in the breakfast room. Her majesty had been an early riser ever since her husband had passed, and when she was ready to attend to business, she expected her advisors to be ready as well. Spencer tugged on the hem of his jacket to straighten it, then allowed himself to be led into the room.

The room was red nearly from floor to ceiling, with enormous velvet drapes framing the large wall of windows. With the matching scarlet upholstery on the furniture as well as the red rug, it looked like a room bathed in blood, hardly one for consuming food. But someone had told her majesty that the color stimulated the appetite, so she'd taken that to heart and instructed her decorators to make it so. Perhaps it was all the blood he'd seen lately that brought the visual to his mind.

"You wanted to see me," he said as he bowed before her. He made no move to take a seat until she offered.

"Yes, sit." She pointed to a chair adjacent to her. Her gray hair was wound in its usual long braid and wrapped into a wide bun that sat at the base of her neck. Winter was weighing on her, stiffening her joints and making her movements slower and more pronounced. England's beloved queen was getting old.

He sat and said nothing as she ate three bites of quail eggs from the gold-rimmed plate before her. Additional food-filled platters and bowls sat on the sideboard behind them, but she offered him none.

She leaned forward and tapped her blunt fingernails on the heavily carved mahogany table. "I'm told that you recently met with an investigator from the Scotland Yard," she said. When he nodded, she continued. "Have they made any headway in finding out who is killing all of my generals?"

"Unfortunately, no. They have no leads." He crossed one leg over the other.

"Well, that stands to reason," she said. "This is a cunning killer they are dealing with, smart enough to not leave evidence. I'm told he uses a different type of gun with every one. Then there was General Carrington, whom the savage beast used a knife on." She chewed thoughtfully for several moments before she spoke again. "I heard whoever is doing this has left me some sort of message."

"I beg your pardon?" he asked. She had called him a savage beast. He evened his breath and clasped the arms of the chair. One day they would all see what he was doing, and they would know it had nothing to do with savagery.

"The killer"—she waved her hand about, her fork dangling daintily from her hand—"he left me a note on one of the bodies."

She believed his message was addressed to her. Clearly that was how the inspectors were interpreting it. Otherwise she would never have heard of it. Fools. Spencer had hoped they'd run the notes in the newspapers as he'd commanded them. But they were idiots and clearly could not follow instructions.

He knew the third guardian lived somewhere in London. His ring flickered too often for the guardian to not be near. The guardian could only hide for so long before he would ferret him out. Then he'd have all of the elixir, as the prophecy required. And immortality would be his.

"A message for you?" he asked.

She rattled on about speculation from the detectives.

Spencer had known this conversation would happen. At some point, he'd expected it. He hadn't informed the queen of the inspector's visit but that didn't mean she would not be concerned or interested in the investigation. Discussing his own crimes without her knowing the truth exhilarated him. What would she do if she knew her favored advisor was single-handedly destroying her military forces? No doubt, have him beheaded.

He caught himself before he smiled. Careful not to show his glee, he forced his features into a frown.

"My apologies, your majesty, for not telling you of the visit sooner. I'm afraid I was called away at the last minute. My aunt is ill." He feigned concern. "We don't believe she has much more time."

"I'm sorry to hear that, Spencer," the queen said, her voice lined with authentic sympathy.

"When the investigator came, he brought along someone," he told her, "the Marquess of Lindberg. Are you familiar with him?" Spencer had done some investigation of the marquess but had not come up with much information. He'd already known the man was a member of London's most exclusive club. Perhaps her majesty would give him some new details.

The queen paused over her breakfast. Then she set down her fork and smiled dreamily. "Maxwell Barrett; yes, I am familiar. Quite the charmer, that one, with a wicked sense of humor." She took a bite of buttered bread slathered liberally with jam. "I presume he came along to assist his friend in gaining an audience with me. I do wish I had known when they were here. It would have been entertaining to see him again."

"You were resting. I didn't want to rouse you. You've been under so much pressure lately," Spencer explained.

A heavy line creased her already wrinkled brow. "I am the monarch of this country," she said in her strongest voice of authority. "I do believe I can handle the pressure. I have thus far."

"Yes, your majesty." He lowered his head and hoped he appeared appropriately contrite. "It won't happen again."

She stood, and a flurry of servants were instantly by her side while she moved to a large wing-backed chair in the sitting area of the room. "Well, don't dawdle, come join me." She beckoned with her hand.

He moved quickly to the seating area and selected his chair.

"Hmmmm. I am most concerned about this current situation. I simply will not abide a lunatic murdering my military leaders." She pounded her fist on the arm-rest. "Soon I will have none to rely on. Precisely how am I to civilize Africa if all of my military leaders are deceased?"

He bristled at her use of the word "lunatic." He was not some common madman going about London murdering just anyone. This was his destiny. Everything had been explained to him, in detail, when he was a small child. His grandfather had seen to it that Spencer had grown up knowing precisely who he was—the Chosen One. When everyone else had failed him, his grandfather had been there to show him the way.

"Well, of course you cannot," Spencer said, continuing to play his role as faithful advisor. "The whole of your empire will feel the effects of the loss of these important men." He crossed his legs. "But we will get this situation under control, and your African missions will move forward as you have carefully planned."

He'd needed to infiltrate her defenses, to make her fear

for the safety of the country. Without having a role in the government, without being close to her, his random killing of the generals would have served no purpose. Just as carefully as he'd orchestrated the kills, he'd created a relationship in which she would rely on him. He hoped the next words out of her mouth would be the ones he'd been waiting to hear.

"I want you to meet with the lieutenant-generals," she said. She sat back in her chair and gripped both armrests. "See which of them is up to the task. I'll get recommendations from others, but you've always had a talent in that area. I need you to help me select who should be the next in command," she said.

There it was, the assignment he'd worked for. All his efforts were paying off. All of the years he'd spent trying to work his way into her cabinet, and then once he'd arrived, the exhausting hours of pandering and fawning over her. They had not been for naught. He said nothing and tried to keep any indication of his excitement out of his expression. So he merely nodded.

He knew precisely which men to contact. He'd already selected them and slipped them elixir in preparation for this very moment. And it was working. The elixir was feeding their aggression, making them stronger and their minds more cunning. Spencer's army would be brilliant and unstoppable.

"I can't very well traipse about in the training field," the queen said abruptly, pulling him out of his fantasy. "I want those five men replaced in two days with the best you can find. I know there are men up for promotion, but I want these hand-selected. By my decree." She tapped her chest.

He smiled; he could not help himself. "Yes, your

majesty, I will get to work on this straightaway." Of course, she'd have two more to replace before all was done, but his plan was falling into place. "I will find the perfect men to lead us into battle," he said.

Soon they'd be ready for his command, and then he would control all of Britain's military just as the prophecy had predicted. And he could see his ancestors' plan through to fruition. Atlantis might not physically rise, but he could ensure an Atlantean ruled all.

"You are dismissed," Victoria said.

He stood to leave.

"Oh, and Cole"—she held one finger up and leveled her shrewd eyes on his—"the next time someone comes to see me about this matter, especially Maxwell Barrett, you are to allow him entrance."

"Of course, your majesty." He nodded, then backed out of her presence. Perhaps Spencer should do something about Max to make sure that never happened.

Chapter Eleven

———— ❦ ————

Sabine knew she was going to walk through that door and break Agnes's heart. To say she was not looking forward to it was a gross understatement. Regardless of how difficult it might be, this was not something Sabine could keep from her aunts.

She stepped into the large bedchamber they all shared. It was the sort of room designed for children, with more than one bed along the expansive wall. But Max had no children, so he'd had the room designed to cater to guests. He'd offered her aunts their own bedchambers, but they'd opted to share this one. They'd always shared a room, and they'd seen no reason to do differently.

It was late in the evening, but her three aunts were still awake. Lydia sat in a reading chair in the corner, book in hand, while Agnes stood behind Calliope braiding her hair. For a moment, Sabine could imagine how they'd been as girls, with her mother right there with them. Four sisters and the best of friends.

"Sabine," Calliope said with a warm smile. "Welcome back."

Agnes immediately walked over. "How was he?" She put her hand to her throat. "How was Phinneas?"

Sabine felt tears prick at the corners of her eyes. "Oh, Agnes, I'm so very sorry."

The color completely drained from her aunt's face, and immediately her two sisters were there by her side as she crumpled to the floor. She clung to them as she wept, and they cried with her. Sabine stood quietly, watching, her tears clouding her vision. There was nothing graceful about their grief; it was raw and intense and utterly unapologetic.

After several moments, Lydia stood. "The Chosen One had found him, then?"

"It appears so. We found Phinneas in his garden. Max made certain to give him a decent burial there."

Agnes swallowed and tried to smile. "He loved that garden."

Calliope and Lydia helped her to the edge of her bed, where she sat. Her head and shoulders hung down in defeat.

Sabine knelt at her feet. She placed the stack of letters in her lap as well as the ribbon collection Max had found. "We found these. We thought you'd want to have them."

Agnes opened her eyes and gasped. "My ribbons. That silly old fool. Why would he keep all of these?" She ran her hand reverently over the bag of ribbons as she spoke.

"Because he loved you," Calliope said.

"I'm sorry, but we read through some of the letters," Sabine said. "We thought they might help us." She shook her head. "I don't know, perhaps assist us in figuring out a way to stop the prophecy."

Agnes looked up. She shook her head. "Don't be. There is nothing I'm ashamed of in these letters." She motioned to Calliope. "Hand me my box."

Calliope reached beneath Agnes's bed and withdrew an old wooden box. Sabine had seen it before, plenty of times. Her aunt had always had it, as far as she'd known, but Sabine knew better than to ask what was kept inside.

Agnes withdrew another stack of letters. "Here are his letters to me. And you're right, perhaps you will find something helpful within them."

Sabine took the letters, both sets. "I'll make certain you get these back." She would share these letters with Max, because they might hold some clue that could aid them in their search. But they also might reveal secrets she'd worked hard to protect. Earlier on the train when he'd asked why Agnes and Phinneas couldn't be together, she'd lied, come up with a false reason about a Seer and a Healer not being free to marry. But it was the only thing she could think of, aside from telling Max the truth about Agnes's being the third guardian.

Agnes wept freely. Sabine longed to say something or do something that would ease Agnes's pain. But she knew there was nothing that could help. When her own parents had died, she'd had to allow time to soften the pain. It still lurked beneath the surface and sometimes would crash upon her, but most days she simply missed them.

"What of the Seer's book?" Lydia asked.

"We found that as well, though someone was coming back after it. We had to run and hide in the woods."

"We're so thankful you're safe. Max took very good care of you," Calliope said.

"Phinneas faithfully wrote all of his visions down in that book," Agnes said.

"I was hoping you could take a look through it," Sabine said, holding it out to Agnes. "See if you can find anything on the prophecy and his interpretation of it. I know he didn't have the entire prophecy, but he knew enough about it to have found the dove."

The aunts exchanged glances.

"Did he say where?" Lydia asked.

"No, it was an incomplete letter to Madigan. It said he found it, but it was safe for now so he didn't want to remove it and risk endangering it," Sabine said. "Max and I have decided we should try to locate it, to be prepared for the battle with the Chosen One."

"Where will you go?" Calliope asked.

"That's what I was hoping you would help with." She handed the book to Agnes, then placed her hand over her aunt's. "I don't want to put too much pressure on you. So if you can't do this, I will do it myself."

Agnes's shoulders straightened. "Of course I can do it."

"The Chosen One will be after you now," Lydia said to Agnes.

"Let him come. I will not fear him," Agnes said.

The following morning, Sabine was surprised to see Agnes join them at breakfast. Her eyes were red-rimmed and swollen, a testimony to a late night spent crying.

"Good morning," Max said to Agnes as he rose from his seat.

Sabine's heart contracted at the show of kindness. As much as he tried to prove otherwise, Sabine knew Max was a good man.

"Morning," Agnes said. She took a seat next to Sabine.

"I'm not hungry, but I wanted to join you. I think I may have found something."

Sabine pushed her own breakfast away from her, making room for Agnes to set down Phinneas's book.

"This is from entries he recorded sometime last year. He plainly says in order to locate the dove, you must go where it all began." She looked up at Max and then Sabine. "I think he's speaking of where the first ship from Atlantis landed. Lulworth Cove. See the part where he refers to the ocean's door?" She pointed to the next page. "That's what our people called the rock formation that looks like an arch. It's near the chapel that overlooks the cove."

"Durdle Door," Max said.

"What?" Sabine asked.

"That's officially what it's called. That rock formation," he said. "Durdle Door."

Sabine read through the words in the book. It wasn't very much to go on, but it was a place to start.

"That makes sense," Lydia said. "Our people began there, though the village has long been abandoned."

"There is more, Sabine," Agnes said. "In other sections, he kept mentioning these numbers. I didn't know what they were at first. I'm not certain he knew what they meant, but he recorded them several times." Her eyes met Sabine's. "Your birthday."

Sabine frowned. "What does my birthday have to do with anything?"

"It is coming up," Calliope said.

"When?" Max asked.

"Next week I will turn twenty-five," Sabine said. "But I don't understand the significance."

"I think it might be a timeline," Agnes said.

"Or a deadline," Max suggested.

"You think the prophecy is somehow attached to my birthday?" she asked.

"Perhaps it is merely a coincidence," Lydia said. "Or the numbers are something else. An address or a location of some sort."

"Perhaps," Agnes said. "But I don't think so. I just want you to be careful." She squeezed Sabine's hand.

"Of course," Sabine said. "I'm always careful."

Max rose to his feet. "You should go pack."

Sabine nodded.

"I have much to do to ready for the journey." He held his teacup up in a salute. "I hear Lulworth Cove is beautiful this time of year."

Shortly after breakfast, Sabine left with Calliope for the shop. It was quite evident that it was far too dangerous for Agnes to venture outside, so they had decided to take turns packaging the remedies for the villagers and handling the local patrons. Sabine and Max had plans to leave London later this afternoon, so she had taken the opportunity to help her aunts, and to get some much-needed distance from Max. The more time she spent with him, the more she craved his affections. She was on a slippery slope, and she knew it.

Sabine sat at the back table, measuring and combining the necessary ingredients, all but the elixir, which Agnes would add later. Spending so much time with Max was weakening her defenses, tempting her to think of not merely what her flesh wanted, but what her heart wanted as well. One night in his arms hadn't been enough, as she'd foolishly thought. But with Max came more than simply passion. No, there were faint whispers from her heart, asking, What about love?

She shoved those thoughts aside and focused on the task at hand. The shop was rather busy this morning, with the tiny bells at the door ringing again and again. But Calliope had been taking care of the customers.

Calliope stepped around the curtain. "Sabine, there's a man out here. Says he won't leave until he speaks with you."

Sabine finished adding the rose oil to her potion, then closed the jar. She stood up from the table and made her way out front.

She entered the shop and immediately spotted the man who'd requested her, as he was the only male in the room. She watched him examine every product on the display. He opened the bottles and jars and sniffed the contents, and he held the glass containers up to the light. The poor soul looked utterly lost, no doubt searching for a gift for his wife, or worse, sent on an errand for her. Still, that was something her aunts were perfectly capable of assisting him with.

"May I help you with something?" she asked.

His frame was slight, and he had thinning hair. He eyed her from behind his spectacles, and his mouse-colored mustache twitched. "I would like to speak to the proprietor of this establishment," he said, his voice pinched and nasal.

"Yes, my aunt mentioned that. Are you looking for a product for your wife?" she asked.

He cleared his throat. "Are you the proprietor?" he asked. He clutched a satchel to his chest.

The back of her neck prickled with awareness. Sabine took a deep breath. There was no need to automatically assume this man was the Chosen One, and it did seem rather improbable considering how ineffectual he appeared.

While he might make a worthy opponent against some women, it seemed unlikely she would not be able to fend him off. And both Madigan and Phinneas were strong men, certainly large enough to have defeated him. No, this man could not be the Chosen One.

"I am the proprietor. Is there a problem?"

He smiled at her. At least, she suspected that slight twitch was his version of a smile. The lasciviousness of that one small movement sent fresh chills across her arms. She rubbed them and hugged them tight to her body.

He picked up a jar of the Tobias Miracle Crème and held it up. "Is this an old family recipe?"

They had put the elixir in all of their products, even the hair tonic for men. Not only that, but Calliope was selling bread to a local bakery, infused with herbs they'd watered with the elixir. They had spread the elixir, covering the largest territory possible, trying to ensure the Chosen One would have a very difficult time homing in on them in their little shop at the edge of Piccadilly Square.

"It is, actually," she said. In truth, they had done nothing more than find a recipe for a facial crème in an old book and added the elixir and some scented oils.

"Interesting." He leaned in closer. His breath reeked. "I'm in the business myself. A chemist by training." He pressed his card into her hand. "Tell me, do you use lanolin?"

"I'm afraid I'm not at liberty to discuss the recipe of any of our products. You understand," she said firmly. She needed to make certain he knew that she would not give away any information.

He looked around the room, fidgeting with the buttons on his coat, when she realized he was missing two of them. He pulled the worn fabric closer around his lean body. "Of course."

He took a step closer to her. A slight twinge of body odor tweaked her nostrils, but she held her ground. There were other customers around, and she could not appear inhospitable. They needed people to continue buying and using their products until the Chosen One was caught.

"It works, you know," he said.

"I beg your pardon?" Sabine asked.

"The crème. It works. Makes women look younger, more supple, lovelier." His watery brown eyes scanned her face. "I see you use it." He reached up with one finger as if he would touch her, but he brought his hand down. "Not a line to be seen on your perfect skin."

She repressed a shiver. "I do not use it," she said. "Sir, I believe I have other customers to whom I need to attend. If you will excuse me."

He nodded, but before she could walk off, his bony hand grabbed her elbow with surprising force. "Any sum you require," he said, his voice shaking with nerves. "I will pay you any sum if you would sell me the recipe."

She attempted to break free from him, but his grip held fast. "I will do no such thing," she said, trying to remain calm and keep her voice low.

"I've tried," he said, his voice cracking. "I've taken apart several jars of this"—he glanced down at the crème in his other hand—"and still I cannot pinpoint all of the ingredients. There is something I simply cannot identify. And I must know what it is."

"I'm afraid you're going to have to remain disappointed, as I will not share our ingredient list. Good day." She jerked her arm free and went to the opposite side of the room to a group of ladies looking at the hair rinses.

The man wandered around the store awhile longer, perusing the materials, and every now and then glancing in her direction. She made certain, though, that she was always with a customer so that he could not approach her again. Eventually he left the shop, though he lingered a moment outside the window before he walked on.

She wondered briefly if she should mention the visitor to Max, though it would seem the man was harmless, probably nothing more than a competitor trying to improve his own products. Still, Max had told her to be on the lookout for anything peculiar, and that man had most definitely been odd.

She eyed the card in her hand—Mr. Bertrand Olney. When she looked up, it was to see Mr. Olney standing across the street watching her.

Chapter Twelve

That evening Sabine and Max were in a coach on their way to Dorset to find some sort of hidden weapon, if in fact the dove was a weapon at all. They had decided to go by coach this time, since the trip was shorter, and they wanted more flexibility in case they encountered another clue and had to travel elsewhere. Not to mention that being in an unmarked coach made it easier for them to be anonymous. Someone was after them.

Max was right. It made far more sense to try to locate the dove, the thing that would supposedly destroy the Chosen One, rather than trying to uncover his identity.

They had essentially no clues to his identity. And Scotland Yard had not had any luck either. Max had received a note from Justin saying that they had followed a lead to a disgruntled former military man, but he had only just returned from a trip to the continent and had been absent during two of the murders.

If they found the Chosen One without the dove, they would not be able to stop him. What bothered her most, though, was that she'd never even heard a rumor about a special weapon or anything that might be the dove. Her people had not had access to the prophecy for many years, but it still seemed that sort of secret would have been passed on through the generations.

Where should they go once they got to Dorset? She knew of the chapel on the cliff overlooking Lulworth Cove. She'd heard her aunts and other villagers speak of it. Historically, Atlanteans had made a pilgrimage there once a year, but during the Crusades it had become too dangerous, so the tradition had ended.

She watched her travel partner sitting casually across from her. He seemed far more accomplished at locating hidden objects than she was. Her people had searched for that map for centuries, and he'd found it when he was little more than a boy.

"It makes sense that something would be hidden at Lulworth Cove," she told him.

"If he'd located the dove, why didn't he go and get it, or at least tell the other two guardians the location, so that they could retrieve it?"

"Perhaps he intended to reveal the location, but he was interrupted before he had the chance. Or he kept it secret for protection. He said the dove was safe for now," Sabine said.

"Meaning at some point it will no longer be safe," Max added.

Of course, neither Phinneas nor Madigan had thought to tell Agnes any of this. Had they planned to simply fight the Chosen One without her? Had Phinneas kept her uninformed in order to protect the woman he loved?

A few moments later, they pulled up to a very old tavern and inn. A few torches lit the drive and the walkway to the front door. When the coach rambled to a stop, they both climbed out. An old wooden sign hung above the door, but only one of the chains remained, so it drooped to the right. The Tudor-style building boasted one stable and a small dining room, which they passed through on their way to the front desk, and they discovered only one remaining room for the evening.

Max paid the grizzled old man, then he and Sabine made their way to their room. Inside they found one narrow bed with shabby, dingy linens.

"This is a child's bed," Max told the man carrying their bags.

He just grunted in return, then closed the door behind him.

"It should be a restful night," Max said wryly.

Sabine stood at the window and pulled back the threadbare curtain and peered into the dark night sky. Only a handful of stars were visible through the evening clouds. "Perhaps it's too dark for us to do anything tonight," Sabine said.

"That's what lanterns are for." He leveled his steely gaze on her. "The night will not be wasted." He sauntered closer to her. "Unless you have something else you'd prefer we do." He eyed the bed with a smile.

She released an unladylike snort. "As if we would both fit in there," she said, pointing to the small bed.

"Did you want to give it a try?" he asked.

"Absolutely not," she said. A complete lie. Narrow bed or not, she knew there was passion to be found within Max Barrett's arms.

She had felt the touch of another man, but with Max she knew it was different. He was a man she intensely desired, a man whose touch made her ache, a man who made her want more than a tumble in bed.

"Do you want to do this or not?" he asked.

More than anything.

But of course, he was talking about exploring the chapel.

"Yes, certainly."

She pushed aside her more lascivious thoughts and considered instead the joys of sneaking around deserted churches in the dead of night. If her birthday marked some kind of deadline, they didn't have much time. Not to mention there was a killer after them—a killer who'd already taken the lives of two other guardians and five of England's military leaders. She ignored the fear bubbling inside her. This was not the time to be cautious. She'd been cautious her entire life. Now was the time to take action to protect the ones she loved.

"I asked the boy at the stable to gather some tools for us, including a shovel. It's been my experience that a shovel can be used for a multitude of purposes, including a weapon, should the need arise," Max said. "And here." He handed her a small stack of folded clothes. "It will make our traipsing around in the dark easier on you if you don't have to lug around forty yards of material."

She explored the stack of clothing he'd handed her. "You want me to wear trousers?"

"Don't you see that it will make our tasks less cumbersome?" He leaned against the wall and crossed his feet at the ankle. "Especially if any of the people who've been chasing us return, and we must again be on the run."

She eyed the clothes warily, then turned and stepped into the dressing corner behind a pitifully short screen.

The room had indeed been designed for a child, as her head and shoulders stuck out above the screen.

It was on her tongue to argue, but she bit back the words. He was right, of course. Wearing trousers and a shirt would be infinitely better than trying to navigate an old churchyard and cemetery in her wool dress. She unfastened her dress and slipped it off her shoulders. It fell to the floor in a pool.

Max never took his eyes off her. He stared blatantly at her bare shoulders; his bold perusal warmed her skin.

"You could be a gentleman and avert your eyes," she said. Her voice came out cool and crisp, completely opposite to the warmth his lusty stare shot through her body.

"I'm not a gentleman, Sabine, and I've never pretended otherwise." His smile was purely wicked. "I'm standing here wondering precisely why I'm not tossing that screen aside and pressing you up against the wall."

She swallowed hard. "Not a gentleman, but what of your title?" Her words came out in a stammer. "Do you not have responsibilities to your family name?"

The muscle in his jaw twitched, and the desire burning his eyes seemed to ice over. "My family is dead. And while I don't give a damn how anyone perceives me or my actions, there's not really anyone left who pays much attention either." With that, he turned away from her. "I'll be outside getting our supplies. Meet me there."

She nodded, even though he could no longer see her. His admission had startled her, and for a few moments after he'd closed the door, she simply stood there—unable to think, unable to move. It was quite evident he did give a damn, despite his protests. He was obviously a man who cared passionately about a great many things. Otherwise he wouldn't bother with the prophecy or her aunts or her.

A lesser man would have walked away from his quest to find Atlantis years ago.

Once she had collected herself, she dressed quickly. The shirt and trousers felt unfamiliar. She'd never encased her legs in anything but stockings, but the pants were surprisingly comfortable. Thankfully she'd brought along her travel boots, so she didn't have to borrow anyone's shoes. She pulled the pant legs over her boots, then rolled them up twice so they wouldn't drag on the ground.

As soon as the clothes were properly fastened, she stepped around the screen and sat at the small dressing table. Quickly she wound her hair up into a knot, then tugged the cap down onto her head. She stood in front of the chipped mirror to get a look at herself.

The masculine clothes hung on her but did nothing to hide her feminine curves. Her waist might not be perfectly accented, but the trousers did not hide her rounded hips, and the suspenders held up the pants but highlighted her breasts. In the light of day, there was no way she'd pass for a man, but by the shrouded evening light, one might not notice with only a cursory glance.

She made her way out to the front of the inn and caught up with Max near the stable. As she stepped into the barn, the color drained from Max's perfect face as he took in her new look. He visibly swallowed.

"What's the matter?" she asked. She smoothed the fabric at her hips, then crossed her arms over her chest.

"There is a reason women wear dresses," he growled. He shifted his stance. The stable boy also stood gawking at her. Max popped the boy on the back of his head. "Keep your eyes to yourself." Then he turned and headed out the door.

The woman inside her wanted desperately to smile. Max

was normally so charming, so smooth, she sometimes had difficulty seeing past the debonair role to the man beneath. Until this moment, she had not gauged the depths of his desire. She knew she had intrigued him, knew he wouldn't say no to a dalliance. But she'd been uncertain if he craved her as she craved him, or if she'd merely been a convenience. Just now, however, she'd seen pure lust in his gaze. Desire pooled through her body in response.

But Agnes's life was in danger. The Chosen One had stolen the elixir from both of the other two guardians, and Agnes had all that was left. Sabine could not afford to be distracted and risk failure in this quest. Firming her resolve, she waited by the gate until Max had collected the items from the stable boy.

The church sat at the very top of the cliff overlooking Lulworth Cove. Walking along the darkened road, all was quiet with only their breath and footfalls to break the silence. They began their climb and immediately she was thankful for the clothes Max had brought her. Her dress would have increased the challenge tenfold. The rocky hill would not be easy to navigate in sunlight. But with only a lantern and the moonlight, it was treacherous. As they climbed, the wind became so frigid, she might have frozen without the pants covering her legs.

The farther they climbed toward the church, the nearer they came to the coastline. Suddenly the wind picked up and wailed around them. The salt air brushed against her face, leaving a stickiness in its wake. Stray hairs escaped the confines of her bun and whipped around her face. The cottage she had shared with her aunts in Essex was near the ocean. The scent of saltwater brought a wave of nostalgia over her, and she found herself longing for the simple life she had led in their village.

Max carried the lantern and walked in front of her, holding his other arm behind him to help guide her along. His grasp was firm and warm, and she had no doubt that he would catch her if she stumbled. Still, she concentrated on her steps so she would not fall. The rocks and cratered landscape beneath her boots made the trek awkward.

Eventually they reached the top and found themselves on a trail that led toward the hollow ruins of the old chapel. The stones to their left sat in piles as if the wall had simply melted into the earth. The grass, uncut for many years, stood long and reedy and clung to their pants as they made their way to the back of the churchyard. A rusted iron fence lined the cemetery and the aging gravestones.

"We'll look here first and then go inside if we need to," Max said.

"What are we looking for?" she asked.

"You tell me. You're the one from Atlantis. If you see something that looks like it's from your homeland, then we've found it."

"That's so helpful," she said.

Waves crashed on the rocks below them. Because of the darkness, it was difficult to determine precisely how high up they were above the surging ocean below.

"You Atlanteans seem to favor cliffside coastlines," he said. "I found the map in a cave at the base of a similar cliff."

"I suppose that after they watched their homeland sink into the ocean, they wanted to be as high above the sea as possible," Sabine said. "How did you know where to look for it?" she asked.

"Determination and a heavy dose of luck." Max laughed. "I had learned about some of the early villages of the Atlanteans, and I went and spent an enormous amount of time in the pubs. Not to mention a hefty sum buying blokes drinks to keep them talking. One night I ran into the right fellow, and he said something so simple, he probably didn't even know how important the information was."

Because Max didn't always act the part, she often forgot he was a scholar of Atlantis, someone who'd studied her people and their ways and had worked extremely hard to find their greatest artifact. There was something attractive about his dedication.

"What did he tell you?" Sabine asked.

"That people had never found the map because the cave disappeared. His words made no sense to me for a long time. But then I happened to be reading an old text and came across a reference to a certain cave that, because of the ocean's tides, only appears every now and again. I tracked the tides and"—he shrugged—"well, we know how that one turned out."

After stepping over the broken gate, Max asked, "What have you heard of this area?"

"Only what I was told in childhood stories. The first of my ancestors came to shore here, and they built this village."

"So these people here"—he motioned to the graves surrounding them—"they are Atlanteans as well?"

She stepped over a broken tree limb that had fallen to the ground. "I believe so. The village changed a lot during the Crusades. But this," she said, motioning to the dilapidated church to their right, "was always my people's chapel."

"A temple to Poseidon?" he asked.

She smiled. "No. A chapel just as any other in England would be."

They continued walking through the cemetery, trying

their best to avoid walking directly on the graves. The tombstones weren't laid out in a grid, though, so that was a challenge. One moment, the wind whipped through the trees, shaking the leaves and emitting a low howling noise, and then it would settle and silence would shroud them. The combination added an eerie feel to the darkened night. Gooseflesh scattered up her arms, across her neck, and then down her body.

"We could get arrested," she said, thinking of a recent article in the *Times* Lydia had told her about.

"For what?" Max asked.

"Stealing bodies for medical research." Sabine looked behind them, but in the darkness she could not see anything but shadows. "They reported in the *Times* just last week about two men who were arrested doing this very thing."

Max stopped walking and turned to face her. He chuckled. "Yes, but in London where there are fresh bodies to steal. No one has been buried in this cemetery in nearly seventy years." He tapped the shovel on the tombstone below them, and the sound echoed across the hill. "There is nothing valuable for medical research here, except perhaps the two of us. Besides, I'm fairly certain we're the only two people mad enough to climb up that hill in the dark."

She glanced around them to again ensure that they were alone, then nodded.

"Take a deep breath, Sabine. We'll make it through the evening unscathed. I promise."

As they moved through the grounds, the earth shifted beneath them. She was careful to match her steps with Max's so she would not fall. She scanned the names on the grave markers, hoping that one would sound familiar or trigger something, but nothing came to mind.

"Why are we not looking inside the church?" she asked.

"Ah, churches are precarious hiding places." His deep voice rumbled through the still night. "Political power shifts. Factions within the church rise and fall. If you have a nosy parishioner offer to dust the rectory, anything could happen. No, churches are useful for hiding treasures short-term. But if you wanted to protect something, keep it safe for a very long time, what would you do with it?" he asked.

She thought for a moment before answering. "Probably bury it," she said.

"Precisely." He nodded.

She scanned the tombstones as they walked, searching for anything that resembled a dove on a carving or a relief, perhaps even something in the Atlantean language that would translate to "dove." She recognized some of the surnames, but nothing that indicated it would lead to the dove.

Max walked slightly ahead of her, but close enough that they could share the lantern's light. He brushed grass away with his boot so she could better see the tombstones. They had moved through the entire cemetery when they finally got to a grave resting against the back fence. The waves were louder here, but Sabine still couldn't see the cliff's edge.

Something rustled in the shrubs behind them. They both stopped walking, and Max reached around to pull Sabine close. This near to him, she could feel the steady thump of his heart beating beneath the warmth of his chest. He held the lantern out in front of them and turned the knob to widen the swath of light.

"Hello," he called. With his other hand, he handed her the shovel, then retrieved his pistol.

The rustling increased. He aimed his gun, just as a large doe walked out from behind the bush. She looked directly at them, chewing. Her eyes glowed in the lantern's light.

Sabine sighed as relief washed over her like warm water.

"Damn deer," Max muttered as he put the gun back in his waistband.

Together they turned back to the grave, and Max held the lantern up so that Sabine could read the name. "I think this is the last one," he said.

But there was nothing remarkable about this grave either. She glanced back at the church.

Together they walked toward the chapel. "We could go in there tonight," Max said, indicating the church. "But without being able to see clearly, and the risk of rotting boards..."

"It seems unsafe," she finished his thought. Still, there was a deadline to consider, but that wouldn't matter much if she fell and broke her neck trying to maneuver through a dilapidated church. "Perhaps we should come back in the daylight. It's only a few hours away." Then as if the mere thought of falling caused it, she tripped, her ankle turning beneath her.

Max caught her arm and prevented her from hitting the ground. "You all right?"

"I'll be fine." She placed her hand on the cold ground to give herself leverage, and she felt something hard beneath her fingertips. "Wait a minute," she said.

Max moved closer, bending next to where she knelt. The lantern's soft glow illuminated an old grave marker, lying flat on the ground, mostly buried by overgrown weeds and grass.

" 'William Travers,' " Sabine read aloud. She shook her head. "That doesn't sound familiar either."

"Move the grass aside," he said. "There's more written on the stone."

She did as he bade, pulling up grass and weeds.

Once he'd moved the light closer, the glow illuminated the entirety of the stone.

"There. See? That's a bird," Max said, pointing to a rough image carved beneath the dates. "Perhaps even a dove."

Excitement coursed through her. "Yes, it is."

Max handed her the lantern, then reached for the shovel.

She grabbed his arm to still him. "What are you going to do?"

"Dig up the grave," he said simply. "Sabine, do you suppose we're to whack the Chosen One on the head with the tombstone?" He didn't wait for her to answer. "Remember, you said yourself you'd bury something to hide it. And perhaps there is no Mr. Travers, and this is merely a false marker."

The shovel hit the old earth, slicing through the ground as if it were nothing more than warmed butter. Sabine concentrated on holding the lantern to provide enough light for Max's work, but she kept an ear out for any sounds around them. That deer had set her on edge and heightened her sensitivity to noise. But the only sounds were the wind, the hiss of the waves pounding the cliff below, and Max's digging. Soil mixed with chalk as he turned the ground over in a pile opposite Sabine.

Max stepped on the shovel to leverage it deeper and hit

wood. "Perhaps I was wrong, and this is an actual grave. I believe we've found Mr. Travers." Max looked up at her and grinned. "Hope he didn't die of the plague."

Sabine eyed him. "You're not amusing." Though she smiled in spite of herself.

He flashed her a brilliant smile. "I think I am. And I'll have you know many others do as well." He kept digging, removing the dirt that covered the wooden coffin. "Particularly others of the female variety."

"I don't believe your sense of humor is what attracts them," she said tartly.

"My rugged good looks then? My virility?"

She rolled her eyes. "Yes, that must be it. Watching you wield that shovel has me positively swooning." With her hand, she pretended to fan herself.

"You were looking rather peaked."

"Finish up," she said.

It took him another five minutes to finish digging around the coffin, then he fell to his knees. "Get down here with me so I can see what I'm doing."

Together they knelt above the grave. She held the lantern close as he scraped dirt away from the coffin. Sabine tried to ignore the thundering in her heart. She'd seen enough dead bodies in the last couple of days to last a lifetime. Yet here she was about to see another one, and this one without any skin. She shivered in trepidation. It seemed wrong to violate a man's final resting place, despite their good reasons.

Max used the shovel as a pry bar to leverage the lid up off the coffin, and with several rusty creaks, he was able to pull it open. There wasn't much left of Mr. Travers. The insects had cleaned off not only his bones but most of his clothes as well. Earth settled around his remains, telltale signs of worms using his final resting place as their new home.

"Perhaps the bird was merely decoration," she said.

"Certainly you're not ready to give up just yet."

"You're enjoying yourself," she accused.

"Of course I am," he said.

"No, I'm not ready to give up. I was just stating my observation." Her hand hovered over the body. She had touched enough wounds, injuries, and infections that nothing should make her feel squeamish. Yet these lifeless bones gave her the shivers. Finally she swallowed her fear and reached into the grave.

Often Atlanteans were buried with possessions from their lives—trinkets and treasures they'd valued. She searched first around the feet and legs, but found nothing.

"Have you done this before?" he asked.

She leaned back and eyed Max. "Desecrated a grave? Absolutely not." She paused, considering him. "Why? Have you?"

"Let's just say that the fine art of searching a grave is not unknown to me." And then he had the impertinence to wink.

"Let's get this over with," she said.

The bones shifted and fell away from their previous position as they searched around the body. There were no pockets in what remained of his clothing. Mr. Travers had lived before that convenience. Max checked beneath the body's torso. He found nothing until he moved Mr. Travers's head. The skull turned toward her, the empty eye sockets locking onto hers, and the lifeless stare pierced her heart.

She swallowed, but could not look away.

"Here we go," Max said. He leaned back, holding a small leather pouch. "Hold out your hand."

Her hands instinctively fisted at her sides. But she forced herself to splay a hand out in front of him. He upturned the bag and poured seven rocks into her palm.

"Rocks," Max said. He looked up at her, confusion furrowing his brow. "Rocks?"

Excitement dissolved in her gut, leaving in its wake the sting of disappointment. "That can't be all," she said.

She poured the rocks back into the bag and shoved it into her trouser pocket. Then she reached back into the coffin. This time, she forgot all about their disrespectful treatment of Mr. Travers's remains. She ran her palm against the bottom of the coffin, giving no thought to the prospect of splinters. She paused.

"Max, should this wood have seams in it?" she asked.

"Where?" He moved the remaining portions of the body out of the way to where her hand lay. With his finger, he ran along the tiny crevice she'd found, and there in one corner, he discovered a small latch. "This is a door."

Chapter Thirteen

———— ❧ ❧ ————

Cassandra St. James stepped into the dimly lit room and paused at the mess. The man she'd hired was rumored to be brilliant, but so far his mind did not make up for the fact that he was rather disgusting. The long table he worked on was littered with small glass dishes and bottles. And the contraption he used to break down the crème looked more like a small torture device than something a scientist would use.

She stepped over a pile of books, and something that appeared to be a moldy chunk of bread, as she moved closer to his work space. "What have you discovered, Mr. Olney?"

He jumped at the sound of her voice. "I didn't hear you come in." He looked up at her, his eyes wide and glassy. "I've broken down all of the key ingredients again. Now I am trying to re-create the material."

"You have been working on this for more than three days," she said. "What could possibly be taking you so long?"

Why must she always wait? She'd searched for this elusive "fountain" ever since Max had told her about it nearly ten years before. The allure of eternal beauty and youth had been too tempting to resist. Women had no power without beauty. Her mother had warned her of that many times. Cassandra had been blessed with a lush body men craved and a face that made other women fume. But time was beginning to take its toll. Lines had appeared around her eyes and mouth, and the soft, smooth texture of her skin was now patchy and ruddy in places.

"It's a complex procedure," he said, his thin voice wavering. "I've had a few setbacks." He glanced at the table in the corner at some mysterious material that had solidified in a jar.

Cassandra's nostrils flared. "I don't have forever." Lately it seemed the skin on her hands had begun to thin, and she'd noticed gray sprinkled throughout her blonde locks. Fortunately for her, her hair was so pale to begin with, few would notice, at least initially. Still, she was concerned. "I'm paying you a large sum of money for this tiny task. You are supposed to be the best!"

"Yes," he said.

She picked up a bottle of gray liquid, sniffed it, then set it down. "I'm told you visited the Tobias shop." With two painted fingernails, she tapped his chest. "What were you doing there?" she asked.

"I . . . I was buying another sample," he stammered, then averted his eyes back to the contraption in front of him.

"Indeed." She glanced around. "Did you forget it?"

A frown creased his high forehead. "I beg your pardon?"

"The sample." She ran a hand over his extraction

equipment. "You said you purchased another, but I don't see any new jars. Did you leave it at the store?"

"Please don't touch that." He hovered over the machine much as a mother bird protects her young. He pointed to the empty jar to his left. "It's right here."

She loathed liars, especially if she was paying them to do a job for her. "I see. Then why were you seen leaving the store empty-handed?" She walked over to him, grabbed his tie, and tugged forcefully on it. "You are lying to me, and I do not care to be lied to by anyone. Especially an employee. *What* were you doing there?"

She stood nearly a head taller than him, and under her gaze, she could see the man's will give way. People did not often succeed in deceiving her. She tended to persuade them that honesty was a far better choice.

"I went to speak with Miss Tobias," he said quietly.

"And?"

He shook his head. "She would not give me any information."

Cassandra laughed. "You asked her for the recipe?"

"I offered to pay her," he said shallowly.

"You offered to pay her. Now don't you think, were that an option, I would have simply done that instead of hiring you?" She paused a moment, waiting for him to give another excuse, but he said nothing. "I was told you were unmatched in your abilities. Evidently someone lied about that as well." She jammed her finger into his chest. "You are an idiot."

"No, I am unmatched. I am the best," he said.

"I have yet to see proof of that."

"Madam St. James, please. I can figure out the formula, I promise. I merely need more time."

"I'm afraid it might be too late for that. We'll see.

Perhaps later I'll be feeling more generous. Right now, however, I'm feeling rather inhospitable," she said.

He straightened his shoulders and tried his best to add height to his pitiful frame. "I am not without threats of my own, madam," he said, his voice wavering. "I might not be able to threaten you with bodily harm as I don't keep company with those thugs you employ. But I do know people, people who would be interested in what you've been up to."

"Is that a fact?" she asked. But he knew nothing. She'd told him she was interested in that crème because a friend who owned a French cosmetics shop had believed her product had been stolen.

"The fountain of youth," he said firmly.

She narrowed her eyes at the man. "If you think—"

"I know precisely what you've been looking for. I do not accept employment from people without thorough research. I know of your previous association with the Marquess of Lindberg and his search for Atlantis as a member of Solomon's." He boldly jammed a finger into her chest. "I can destroy you."

"Don't touch me again," she said slowly. "You know nothing." But the nasty little man did. He'd uncovered her secrets, and she could not have anyone know what she was after. "I'll be in touch, Mr. Olney."

She walked back over to the door and slammed it behind her. He couldn't do anything to her, she reminded herself. Still, it would seem that he knew more than he should. She needed to call Johns. There was a mess here only he could clean up.

"Well, open it," Sabine said. "What the devil are you waiting for?"

Max shrugged. "I thought you might like to warn me about what could happen if I pulled the latch."

"There's no time for warnings," she said.

"Here goes." He smiled and yanked hard. The wood creaked and moaned as it loosened and opened to reveal a staircase.

Their eyes met. She nodded and he stepped in, putting one foot on the step.

"Seems sturdy enough," he said. "Though it's going to be a tight squeeze."

He was correct in his assessment, as he had to shift his body to get his shoulders through the opening. She followed him down. Their lantern lit the area around them enough for her to see that they stood in a small, carved-out room.

"Ah, perfect," Max said. He stepped away from her, leaving her momentarily shrouded in near darkness. But soon light filled the area. "Torches," he said with a smile as he lit a third one. "Always useful."

The wooden walls of the shelter were plain and solid, with no markings or cutouts. The ceiling, aside from the hole at the entrance, was much the same. On the floor, however, lay stone tiles of different sizes, all painted with images. The brightly colored floor stood out against the rest of the surroundings.

"What is that?" Max asked, pointing to something in a corner of the room.

She followed his movement and found a pole with a small wooden box perched atop. She looked back at the floor, then felt for the leather bag in her pocket. "It's a game," she murmured as she poured the stones into her palm.

"This doesn't look like a game," Max said. He bent

to the floor and ran a hand over one of the painted tiles. "They're reminiscent of stained glass. This looks more like a tomb or monument of some sort."

"No, it's Thistle. I know this game," she said.

"You've played before?"

No, she'd never played it before, but she'd watched the other children in the village for hours. Nose pressed against the window, she'd sat and stared at them while they'd laughed and skipped and tossed their rocks, until her breath would fog the glass. She'd longed to play as the other children had, but she had been born to a guardian so she'd had studies. And she'd had to be protected from injury and accidents that marked others' childhoods with tiny scars and scuffed knees. Though all of that sacrifice had seemed foolish and presumptuous when she hadn't been selected guardian.

She took a steadying breath. "Not precisely."

"This is an Atlantean game?" Max asked.

"Yes, and I've seen it played many times." She looked directly at Max. "I can do this."

He opened his arms in a welcoming motion, then stepped away from the painted tiles.

She took another look at the small rocks in her hand, and then she released them into the box. They scattered and rolled until eventually they stilled.

"Three," she said. She moved over to the painted tiles and studied them. Max was right. They did resemble stained glass, with their portrayals of people in everyday life. On one, a woman hung laundry on a line to dry. Another showed people harvesting in a field. "Three," she said again.

Before she began, she looked at Max. "Whatever happens, don't touch the tiles until I've completed the game."

He nodded.

She stepped forward onto one of the tiles. Then moved to the next. Before each move, she studied the images, always choosing ones with patterns of three, to select her next step.

Max stood quietly, watching her every move.

In her mind, she could see the girls and boys playing together, laughing and teasing. Some days they had waved to her, sitting in her window. But most days, they'd simply ignored her.

Another four moves, and she was halfway across the board. She examined the next option.

She shifted one foot forward to touch the next tile, the image of children playing with three balls. As her foot touched the stone, it shattered and fell below, leaving a gaping cavern in its wake. Her balance shifted, but Max caught her, holding her steady without walking onto the game board himself.

"You all right?" he asked.

"Wrong move," she said, her voice shaky. "I must have missed something in that picture. An extra ball, perhaps."

"Does that always happen if you mess up?"

"No, normally you die, meaning you lose your turn. This one seems a little different from the Thistle the children play. Here it doesn't seem to be a metaphorical death."

"Right." He made no move away from her, still holding her up and assisting her balance.

"I can finish now," she said with a nod.

"No more mistakes," he suggested.

She smiled. "I'll try."

She didn't know how much longer it took her to work

through the game, but eventually she came down to her last move. She closed her eyes and concentrated, then examined the remaining tiles. "Last one," she said.

"Are you certain?" Max asked.

"More or less," she said as she took the final step. The tile did not break, but instantly the box, in which she'd cast her rocks, began to shake.

Max made his way over there. "The box opened," he said. He reached down into it and pulled something back. "It's a letter."

"What does it say?" she asked, standing still, afraid to move.

He met her eyes. His own sparkled with excitement. "It's another clue."

They made their way down the hill. Sabine moved more quickly in their descent, clearly eager to get back to their room. Max had no difficulty keeping up with her pace, but twice he had to grab her elbow to steady her when she hit a rocky portion of the hill. They walked in silence into the tiny inn and had barely closed the door to their room before Sabine grabbed his arm. "What does it say again?" she asked.

Max unfolded the parchment again and read aloud: "*'At the Virgin's rock, the dove bathes where the ancients found tranquillity.'*"

Sabine sat on the edge of the bed. Deep creases settled into her brow. "It's a riddle," she said.

"So it would seem." Max eyed the handwritten note again. It was written on papyrus, but anyone could purchase the antique paper. So the question was, how old was this particular note? The ink had faded, but was still legible. And the note had been scrawled in Greek, not the native Atlantean language.

Max sat next to her on the bed, and beneath both their weight, it creaked and moaned.

"If the Chosen One has a copy of the prophecy, which I'm assuming he does in some form or another, then he knows about the dove, too," Sabine reasoned. "He will undoubtedly be looking for the dove as well. Or has looked for it in the past."

Max nodded. "And what better way to keep him from getting his hands on it than to hide it with a series of puzzles."

"But we solved the first one," she said.

"No, you did. I wouldn't have known how to play that game. Hell, I didn't even know what it was," Max said.

"I almost failed," she said, her voice barely above a whisper.

"But you didn't."

"Let me see the note," she asked.

He handed her the note, then scooted backward so that he lay on one side of the bed, if there could actually be sides in a bed this small. He folded his arms up behind his head. In this position, his feet hung off the bed past his ankles.

She still wore the men's clothing he'd given her, and he tried not to let his eyes linger on the way the suspenders cupped her breasts, or the way her hips and bottom seemed even rounder in those pants. Her hair bound up in that cap gave him a clear view of her tender throat.

"Virgin's rock, I don't know what to make of that," she muttered. She turned to hand the note back to him. Her head cocked to one side. "Where am I supposed to sleep?"

He patted the empty portion next to him. "There's plenty of room."

She snorted. "For elves, perhaps, but not for grown people."

"We might have to snuggle." He wiggled his eyebrows at her.

The edge of her lips curled, but she did not fully smile. "You are incorrigible."

There was a long pause as she eyed him warily. She glanced at the bed, then finally resigned herself to lying next to him. He busied himself by reading the riddle again and again. Or rather he simply stared at the note pretending to read while she settled her warm, luscious body next to his.

Once she stopped moving, he rolled over and braced his arms on either side of her so that he leaned above her body. She looked up at him with molten amber-colored eyes. Her lips parted in a protest, but she said nothing.

He moved even closer, putting no more than a breath of distance between their mouths. Her eyes widened, then fluttered closed as she waited for him to kiss her. But he did not. She wanted him, too. Satisfaction surged through him.

"I've thought about that night on the train again and again," he said.

She said nothing in response, but made no move to retreat.

"I know you have, too," he ventured. He lowered himself onto her. They were fully clothed; still he could feel her soft curves below him.

He kissed her. Not a slow, gentle, romantic kiss intended to seduce, but rather one full of the pent-up passion and desire he'd felt since the moment he set eyes on her. She didn't shy away from his advances. She wrapped her arms around him and kissed him back.

He moved against her, his erection rubbing against the juncture of her thighs. Her legs parted, pressing him closer to her. She kissed him more deeply.

With one hand, he reached up and cupped her right breast. Her nipple pressed hard against the fabric of her shirt, and he stroked it with his palm. She arched beneath him, pressing herself into him.

Damn, but he wanted her. As he'd never wanted another woman. He tugged on her shirt, pulling it up from beneath her waistband, and then slid his hand up to touch her bare breast. He rocked against her again, feeling more like a boy touching a girl for the first time than the man he was now. His fingers fumbled across the buttons on her shirt, but he managed to get it unfastened.

Her breasts were perfect. Round and pert with dark rose-colored areolas. He dipped his mouth to one, covering the tip. She cried out. Her nails dug into his arms. He laved kisses from one breast to the other and all in between. Her soft, olive-colored skin was warm beneath his lips, simply delicious under his tongue.

"Wait," she whispered.

He stilled, listening for her next words. Her eyes met his.

"I can't." She shook her head. "I'm sorry. I didn't mean to..." But her words died out.

He rolled off her. Lying on his side, he stared at the wall. He was not above seducing a woman into his bed, but he would not take what was not freely offered.

"I'd be a liar if I said I didn't want to," she said with a humorless laugh. "But I just can't. You make me want more... ," she said quietly, her words trailing off.

Max didn't say anything else. He wanted more, too. More touching, more kissing, more passion. But he didn't think that's what she'd meant. He couldn't offer her anything more than an affair.

He got up from the bed and made his way to the small window. The first hint of morning peeked out from the horizon in a soft golden glow. There was nothing to say; nothing more to discuss. She could rest, and in the meantime, he would try to decipher the riddle to figure out where they would go next.

He found a chair behind the dressing screen and pulled it out beside the fire. Sabine rolled over to face away from him, but said nothing. With no cover and the way her legs curled up, those trousers molded to her backside, leaving nothing to his imagination.

For more than an hour, he sat in that plain wooden chair. *At the Virgin's rock, the dove bathes where the ancients found tranquillity.* He read it again and again. The fire in the hearth died down to a handful of embers. A chill settled on the room. He didn't know if Sabine had fallen asleep or just lay there in silence.

He leaned the chair back against the wall, pulling the two front legs off the floor. Virgin's rock. Bathes. Weapons did not bathe, though. Perhaps it was the site of a previous battle, a stream where warriors would have washed their swords. But what did that have to do with tranquillity? What if they meant bath as in a Roman bath? Then how did Virgin's rock fit in?

Damnation!

He let the chair fall forward. Could it be that simple? If he was right, they had a lengthy drive ahead of them. He glanced out the window to find that the sun had fully risen now. They needed to leave.

Gently he nudged Sabine's shoulder. "Sabine," he said.

Her eyes opened, and she sat upright. "What?"

"I think I've figured it out. But we need to leave now."

She nodded and stood. Quickly she buttoned her shirt and tucked it back into her pants. He boldly watched her, but said nothing and made no attempt to touch her.

"Where are we going?" she asked.

"Kent, to Maidstone."

Chapter Fourteen

Several hours and two very sore backsides later, they found themselves in the bustling town of Maidstone. They had not spoken much in the carriage, other than to exchange theories about who might have set up the clues leading to the dove.

Max didn't know precisely what had made her pull away from him. He supposed most women wanted more from a relationship than a passionate night spent in a dingy hotel. After his family died, he'd decided then and there, he'd never again get close to anyone. And he'd never even been tempted—*until now*, echoed through his mind, but it was only her kisses that tempted him. Nothing more.

Now they were walking the streets, and the late-afternoon crowds were thinning out. The shops prepared to close for the day.

"If the clue pointed to a Roman bathhouse," Sabine said, "it stands to reason that Bath is where we should have gone. I don't recall ever hearing of a bathhouse in Kent."

"Nor have I," Max said. "But Bath would have been far too obvious. Additionally, Bath wouldn't explain the mention of the Virgin's rock, which clearly points to Maidstone. If I'm wrong and we find nothing, we will go to Bath. And you'll have my permission to box my ears. Does that make you feel better?"

She paused awhile as if considering his offer. "Perhaps. I have wanted to do that on occasion."

He chuckled, but said nothing more on the subject. "We're looking for anything having to do with bathing or tranquillity or ancients."

They got to the end of the cobblestone street and turned down another. There were fewer people here, fewer carriages, and eventually the road stopped at an alleyway.

"A dead end. Where to next?" she asked.

Max looked down the alley. Farther up on the right sat an old three-story redbrick building with a rounded turret of windows. Something about the design, different from the Tudor-style buildings that housed the other shops, drew his attention. And there was that niggling feeling at the base of his stomach—instinct, the men at Solomon's had called it. It had been his experience that if something stood out, was the exception to the rule, it often warranted inspection.

"I think we should visit that building." He pointed, and she nodded, then followed him down the alley.

The cobblestones here were irregularly shaped and uneven, clearly older and less maintained, so navigating to the shop proved challenging. Max held his arm out for Sabine, and much to his surprise, she took it, her delicate fingers wrapped onto his forearm. Her touch, though innocent, sent desire charging through him.

There were several different types of chairs crowding

the landing of the shop. Though he would have sworn he saw a light burning in one of the upper-story windows, there was no other indication of life in the old place. Another sign hung over the front door that read *The Ancient and Unique*.

"Ancient. This could be it," Max said.

Sabine stopped walking and looked up at the building with a perplexed expression. "This certainly looks nothing like any bathhouse I've seen."

Max pointed to the sign. "The riddle said something about where the ancients go."

"Ancient is a common name for antiquities shops," she said as she climbed the steps. She looked unconvinced, but followed him nonetheless. "I suppose it is worth a look. Though I wouldn't think it would be old enough for this clue."

"We don't know when this hunt was established, though," Max said.

She thought a moment before speaking. "True. I suppose any of my ancestors could have hidden the dove for protection. Just as they did with the map." They reached the front stoop and Sabine peered into the windows.

There were no lights downstairs that he could see, and the front door was locked. But he never traveled anywhere without his tools, so he reached into his pocket and retrieved them.

"Is that how you got into my shop?" Sabine asked from over his shoulder as he slid the first pick into the lock.

"It is." He smiled at her.

"You are a criminal, Maxwell Barrett." She crossed her arms over her chest.

He chuckled, but continued working on the lock. "Do you have a better idea?"

"No, I do not. But don't you think someone might see us?" she asked.

"I doubt it. We are in an alleyway, and most of the shops have closed for the evening."

"Probably," she muttered. "Very comforting." She continued to pace the porch and look out at the alleyway, checking for passersby.

The lock gave way, and he was able to open the front door, though not all the way. Something blocked the door from the other side. With difficulty, each of them squeezed inside. A curio cabinet partially obstructed the door.

"Obviously they don't want people inside," Sabine said.

Max closed the door behind them. "Stay close," he said.

Ancient and Unique appeared to be an appropriate name for the store, Max thought, as they made their way through the front room. Every odd thing one could imagine filled every open space available. There was an entire shelf on one wall that appeared to be filled with different types of potions and restorative cures or some such nonsense, then a corner with an array of odd musical instruments. Another shelf housed navigational tools, including several different sizes of compasses. Copper pots and clay pottery cluttered a bottom shelf.

They moved through the room and toward the back of the house. Each room was much of the same, filled to the brim with one oddity after another. Finally they came to a staircase at the very back of the building that went downward. Two of the wooden stairs were missing completely, so Max had to assist Sabine down to the bottom.

"Do you think it's merely a storeroom?" Sabine asked.

"Should we search through all of the items in the shop to see if we can find something hidden there?"

"I say we search the building first, see if we can find a chamber down below," Max said. "If nothing comes of that, we can dig through all of these treasures. Though I'm not certain we'd find anything of worth. There's nothing bath-related in all that stuff."

"Perhaps we'd find a bathing tub," Sabine suggested. "Though I'm not sure how that would help. Perhaps we could drown the Chosen One."

Max stopped walking. "Sabine, did you just make a joke?"

"Shut up." She punched his arm. Then they kept moving.

They reached the storeroom, but there was something different about it. For one thing, it was made entirely of stone, and for another, there was nothing stored inside. All of the rooms above were packed to the ceiling and yet this, a room typically designed for storage, was completely empty.

Dampness seeped up from the floor, chilling the room. It smelled musty and stale. The walls were nearly bare except for an old bulletin advertising a Shakespearean play. Max walked the length of the room, running his hand over the wall as he did.

"What are you doing?" she asked.

"Looking for a lever or hidden notch that will open the chamber," he explained. He kept moving. The stones beneath his fingertips were smooth and cold, but nothing out of the ordinary.

He came to the last corner, and as he slid his hand over the stone, he realized he'd found a gap. "It is an optical illusion," he told Sabine. "Look, it's painted to appear to be another corner to form a perfectly square room."

She walked over and leaned to see the area behind his arm. "That's a hallway. A long and narrow one, but a hallway nonetheless." She smiled broadly.

"Shall we?" Max asked. He held his hand out to Sabine and she followed.

They continued moving through the underground tunnel, unsure of where they would end up. Max hoped he was correct in deciphering the riddle, and that they hadn't simply stumbled upon a very strange house.

They came to another set of stairs leading farther downward, though these were made of stone. It was not a long staircase, but it wound to their right until they were deposited into a large rectangular room. Columned archways lined the perimeter of a spacious pool, just like those in Bath.

"You were right," Sabine said, wonder filling her voice.

"It would appear so. But you don't have to sound quite so surprised."

The sunken pool was empty, the spring that fed the bath having long since dried up. Some statues remained intact, although a few had begun to crumble. Along one side of the pool were four stone women, naked from the waist up, leaning forward and pouring water from large amphoras into the bath. At the height of this Roman bath's day, it would have been luxurious and decadent to have water fall into the pool in such a manner. Quite sophisticated engineering as well.

"It's beautiful," Sabine said. She stepped around him, walking through the archway and near the edge of the pool. "The dove? Where would they hide it?" she whispered. She made her way over to the steps that led into what would once have been a refreshing pool of water.

"Search all around," he said. "It looks as if we have a large area to cover." His voice echoed in the solid stone surroundings.

She nodded and stepped down into the empty pool.

Max glanced around and decided to start over by the four statues. He stood behind one, searching the marble carving for any clue. The cloth draped over the woman's hips below her navel, then fell to her bare feet. It was an exquisite piece of work, with realistic details, from her toenails to the delicate curve of her cheekbones. Around the front of the woman's body, he found a small harp dangling from a tie at her waist. Her hair fell in loose curls around her face, and a handful of them sat like marble springs over her round, pert breasts. Her slight smile was forever immortalized in the stone. But he found no sign of a dove or any other bird, so he moved on to the next statue.

She was much the same, with only a few small differences. But he continued his perusal—one never knew where one would discover the unexpected. After several moments, he heard Sabine make an exasperated little huff. He turned to find her glare aimed right at him.

"What?" he asked.

She walked toward him, but stayed in the pool looking up at his face. "We are searching for a clue, and all you can do is ogle the naked women?" She pointed at the statues.

He glanced back at the statue he'd been examining. "I *was* looking for the clue."

"By staring at their breasts?" Sabine nodded knowingly. "You're certain to find the dove there," she said drolly.

"Are you embarrassed?" he asked. He cupped the statue's breasts for emphasis.

"Embarrassed about what, precisely?" She propped her hands on her hips in what Max considered the universal stance of disgruntled women. "Your juvenile behavior?"

He jumped down from the edge into the empty pool. His boots made a great thump as he landed. "I can assure you I've seen more than my fair share of breasts, real ones," he reminded her. "Not ones made of stone. And should I desire to again see them in the very near future"—he let his eyes drop to her own chest—"I will find no difficulty." He had closed the distance between them and stood merely a breath away. A wolf with his prey, he had her cornered.

She swallowed visibly. "Are you threatening me?" she asked, her voice barely a whisper.

"I would never threaten the virtue of a woman." He flashed her a smile.

She took several steps away from him. "Clearly, my virtue, as it were, is no longer an issue. Though I *never* claimed to be a virgin." She turned to examine the far end of the pool. Bending, she followed the engravings that lined the stone's edge.

He had wondered, but there were lines even he wouldn't cross, so he'd never asked. It mattered not to him. He found her demure attitude while making such a bold admission intoxicating. She was a divine mixture. Saucy minx cleverly matched with her fierce determination. "So you admit that you have had lovers," he said.

"I admit no such thing. My personal life is of no

concern to you," she said tartly. "Which is precisely my point. You shouldn't make assumptions."

"And you've never made assumptions about me?" He cocked one eyebrow. "How about just now when you assumed I was standing up here wasting time gawking at the statues?" She said nothing, but had the grace to look appropriately guilty. "Your veiled denial gives me plenty of information," he said. "Someday perhaps you'll tell me about those previous lovers."

She said nothing.

"Shall we continue our search?" he asked.

He stepped out of the pool and back over to the statues he'd been examining. He knew she still stared after him, but he pretended not to notice. He'd flustered her and that pleased him. More than he was willing to admit.

But he also needed his distance from her. His focus on her breasts had begun a string of fantasies flowing through his mind. Images of Sabine naked and writhing beneath him, or beckoning him into a pool like the one she stood in now—only with water lapping at her naked breasts, flesh and not carved of marble. He felt himself grow heavy with desire. Damned if he wasn't behaving as a randy schoolboy would.

He turned around and found himself facing the fourth nude statue. A lute hung from her waist, and like her three sisters, she had been sculpted by a master's hand. But again Max found no sign of a dove or bird of any kind.

From his vantage point, he watched Sabine continue to study the engravings that lined the inner rim of the pool. She moved along the edge until she ended up where she'd begun. "Nothing," she said. "No sign of a dove anywhere."

"It's got to be here somewhere," Max said.

She climbed out of the sunken pool and walked to the far side of the room. "Unless you were wrong." Sabine tossed him a sweet smile from over her shoulder that he knew meant quite the opposite.

"I was right about there being a bathhouse here. And I do have experience finding objects other people have been looking for." He winked at her. "You've said that yourself."

She glared at him, then stepped back through the arches to the next adjacent room. He followed her, and they found themselves in what he assumed had been a steam room where the water had been heated for a plunge bath. Another statue of a woman occupied this room, though she was larger than the four by the pool. She looked vaguely familiar. Again she stood draped with a sheet hanging seductively on her hips, the rest of her bare. But instead of an amphora, she held a scale.

More carvings covered the stone walls. There were tributes to the gods and goddesses: Zeus, although the Romans would have called him Jupiter, on a chariot led by winged horses; Venus reclining while a throng of men fanned her and fed her grapes; Diana with her bow and arrow aimed at a boar. The walls were covered with such images from floor to ceiling.

They moved through the room in opposite directions, each carefully scanning the images lining the walls. He was examining an image of Achilles toppled over with a spear in his ankle when Sabine gasped.

"Max, I think I've found something," Sabine said.

He made his way over to her. She leaned in close to the stone wall and pointed. There, in another carving of the god of the underworld and Cerberus, his three-headed dog, was a crude rendition of a dove—the same rendition they'd seen on the tombstone.

"That's it," he said. "It was clearly added later than the rest of these carvings. It's not as expressive or detailed."

"There aren't any words anywhere near here. Perhaps there isn't another clue, and we've actually found it," she said. "Do you have anything we can break the stone with?" She searched the area around her feet, scanning the floor for an item she could use.

Max smiled at her. "We might want to be careful before we bust through the wall. We don't want to be trapped down here indefinitely. One wrong move could bring the whole building down on us."

She looked up at the stone ceiling above them. A frown creased her forehead. "Excellent point."

Max felt on the wall around the dove carving, pressing into the stone, but nothing moved beneath his hands. "There has to be a compartment or something around here," he muttered.

She followed his lead and began running her hands over the stone. Her delicate hands ran inquisitively over the walls, and Max couldn't help but imagine those same hands exploring his own body. The way she'd run her finger down his chest, her nails biting into his flesh, the way she kissed. His stomach tensed.

Damnation!

He stepped forward and pressed directly onto the dove. Nothing. He leaned into it and suddenly he felt the floor beneath his right foot shift. The stone where the dove sat slid downward, opening up a compartment.

"Max!" Sabine said.

In the compartment sat six bottles of different shapes and sizes.

"Interesting," Max said.

"What do you suppose we're supposed to do with them?"

"I'm not sure." He leaned closer to better examine the bottles. "Poison," he muttered. "No, that can't be it. There has to be something else."

"The last clue dealt with an Atlantean game." Sabine turned around in the chamber. "Nothing here looks familiar to me, though."

Max followed Sabine's lead and surveyed the room again. The statue and the bottles—there was nothing to be done there. He narrowed his attention to the scale. He'd seen that scale before—that's what was familiar about that statue. He stepped over to it. "I know this scale."

"It looks like any other scale would," Sabine said.

"No, see the symbols here." He pointed to the engravings at the apex between the two plates. "I've seen that. In a book?" No, that wasn't right. He glanced back at the bottles in the secret compartment, then back at the scale. "That's it."

"What's it?" Sabine asked.

He gathered the bottles, one by one. "This image, the scale with bottles on it." He met her eyes and smiled. "It's from the map."

She motioned to his bag. "Well, get it out, and we can match this scale to the illustration."

He shook his head. "With all the people we've had chasing us, I didn't think it would be safe. I left it at my home."

"Do you remember it then? The exact placement?" she asked.

"It's not just about the bottles. We have to fill them with water. The weight needs to be evenly distributed."

"So we have to find water," Sabine said. "I wonder if that pump in the main room still works." She turned and strode out of the chamber and into the pool room. Back behind the four statues sat an old pump.

"Here, let me. You hold the bottles." He handed them to her. It took several cranks to get the pump moving. The water creaked and moaned through the pipes beneath the floor, then shot through the pump.

Sabine held each of the bottles under the flow, allowing them all to fill.

Once they'd completed that task, they went back into the chamber. They stood before the statue with the scale. Max closed his eyes, trying to envision the image of the scale with the bottles. While these bottles were also all different sizes and therefore held different amounts of water, they were not exact replicas. The bottles on the map were all different colors. With his eyes closed, he could imagine them: a short red one and a tall purple one, a narrow green one. But the bottles here were all made from the same yellow glass.

"Where do they go?" Sabine asked.

"This one," he said as he picked up the tallest one, "goes here." He set it down on the left scale plate. The scale itself did not move, as it was carved of stone. But when he placed the second bottle, the sound of chains pulling through metal sounded from behind the statue.

Sabine nodded. "So far, so good. Do you suppose if you get one wrong the flooring in here collapses as it did in my game of Thistle?"

"Let's not find out." He lifted another bottle and eyed both sides of the scale, then finally set that one back down and retrieved another one.

Carefully he placed bottles, and each time they heard

the chains. Finally only one bottle remained. He leaned forward, and Sabine put her hand on his arm. "Wait. Before you set it down, examine them all and make certain you're correct."

He heeded her advice and checked all the bottles he had already placed. The one in his hand was short, but very round. He looked again at the scale, and the tallest bottle caught his attention. He picked it up and tried to weigh each on his palms.

"I think this is right. Four on this side"—he set down the round bottle from where he'd retrieved the tall one— "and two on this." He placed the final bottle, and both Max and Sabine stood still waiting for what would happen next.

The chains creaked and through the wall another compartment opened. Inside was a small leather pouch, much like the one they'd found in Mr. Travers's grave.

He reached in and grabbed the wrapped packet, then handed it to Sabine. "You read this one," he said.

Sabine reached for it to unwrap it at the same time as the stone shifted back into place, and then the ceiling began to move, shifting downward.

"I think we've fallen into a trap," Max said.

The ceiling had closed in on them so quickly that Max already had to hunch over. He grabbed her hand and pulled her out with him into the spring-fed pool room. Stones fell from the columns, and the amphoras, as if in unison, broke free of the women's sculpted hands and crumbled into the empty pool beneath them. The pool itself split as if the earth sat ready to consume the entire space.

"We've got to get out of here," Max said.

"Quickly," Sabine added. Her heart beat so furiously

she was certain she'd choke on it. She moved as fast as she could behind Max as he continued to drag her along.

A large stone fell right beside her. She screamed. They kept moving.

The floor shifted, and they both fell. Max sliced his arm on a broken piece of marble, and blood immediately appeared on his sleeve.

"Max, you're bleeding," Sabine said, reaching out to touch his forearm.

"We don't have time." He pulled her to her feet and out of the arched area just as three columns crumbled to the ground. "This whole place is falling apart. If we don't get out of here before that happens, we'll be buried alive."

They reached the tunnel, and the very walls of it shook. The instability of their surroundings frightened Sabine to her core.

"Run, Sabine," Max yelled.

She ran. Behind her, the tunnel seemed to disappear into the ground. But she kept moving forward, her heart pumping so fast she felt certain it would explode.

Finally they reached the stairs that wound back up to the storeroom. Max ran up the stairs, and Sabine was right behind him, but once she hit the second stair, something shifted beneath her feet and suddenly she was falling. Strong arms grabbed her wrists, and she met Max's gaze.

"Do not let go," he said.

Tears gathered at the corners of her eyes as her legs dangled under her. The floor beneath her completely disappeared, and in its place was a gaping hole that was swallowed in darkness. "Max!"

"I won't drop you. Hold on." He leaned on the floor above where the stairs had been and pulled her upward.

Her stomach scraped across the rough edge. She drew her legs up, struggling to find her footing.

Once she was able, she pushed herself up onto the floor and fell against him. Their labored breath mingled.

"Thank you," she said.

"Any time. Now, let's get the hell out of here."

Chapter Fifteen

⊰·⊱

They ran out of the building, Max still holding tightly to her hand. Then they jumped off the front stoop. The wood creaked, and the red bricks started to crumble and fall. Together they stood back and watched as the house shifted to the right, then fell in on itself, until it was nothing more than a pile of wood and bricks.

Sabine swore.

"I'm beginning to wonder if this quest isn't meant to kill us rather than provide something to save us," Max said. He took a deep breath. "Where's that clue?" he asked.

Thankfully she'd stuffed the bag in her pocket when the ceiling had begun to crumble. She peeled away the leather and found inside another papyrus note, written in the same handwriting. "'*Bathed in blood, the dove commands by blade,*'" Sabine read. "Perhaps we are to kill him with some sort of knife or sword."

Max nodded. "I think this confirms that the dove is a weapon. We should get to the carriage before it gets any darker. Hopefully our driver has waited for us."

"You paid him well enough to wait an entire year," Sabine said.

They walked in silence for several moments before Max spoke again. " 'Bathed in blood'?"

"Well, that's not a clue. Where are we supposed to search for a weapon?" she asked impatiently. "There are millions of them all over the world," Sabine said.

She was not the guardian, but Madigan had sent her to find the map. He'd essentially set her on this journey and whether she felt prepared did not matter. Agnes needed her help.

"Yes, there are weapons all over. But this quest was created by your people, so I believe we're dealing with only those here in England. And we can assume it's old. Judging by the age of that house, I'd guess these clues are about three hundred years old."

She took a sobering breath. He was right. They would persevere. Training or not, she had to succeed in this. And so far, they had managed to accomplish all the tasks set for them. As much as she didn't want to admit it, they made an excellent team.

"We can start at the British Museum," Max suggested. "They have a rather large weapon collection."

Sabine and Max made it safely to the confines of their carriage and set out on their way back to London. They had a few hours' ride ahead of them, and it was already late. Her heart still beat wildly, pounding in her ears.

Max sat across from her, his legs taking up most of the space between them. "Are you all right?" he asked.

"A little scared, perhaps, but I'm in one piece."

"Always a good sign."

Blood still oozed from his wound, so she leaned forward to examine his arm.

"It's nothing," he said, trying to pull it away from her.

But it looked deep enough for some concern. "Hold still," she told him. She grabbed the fabric of his sleeve at the seam by his shoulder and pulled. It ripped, and she kept tugging until it slid off his arm.

"That was my favorite shirt," he said.

She rolled her eyes. "You can buy another." She used the inside of the sleeve to wipe the excessive blood away. "This doesn't look good." She rummaged through her bag but there were no supplies for stitches. "If we don't attend to this, it will become infected."

"No. It will be all right. I'm certain I've had worse," he said, but she could see the pain around his eyes.

She didn't want to use the elixir, and she wasn't truly authorized to do so outside of assisting the Healer. But she had no choice. If she did nothing, they risked the wound festering until infection poisoned his blood. So she reached into her bodice and pulled on the gold chain attached to the small vial. She removed the necklace, then popped off the lid. She twisted his arm so she had a better view.

"What is that?" he asked.

She met his glance, but said nothing as she poured one drop onto the wound.

He jerked his arm away. "Bloody hell, that burns!"

"Hold still," she said. She placed another tiny drop onto his arm, and he didn't move.

"That's elixir," he said. He leaned forward and craned his neck to try to see the vial she held.

She replaced the lid and quickly dropped the necklace back inside the bodice of her dress.

"Do you always carry elixir with you?"

"We like to have some in case of emergency," she said, trying to keep her face void of expression.

Cassandra lounged on her chaise, sipping brandy. Moonlight poured in off the balcony of her bedchamber, giving her skin a luminescent quality. She wore nothing but a filmy dressing gown.

Johns knocked once, then came into her bedchamber.

She smiled at him, loving the way his eyes darkened as he took in her nearly nude state. "Did you take care of Mr. Olney?"

"I did. He fought me, or tried to, so there was some noise," Johns said. "The authorities should find him tomorrow."

"And you?" she asked.

He shook his head. "No one saw me."

"Excellent. Now then, tell me about your other assignment." She shifted her position, allowing the dressing gown to open, giving him a full view of her breasts.

He gaped at her display, then swallowed. "We can't get to the girl," Johns said.

"You've been to her shop." Cassandra stood and walked over to her full-length mirror. The folds of her dressing gown flowed behind her as she moved. "You know where she is. What do you mean, you can't get to her?" Cassandra patted her hair, then stepped away from the mirror.

He nodded. "She doesn't appear to go to the shop much these days. We've followed her several times, but she is never alone."

"Yes, yes, her aunts, I know. But you cannot find some way to dispose of three elderly women to get to the girl?" Cassandra was impatient; she knew that about herself. She'd never been good at waiting for what she wanted.

But this was getting ridiculous. That idiot chemist had proven to be a complete waste of time and money. Then he'd had the nerve to think he could threaten her.

"It's not the aunts," Johns said. "Though they leave the shop each evening. They are no longer staying above the store."

"Every night? Where do they go?" Cassandra faced Johns and was struck by the sheer masculinity of him. It intrigued and annoyed her that after all these years she still desired him.

"That man you know. The blond fellow."

"Max," Cassandra whispered. So he had brought the whore home with him. "They all go to his townhome?"

"The aunts. The girl and Max left London. I sent Beaver and Platt to follow them. They lost them on a train. But Max and the girl are back in London."

Platt and Beaver were idiots; they would never be able to find anything on their own. "Tomorrow I will go with you to watch them. I want to know what they are up to." She walked up to him and ran her hand down his chest to the front of his trousers. Already he was hard for her. "Perfect."

She shrugged out of her dressing gown.

Spencer made his way into the man's study. Jennings was an ambitious sort, but neither skilled nor connected enough for those ambitions to take him far. He'd been an easy first choice for a lieutenant-general and now they were days away from his promotion.

"Cole," he said as he stepped around his desk. "Good to see you again." He closed the door behind Spencer. His mouse-colored brown hair lay flat against his head, trying in vain to cover his premature balding. Jennings was older than Spencer by at least ten years, but he was neither as cunning nor as gifted, though the man somehow had a brilliant military mind.

Spencer sat on the large leather sofa before he'd been invited to do so. He crossed his legs, resting one foot atop his other knee. "How are the plans coming along?"

Jennings jumped into motion. "I have maps." He retrieved several maps from his desk and rolled them up, then handed them to Spencer. "We have several alternatives as far as where to land in Africa, and which countries to take control of when. Once we have the native soldiers trained, we shouldn't have any problem occupying the continent. We'll have them vastly outnumbered."

"And with the elixir," Spencer commented.

Jennings's eyes nearly glazed over as he stared at the vial Spencer held. "Yes, yes," the man said. "With that, anything is possible." He took a step toward Spencer. "May I?"

"One small drop," Spencer said.

Max and Sabine had no choice but to take time to bathe and change clothes before heading to the British Museum. While they were at Max's townhome, Max's chief of security told him about some men who had been spotted outside the building. And they'd also been seen outside Sabine's shop. They matched the description of the men he'd fought with that night in the shop, the same ones they'd evaded on the train. Whoever had hired those thugs had not relented in their search.

As Max and Sabine approached the museum, they saw that it was full of patrons today—evidently a new mummy exhibit had opened recently and people were flocking to see it.

"Max," someone called to him. It was a familiar voice, as Max knew only one Scotsman who would call him by his Christian name.

Max turned, and there walking toward him was Graeme Langford, Duke of Rothmore. A longtime member of Solomon's, Graeme was one of the few people Max trusted implicitly. They shook hands and exchanged pleasantries.

Sabine stopped moving as well, but stood a few paces ahead of them.

"What brings you to the museum?" Graeme asked. "I thought there was nothing of value here for your research."

Max nodded to Sabine. "I was helping a friend. We are trying to locate a specific sword."

"Or knife," Sabine added. "Some sort of blade."

A low whistle escaped from between Graeme's teeth. "That's quite specific," he said, his Scottish brogue lilting on each vowel. Graeme turned and looked at the museum doors. "They have a good armory here, but nothing compared to Mortimer Flynn's," Graeme said.

"Flynn," Max said, "I had forgotten about him. That's an interesting idea."

Graeme took a step closer to Max and lowered his voice. "He doesn't live too far out of London. You might pay him a visit." Graeme eyed Sabine, then added, "Quietly."

Max knew what the man meant. Mortimer Flynn was an exiled member of Solomon's, and chances were he wouldn't take too kindly to anyone from the club paying a call on him. They would have to find an alternative means of entry. Not altogether unfamiliar territory for Max.

"Thank you," Max said.

"You haven't been by the club in a few days," Graeme said. He looked at Sabine again. "Busy?"

"Generally speaking. I'll be by soon enough," Max said.

"Is that the wee lass who shot you?" Graeme asked.

Sabine burst out laughing, but said nothing.

Graeme held up his hand. "That's answer enough. I heard at the club that Marcus is nearing the end of his design. Are you really going to ride in that sunken machine?"

Max eyed Sabine before answering. "If I can persuade him it's a worthy journey."

"Good luck then, Max," Graeme said. "Oh, and should anyone need me, I'll be in Scotland for a while." Then he walked away.

"Graeme reminded me of a better collection we should start with. Besides, with the crowd here today, we'd be hard-pressed to truly search as closely as we need to," Max said. Max and Sabine walked to the carriage, which waited for them across the street.

"What club was he speaking of?" Sabine asked as he lifted her into their rig.

"There is a club here in London specifically for people, like myself, who study and try to find ancient or mythical artifacts." The carriage rumbled down the street toward his townhome. Max had some investigation to do before they could go to Flynn's estate.

"That Scotsman is in this club of yours?" she asked.

"He is. As well as many others."

She sat directly across from him, her eyes wide with curiosity and interest. "Are there others who study Atlantis?" she asked.

"No, I am the only one."

"What is a sunken vessel?" she asked.

"You shouldn't eavesdrop on others' conversations," he said.

"You should tell your friends not to talk so loudly. What is it?" She smiled sweetly.

"It's a boat. An underwater boat."

Her breath caught. "And you could take it to try to find what remains of Atlantis?"

"Something like that."

A bump in the road shifted the carriage, and she fell forward. He caught her, pulled her close to him, and pressed his mouth to hers. She had once kissed him to create a diversion, and he could bloody well do the same. He would not discuss the submersible boat with her. As she kissed him, his motivation turned into something far more primal. Not to mention more enjoyable.

Her hands clasped his shoulders as she opened to the kiss. Her eagerness and greedy passion fueled his desire, and he pulled her onto his lap. He deepened the kiss, plunging his tongue into her mouth.

His hand dipped into the bodice of her dress and cupped her breast. She leaned into his touch, and the tip hardened beneath his palm. Hot, thick desire surged through him, pouring into his groin. His erection pushed urgently against his trousers. He moaned into her mouth.

And then the carriage rumbled to a stop, but Sabine didn't move, so he continued kissing her, caressing her, tantalizing her. The driver tapped on the door.

Sabine sat up abruptly, then pulled herself off Max's lap. She swiped at her mouth but would not make eye contact.

"Sabine," he began.

But she leaped from the carriage and was up the steps

to his house before he could finish. Which might have been for the best, because for perhaps the first time in his life, he had no idea what to say.

Johns stepped into the carriage Cassandra had waiting a block away from the British Museum.

"Well, did you find out anything?" she asked.

"They're leaving tonight to see some man," Johns said. "Mortimer Flynn. That's all I heard. That Scottish bloke looked in my direction one too many times. I didn't want to get nabbed."

"Truly?" Cassandra asked, not believing her good fortune. "Mr. Flynn lives only four miles away from my country estate. I think it might be time for some refreshing air away from the bustle of London."

Chapter Sixteen

Graeme's suggestion had been a good one. Mortimer Flynn, a former member of Solomon's, was said to have one of the largest and most extensive collections of unique weapons in Great Britain. It might be another futile search, but perhaps luck would be on their side. Flynn's estate was a two-hour drive from London, and exhaustion overcame Sabine during the ride. They hadn't gotten much sleep the past few days, and no doubt it was wearing her down. As the carriage rumbled to a stop, Sabine awoke.

Sabine looked weary, but so beautiful. Her hair was rumpled, and she had a hand imprint on her cheek from her nap. Still, she stirred him.

"Where are we?" she asked, peering out the small carriage window.

He climbed down from the carriage and held his hand out to her.

"In Kent at the weapon collector's estate," Max reminded her. She'd evidently slept so deeply in the short period of time that she'd forgotten their destination.

"Oh, right. And this man, you and your Scottish friend know him?"

Max looked out the window. "Not precisely."

"Not precisely?" she repeated. "What does that mean?" She looked around at their surroundings, trees lining the small road. "Why did we not pull into his drive?"

Max took that exact moment to check his pistol.

Her eyes widened as she eyed his gun.

"He used to be a member of my club," he said.

"You've never met him, though."

"No, he was gone long before I joined." He shrugged. "But I know of him," Max said.

"And you think that small affiliation will grant us an invitation into his home?" The pitch of her voice rose.

"Of course not." He moved closer to a tree. "We don't need an invitation."

She followed. "Why is that?"

"We're going to go in unannounced and look around." He peered through a clearing in the trees. Flynn's house sat straight ahead of them, though they'd have to maneuver through the remainder of the trees and scale a stone wall to get onto the property. Then it would be a matter of finding the right door.

"Do you ever go in through the front door with an actual invitation?" she hissed. "I should have known you were planning something like this when we left London at such a late hour."

"We need the weapon, do we not? Do not worry, he'll never even know we were here," he said.

They moved along the shrubbery, careful to conceal themselves in the darkness. The grand estate before them swept across a hillside, staking a clear claim on all the land below. The gray stone looked dark and menacing in the night sky. Ivy crept up, covering one entire side of the building.

Soon they found themselves against the stone wall that surrounded the perimeter of the house.

"We should try a door in the back," Max whispered.

Together they moved along the wall, across the front, and around the side. Max stopped.

He pointed to the single door on the west side of the house. "That's even better. A servants' entrance. He'll never know."

"And I suppose if we find the weapon we're just going to borrow it," she said tartly.

He thought a moment, then nodded. "Precisely."

"Is breaking into people's homes some sort of misguided hobby for you?" she asked.

"When the task calls for creative measures. Come." He hoisted himself to the top of the wall. When he turned to help Sabine, she was already halfway up. He assisted her the rest of the way, then jumped down and helped her land on her feet. They used a grove of trees to maneuver closer without being seen.

"How are you not rotting in a prison cell by now?" she whispered. But he saw the hint of a smile teasing her lips.

"I am the Marquess of Lindberg," he said simply. That, and he excelled at smoothing over bad situations. A smile here, a banknote there, and people tended to forget their worries. He made his way to the door. At this hour, the servants would all be in bed. With his tools, he was able to pry open the lock. He saw Sabine still hiding behind a tree. "Are you coming with me or are you planning to hide out here?" he whispered.

Her lips tightened into a thin line. She said nothing as she strode past him into the house.

Max smiled and followed behind her.

They stood completely still for several minutes, allowing their eyes to grow accustomed to the dark room. It appeared to be the kitchen, as the scent of bread permeated the area. Sabine's warm breath breezed across his neck. She leaned in closer and that same warmth blew against his ear.

"How do we know where to look?" she whispered.

Bloody hell, but he wanted her. Right here in this stranger's kitchen. Pushed up against the cupboards, hot and fast or painfully slow. He didn't care which. Maybe both.

Quietly they crept across the kitchen and into the pantry area. Max held his arm out to stop Sabine's forward movement. He pointed down at their feet. There sleeping on the floor were two scullery maids. Sabine's eyes grew large. Max nodded to reassure her. He held her hand as they climbed over the girls' sleeping forms. One of them stirred, and Max and Sabine froze. But she turned over and continued to sleep.

They exited the pantry into a hallway with a staircase, because if they didn't keep moving, Max just might take her on the floor. "He keeps most of them on display in the great hall," he said quietly as they began their climb.

She tugged on his shirt to stop him. "Then why couldn't we have simply asked him if we could take a look?"

"On display for himself. He doesn't like to share."

"I see."

"This way." He grabbed her hand, ignoring the way it fit perfectly within his.

He led her through a darkened parlor into a hall and

across a marble floor. They walked slowly to avoid making too much noise, crept up another staircase, and down to the right until they entered what Max thought to be the great hall.

Two large windows allowed the moonlight enough entrance to give them a clear view of the room. In addition, there were oil lanterns flanking the sides of the huge mantel. Enough oil remained for another couple of hours, though Max suspected a servant would be by in that time to douse the lights. They would have to work quickly. Suits of armor stood guard in all four corners and display cases featured weapons from every era and country. Swords and knives and guns covered every surface, the larger ones hung on the walls.

"Oh, my," Sabine said. "I should hate to make this gentleman unhappy."

If the rumors Max had heard of Flynn's temper were true, then they certainly did not want to make the man angry, but he said nothing of that to Sabine. "Let's make quick work of this. You start over there." He pointed to the right side.

"It could potentially take us three days to make our way through all of this," Sabine said. "There are so many inventive ways to kill a person."

"We know we can ignore all of the shields and armor and concentrate only on the knives and daggers and swords," he said.

"Anything with a blade," she said.

"Precisely."

Max walked past samurai armor, horse armor—and it would seem an entire regiment of muskets—before he even found a glass case with swords in it. There he found them in several shapes, made of gold and silver and bronze and iron, but no sign of the dove carving.

"I would think it would be Greek in origin," Sabine said. "Or at least appear to be. That's the closest civilization to Atlantis." She reached into her bag and withdrew a magnifying glass.

"Ancient Greek or older," he said. He frowned and pointed at her hand. "Where did you get that?"

"From Calliope. I thought it might make it easier to find what we're looking for. So far we've found the dove engraving on a tombstone and the wall in the bathhouse, but those are both rather large in comparison to the hilt of a sword." She shrugged. "I wanted to be prepared."

He smiled.

"Why, did you want to borrow it?" she asked. She held it out to him.

"I can see quite well on my own. I don't need your lady's tool to assist me."

She braced her fists on her hips. "Let me know if you change your mind. You might run across another statue and need it"—she waved the magnifying glass—"for a closer examination of the breasts."

Max laughed quietly. "Carry on," he told her.

They looked for over an hour and had only scoured half the room. Max had seen pieces from what he believed to be the Byzantine Empire and perhaps even one of the early dynasties of China. Fascinating though the collection might be, he could see why the men of Solomon's had decided to remove Mr. Flynn from their roster. He was not interested in any particular legend or myth, but rather was simply a collector of all kinds of weaponry. A fine hobby, but not the stuff of the legend hunters, as some outsiders referred to the men of

Solomon's. Also, he was known to use his collection regularly. The threat of violence was more than enough to disqualify him. He'd been asked to leave the club and had subsequently left London, and as far as Max knew, had never returned.

"Max," Sabine whispered. "I think I've found something."

He moved to where she stood, near one of the windows in front of a small display case. Inside was one single dagger, the hilt carved with a crude rendition of a bird. Engraved on the blade was an inscription in Greek: *The Great army is commanded as the ten were done.*

"That has to be it," Sabine said.

Max eyed it carefully, then with his own much smaller knife, reached for the lock at the base of the display case.

"What the hell do you think you're doing?" a voice called from behind them.

"We're in grave danger, sir," Sabine began. "And we need this weapon." She pointed to the dagger encased in the glass box. "We will certainly return it when we are done." It was probably futile to try to bargain with the man; he didn't seem congenial in the least.

"I don't bloody well care if you're the queen, you're not getting my knife," the man growled. He was tall, taller than Max, though not as broad. His long, brown hair was scruffy and straggled past the man's shoulders. His beard was full and gray and covered worn, wrinkled skin that had seen far too many hours in the sun. Coarse wool on aged leather. "I found that one myself, dug it up from beneath a castle in Gloucester. Nearly lost my leg, I did." Then, as if he'd realized he was conversing with them, he shook his rifle.

Max took a step forward. "Mr. Flynn, I can assure you—"

Flynn pointed his rifle directly at Max. His narrow eyes squinted until they were nothing but angry slits. "You're one of them, aren't you?"

"I don't know what you mean," Max said.

Sabine watched Max's demeanor change. Gone was the seductive charmer she was used to, and in his place was a deadly calm protector ready to negotiate and bargain their way out of this.

"From Solomon's." Flynn's eyes narrowed, and he snarled. "They've always been after me. Did they send you for that piece in particular or were you planning to take everything the two of you could carry?"

Max nodded slowly. "I am a member of Solomon's, but that is the only reason I even knew of your name and your collection. We were looking for a rare piece, but it doesn't appear that you have it." Max slid his hand into Sabine's and pulled her closer to him. "We are terribly sorry for bothering you at such a late hour." He moved them closer to the door. "We'll be on our way now." His smooth and steady delivery nearly convinced Flynn, or so it seemed. Max had even managed to direct Sabine a couple of feet closer to the door.

Then Flynn shook his head. "I don't think so," he said. He held his gun steady, aimed directly at them. "This way. You walk slowly and don't try anything or I'll shoot you first," he said to Max, "then take my time with the girl and shoot her, too."

Sabine swallowed and involuntarily squeezed Max's hand, pulling it tight to her side. The warmth from his body offered no actual protection, yet gave her a measure of comfort, though she realized that if this armed man behind them chose to do just as he said, they'd have little defense to prevent him.

"Keep walking," he said. Eventually he closed the distance between them enough so that he could alternately press the end of the rifle into Max's back and then her own.

He marched them upstairs and into a bedchamber, where he shoved them inside. "I've already sent for the local magistrate. I saw you creeping across the lawn and knew you were up to no good. But I waited to see what you would take. He's on his way to have you both hauled off to jail. I called for him first, so I can't kill you myself," he said, then slammed the door. The lock turned behind them. They heard something large scrape against the floor, then bump the door.

"He's braced it with a piece of furniture or something. I'm surprised he didn't toss us into the dungeon," Sabine said.

Max looked away from the door, where he was currently trying to dismantle the lock, and smiled at her. "Now wouldn't that have been an adventure."

"Not one I would relish. I can assure you that," she said.

"Check the windows," Max said.

Sabine made her way to the opposite wall to the four windows. "They have bars on them."

"Check to see if we can remove any of them."

"If only you could have pocketed that dagger before he found us," she said.

"It wouldn't have mattered," Max said, going back to the lock.

She checked the first set of bars, but they would not budge. "Why ever not?" she asked. "The prophecy states that the dove is the only way to stop him. How are we to do that with the blade locked up here?" She had to save Agnes.

"That wasn't the correct weapon," he said plainly. "I was not lying to Flynn."

"Of course it was. It had a bird carved into its hilt. The same bird we saw in the cemetery and again in the bathhouse." She checked the next window and again found the bars immovable.

Max turned away from the door and walked over to her. "I know it looked as much, but it was merely another clue. Sabine, trust me when I say it wasn't the right one."

"How can you be so certain?"

"Wrong time period, for one. That dagger was Turkish, from the Ottoman Empire, far too young to have been something made in Atlantis or at least made in the time of Atlantis." He reached down and tilted her chin up. "That doesn't mean it wasn't the correct clue, though."

For a moment, she forgot herself and allowed his sympathy to squeeze at her heart. Tears pricked at her eyes. More than anything she wanted to lean into him, give herself over to the attraction between them, and for one night, forget the prophecy. But she was afraid that if she gave in to him again, even one more time, she'd never be able to walk away from him. So she moved to the next window.

The windows looked out over the front of the house, and she could see the circular drive off in the distance. The moon lit the forested area lining the estate, and the grounds were lush and well landscaped. When she opened the final window, she shoved on the bars as she had done on the others. This time, they moved.

"Max," she whispered as she straightened. "These bars shifted. Perhaps we can somehow remove them."

He sauntered over to her, then pushed at the bars. They moved some more. "Stand back," he told her before he kicked at the bars. They broke away and fell to the grass below. "We're on the second floor." He leaned out, looking at the ground. "It's quite a drop."

She judged the distance herself. "The grass looks plush enough. And there are those rounded shrubs."

He cocked one eyebrow.

"At least we are not on the third level," she said.

"I could do it, but you might break something," he said, then peered out the window again. "Several somethings."

"What about you?" she asked. "If you can make the jump, so shall I. You're certainly not going to leave me here alone."

"I don't suppose we have any other options. Unless we want to wait for the authorities and hope we can talk ourselves out of a prison sentence."

"But we did break the law. They won't simply let us go. I don't care who you are." She shook her head. "I think we jump."

"All right. I'll go first and then I might be able to help you down easier," he said.

It was those moments that annoyed her the most. Just when she'd about convinced herself that he was an utter cad, he'd do or say something so gentlemanly that she knew no matter how much of a scoundrel he might be, there was a good man inside him.

"Very well," she said.

He positioned himself in the window, but facing her. Deftly he sprang from the window, but his fingers remained grasping the ledge. He was stretching himself down so that the actual jump would be as short a distance as possible. Then he let go.

She looked out the window in time to see him land on his feet. He looked up and smiled at her, and that wicked smile stole her breath. She suspected that Maxwell Barrett, like a cat, always landed on his feet.

"Come on," he said into the darkness. "I'll catch you."

The amount of space between his outstretched arms and the window seemed enough for her to fall and break her neck. What if she couldn't bring herself to do it? What if she couldn't jump?

The answer came for her in the form of footsteps in the hall, followed by male voices.

"I caught them in my display room," Flynn said.

The furniture outside the door scraped against the floor. She glanced behind her just as the lock turned, then she closed her eyes and jumped out the window.

Max caught Sabine, and the weight of her landing knocked them both to the ground.

"Look, down there," Flynn yelled.

A man, presumably the magistrate, leaned out the window beside him. "Stay right there," the man ordered. He pointed at them and then disappeared from the window.

"Run," Max said as he grabbed Sabine's hand and quickly pulled her to her feet.

Fortunately, Sabine's long legs afforded her the ability to keep pace with him as they made their way across the grounds toward the main road. He scaled the wall, then pulled Sabine over. They ran into the woods lining the property.

Max could hear voices behind them, but they'd had a decent head start, provided the two men didn't chase them on horses or in a carriage. They might be able to make it to the road and then get back to their own rig.

"Are they coming?" Sabine asked, her voice husky with exertion.

"Yes. This way." He pulled her along, and she made no complaints as she followed closely behind him. "Our carriage should be waiting just over this bluff."

The voices behind them became louder, shouts actually, and Max realized that the men had, in fact, jumped into a carriage to chase them.

Max and Sabine burst through the trees and onto the main road, but the rocks would provide no easier terrain for them to navigate on foot. And their carriage was not there waiting. Had he gotten turned around in their escape and gone in the opposite direction? He didn't have time to figure it all out. Perhaps he'd misjudged the distance, and their rig was farther down the road.

"They're getting closer," Sabine said.

They fled as quickly as they could, but the noise of wheels grew louder, the horses' hooves bearing down on them as they clopped along the road. The carriage drove up beside them and pulled to a stop. But instead of the men who were chasing them, a familiar voice came from the inside.

"Max, what a pleasant surprise. You and your friend"—the female voice stumbled over the last word—"seem to be in a pinch of trouble. Might I be of assistance?"

"Cassandra, you have impeccable timing, as always." Max helped Sabine into the carriage, and it rolled off into the darkness in the direction opposite the men who pursued them.

"My country home is not far from here. I will be glad to offer you sanctuary for the night." She smiled. "I take it you had a disagreement?" she asked, and a delicate brow arched over her right eye.

"Minor," Max agreed.

"You always did have a knack for causing trouble." Cassandra's cool gaze fell to Sabine. "Aren't you that girl from the shop in Piccadilly? Having to resort to peddling your wares in the country now?" she asked, doing nothing to hide her acerbic tone. Cassandra never did hesitate to show her claws when the mood struck her.

But Sabine did not allow the insult to affect her. Instead she held her head high and gave Cassandra a luminous smile. "I am. I believe it might be time for you to purchase some more of my products." Sabine touched her own smooth forehead, then nodded in Cassandra's direction.

Cassandra's hand immediately moved to her own head to rub at the skin.

"I'd be happy to send you a few jars to any address," Sabine offered.

Max wanted to laugh, but didn't dare. It would not help matters if Cassandra scratched out Sabine's lovely eyes.

Chapter Seventeen

———❧ ❧———

Cassandra had graciously put them up for the night and offered a carriage for them to ride back to London in the morning. Max hoped his own driver had had the good sense to flee from the magistrate. Currently Max stared out the darkened window of his borrowed room, a glass of scotch in his hand. He still hadn't deciphered the next riddle, but the words kept running through his mind. He wasn't certain that Sabine believed the dagger was not the one they were looking for, but he felt certain. Whoever had hidden the dove had gone to great lengths to keep it hidden, ensuring that only those willing to seriously search might actually find it. Yet there was something about the ordeal that felt off. Perhaps Sabine's aunts might know more about who had created this quest.

A slight rap sounded on his door, then it creaked opened.

"I was wondering if I'd see you tonight," he murmured as he turned around. But instead of finding Sabine, Cassandra lingered in his doorway.

"Cassandra," he said, unable to keep the surprise from his voice.

"Were you expecting someone else?" she purred.

He gave her no answer.

Dressed head to toe in some silk confection the color of blood, it left little to his imagination. But then he didn't need to speculate when it came to Cassandra. He knew her body, knew every contour, even though the last time he'd touched her, they'd both been younger. They'd had an affair nearly ten years before that had lasted for about eight months. He'd almost fancied himself in love with the blonde beauty, but then he'd found her in bed with another man. A man she'd claimed was a servant. It had been the last time Max had kept a woman in his bed for any length of time.

"Quite fortunate I came upon the two of you this evening," she said. His bedchamber door shut behind her.

"Indeed. We appreciate your assistance." Her rescue was timely and most convenient, though Max knew he would have been able to get them to safety one way or another. Still, it was nice to know Sabine was safe, and they had comfortable beds for the night.

Cassandra closed the distance between them, then took hold of his glass and slowly sipped some of the contents, her icy blue eyes never leaving his own. "What is this thing between you and that woman? Is she your new lover?" She did her best to sound nonchalant, but Max knew better. There were no sentimental feelings involved, but were it up to Cassandra, no other woman would have Max. She was just that kind of woman. Possessive even of the things that were no longer hers.

For a moment, he considered lying, telling her that Sabine was his mistress, but that would only serve to anger

Cassandra. There was no need to add fuel to that fire. "No. She hired me to assist her with a certain matter."

"Oh, I see." She set the glass down, then proceeded to deftly unbutton his shirt. "You are a man for hire now, are you?"

"Cassandra," he protested.

"Relax. No one has to know." She leaned in and pressed wet kisses on his chest. "Remember how it was between us, Max? How passionate and hot we were together?"

It was difficult to forget. Not the passion, per se, but Cassandra in general. She was no shy violet, hiding in the shadows hoping a man would notice her. No, she demanded attention, and she got it. Plenty of it. He remembered mostly how she'd flirted with other men, shamelessly, then insisted they meant nothing to her. He'd been young and foolish, but he'd never make that mistake again.

"One more night together. To reminisce about how it used to be," she said.

He grabbed her wrists to still her hands before they unfastened his trousers.

Her eyes flashed, and a wicked grin spread. "You want to play a little rough tonight?"

"No," he said flatly.

"I don't understand," she said. She pressed her body against him, and her plush curves melded against his frame. He didn't want to respond, but he'd have dared a man of the cloth not to have a reaction to her bold invitation. Still, it mattered not if his body stirred at her touch; he did not desire her.

"Cassandra, have you so easily forgotten our past?" Still he held her wrists firmly. "I told you never again."

She gave him her best pout, her perfectly painted lips

pursed outward. She looked up at him through her lashes. "You still haven't forgiven me for one tiny indiscretion?"

He chuckled. "I suspect he was not the only one, simply the man I caught you with," he said. "And it has nothing to do with forgiveness."

She shrugged casually, but there was never anything casual about Cassandra. She did not like being told no. "Perhaps. I am a woman with a voracious appetite for pleasures of the flesh," she said tartly. "I cannot help it if one man is not enough to satisfy me."

"Classic Cassandra." Max smiled. "If you do not get your way, it is better to insult the other party rather than graciously accept defeat."

One delicate eyebrow arched. "Defeat? How am I defeated? I do not need you, Max. I have men all over London waiting for an invitation to my bed. I only thought you might want to remember what it was like to be with a real woman. Not that waif you're with now. Rather plain-looking, don't you agree?" She inspected her nails, but Max could see a rise of color up her pale throat. Cassandra was angry.

"Actually, I find Sabine rather beautiful, exotic even," Max said. He could have said those words simply to further annoy Cassandra, but he'd meant every word. To him, there was no greater beauty than Sabine. And Cassandra could see it, too. Everyone could. Sabine was ethereal. The Mona Lisa come to life, with her olive complexion and a face that could have been carved by the gods themselves.

"Age has done nothing to hone your taste in women, Max," Cassandra said bitterly. "You could have had me tonight." She looked at him meaningfully, allowing her eyes to travel the length of his body. "Your carriage will be ready first thing in the morning. Before breakfast," she added.

"Thank you, Cassandra."

Sabine stood still as Cassandra stepped out of Max's room, flowing red lingerie her only covering. The woman gave Sabine a wicked smile, then wiped the corners of her mouth.

"He's all yours," she purred as she walked past.

Sabine turned to go, but Max must have heard the brief exchange, because he opened the door. "Wait," he said. "That was not what it looked like."

Sabine stiffened. She turned to watch Cassandra turn the corner at the end of the hall. "It matters not to me who you have relations with. I've made no claim on you, nor do I want one." She knew her tone was rude, but she did nothing to soften it. A line from Shakespeare's *Hamlet* floated through her mind: "The lady doth protest too much."

He sighed, and for a brief moment weariness settled in his eyes, but then it was gone. "Did you need something?" he asked.

"I wanted to further discuss the dagger."

"I expected you would. Come in," he said.

She tried not to notice how his shirt was completely opened to reveal that chest of his. She'd seen it before, but still the taut muscles left her mouth dry and her mind blank. Once they were closed in his room, she said nothing.

She turned and found herself looking straight at the large four-poster bed. It was still made, not even a pillow out of place. There were no pieces of clothing dropped on the floor as if forgotten in the rush of passion. Perhaps he'd been telling her the truth. Sabine had certainly seen enough to know that Cassandra was a woman used to getting what she wanted. It seemed of late, the woman wanted Max. Well, Sabine would certainly not stand in the way.

"Sabine," he said, his breath hot on her neck as he stood too close behind her. "I didn't touch her."

"I told you I do not care," she bit out. But she couldn't ignore the thrill that swept through her at his admission.

He turned her around to face him. "It matters to me. Damned if I know why, but it does. I won't lie and say I don't have a past with Cassandra, but she means nothing to me. And hasn't for a very long time."

Did that imply that she herself meant something to him? "Max, you and me, we're not together," she said again.

"From the moment I first laid eyes on you, I've wanted nothing more than to strip every piece of clothing off your perfect body and spend hours laving kisses across your flesh." His crystal-blue eyes never wavered from her own. "That night on the train was too hurried. And you stopped me in the inn, but I know you didn't want to."

Why did she crave him so intensely? What was it about him that captivated her so?

"This is highly improper," she said, wishing she had a cloak about her to pull close around her. Instead she hugged her arms to her body. She was weak when it came to Max. Give her one tiny taste, and she wanted the entire plate. She didn't want to want him. She didn't want to need any man, but damned if this one didn't pull at her as the moon pulled the tide.

"I know you want me, too," he said, his voice no more than a whisper.

She bristled. "You know no such thing." Evidently she had not done as good a job as she'd thought of keeping her desire a secret.

"You can deny it, if you choose, but I know the truth." He passed behind her, his breath ruffling through her hair. "You want me."

"Stop that." She swatted at him as she turned and put distance between them.

"You won't be able to fight it forever. Eventually this sort of desire always"—he paused, letting his eyes slowly move down her body—"combusts."

"Clearly you have far more experience in this sort of thing than I do, but I can assure you I do not feel as if I'm going to combust. Quite the contrary."

"So when I grab you this way and pull you to me"—he did as he said, pressing the length of her body against his own—"you feel nothing?"

She swallowed slowly. "Correct."

"And there is no rise in your temperature when I do this?" His hand lifted her slightly by squeezing her bottom, then he nuzzled his face into the crook of her neck. The day's growth of beard scraped tantalizingly against her collarbone as he took small heated nips along the tender flesh.

"Nothing at all," she lied.

"I see." He placed both hands on the sides of her face, then leaned in and kissed her. Not any kiss, but a kiss intended to imprint itself on a human soul, so tender, so full of yearning, she could not help but cry out. The sound was muffled by his mouth's covering. His tongue slid against her bottom lip, and she opened to him, and lost were her protests as she melted against his body.

Good gracious, but Max was a good kisser.

His hands kept her in place, but she was in no rush to move. Not yet. She could endure a little more.

Then he was done, pulling back from her with small kisses directly on her lips. Achingly sweet.

"And now?" he murmured.

She swallowed and kept her eyes closed, but managed to say, "Nothing."

"As I expected," he said.

She opened her eyes to find him grinning ruthlessly at her.

One eyebrow cocked. "Nothing?" he repeated. She took in the length of him, standing there with his shirt open and that wolfish grin. Not nothing, but everything. When he touched her, the world stilled and only the sensations gave her breath.

She so wanted this. Wanted him.

Without another thought, she crossed to him and kissed him. She yanked his shirt off his arms and ran her hands over his torso, touching every hard, sinewy line on his chest. She couldn't deny her desire for him any longer. She simply wouldn't.

Impatiently she unfastened his trousers. Her body positively hummed with lust. Everywhere he touched, fire lit under her skin and blazed through her. Her nipples peaked. She was wet for him, wet and simply aching for his touch. For him to be inside her.

He stilled her hand and met her eyes. "Sabine, I can't offer you anything more."

His words tugged at her heart, but she ignored them. He couldn't offer, and she wouldn't ask. "I don't need anything else."

She finished undressing him until he stood before her as God had made him. So handsome, so rugged, so perfect.

She wanted to touch him everywhere. She stepped away from him, but not far, and quickly removed her own clothing. Max's eyes trailed the length of her naked body, his blue eyes turning the color of warm steel.

"You're so beautiful," he said, his voice raw with desire. He grabbed her hand and pulled her back to him so that their bodies pressed together. Flesh upon flesh.

His hands cupped her bottom, pressing her to him, pressing her into his erection.

She kissed him again, and this time he picked her up. Cradling her as he carried her to the oversized bed, he didn't even pull the coverlet back; instead he simply laid her on the velvety softness. She wrapped her legs around his waist, encouraging him to get closer, to lose himself inside her.

It was all the encouragement he needed. With slow and steady movements, he entered her. The fullness of him felt so right, so exactly what she needed, what she craved.

His movements were deep and sensual, and her climax began to build almost immediately. Swifter and swifter, she climbed until she couldn't hold it any longer, and the world seemed to shatter in a million glassy fragments all around her. She clung to his shoulders as the pleasures rocked her, and she was vaguely aware of his own climax as his abdomen tightened against her.

She lay sleeping, curled against his side, her breathing slow and even. Sabine was a passionate woman. It had been good on the train, but damn, that had been explosive and powerful. He caught sight of the small vial glistening between her breasts.

She had proof of Atlantis, and he'd seen it work. Twice now. She had it on that necklace she wore.

His gunshot wound had healed faster than some shaving cuts he'd endured, and then after his injury in the bathhouse, she'd poured the elixir directly onto his wound, and it had healed almost instantly.

Marcus would be able to tell there was something unique about it. It would be the necessary proof Max needed to borrow Marcus's submersible boat. Then he would be able to locate the lost continent and see it for himself.

Max's family was long dead and buried. That was a reality he'd accepted long ago. Only in his most maudlin moments did he let himself linger over regrets. His family would never know what he'd accomplished. They could never enjoy his success or acknowledge his achievements. It was the most bitter reminder of how solitary his position in the world was. Of course, he would always have the men of Solomon's, men who could appreciate his success as intellectual equals.

And he would have Sabine in his bed. That would be enough for her and for him. It would have to be, because he could not give her his heart.

The following morning as they rode back into London, Sabine wanted to make certain they concentrated on the task at hand, that they didn't get distracted by their night of lovemaking. He'd taken her a second time before they'd fallen into a deep sleep. When they'd awakened, it was to find their hostess had already left the house, but had readied a carriage for them as she'd promised.

Neither had spoken about the night before. It wasn't as if she'd expected Max to fall to his knees and recite poetry or whisper proclamations of love. It wouldn't matter if he had. They couldn't be together.

She was Atlantean, and he was English. She could sit here and think of many reasons why she wanted to be with Max. But choosing him would be the same as walking away from her people, and she could never do that. Just as Agnes had chosen her duty over the desires of her heart, so would she. Not that she loved Max, she didn't, but she did desire him.

And he'd made it all too clear he was not looking for a wife. Not only that, but after watching her mother grieve for Sabine's father and now Agnes for Phinneas, Sabine knew that love only brought heartache.

This line of thinking would get her nowhere. They had a weapon to find, and if her aunts were right and her birthday had something to do with the timeline of the prophecy, then they only had four more days. He sat opposite her, his legs stretched in front of him, but completely avoiding contact with her. Did he regret last night?

The carriage jerked, and when it did, her bag slipped off the seat and was dumped onto the floor.

She knelt to pick up the contents.

He leaned forward to help her.

"Here, you missed this." He held a calling card out to her, but before she could grab it, he'd snatched it back. It was the card of the chemist who'd come into her shop a couple of days before.

He looked down at the card in his hand. "Bertrand Olney. Why does that name look so familiar?" He looked up at her. "Where did you get this?"

She frowned. "He came by the shop that day I went in. He'd handed me the card, and I guess I stuffed it in my bag. I'd forgotten all about him."

"What did he want?" Max asked, suspicion sharp in his voice.

"He's not the one we're looking for," she said. "He wasn't strong enough."

"I've seen his name." He shook his head. "I can't place it, though."

"It's nothing. He was a chemist; offered to buy the recipe for one of my products."

"A chemist? That's where I've heard of him. In the *Times*," he said. "There was a story about how chemist Bertrand Olney had been murdered the previous night in his home. It did not appear to be a burglary."

"What?" Sabine asked.

"He was murdered."

She didn't know what to think about that. Should she feel remorse or compassion for him, despite the fact that he'd appeared to be a dishonest little man? She supposed she should, yet she felt nothing. So she changed the subject.

"How can you be so certain the dagger we found was not the dove?" she asked.

"I told you, wrong era. It was crafted far too late to have come out of Atlantis or anything near that time period. And the engraving on the blade gave another clue," he said plainly.

"Yes, you mentioned that last night, but I saw no such thing."

"*The great army is commanded as the ten were done*," he said.

"Great army. That could refer to the armies of the Great War."

"You've mentioned the Great War before. Tell me about it," he said.

"Atlantis invaded many countries, destroying most of them. The military abused the elixir, making them nearly undefeatable. That's when the guardians and their families fled. They took the elixir, and eventually the army weakened. Poseidon punished them for their greed, and he commanded the ocean to swallow the island," she said.

"No one was punished, Sabine. It was merely an earthquake or volcano that destroyed the island," Max said.

"That is not what my people believe. The elixir was a gift to us, and we did not obey, therefore we received retribution."

"A biblical plague," he said.

"If you want to view it in such terms," she said.

"Well, soldiers from the Great War is a good theory. What I focused on was the 'as the ten were done.' I believe it refers to the Ten Commandments."

"Thou shall not commit murder," she said. "Tell that to the Chosen One."

"I don't believe it's referring to any one of the commandments in particular, but rather to how they were presented to the people," Max said.

"From a mountaintop?" she asked.

"No, on stone tablets. I think our next quest is to locate a specific tablet."

She thought on it a moment. "The Rosetta Stone," she suggested, then shook her head. "What good will a tablet do us?"

"Another clue?" he suggested.

"At this rate we could chase after clues for the next one hundred years," she said.

"Consider this an adventure, Sabine."

"Perhaps we do not have time for an adventure. There are lives at stake," she said. Hers included.

"Indeed there are. Not only the remaining guardian,

but the rest of our military leaders, who protect the rest of us." He nodded. "Yes, there is much at stake."

"Why do you care so much?" she asked, unable to hide her curiosity.

"My club," he said without missing a beat. "It is not our intention or prime purpose to guard the crown, but Solomon's has on occasion been given the opportunity to protect our monarch and our great country."

She didn't believe that for a second, but Max always had an answer for everything. "So you do it for patriotism?"

"And perhaps for other, more personal reasons." He shrugged. "I cannot help but be intrigued by anything related to Atlantis. You included."

Her heartbeat faltered. She watched his clear blue eyes and the amusement, intelligence, and passion they held.

He'd found their map. Phinneas had once had a vision about that very thing, "a great one." Max would not be satisfied with that one artifact forever, though.

"But if given the opportunity to find proof," she said. "You would do it?"

"Yes, I would," Max answered without hesitation.

She knew that, in and of itself, should frighten her. The guardians worked tirelessly to hide and protect the elixir to avoid its exploitation and ruin. He knew about the elixir and had seen its powers firsthand. Max, if he so chose, could ruin them all.

Chapter Eighteen

⚜

Sabine and Max climbed up the wide staircase, and this time they actually walked through the pillared entryway of the British Museum. They were here to visit the King's Library.

"Are you certain the next clue leads us to Alexander the Great?" Sabine asked.

"No, not certain at all, but if I'm right we'll see the truth in moments," Max said.

"You're beginning to sound like a riddle yourself," she said, with a smile. She'd been smiling a lot more lately. Strange, considering life had become more complicated and dangerous in the last two weeks. But Max made her laugh.

"Great army—Great's army. It was capitalized. Shortly before he died, Alexander the Great made one final decree," Max said.

"And put it in stone?" she asked. "Not precisely the medium they used during that time period."

"On the contrary, there were still official proclamations made in stone," Max said.

They crossed through a quiet corridor, and she kept pace to walk next to him. "I suppose I'm more familiar with the history of my own people. Was our civilization really so much more advanced than the Macedonians' that we were using scrolls when the rest of the world was still using tablets?"

"Perhaps we might all still be whittling in stone had it not been for the few Atlanteans who came along to civilize the rest of us," Max said drolly.

"You are truly hilarious," she said.

"Thank you."

They walked past the reading room and a few exhibit halls. Finally they came to the library. It was dim, with very few lamps. Windows surrounded the top of the room like a ribbon of light, but with today's clouds, they didn't provide much illumination.

Aside from that, the library was magnificent. Books and scrolls and other artifacts, including King John's Magna Carta and the Rosetta Stone, surrounded them. And perhaps a piece of her own people's history was here among Britain's most valuable treasures. Pride swelled within her. If she survived this prophecy, she should come back here someday to enjoy all of the artifacts.

She paused and glanced back at the Rosetta Stone. "Just to be certain," she said as she walked over to it.

"You know, this actually dates a little more recent than Alexander's decree?" Max said.

"You are a font of information,"

"A member of Solomon's found it," he said.

She circled the display, looking closely for any sign of the dove. "I thought a Frenchman had discovered it."

Max shrugged. "He claimed it. But whose museum is it in?"

There were no symbols resembling their dove. "Nothing. Shall we?"

They walked into a smaller room, and there, atop a podium, was a large stone tablet.

"Some theorize," Max spoke in a low voice, "that Alexander was attempting to put himself on the same level as God and thus chose the same medium to proclaim his own commandments."

As they moved closer, Sabine could see the Greek inscription carved into the granite. She read the entire decree, and it was, in fact, about war, an extended battle cry and promise to be ruler of all.

"That mentions nothing about a dove or a specific weapon," Sabine said.

"No, it doesn't. But..." Max turned around to ensure they were alone before he picked up the massive tablet and turned it over. The stone had chipped in a few places and wasn't entirely smooth, but there were no significant marks on most of the surface. "There," he said, pointing.

On the right-hand corner was another inscription directly below the now-familiar carving of the bird. The letters looked familiar, but something was peculiar about them. And without proper lighting, it was far too difficult to read.

She reached into her bag and retrieved her notebook and a pencil. With a firm yank, she pulled a couple of blank pages out of the notebook, then handed them to Max.

He set the tablet facedown, then spread the sheet of paper over the inscription. As he moved the pencil across the stone, Sabine watched the message appear on the parchment.

A scholarly-looking gentleman with spectacles entered the room and eyed them disapprovingly. He cleared his throat. Sabine ran a hand seductively down Max's back, then leaned over to his ear pretending to whisper something.

Max stopped what he was doing.

She brazenly winked at the other man.

The scholar's eyes rounded, then a bright shade of red covered his entire face, and he quickly turned to go.

"I apologize," she said to Max when they were alone again. "It was the first thought I had to get him out of here. It worked," she said cheerfully.

"Next time think of an alternative solution that doesn't involve touching me." Then he turned to meet her eyes. "Unless you fully intend to finish what you start."

She started to chuckle, but then she caught sight of his expression. He was deadly serious.

She swallowed, but said nothing in response. While Max took an impression of the entire inscription, she stood watching and smiled sweetly at any passersby who happened into the room.

"Done," Max whispered. He handed her the two sheets of parchment, which she tucked neatly into her bag.

"Let us be done with this place before we attract any more attention," she said.

He nodded as he gently turned the tablet back to its original position. "Lovely piece," he said to a lady and her two young sons as they entered the room. Then he and Sabine made their way out of the library.

Their waiting carriage took them directly to Max's home, and they made their way into his study. It was late afternoon, Agnes was probably upstairs while Lydia and Calliope were still at the shop. Momentarily she felt a pang of guilt for leaving them to do the menial work when it had been her idea to begin with. But she had been set on this course, and she felt it was her duty to stop the prophecy and protect Agnes.

He laid the pieces of parchment on his desk then read them aloud. "*'Deception is deceiving,'*" he began, then finished the inscription, though it wasn't very cohesive.

"Well, that doesn't make very much sense. Are you certain you translated that correctly?" she asked. She came around the desk to look for herself.

"It's the first line," he said.

She stared from one page to the next for several moments and again was struck by the familiarity. "Wait a moment." She picked up the first sheet and held it upside down. Then she smiled. "Do you have a mirror?"

"Why?" he asked.

"Trust *me* for a change," she said.

He nodded. "This way." He led the way out of the office and up the stairs. They went down a hall and then another until they came to the end and entered a room.

"Is this your bedchamber?" she asked, still standing in the hallway.

"You asked for a mirror, and it was the first one I thought of." He pointed to the full-sized framed mirror in the corner of the room.

Even though it was a very large room, the massive bed commanded her full attention. Covered in the lushest of blue silks, it beckoned to her as she breached the threshold. She quickly turned away and walked right up to the mirror. She turned over the sheet of paper until it was upside down and the reflection shown in the mirror. "That's it," she said. She smiled broadly.

Max peered into the mirror and saw what looked to him to be upside-down Greek letters. "That's what?"

"It's written in Atlantean," she said. "I don't know how I missed that before. Hand the other one to me."

He held the sheets to the mirror as she scribbled the translation into her notebook.

"So what does it say?" he asked.

"*Your task is nearly complete, and the reward is near. The dove is before you, if you have the right eyes to see.*"

"What the hell is that supposed to mean?" he asked.

"I have no idea."

Spencer stood near the French doors enjoying the evening breeze while the music played and couples littered the ballroom floor. His fellow guests jested and laughed about other men in Parliament or the latest scandal. On occasion, he'd nod and chuckle to remind them he was participating, that he was one of them, even though he knew that wasn't true.

He was better than every one of them, far more important. It mattered not that his title was lower, and his coffers might not be as full. When it came to importance, he ranked at the top, and whether they realized that now or not had no bearing on the truth. The truth would be revealed soon, and then everyone would know.

His signet ring weighed heavily on his hand, reminding him of his purpose tonight. He had not made any headway in locating the third and final guardian. So he'd come out among Society tonight in hopes of uncovering that person's identity. He had very few clues, but he knew London was the correct location.

Spencer's birthday was rapidly approaching, only three days away, and he had to complete the prophecy by then or he would fail. Two more generals and the final guardian and then all would be set.

"Pardon me," he said to his companions; he could scarcely consider them friends. "I believe I'll retrieve some refreshments." It was an excuse to roam the room and get as close to as many people as possible. The women were not the problem. He could dance with any woman in the room. They'd respond to him, he knew that. He was a handsome devil, and women always craved his attention. That and being her majesty's faithful advisor usually ensured that he made a rather popular dance partner. But he preferred situations in which he wouldn't have to play the charming rogue and could instead be silent and focus on his work.

The closer he got to the table and the crowd of women to his left, the more the ring glowed bright red. The guardian was here. Only elixir caused his ring to blaze. Deftly he poured himself some lemonade—dreadful stuff, but it was the only concoction available at the table. So he forced the drink down and poured more. Then he slowly walked toward a group of women standing not too far away from him.

The redness deepened. A female guardian, that was something he hadn't considered. He found himself searching the women's faces looking for some other sign. No doubt, she'd be beautiful. At least, he imagined she would be, and as he looked into the eager expressions of the girls standing together—their desire for him to invite them to dance etched painfully across their faces—none of them seemed particularly beautiful to him.

And the ring, while glowing, was not nearly as red or bright as it had been when he'd found the other two guardians. He didn't bother smiling at the women as he moved around the perimeter of the room. Sitting in a tight clump directly opposite the band, he found another group of women. Again they were all pleasant-looking, but not so much so as to stop him in his tracks. The ring brightened, but the ruby-red color it had taken in the presence of the other guardians did not appear.

He took a slow walk along the open balcony, but discovered only couples hiding in darkened corners. As he made his way back into the ballroom, he stopped as the color of blonde hair caught his attention. It was nearly white, it was so fair, and the woman it belonged to was nothing short of exquisite. She was in the arms of an older gentleman, one he knew from some circles. She laughed at something the man said, and the throaty sound purred up Spencer's extremities.

"Behave," she said, "you wouldn't want my lover to get jealous."

"Your lover, and who might that be?" the man asked.

"The Marquess of Lindberg. Maxwell and I have been together for years," she said.

So she belonged to the marquess. Perhaps this was the woman whom Spencer had seen with Max at Phinneas's cottage.

He waited until the dance was complete, then made his way to her side, champagne in hand. The closer he got to her, the deeper the red shone in his ring. This was her. She had to be the third and final guardian.

"A drink?" He held it out to her.

She looked up at him from beneath long, kohl-covered eyelashes. "Thank you. I don't believe I've had the pleasure." She held her hand out to him, waiting for him to press the scandalously ungloved skin to his mouth. "Cassandra St. James."

"Beautiful name," he said as he kissed her warm hand.

"And do you have one?" she asked. "A name, that is?"

"I do. Walk with me." It was not a request. Though Spencer sensed Cassandra was not a woman who took orders lightly, her curiosity got the better of her, so she took his arm and together they stepped out of the ballroom.

Max said nothing more and instead turned his attention to pouring them each a glass of brandy. He handed Sabine the amber-colored liquid, then downed his own glass. "At the moment, I'd like to find those ancestors of yours and throttle them. Damned riddles and clues and dead ends," he muttered.

"Agreed. There has to be another way to stop the Chosen One than to traipse all over the country breaking into people's homes and digging up graves."

He poured himself another splash, then turned to find Sabine staring at him.

She boldly made her way over to him, took the drink out of his hand, and set it on the occasional table behind him. He said nothing, merely kept his eyes on hers, as she made quick work of the buttons on his shirt.

"You told me not to start something I didn't want to finish. Well, I'm starting something," she said.

He didn't wait for more of an invitation. His hand wrapped around her waist and pulled her tight against him, then he swept his mouth across hers.

While they kissed, she ran her hands over his torso, tracing every muscle and hair with exquisite torture. He could not lose control, he reminded himself. Tonight he would slowly indulge her every need.

"Sabine," Max said, his voice ragged with his own need.

"I merely need to forget," she whispered. "If only for a short while."

The dead end they'd come to on the quest was wearing on her. She'd been through quite an ordeal over the last several days, and her life had been threatened repeatedly. She deserved to forget for a moment that danger still lurked around the next corner.

He moved to stand behind her, and while she held her hair out of the way, he unbuttoned her dress. Though there were only twelve buttons, he took his time, kissing each new portion of skin as it was revealed. Then he slowly slid the bodice off her shoulders and down her arms.

He stopped at her wrists, imprisoning her arms at her sides. He nibbled at her neck and the tops of her shoulders. Her soft moans drove him wild, and he wanted nothing more than to bend her over and take her hard and fast. But she deserved slow and patient and he wanted to give her that.

His hands went around and cupped her breasts over the thin fabric of her shift. Her nipples immediately hardened at his touch, and they pressed against the cotton material. She rubbed against his palms. He caressed her breasts while he feathered hot kisses across her neck. Her desire was palpable. Her breath came faster until she exhaled in a soft gasp.

She leaned her head back on his shoulder, an act so simple but so full of trust that it nearly knocked him over. He released her arms, and immediately she reached behind her and ran her hands across his thighs. He pressed his erection against her, loving the feel of her curvaceous backside.

He swept a hand softly down the side of her face. With as much tenderness as he could manage, he leaned in and pressed a kiss to her cheek, then found her mouth again. Raw need mingled with curiosity as he deepened the kiss. He needed her tonight as much as she evidently needed him.

With one swift movement, he pulled the shift over her head, then removed the rest of her undergarments until she stood before him completely nude save for her stockings and shoes. The sight of her long legs encased in those sheer stockings nearly sent him over the edge.

"So perfect," he said as he grazed her right breast with his thumb. He cupped her, and she closed her eyes against the sensation. He went down on one knee and pressed kisses to her breast. His tongue flicked against her nipple, then he suckled it into his mouth.

"Max, please," she said. Her fingers knotted in his hair.

"Do you want me?" He stood as he asked the question and looked directly into her eyes.

She swallowed, but her brown eyes never wavered. "Yes."

"Say it." For reasons he did not understand, nor wanted to, he needed to hear it from her.

"I want you."

"Again," he insisted. He closed his eyes and listened to her soft, sultry voice.

"I want you, Max."

He moved past her then and yanked back the coverlet on his bed. The creamy sheets looked welcoming and soft as they always did. But tonight was not a night for sleeping. Tonight was a night for loving.

She had been with other men, she'd all but admitted that. And it didn't matter to him. Tonight he would make her forget that any other man had ever touched her. After this, she would remember only his hands, his mouth, his body.

Deftly he removed his own clothes, then walked toward her. She stood still beside the bed, and gently he picked her up and set her on the mattress. He slid a hand up her right thigh and she sucked in a sharp breath. But he stopped at the top of her stocking and rolled it down her leg, knocking off her shoe, then peeling the stocking off. Then he did the same with her other leg.

The hair between her legs glistened with her desire for him. He nibbled at her inner thigh, laving kisses on her warm flesh. Then he covered her center with his mouth. She was hot and wet, and her musky scent drove him wild. Her fingers threaded through his hair, her nails scraping over his scalp.

He dipped his tongue in, and she bucked against him. He grabbed her hips to keep her still as he licked and suckled her folds. That sensitive little nub got most of his attention, and Sabine's fitful cries let him know her release was near.

And then she climaxed. She cried out his name again and again as she shook beneath him. Her hands fell away from his head, and she lay there completely spent. But he was not done with her.

He crawled up beside her and kissed each breast and then her collarbone.

Still her breathing was labored, but she was smiling.

"Touch me," he whispered. Then he moved her hand downward until her fingers brushed against him.

She encircled him with her hand. While she explored his body, his hand ran down her stomach to the apex of her thighs. He cupped her, threading his fingers through her hair until he found that sensitive nub. He slid one finger across her opening, and she spread her legs farther, inviting him to touch her more.

Gooseflesh spread over her body, her nipples growing larger. She gripped him tightly, and he tossed his head back with a groan. She moved even closer to him.

"Now," he said firmly. He placed himself on top of her, her body plush and warm beneath him.

He intertwined his fingers with her own, pressing her arms to the bed as he slowly entered her. Her knees came up, and she wrapped her legs around his back, clasping her feet and pulling him even deeper inside. Still he held her down and moved in and out, grinding against her.

Her nails dug into his back, and her breathing became tighter and shorter. Her release was very near. She teetered right on the edge, so he moved deeper and deeper and increased his speed.

Her body rocked with pleasure.

His own release wasn't too far behind. His abdomen tightened as wave after wave shot through him. Then he collapsed on top of her.

They lay in comfortable silence for several moments, and for the first time in so very long, Sabine actually felt at peace. A sharp contrast to the realities around her—the prophecy, the quest, the Chosen One. Yet in this moment, lying in Max's arms, it seemed as if all would be well. She knew it was the worst sort of deception, the kind you weave yourself. It was what her mother had done, ignoring the truth around her, and in the end she'd paid the ultimate price.

She snuggled deeper into his side, knowing tomorrow would be a different day, and this intimacy they were enjoying would be shattered. She could not have a lover, especially not someone who stirred her soul so. She could easily fall in love with Max, and that terrified her because she knew love, in the end, only brought pain. The thought seemed to paralyze her heart, and for a fleeting second, she would have sworn it stopped beating.

"Why have you not married?" she asked him. She needed conversation to empty her head of those thoughts.

"I am not the marrying sort," he said.

"So you've settled yourself on being a bachelor?"

"Something like that."

She absently ran her fingers against the hairs curling across his torso. "But what of your duty to produce an heir?" she asked. "Without an heir, your name will die out."

"There are enough bastards, legitimate and otherwise, in the world without me adding to them." He shrugged. "If the name dies out, so be it. There's nothing inherently magical or important about my family name."

"What if your own family had had that attitude? Then you would not exist. Shouldn't that count for something?" She could not understand a man who could so passionately commit to his quest for Atlantis, yet felt no pull of familial duty. Her entire life was about familial obligation; it was all she knew. How could she be drawn to a man who was so foreign to everything she understood?

"It should, but it doesn't." He rolled over to face her, and his expression was stern, all lines and contours, but he placed his hand on her hip and his touch was gentle. "My parents got married young and successfully had three children right away. One girl after another. Not exactly what a marquess wants for his family name, but at least my sisters presented opportunities to marry well and bring more money and prestige to the family."

Sabine said nothing, simply allowed him to talk and rub his hand down her hip. When he wasn't using his charming façade, there was a man beneath—a man with emotions and scars, and in this moment she was getting a glimpse. Like a hunter in a deer's path, she didn't dare move and risk spooking him.

"Five years after my last sister was born, my brother came along. Finally the heir," he said with much formality. "The family was complete." His eyes darkened, and his hand on her hip stilled. "Then another three years, and it was my turn. The leftover child—they already had their heir—and I would never bring them money as my sisters would, instead I would cost them. They had to send me to school. Pay for me to marry."

He said nothing more for several moments. So she ventured, "You once told me you were alone, that you had no family. What happened to all of them?"

"Our family estate in Devonshire was destroyed in a fire. It was at night, while everyone slept. They were all inside," he said.

"And where were you?" she asked.

"I was off digging in a cave looking for an ancient map." He smiled ruefully. "I was trying to do something, anything that would garner their attention..." His voice trailed off.

"How old were you?" she asked quietly.

"Seventeen. We lost everything." He laughed, though his chuckle held no humor. "All but that singed spear I keep in my office. Everything else I have, I built."

A boy, not yet quite a man, and he had come home with such hopes only to discover his entire family had perished.

On top of that, he'd inherited a title and duties he'd never asked for. But instead of forging ahead and embracing his duties, he'd gone in the opposite direction—tried to sever all ties he had with anyone so that child he'd been would never again experience pain and loss.

She knew a little about that sort of thing.

Chapter Nineteen

He hadn't told many people that story before and knew he had probably revealed more than he had wanted. Yet he'd felt compelled to share it with her. So often he smiled or quipped and shifted the subject away from the uncomfortable parts of his life. But she'd asked as if she truly cared, as if she'd wanted to know the man he was beneath the legend hunter.

She looked up as if she had an additional question.

He might not regret sharing what he'd just told her, but he was done opening old wounds for the evening. Sabine had her own secrets that she still had yet to reveal to him. She hadn't trusted him, not truly. Damned if that didn't infuriate him.

"Your mother was a guardian," Max said before she could speak.

She sat, clutching the sheet to her chest and looking at him, her expression one of great surprise. "How did you—"

"Those letters we found in Phinneas's house. I've been

reading through all of them. I've found the letters from Phinneas the most helpful, but a few of Agnes's were useful, too," he said.

She frowned. "But those were simply love letters," she said softly. "I've read through most of them, and while I found their love story intriguing, there was nothing helpful. And I don't recall seeing anything that stated that my mother was a guardian."

He propped himself on one elbow. "True, but they spoke of other things. Hidden within the letters. I discovered their code. In more than one, your aunt mentions her eldest sister and how the village was scandalized when she was revealed as the guardian."

"The first female guardian my people had ever had," Sabine said, obviously resigned to no longer denying the truth.

"At first, I thought she meant Lydia, but in another letter she used her name," he said.

"Isadora," Sabine supplied. "What code?" She frowned. "Agnes mentioned nothing of a secret code. I read them only as love letters."

"Oh, they are love letters," he said. "But I'm coming to realize that when it comes to Atlantis, things are not always what they appear. There was more, plainly hidden."

"She didn't tell me," Sabine said again.

"She was probably trying to protect you. She knew I'd be reading them." He tucked a stray curl behind her ear. "Your mother, what happened to her?"

"She was weak and an utter fool." There was no denying Sabine's anger in those short words. "She did not take her duties as guardian seriously. It is the guardians' duty to pass on their ways to their successors. In my mother's case, that was me, her only child. Historically the guardianship passed through the bloodlines, even though there is a ceremony to name a new one. When her father died, the people in our village begged the elders to change the ceremony. Never before had a woman been named guardian. But she came forward and pled her case, promised to fulfill her duties just as a man would, and the ceremony confirmed her.

"And initially she did just as she'd vowed. She married, they had me, and she was as good a Healer as our village had seen. She trained me every day, too. And then my father fell ill." She shook her head. "It changed everything. My mother adored my father, they adored each other, and his illness rocked her to her core. She prepared his treatment, but she did something wrong, something horribly wrong. Within a day, he was gone. Not even a year later, she had died, too. I was thirteen."

Her tone was etched with bitterness and anger and spoke of the hurt child she'd once been. He was almost sorry he'd pressed the issue. But he'd shared truths about his family he'd never told anyone else. And so far Sabine hadn't stood to leave. "How did she die?" he ventured.

"A guardian must consume a small portion of the elixir every day. It is part of a guardian's duty and strengthens the connection with the elixir, with our homeland." Sabine shook her head. She was no longer looking at him. Instead she stared at the sheet wrapped around her. "She just stopped. Wouldn't take a drop. Eventually her body succumbed, and she died."

"And you've been with your aunts ever since?"

"Yes. They were there all along, trying to assist my mother when things started to go badly, but she was intent on destroying herself."

"What about other people? Can they directly ingest the elixir? Or can it only be used on injuries?"

"It's far too dangerous for others to consume except in extremely small quantities, and only in dire emergencies. It is very dangerous." She paused for a moment. "Our people are careful with the elixir. We don't want history to repeat itself."

He'd have to be certain to give Marcus all of these warnings when he brought the sample to him for testing. Marcus would respect the boundaries, but Max wouldn't want word to get out about the elixir. That kind of power would be too tempting to resist for any number of criminals.

Max was quiet, thinking of all she had said and about how they both had lost their families at a young age. He could understand the anger she had for her mother. Sabine still viewed her mother's death through a child's eyes. Grief could distort reality. But so much of what she'd said tonight and the last few days came together for him. She never said "us" or "I," instead she always used "they" as if she were not part of the guardians.

"You told me you were the third guardian," he said softly.

Sabine pulled the sheet up to her chin, but said nothing. Nevertheless, he could see the truth in her expression. The moment of surprise before she carefully capped her emotions. He'd guessed correctly.

Still she was reluctant. "Your cards are showing," he chided her. "You've lost the hand. Why won't you simply tell me the truth? You owe me that much."

"Why?" Her amber-colored eyes sparked with indignation. "Why do I owe you anything?"

Her words stung. How could she ask such a thing? After all they'd been through together. After he'd taken her to bed. Not once, but several times. And here she was, treating him as nothing more than hired help.

He shook his head in frustration. "Without me, you wouldn't have had access to the full prophecy. Not to mention, I've offered protection to you and your aunts. And I've assisted you in deciphering the clues." He raked his fingers through his hair.

"Of course. I didn't mean to seem ungrateful," she said.

"This isn't about gratitude." He propelled himself from the bed, reaching for the pants he'd discarded on the floor in his earlier passion. "You don't trust me. And you never have."

"It's not that," she said.

"Yes, actually it is," he said, knowing his anger was evident in his tone. But he didn't care. Yes, he was angry. He'd done everything right to deserve her trust, yet she had lied to him.

He shoved his feet into the legs of his pants. He shouldn't even give a damn about her bloody secret. She was a pastime, nothing more. He wouldn't make the mistake of forgetting that again.

No, he didn't want harm to come to her, but that didn't mean that he would forsake his own ambitions simply because of a secret she wanted to keep.

"Just tell me the truth, Sabine. I already know, but I want to hear you say it." His voice sounded weary to his own ears. Earlier, he'd been ready to take her again, his body heavy with desire. But now ice ran through his veins, cooling his need.

Why did he care so much whether she was honest with him?

He simply could not abide dishonesty. That's all it was.

He needed all the facts when he was in the middle of a situation.

"No," she said fiercely. "Does that make you happy? I am not the guardian."

"It's Agnes, isn't it?" he asked.

She took a shaky breath, then nodded.

"But what of your being your mother's heir? Shouldn't you have been the next in line?" he asked.

"Yes, but the ceremony named Agnes as guardian."

"You were a child at the time."

"That wouldn't matter. Some had been named guardian at even younger ages. The fact of the matter was that I was not chosen. Whether that's because of my mother's failure or some deficiency in me, I do not know. I only know that I was not worthy to bear the duties of the guardian."

He disagreed with her, but he understood why she would believe it. He'd inherited a title he'd no right to claim. His brother, Phillip, had been heir. But he had died, they'd all died, and now Max was the marquess, whereas Sabine had been the rightful heir, yet she'd been stripped of that honor.

"Why is it then that you wear that vial of elixir?" he asked.

"Agnes gave it to me several months ago. I think they're trying to train me, trying to prepare me so when the time comes around for the next guardian, perhaps I'll be chosen. They're fooling themselves, but I hate to disappoint them," she said softly. "So I wear it."

Something in his chest caught, but he shoved it away. He didn't have tender feelings. Not anymore. Despite that, Max couldn't help but feel some measure of relief that the Chosen One wouldn't be after her.

Still, it was important for him to know the truth. He sat

back down on the edge of the bed. "I need the truth if I am to protect you and your aunts," he said.

"You can be angry with me for withholding it from you, but it's not as if you trust me either, Max." She scooted farther away from him, making her way to the edge of the bed. "You haven't exactly been forthcoming with your motives. You can't possibly be helping me simply out of the goodness of your heart, or merely because you're a patriot. You're a scholar of Atlantis, and simply by offering your assistance, you have four Atlanteans currently residing under your roof. Rather convenient, don't you think?"

She was right. There was something he wanted, and it was in his house right now. She was in possession of the very thing he sought. The one thing that would prove the existence of Atlantis. The elixir. He knew he couldn't take Agnes's away from her because she would die. But he could take Sabine's necklace.

She climbed out of the bed with her back to him and bent to retrieve her clothes. Quickly she pulled on her shift. She turned to face him, her shoes bundled in her arms. "Is that the only reason you wanted to know the truth?" she whispered. "Because of the prophecy?"

He eyed her for a moment, searching her face for something she wasn't saying. For any hint of what she wanted from him. What did she expect? "What else would there be?"

He all but held his breath, waiting for her answer.

She seemed to be searching his face as thoroughly as he'd searched hers. Whatever answers she found there must have offered no consolation.

"Nothing else," she said tersely. "You're right, there's nothing else." She turned to go.

"Sabine?"

She faced him.

"Tomorrow we'll finish this bloody quest. We'll find the dove."

She nodded but said nothing as she slipped out of his room.

The only thing that stood in the way of his proving the existence of Atlantis was Sabine. But in order to do that, he would have to betray her. He knew that. That was what had given him pause. Normally she wore the necklace, but lately she'd taken to carrying it in her bag.

She'd trust him now. She had no other options now that he held their secrets. He'd pushed and pushed until she'd had no choice but to tell him everything. And eventually, he'd have to betray that trust.

He was a bastard.

Sabine and her aunts sat eating breakfast together the following morning, and across the table, Max sat quietly reading the newspaper while sipping his tea. Aside from wishing them all a good morning, he hadn't said another word.

There was nothing further to discuss, she reminded herself. Still, their argument from last night lingered in the room like stale perfume. But more than the fight, she thought of the way he'd touched her, so gentle yet so full of passion. The way he'd said her name and whispered in the dark. The feel of him inside her, his skin pressed against hers.

His icy blue gaze looked up and locked on hers. He'd caught her watching him. Those intense azure eyes of his pierced through her.

She took a bite of her bread, not even tasting the melted

butter, but she wanted something to do other than stare at Max.

"Sabine, what did you do last night?" Lydia asked.

Sabine nearly choked on her food. She coughed and took a sip of tea.

Max set his newspaper down. "We went to the King's Library. Found yet another riddle to be solved," he said.

"Indeed," Agnes said. "And have you solved it?"

"Nearly," Max said.

Sabine recovered enough to speak. "The riddle told us we needed to look at what was right in front of us. Something like that." She glanced at Max. "Perhaps we need to go back to the library, stand near the tablet, and see what it could possibly mean."

"To see what was right before you?" Agnes asked.

"Something similar," Max said. "The library." He frowned. "No, that won't work."

"Of course not," Sabine said as realization hit her. "That tablet was found elsewhere. Foolish." She shook her head.

"This riddle business isn't easy," Calliope soothed. "It is more a job for the Seer," she said, then her eyes widened as she remembered Max sat at the table.

Sabine shook her head. "It matters not, he knows everything," she said.

Lydia's expression tightened. Sabine knew her eldest aunt was angry, but that could not be helped. The truth was, Max had assisted them, saved them really, and kept them protected. She owed him much. They all did.

"Only two more days until your birthday," Agnes said.

They were running out of time.

"During the Crusades. That's when the tablet was

discovered on the Isle of Rhodes," Max said, redirecting the conversation back to the clue. He stood. "And I can think of only one other important piece that was found right there with it." He flashed Sabine a smile. "Achilles' sword."

The huge manor sat prominently in Hyde Park. With a recent façade of Bath stone, the three-storied house was grand and ostentatious.

"Who lives here?" Sabine whispered to Max. She held up her skirts as they climbed the stairs to the large estate. Earlier that day, Max had come home with a gown for her to wear to this ball, a stunning dress he'd selected just for her. It was a startling bright blue silk accented with darker blue velvet trim, and cut perfectly for her frame.

"The late Duke of Camden. Now his widow primarily resides here," Max said. "I should warn you"—Max leaned close to her ear—"this isn't your ordinary ball."

She wasn't certain what he meant because she'd never been to any ball before. It was on her tongue to ask, but they, along with several other guests, were met at the front door by a footman. "The Marquess of Lindberg and guest," Max said to the man, who then announced their entrance to the entire crowd. The entryway was enormous, and the ceiling seemed to reach into the heavens. Candles and petite roses surrounded the area.

"Maxwell, what a surprise. I did not realize you were planning to attend." It was a woman, middle-aged, with a thick head of red hair piled on top in a crown of curls. Her low-plunging gown revealed a more-than-ample bosom, and sitting right at the top of that deep crevice was a huge pink diamond necklace.

Max bent over her hand in an unexpected display of

gallantry. "My response must have gotten lost in the post," Max said with a wicked grin.

"Indeed," the woman remarked, her own smile full of wit and charm.

"Might I introduce you to Miss Sabine Tobias," Max said. "She and her aunts are relatively new to London, and we've recently become acquainted." Innuendo seemed to linger with his last word. Then he turned to Sabine. "The Duchess of Camden."

Sabine thought to correct him and further explain their relationship, but how many people would find it less offensive (if not unbelievable) for them to be embroiled in an ancient prophecy rather than a common liaison? So she said nothing other than to exchange pleasantries with the duchess.

"Welcome. Come in and enjoy yourselves," the woman said. Then she turned to greet other guests.

As Max led Sabine off, he pulled her close to his side. "Her late husband was an avid antiquities collector. He bragged often about securing Achilles' sword. Now we only have to locate it."

They walked arm in arm through the foyer. Halfway to the ballroom, they'd already passed two swords on display, hanging high on the walls. "How will we know which one it is?" Sabine asked.

Max nodded to a couple as they passed by, but waited until they were out of earshot before answering. "It is rumored to be rather large and ornate. Forged by the gods, they say," Max said with a smile.

"Yes, of course." She shouldn't snicker. Didn't she believe that the elixir she protected had been somehow handed to the Atlanteans by Poseidon himself? In actuality, she hadn't ever given it much thought.

The ballroom was empty, not of people, but of any weaponry. That was probably a good thing, considering how much champagne was floating about. It would be most disastrous if two gentlemen were to be angered by each other; having weapons handy could have dastardly results.

"Did you want to dance before we look elsewhere?" Max asked.

His simple and probably not-altogether-serious request gave her pause, causing her heart to flutter. She wasn't certain she knew how to dance, at least not the way that proper English Society preferred. But now was not the time to indulge such frivolities. They had a task at hand, and the clock was ticking.

"No, thank you," she said.

They made their way to the second floor. The landing balcony overlooked the ballroom below. Couples moved together, swaying rhythmically to each pulse of the music. The band played a waltz, and the dancers held each other close, but more than a few openly caressed their partners or nibbled on a neck or an earlobe. She was quite thankful she had declined Max's offer to dance.

This was a slightly different crowd of London Society than those who'd shopped at her store. They were a little older, not necessarily in age, but in experience—perhaps wiser or more worldly would have been a more appropriate description. The women moved their bodies sensually as if they were used to lovers watching their every move. There were no shy virgins among them.

Likewise the men openly viewed their women, not in sly glances, but in brazen appraisals. This was a different London than the one she'd seen. Max had warned her, but still it was surprising to watch. Everything she'd seen and heard about Society indicated that they valued propriety above all other things.

"Sabine," Max whispered from behind her. His muscular body was but a breath away from her own. It wouldn't even take a full step for her to walk back into his arms.

"Sorry, I..." But she stopped. What could she say? That she was caught by the sexual air thrumming through the party? That already she felt awareness flit through her body, so that her very nerves seemed to sit on the surface of her skin?

"It's a lovers' party." His voice brushed past her ear.

She whipped around. "What?"

He chuckled lightly. "I don't suppose that is the official name, but that is what this is." He ran his hand down her arm. "Ever since the duchess was widowed, she's indulged in a rather unorthodox life."

"So now everyone here believes we are lovers?" Sabine said.

"Absolutely." He did little to hide the smile that pulled at the corners of his mouth.

"Splendid." But they were. And did she truly care what any of these people thought of her? No, she didn't. But she felt as if she should be incensed. Being here on Max's arm filled her with pride rather than embarrassment. "You're enjoying this, aren't you?" she asked.

He forced a frown. "Not even a little bit."

"Shall we find that sword?" She grabbed his hand and pulled him forward.

"Of course."

They found a study with other collectibles, mostly vases and other pieces of pottery, but no weapons at all. The rest of the second floor was more of the same, but nothing that resembled a sword and no sign of the dove.

"You didn't seem to mind playing the part of my lover at the King's Library," Max said. "You scandalized that poor man."

At first, she'd thought he would mention last night. She'd been brazen, an utter wanton, and she didn't want to examine why. She told herself it was because she was weary, exhausted from their futile search for the dove. But there were other reasons. She'd come to rely on Max, and last night when she'd so desperately needed comfort, she'd fallen into his arms.

But he'd mentioned the library. "I was merely trying to prevent you from being arrested. If that man had cried foul, you would have been in serious trouble, handling the tablet that way," she said. "It was a role I played. Nothing more."

He stopped in his tracks and eyed her. She searched his face for meaning behind his odd expression, but he gave her none.

"Merely a role." He said. "Onward to the next floor."

She nodded.

Up the staircase to the third story they climbed. They passed a couple in a passionate embrace at the end of one darkened hallway. The man had his lover pushed up against a small table, her legs wrapped around his waist.

Sabine and Max kept walking. One by one, they checked the doors until finally they stepped into a grand bedchamber. Large and elegantly decorated, it had to be the late duke's personal room. Hanging above the bed was a grand sword. Gold from hilt to tip, it was elegantly carved, and as Max had predicted, quite large.

"That's it," Sabine whispered. At last, they had found the dove. After traipsing across the whole of England, they had found their reward.

In one swift movement, Max had climbed atop the bed. He held his hand out to her. "Here."

She placed her hand in his, and he pulled her to stand next to him on the plush mattress. Max kept hold of her hand as he led her to the headboard.

The gold of the blade shimmered in the candlelight. The brackets holding the sword in place locked the treasure to the wall. It was going to be slightly more challenging than simply sneaking it out of the house. They'd first have to figure out how to remove it from its mounting.

Max tugged at the bracket, running his hand along the metal, looking for a catch. "Interesting. I can't find any kind of lock mechanism." He looked around the room. "I think I'm going to need something to break those off."

He jumped off the bed, then reached up to pull her down. She braced her hands on his shoulders as he brought her down to the floor. His movement was slow and intentional, placing her strategically between his arms, pressed against his chest.

With one wicked grin, he leaned in and captured her mouth. His kiss was hot and needy.

But she pushed against him. "Max, we shouldn't," she said.

"I never have paid much attention to what one ought or ought not to do," he said.

She considered him a moment longer, knowing that more than anything she wanted to press herself against him and lose herself in his kisses and caresses. But she could not do that. Making love to Max didn't change anything about the prophecy. And it didn't make her forget anything. Quite the contrary, it flooded her mind and heart with dreams and wishes for so much more. Family and love, he could not and would not offer her. He'd said as much last night.

"The fire poker," he said.

"Will that work to pry the brackets off?"

He nodded, but said nothing as he went to retrieve the poker. Again he climbed onto the bed, this time armed to remove the brackets. It took several tries, but he was able to pop one of the brackets off the wall. There were four others. Max had placed the poker into the second one when they heard fumbling at the door. The knob turned.

"Hide," Max said.

Chapter Twenty

$\sim\!\!\sim\!\!\sim$

Max jumped off the bed and raced toward Sabine and the door she'd opened. He barely made it into the over-sized dressing closet and closed the door behind them before the other people entered the bedchamber.

Max leaned against the closed door with a heavy sigh and set the poker down. A gentleman's voice, followed by a woman's throaty giggles, filled the room and echoed into Max and Sabine's hiding spot.

He cracked the closet door to peek out into the room. The woman pushed the man onto the bed with a lusty laugh, then proceeded to push down her bodice to uncover her ample breasts. Max pressed the door closed. This would be interesting.

"Who is it?" Sabine whispered.

"Just a man and a woman."

"What do they want?"

"Each other," he said simply.

Recognition lit Sabine's molten eyes and her features softened. "Oh," she said soundlessly.

As if punctuating his meaning, sounds of passion began seeping through the door. Sabine's lips parted, and color stained her lovely neck. Blood surged through Max, intensifying his arousal.

"Oh, yes!" the woman yelled. Another moan, and then several trills of laughter. "You're so naughty," she said, then giggled again.

Moments before, Sabine had been in Max's arms, kissing him back. And though he knew she desired him, she'd pulled back. Their work was nearly done. He'd helped her find the dove, and it was only a matter of time before they were able to stop this Chosen One. She wouldn't need him anymore after that. And hadn't she just said it was a role she had played, his seductress?

With other women, he had always been the one to slip from the bed after a night of passion. Last night had been different, though. And it had stung when she'd closed the door behind her. True, they had argued, and he'd been angry. Still, she had just walked away.

Damn but he wanted her again. And it didn't help that the noises of the other couple's lovemaking were growing louder and more pronounced. The wooden headboard slammed against the wall in rhythmic beats. The man grunted, and the woman continued with her chorus of "yeses."

Sabine had closed her eyes. Max didn't know if it was to try to remove herself from the potentially embarrassing situation or if she was attempting to listen, closing out everything else to focus on the amorous noises just beyond the door. Perhaps she was aroused as well, standing there wondering when he would reach out and touch her, kiss her.

He stepped closer to her, and still she did not open her

eyes. The woman in the bedchamber released a throaty moan and Sabine's breath caught. *Bloody hell!* She *was* listening to every sinful moan. Her lips parted, and her tongue darted out, moistening her bottom lip, then she bit down. A sensual flush spread across the flesh exposed at Sabine's throat, and the appealing blush disappeared beneath her gown.

She looked lovely tonight, wearing the blue gown he'd bought her. He'd known it would look perfect on her.

The pounding of the headboard became faster; the man's grunts more steady. Max's erection pressed painfully against his trousers. Sabine still stood completely still, though her fists had gathered fabric from her skirts.

He had to have her. Right now.

He swiftly pulled Sabine to him and slammed his mouth onto hers. Her breath caught in surprise, but she kissed him back. Fervently, passionately. She snaked her hands up his neck, and her fingers slid into his hair, pulling him down to her. Harder, firmer. She wanted him.

Again the woman outside moaned louder and louder, this time releasing a litany of curses as the bed groaned in rhythm with their thrusting. Max reached into Sabine's bodice and found her nipples already hardened for him. She moaned into his mouth. He pushed the dress down as far as he could and freed her breasts. Slowly he laved kisses down her throat to her collarbone and finally onto her breast, where he suckled her nipple hard in his mouth.

He slipped his free hand up under her skirts, feeling along her long, shapely leg until he found the slit in her drawers. She was slick with desire for him, the surrounding fabric saturated with her need. He nearly went mad with want. She sucked in her breath sharply as his finger entered her. She bucked against him as he slid his finger in and out. With his other hand, he unfastened his own pants and freed himself.

In one swift movement, he bunched her skirts up, then pressed himself into her. She wrapped her legs around him and her fingernails bit into his back through his jacket and shirt. She was up against the wall, wrapped tightly around him. And he took her with no mercy.

There was no control, no patience, only want and need as he thrust into her. But she met him with a passion that was only Sabine. He felt her climax around him as she tossed back her head and cried out. His own release was not even a moment behind hers and rocked through him so fast and so hard he nearly fell to his knees. But he kept his stance and kept her bundled around him.

For a moment they stayed like that, holding on to each other, breathing hard. Then she slowly lowered her legs to stand on her own. They'd given no thought to being discovered. But he doubted a couple making love in the closet would even raise an eyebrow at this party.

All he could think of was that he'd never lost control with a woman before. Never. Not even his first time; he'd always been able to keep his need at bay. It was easy to pretend he did so because he was a generous, patient lover. But that was a lie. He focused on a woman's needs because it made it easier to keep his heart detached. But not tonight. Tonight he'd forgotten everything except how much he wanted her. Sabine. Only Sabine.

Sabine cracked the door to peer out into the bedchamber. "I think they're gone," she whispered.

He saw her reticule tossed aside on the floor and picked it up. He'd nearly handed it to her when he remembered what he'd once seen her pull from within. Quickly he stuck his hand inside the bag and felt around. It didn't take long for his fingers to brush against the glass vial. He snagged it, then dropped it into his pocket.

"Sabine, don't forget your bag." He held it out to her.

Quickly they finished removing the sword, and it took all of Max's strength to lift it from its anchors. Sneaking out of the party with a blade nearly as long as Max's leg was tricky, but they managed to get back to their carriage without being seen.

Finally, they had the dove.

Only two more and then the military would finally be his. Tonight's would be the most challenging. This man Spencer knew. Some of the others had recognized him because of his position, but had not truly known him. This man, though, was actually a friend. Well, as much as he was able to call any man friend.

He had been in this house many times before, so breaking in and making his way through the house had been simple. He'd made certain that none of his friend's servants had seen him enter the man's study. For the last two hours, Spencer had waited quietly in the dark, sipping on some borrowed and rather expensive port.

The room had been wired with electricity, something the man could afford with his family's wealth and the additional commendations from her majesty. And the power crackled as the man turned on the switch. It took a moment for the light to fully illuminate the space, and still Spencer waited in the shadows, waited until the man walked completely into the room and closed the door behind him.

He was the perfect soldier, Spencer lamented. It really was a shame he could not afford to keep the man around.

But Spencer knew this man in particular would not accept any such offer. His loyalty to the crown could not be tempted or purchased. So Spencer had no choice but to kill him.

The soldier stepped forward to his desk just as Spencer stepped out of the shadows. "Spencer," the soldier said with great surprise. "Did we have a meeting set?"

"No." He paused, waiting for fear to cross the man's face. There was only caution in those slightly elevated eyebrows. "I wanted to discuss something with you. A proposition." He knew the fear would come eventually.

The soldier nodded. "Have a seat." Then he smiled. "I see you already helped yourself to the port."

"Indeed." Spencer allowed himself a slight chuckle. "I hope you don't mind." He enjoyed the pleasantries, knowing that in moments he'd watch as the man breathed his last.

Max stood at his study window watching Johns on the next block over, leaning against a brick building and trying to look in a different direction. He'd seen the same man following them on several other occasions, and now he realized how he knew him. It was the same man whom Max had caught Cassandra in bed with those many years ago. Her man Johns—not a man of title and wealth, but one who definitely turned the heads of the ladies with both his face and his body. Cassandra would never choose him in public, but in private he was, or had been, her lover.

Now Johns was evidently doing other tasks for Cassandra, namely following Max and Sabine as they searched for the dove. The man would make a wretched spy. For one, he stood out too much. He was at least a head taller than everyone else around him and broader than most men.

What interest would Cassandra have in an ancient weapon? Unless, of course, that's not what she was after. Surely it wasn't jealousy of Sabine. He hadn't had a relationship with Cassandra in more than a decade.

No, it had to be something else.

Then Max remembered Sabine's crème that was selling so quickly and how he'd seen Cassandra in her shop that first time purchasing some. She'd always been vain; anyone who knew her could see that. He'd been twenty-two when they'd been lovers and still devoted to his Atlantis research. He vaguely recollected speaking with her about Atlantis. Perhaps he had told her about the fountain of youth.

But was it possible that Cassandra had something to do with the deaths of the military officers? Johns was definitely strong enough to take those men down. What purpose would Cassandra have for such deeds?

Had she somehow found a copy of the prophecy and sought to play it out in hopes of gaining the elixir? Max doubted she was clever enough to come up with that sort of plan. But it would explain how the officers had been reached so easily. Any man would allow Cassandra a visit if she asked for one.

Perhaps it was time for Max to pay a visit to his former mistress and see what information she had for him.

Cassandra was tired of waiting for proof. She had also lost her patience with relying on others to do the job she'd hired them to do, and then never completing the task. It was past time she saw to matters herself and went after the fountain. She knew that woman, Sabine, had it. Soon Cassandra would possess it and all the magic it held.

Cassandra opened the shop door, and the bell jingled above her head.

"I'm sorry, we're closing now," came a voice from the back.

Cassandra ignored it and continued into the shop.

An older woman peeked around the corner. "I'm sorry, madam, but we are closed for the evening. We'll reopen again tomorrow."

Doing what she did best, Cassandra gave the woman her warmest smile. "I'm a friend of Sabine's. I've only come for a brief discussion."

"A friend of Sabine's?" the older woman repeated. She nodded, but did not look convinced. "I'll let her know you're here."

"I'm not expecting anyone, Calliope," Sabine said as she walked around the curtain to the front of the store. Her eyes lit on Cassandra. "Oh, Madam St. James, how unexpected of you to drop by. Did you not receive the shipment I sent to your house?" The woman never missed a beat. She kept her smile in place and her tone friendly as she would for any customer, but Cassandra could see congeniality never made it to Sabine's eyes.

"I did," Cassandra said. "Why don't the two of us skip the pleasantries. I can certainly tell you don't like me any more than I like you."

"Very well," Sabine said. "What do you want?"

"I want the fountain of youth." She smiled and held a hand up to stop Sabine from denying anything. "Don't pretend you don't know what I'm talking about. It's your secret ingredient for your facial crème, is it not?"

"You hired the chemist," Sabine said.

Cassandra shook her head. "Worthless man. He actually had the audacity to threaten me."

"And you killed him," Sabine said.

"He might not have figured anything out, but I'm no fool. I know you have it. And I want it." She punctuated the last sentence by pulling out her pistol and aiming it at Sabine.

Sabine visibly swallowed, but showed no other sign of fear. "I see," she said slowly.

"What did she want?" Calliope asked as she stepped around the drape, then stopped short when she saw the gun. "Oh, dear."

"Calliope," Sabine hissed. "Why did you not stay behind there?"

"It matters not," Cassandra announced. "We're all going back together. Come along, ladies, nice and slowly."

Together Sabine and the old woman walked into the storeroom, with Cassandra close behind. She couldn't help but notice Sabine's dress and her worn shoes. The woman was beautiful, Cassandra could tell that much, but her apparel did nothing to aid in her appearance. She also did not wear her hair in the appropriate manner. Instead of wearing her hair up as most women of good breeding did, she allowed her mahogany-colored locks to fall down her back in a cascade of waves. Highly improper. While her dress was not at the height of fashion, the green material fit the woman well, accenting her lush curves.

"I would think you would earn enough coin here to buy yourself some decent shoes and dresses," she said disdainfully.

Sabine looked down at her feet. "I'm far too busy helping those with unfortunate complexions to go shopping."

"You've got a cheeky mouth on you," Cassandra snapped. "It's not very becoming."

"Have you come to give me lessons then? On how to be a courtesan?" Sabine asked.

The old woman swallowed a giggle, which infuriated Cassandra even more. "Shut up." She glared at Calliope, then turned back to Sabine. "Are you having trouble satisfying Max in bed? Or perhaps you can't lure him between the sheets at all." She smiled. "I suppose I could pass along a few tips."

Sabine's brows pinched together. "Max is quite satisfied, actually."

Cassandra felt her temper rise. Her ears grew hot, and her palms itched. She forced herself not to take the bait. The bitch was lying, and Max was *not* the reason Cassandra was here.

"I don't want to kill you, but I will. Now where is the fountain?"

"What fountain?" Calliope asked.

"She's after the elixir," Sabine said calmly, then faced Cassandra. "It's not here."

"What do you mean, it's not here? Where is it?"

"I don't have it," Sabine said.

Cassandra was no fool; she knew when someone was lying to her. She walked up to the old woman and pressed the gun against her wrinkled neck. "Where is it, Sabine? Tell me, or your aunt will get a bullet in her skull."

Sabine's eyes darted to her aunt, then to her left, then quickly back to Cassandra. Sabine probably didn't even know she'd done it, but she'd just shown Cassandra precisely where the precious elixir was.

Max watched Cassandra's London estate come into view as the carriage made its way up the drive. Sabine had gone into the shop to help Calliope today, so Max had taken the opportunity to pay Cassandra a visit. It had been years since he'd been here, but the stone structure looked the same—still large and ornate and hideously grand. Ten years ago, he should have known simply by looking at her house that she was not the right sort of woman for him.

But there was no right kind of woman for him. He was only interested in a few nights of pleasure, here and there, nothing long-term, nothing serious. Though it seemed he would never tire of Sabine. But that had no bearing on anything. He'd promised himself a long time ago that he'd never have a family again.

He rapped on the heavy wooden door and waited. A few moments later, it swung open to reveal Johns. The man's eyes widened. "What do you want?" he asked.

"Where is Cassandra?" Max asked. He elbowed his way into the foyer and walked down the hall.

"She's out." Johns's voice echoed down the high-ceilinged hall.

Max turned to face the man. "And she left you here alone?"

"I don't know where she went."

Max started to argue, but for some reason he believed Johns was telling the truth. It could have been that he questioned whether the man was bright enough to formulate a lie, or perhaps it was simply the honesty in his expression.

Max stepped back over to the front door. "If I find out that you and Cassandra are behind all of these murders—" He paused and took a deep breath. "Leave Sabine and her aunts alone." Then he strode out the door.

Chapter Twenty-one

Silly girl," Cassandra spat as she walked over to the cabinet.

Cassandra was right, Sabine realized, she was a silly girl. Of course, they kept some of the elixir here at the shop to use when putting their concoctions together. A guardian could always separate the elixir, but the amphora with the main supply had to remain safe. She was thankful that was safely tucked away at Max's house. Still it appeared the small amount here was in danger of being stolen.

"I don't know what you're talking about," Sabine lied, though she knew it was too late to fool Cassandra.

Still aiming the gun at both Sabine and Calliope, Cassandra knelt at the cabinet and opened the drawers.

Sabine had never considered that the Chosen One might be a woman. Foolish, really, considering her mother and now aunt had been guardian. It would take Cassandra a while to locate the bottle; still it seemed unlikely that tonight would end well.

Cassandra had obviously figured out the connection Sabine had with Atlantis and thus believed she was the remaining guardian. Evidently she thought Sabine kept the entirety of the elixir here at the shop. Once she realized that the rest of it was elsewhere, she would, no doubt, return.

Or perhaps Cassandra would simply shoot both Sabine and Calliope and be done with it. Thankfully Agnes and Lydia had remained at the townhome today with Max's guards to protect them. So at least they were safe.

Cassandra withdrew the baskets of scented oils, herbs, and other ingredients for the beauty products Sabine sold. With a basket in hand, Cassandra made her way to the table closest to Sabine and Calliope. She picked up a couple of bottles, examined them, then placed them back.

"How do you tell what is what?" she asked tartly. "None of these bottles are labeled."

"It is not difficult to know the difference between rosemary and rose oil," Sabine said.

Cassandra eyed her for a moment, then recognition lit her icy blue eyes. "The scents." She stood and walked back to Sabine and Calliope. "But first, we need to make certain that the two of you hold still. We can't have you trying to be brave while I'm distracted. Where is some rope?" she asked.

"Why should we help you tie us up?" Calliope asked, then crossed her arms over her chest. Her diminutive frame did little to make her appearance formidable.

"Because, old woman, if you don't, I'll simply shoot you and then I'll know the girl here will hold still. Should I just do that instead?" Again she held the gun to the woman's throat.

"No, please," Sabine said quickly. "There's rope, under

there." She pointed to a shelf to their right. "On the bottom. I'm afraid it's rather thin, since we only use it for parcels. We're currently out of rope for tying up people."

"Watch your tongue and don't move," Cassandra said. She walked over to the shelf Sabine had indicated and bent to search for the rope.

Sabine wasted no time in seizing the free moment and picked up a chair, slamming it down over Cassandra's back. The woman screeched and dropped the gun. Sabine dove for the weapon, slamming her body onto the hard floor and reaching for the pistol.

"Bitch!" Cassandra yelled. She clawed at Sabine, holding her ankle and preventing her from getting any closer to the gun. Calliope jumped on Cassandra's back and tried her best to choke her. Cassandra stood and grabbed Calliope's arms. The older woman was no match for Cassandra's strength as she flung her off and onto some shelves in the corner. Sabine had nearly wrapped her fingers around the gun when she heard Calliope's cry.

She looked over to find Cassandra leaning over her beloved aunt with a small dagger pressed to her cheek. A drop of blood dripped down her aging face where the woman had cut her.

"Leave the gun alone, Sabine." Cassandra's cold voice filled the room.

Sabine stilled. It was too risky to attempt to snatch the gun, turn, and fire. She couldn't be certain she'd hit her mark, because she'd never shot a gun before.

"Get the rope," Cassandra said.

Sabine complied and stood with the rope.

"Now then, if you two can agree to not do anything stupid, I would prefer not to bloody my hands tonight. It's not that I won't do it." She jerked Calliope to her feet and led her to a chair. "But I much prefer to have these sorts of tasks done *for* me rather than doing them myself. If you comply with the rest of my wishes, I won't send my man back here to finish the job. Do we have an agreement?"

Sabine met her aunt's eyes and saw raw fear filling the blue depths. "Yes, you have our word," she said firmly. She tried to smile reassuringly at Calliope, though doubted she managed it with any confidence.

With no more conversation, Cassandra tied them both to chairs, with the backs against each other.

"Where was I?" she asked once she was finished. She made her way back over to the bottles. "Ah, yes, the smells. I don't want to trust you to tell me which bottle, considering you might try to poison me."

"I might," Sabine said honestly.

"I can still call out my dogs," Cassandra said. But she said nothing more as she went about pulling the corks and smelling one bottle after another. "Lavender, thyme, lemon, rose."

Sabine could see the bottle with the elixir. It was a small bottle made of blue glass, buried in the midst of the scented oils.

Cassandra picked it up, popped the cork off, then held the bottle to her nose.

Sabine held her breath.

She put the cork back in and moved to return the bottle.

Sabine relaxed.

Cassandra stopped. She pulled the bottle back to her nose and inhaled deeply. "This one has no scent." Then she turned to face Sabine. "You can't imagine what I've gone through searching for it. Countless hours and more money than I'd care to consider. This is it, isn't it?"

Sabine said nothing.

"It is, I know it. I can feel it." Cassandra's smile had changed from one of glee to the wild-eyed grin of madness. "Do you have any idea how long I've searched for this? I won't let you or anyone else steal this from me now."

Again Sabine didn't answer. There was no need to engage in a conversation with the woman. It was best to keep quiet and maybe she'd leave them here, safe, as she'd said she would. Though Sabine doubted Cassandra's word meant anything.

"Ever since Max told me about the fountain of youth that ran through the center of Atlantis, I've wanted to possess it. I knew he'd find it eventually. And he did. He led me straight to you."

Sabine's heart contracted. Had he told this woman about the elixir and where to find it? Were they working together, setting a trap for her that she'd willingly stepped right into? The thought sickened Sabine. She'd given Max her body, had nearly given him her heart.

Cassandra set the cork down on the countertop and brought the bottle to her lips.

"Don't drink it!" Sabine said.

"Why wouldn't I drink it?" Cassandra asked. "It will make me young and beautiful forever. Women everywhere will crave my secret." She clicked her tongue. "Too bad I'm not interested in sharing."

"Too much elixir will kill you."

Cassandra smirked. "Nice try, but I'm not going to fall for that." Then without another word, she tipped up the bottle and drank the entire contents.

Max had knocked three times at the back door of Sabine's shop with no one answering, but he knew they were inside. He could hear their muffled voices through the heavy wooden door. If Sabine wasn't answering, something was wrong. It took only one great kick for him to burst through the lock. The door to the shop swung open. Inside the storeroom, he saw Cassandra standing over by the cabinets, a bottle to her mouth.

He scanned the room searching for Sabine and finally saw her with Calliope tied back to back in two chairs.

"What the hell is going on here?" he demanded.

"Max, darling," Cassandra purred. "Come to rescue your whore?"

He saw the pistol she had dangling from her pale hand. She straightened her arm and leveled it at him.

His stomach clenched. "Cassandra, what are you doing?"

"Taking what is rightfully mine. I've been looking for this for years, and now I'll have eternal beauty." She smiled broadly as her glazed eyes focused on the blue bottle in her hand.

"Sabine, are you and Calliope hurt?" Max asked, not taking his eyes off Cassandra.

"No," Sabine said. "We're all right. Max, she shouldn't have drunk all of that elixir."

"What's going to happen to her?" he asked.

"She's going to die," Calliope said. "That much will most certainly kill her."

"If you are trying to frighten me, it won't work." Cassandra set the bottle down and walked toward the restrained women. "I feel wonderful." She looked down at her hands. "Look how smooth and lovely my hands look. Where can I find a mirror?" she asked Sabine.

"There is a handheld mirror in the drawer of the desk," Sabine said. She motioned to the corner.

Max took the opportunity, while Cassandra was retrieving the mirror, to make his way closer to Sabine. "How long will it take?" he asked softly.

"I'm not certain. I've only known a handful of people to ingest it directly, and only because of grave injuries or disease, and then in very small quantities. A drop or two at the most, but an entire bottle, even a small one, will..." Her voice faded as she shook her head.

"It won't be long now," Calliope said knowingly.

"Oh, it's working," Cassandra said, her voice full of awe and glee. "Look at my face. Look how lustrous my skin looks, how healthy." She stared into the mirror, as if entranced by her own reflection.

"Is there anything we can do to stop it?" Max asked.

Calliope shook her head. "No. And it will be painful for her. Vanity is not a pretty way to die."

As if Calliope's words had commanded the elixir into action, Cassandra screamed in pain. She grabbed her face as the skin began to wrinkle and bubble.

"What's happening to me?" she asked.

"We tried to warn you," Sabine said. "The elixir is far too dangerous."

Cassandra's hands gnarled, and her face contorted in pain as she fell to her knees. Then she screamed, a noise so loud and so full of excruciating pain, it actually hurt Max's ears. He made his way to Sabine and stood in front of her, holding her face against his side to block her from the sight of Cassandra's painful demise.

"You did all you could," he told Sabine.

"Max! Do something!" Cassandra screamed.

"I taunted her," Sabine whispered.

"But you warned her. You couldn't have prevented this."

And then the screaming stopped, and Max knew that Cassandra was dead.

Spencer had followed Cassandra St. James's carriage as it led her to Piccadilly, and she went into a small shop. Two hours later, and she still had not come out. He knew his lovely lady wasn't the guardian. He'd spent several hours in her company the other evening, and after a while, his ring had dulled in color. And he'd known from that day in his office that the marquess hadn't been the guardian; there had been no change at all in his ring that day.

The only explanation he could come up with was that somehow she had been exposed to the elixir. He'd decided to follow her and see if she didn't lead him straight to his target. It was well past closing for those businesses. After an hour of waiting, Spencer had moved to the alleyway. There he stood across the street, shrouding himself in the darkness as he hid on the stoop of a milliner's shop.

A man had entered a little more than thirty minutes before, and now another man, followed by a constable, stepped into the small shop. Something was happening in there, something he knew had to do with the prophecy. He could feel it. She was nearby. The guardian was in that shop.

Quietly, he walked across the street and kept his body up against the wall so he was not seen. He looked down at his hand, and the ring glowed bright, the color of fresh blood, just as it had done when he'd found the other two guardians. This was the place.

His grandfather would be so proud. Finally he would fulfill what his ancestors had begun. Atlantis had once been a handful of battles away from becoming the ruling nation of all, and his ancestors had been part of that. But then the guardians had fled, taking their elixir with them.

And the military had suffered. Without the elixir to give them extra strength and cunning, they had failed and ultimately been destroyed and defeated.

But he had been selected as the Chosen One to see their plans through to completion. And now he was very close. Satisfaction and excitement surged through him.

Now he needed only to bide his time until he could get her alone. Or perhaps he didn't even need her, only needed to get into that shop and find her amphora. If she was not sleeping here, she might not have the elixir with her. No, it was best if he followed her until he could have a few moments alone with her.

He had found the third guardian, and finally the prophecy would be fulfilled.

A couple of hours later, Sabine and Max finally arrived back at his house. The police had come and taken Cassandra's body away. Thank God, Max had called on his friend Justin to come to her shop. She could only imagine trying to explain Cassandra's death to an inspector. No doubt Sabine and Calliope would have been accused of poisoning the woman. But Max had given his statement swearing that when he'd arrived both she and Calliope were tied up, and Cassandra had consumed the liquid of her own volition.

Justin had referred to the liquid as poison in the official documentation. He said it would be easier than attempting to explain the mystical elixir from Atlantis.

Weariness settled on Sabine's shoulders like a great overcoat, heavy and cumbersome, as she followed Max up the steps into his townhome.

Behind them, carriage wheels rolled to a stop. "Max," a man said. They turned to find Justin.

"What is it?" Max asked. "Surely you're not here to arrest her."

"No, of course not." Justin made his way up the steps and into the entryway. "I wanted to let you both know that we picked up Johns, Cassandra's man. He's already confessed to a murder."

Relief washed over Sabine so forcefully she nearly collapsed. "Truly?" she asked. Could it possibly be over even without the dove? Had the Chosen One simply destroyed herself through her own vanity? Perhaps that had been it all along—the elixir was the dove.

"The generals' murders?" Max asked.

Justin shook his head. "He hasn't given us any specific details, but I think it's only a matter of time before it all comes out."

"Still doesn't make much sense," Max said. "I don't understand why Cassandra would kill military leaders."

"The prophecy," Sabine said. "If she was the Chosen One, it was commanded of her."

Max nodded. "I can't argue with a confession. And this is Cassandra; she hasn't always made a lot of sense to me."

"I thought you would want to know tonight," Justin said.

"Appreciate it. Oh, and Justin, if Johns says anything about the prophecy, let us know. Perhaps we have it backward, and he was the Chosen One, and Cassandra was helping him. I just want to be certain."

"Absolutely," Justin said. "Well, you two have a lovely evening." He smiled and gave Sabine a wink before he left by the front door.

Together, she and Max made their way to his study.

"Do you really think it's finally over?" Sabine asked. "The prophecy, the Chosen One, all of it?"

He closed the door behind them. "Yes, I think it's over. Would you care for a drink?"

"Perhaps a small one." She stood in the center of the Persian rug. "Should we return that sword?" She motioned to the massive blade leaning against his desk.

He smiled. "Perhaps we'll hold on to it for a while longer."

He handed her the glass, and she took a small sip, allowing the brandy to slide down her throat slowly before she took another.

"I don't know how Cassandra found out about the prophecy," Max said. "Maybe I told her once." He turned to look at the map. "I can't imagine she saw it in there, though she has been in this very room many times. Hell, I don't even think she can read Greek." He rubbed his hand across his neck. "I know we talked about Atlantis a lot back then, it was nearly all I ever talked about. I was young and stupid and not very discreet."

"This isn't your fault," Sabine said. Somehow she'd known he would blame himself.

His eyes met hers, and gone was any hint of humor or charm. This Max looked intense, almost deadly. "Yes, it is. She would never have found you had it not been for me." He swore loudly. "She could have killed you."

"But she didn't." She touched his arm. He didn't push her away, but he didn't turn in to her touch either.

"She came into my shop the first time the day you did. After the poker game. I don't believe she was following you. Vanity does cruel and terrible things to people," Sabine said. But she knew he did not hear her. At least he did not believe her.

There was no point in arguing with him. There would be no consoling him. Frankly, she couldn't blame him.

But Agnes was safe. The elixir was safe, and Sabine should feel enormous relief. Yet anxiety still flowed like water through her veins.

She set her glass down, then made her way over to him. Quickly, before she could lose her nerve, she wrapped her arms around him and squeezed. "I just wanted to say thank you. You've done so much for my aunts and me, and you didn't have to." It was one thing to seduce a man, to touch him as a lover would, but to embrace a man with no other intention than to console him, that was an entirely different matter.

His arms tightened around her and pulled her closer to his body. He nuzzled her neck. Before Sabine knew it, they were kissing. Slow and gentle at first, like lovers kissing after a long time apart. Then their hunger increased, and the kisses became hotter, wetter, more intense.

Desire bubbled in her abdomen and radiated down between her legs. She felt herself grow wet for him.

Sabine tore at Max's shirt, ripping it open. Buttons flew in several directions. She didn't care, though; she needed to touch him, feel his strength. Next were his trousers. The other time he'd been nude with her, she hadn't paid close attention; she'd been so focused on her own feelings and sensations. Now she looked, took in her fill. Long and rigid with muscles, his sculpted thighs looked like a statue of Adonis.

They couldn't wait to move to the bedroom, so instead she pushed him down on his sofa. He sat and smiled up at her, raw desire apparent on his face. And she would have sworn there was something else, something far more tender, but she shoved the thought aside. Wanting more from Max would only lead to a broken heart. But for now she was finished trying to resist him. Their affair would be brief, he would tire of her after too long, but at least she would have experienced this kind of passion.

She straddled him, and the rock-hard sinew of his thigh twitched under her touch. She reached under her skirt, pulled aside the hole in her drawers, and glided down on top of him.

His hands encircled her waist as she began to move. Then he cradled her face with his hands and kissed her. Kissed her as if he loved her. Her heart soared. She tried to remind herself that actions could be deceiving, and no matter how it might seem in this very moment, Max did not love her. But she realized with a sudden, fierce certainty that she loved him.

She did not need him to love her. She said the words again and again in her mind, trying to brand them on her soul. Still, tears pricked her eyes as she made love to him. When they climaxed together, the world seemed at peace, in perfect union. She kept her eyes closed and laid her head on his shoulder.

This was a moment out of time for both of them. Merely an adventure for him, and for her, the last time she'd devote totally to herself.

As much as she'd tried to avoid it, she wanted more. Wanted Max. With his sharp tongue and wicked sense of humor, he was everything she never knew she wanted in a man. He made her laugh, and he made her feel secure.

But she would not repeat her mother's mistakes. Loving Max did not mean she would build a life with him.

Chapter Twenty-two

~~~~~~~~~~

S*abine Tobias.*

She was the third and final guardian. Spencer had followed her and the marquess back to his townhome in Mayfield. Now he knew where to find her, and how to get to her. All along, she'd been there, safe with her lover, Maxwell Barrett. If only Spencer had paid closer attention that day when Max and the detective had come around to ask questions. He'd known that the marquess was involved in some capacity, he'd simply picked the wrong woman.

But the timing was perfect. He had one more general to take care of, then he could pay Miss Tobias a visit. And he'd make certain that Max had other plans.

Now, though, it was time to retire poor General Radcliffe. Spencer had been waiting several hours for this last and final kill. The officer had been expected home hours before, but here it was nearly five in the morning and he was only now arriving home. Spencer was unfamiliar with this man, having never met him before, but he knew he was younger than most other officers of his rank and exceedingly headstrong.

Spencer could tell by the man's wavering walk that he was drunk. Perhaps this would be easier than he anticipated, an unexpected benefit, considering how long he'd been sitting here in the dark. He stood now and moved to the darkened corner as the drunken officer entered his study.

Men were so predictable. He'd come in here and pour himself another drink, then probably pass out on the sofa. And hours later, his wife would find him in here, only to assume he'd been here all evening, working on some high military secret. They were all fools.

Unlike all those previous mornings, this time when his wife found him, she'd find him dead.

The officer made his way into the study, and after lighting the lamp on his desk, moved to the sideboard and poured himself a hearty glass of scotch. He took a swig, then turned and came face to face with Spencer.

"Who the devil are you?" he asked, his speech not altered by the drink.

"Who I am does not matter. Only who I will become."

The man blinked at him. "Damned crazed bedlamite."

Spencer considered for a moment the term, then pulled back and punched the man square in his face. Blood spurted off his nose, and he stumbled backward. It was to be his final kill, so perhaps this once, he would indulge himself. Get his hands dirty.

But the officer recovered more quickly than Spencer had expected. The glaze on his eyes cleared, and in an instant, it was as if he'd become completely sober. "Bastard." He slammed his fist into Spencer's stomach, then landed another blow on the back of Spencer's neck when he bent forward.

So much for wishing this would be an easy kill. Even drunk, this man was a deft fighter. No wonder he'd been promoted through the ranks so quickly. Spencer used his own fighting skills to quickly bring the man to his knees. But his advantage didn't last long. Spencer was knocked off his own feet and found himself sprawled on his back, the breath knocked out of him.

The officer straddled Spencer and pounded his face. His nose broke, and the crack made a sickening sound as pain shot through his body and blood spurted like a fountain. *No*, his mind screamed. He had not worked this hard to be taken down by mere brute strength. His body wailed in protest, but somehow Spencer found the strength to reach up and grab the man's throat. He squeezed so tight the man stopped hitting him. This gave Spencer enough leverage to flip the officer over onto his back, and then he wrapped both hands around his throat.

"This is my destiny," Spencer told the officer. "Neither you nor anyone else will stop me." He leaned over him, squeezing the life from him. Spencer watched myriad emotions flit through the man's eyes: fear, pain, anguish, panic. And then life slid completely out of the man's eyes, and they stared blankly up at him.

Finally it was finished. Power surged through him. He was the Chosen One; this was his destiny. He had been selected among generations of men to be the one to redeem his people. Now he only needed to find that Tobias woman's elixir. Then the prophecy would be complete. And the whole world would know he was the Chosen One.

*   *   *

Sometime after breakfast, Justin burst into Max's study. "We found another one."

"What do you mean?" Max asked, coming to his feet.

"Another body. This time General Radcliffe." Justin looked as if he'd been at Scotland Yard all night; dark circles beneath his eyes were a testament to his sleepless night. He wore no jacket and his sleeves had been rolled up to his elbows.

"Could he have been killed before you apprehended Johns?" Max asked.

Justin shook his head. "It doesn't look that way. His wife found him about three hours ago. She said he was still warm. The coroner agrees that it was a recent death."

"You still have Johns?" Max asked.

"We've had him in custody all night," Justin said. "And while he's confessed to the one murder—some chemist— he claims to know nothing of the military officers."

"Son of a bitch!" Max swore. "The bastard is still out there."

"What's happened?" Sabine's voice came from the doorway. She searched Max's face.

He said nothing, merely looked at her and willed her to understand. It still wasn't over, and Agnes wasn't safe. And yesterday, when he'd come in to find her tied up and Cassandra armed with a gun...He thought he'd almost lost her, and it had scared the hell out of him.

"It isn't over," she said plainly.

"No," Justin said. "We found another dead officer this morning. This time the note was addressed to you specifically."

"To me?" Sabine asked.

Max came around the desk, approached Sabine, but

stopped. What did he plan to do? Console her? He didn't know the first thing about comforting a woman. "Why the devil didn't you tell me that before she came in here?"

"I hadn't gotten that far," Justin explained.

"What does it say?" Sabine asked, her expression solemn.

Justin exhaled slowly. "Simply that he knows who you are, and that you're next."

"He believes me to be the guardian," she said after Justin had left.

"Yes, but he doesn't know where you are," Max said.

"We don't know that," Sabine argued. "I want my aunts to be safe. Can you assure me that they're safe here?" For the first time since she entered his study, her voice wavered. But she would not cry, she refused to. If that bastard thought she was the guardian, then let him come after her. It was Agnes's safety and that of the elixir that truly mattered.

"I can assure you that you are all safe here," Max said. "I'll add more guards around the house."

"I want this over with now. At least we have that damned sword," Sabine said.

He stepped over to her and grabbed her upper arms. "What do you think you're going to do?"

"I'll go find him. Or I'll sit at my shop and wait for him," she said defiantly. "I need to be alone right now. I need to think."

He held fast to her arms, trying to stop her. "Sabine."

"Damnation, Max, you can't fix everything, and you can't protect me from something greater than you and all your guards." She exhaled slowly. "I don't mean to sound ungrateful." She shook her head and walked away.

She stepped into her room, noting the trunk at the foot of her bed, half-filled with her belongings. Sabine had been packing when she'd gone downstairs to discover Justin in Max's study. Now it seemed futile to continue. They weren't leaving, not yet.

She wanted to throw something, but that wouldn't solve anything. Instead she went back to the pile she'd made on the bed. Slowly she returned her possessions to their proper places. Her hairbrush went back on the dressing table with her combs and few pieces of jewelry.

From her reticule, she pulled out some money and a pair of earrings she'd worn to the party the other night. But something was missing. She felt around to the bottom of the bag, but the necklace wasn't there.

She tore through the dressing table, picking through each item, one by one, to find it. But it was not there. Still clutching the earrings, she searched the rest of the room.

The bed was empty, so she checked the floor, and still she could not find it. Her elixir was gone. The small vial Agnes had given her. The one she'd used on Max when he'd injured himself in the bathhouse.

She sank to the bed, sitting right on the edge. The earrings dangled from her hand. It was a few nights ago, after they'd made love, and he'd handed her the reticule. That must have been when it happened.

Damn him! He'd stolen it. The earrings fell to the floor with a clang.

He hadn't wanted her, Sabine realized. He'd been after the elixir the entire time and had seduced her as a distraction! She'd known she'd been nothing more than a diversion, a dalliance, but she'd never doubted his desire for her. How could she have been so wrong?

The other night she'd given him every opportunity to

tell her that he cared about her above and beyond his quest for Atlantis. He'd been angry with her for lying about her being the guardian. And she'd thought for a moment, she'd hoped, his anger stemmed from deeper feelings for her. That she'd wounded him because he cared. But that was only what she wanted to hear; it wasn't the truth.

Did Max have intentions of stealing the rest, only he hadn't been able to locate Agnes's amphora? Would he take it, then simply watch her aunt die? He'd always expressed doubt that the guardian's mortality was mystically attached to the elixir. He'd suggested the Chosen One had killed them. But she knew different.

What hurt the most was knowing that despite this, she still loved him. She still wanted him to come to her, pull her into his arms, and tell her it would be all right, that the Chosen One wouldn't win, and that she and her aunts would survive this. She wanted him to tell her that he loved her, and he'd never let harm come to her. And that somehow, they would manage to find a fairy-tale ending when this was all over.

But all of that would be a lie. He couldn't protect her now. It was time for her to take matters into her own hands and fight the Chosen One. She couldn't allow Agnes to risk her life, so it was up to Sabine to bring about this madman's destruction.

If only she knew how to find him.

She swiped at a tear just as her aunts entered her bedchamber door. She tried to smile, but she knew they'd seen her.

"Sabine, what's the matter?" Calliope said as she came over to hug her niece.

"I'm tired, that's all," Sabine said.

"We saw the inspector leaving as we arrived," Lydia said. "What happened?"

Sabine's shoulders sank. "The man they arrested is not the Chosen One; neither was the woman. He's still out there."

Her other two aunts were by her side instantly. Hugs and squeezes and words of encouragement surrounded her.

"I feel as if I've failed," she said quietly. "We tried to find the dove, and we did. We even have that bloody sword. But how am I to find the Chosen One and destroy him?"

"No one expects you to," Lydia said.

"That sword might help, but you already have everything you need within you to defeat him," Agnes said.

Sabine shook her head in frustration. "I appreciate the encouragement, but now is not the time for platitudes."

"No, Sabine, she found something," Calliope said. "In Phinneas's book."

"The quest," Lydia said, "was not meant for you and Max, but rather for the Chosen One. A diversion, you see, created by our ancestors. But you stumbled upon it by mistake."

"What are you talking about?" Sabine asked.

Agnes stood and retrieved Phinneas's book from the chair where she'd set it. "That's why the first clue, the one that sent you to Lulworth Cove, was so simple. It was meant to be blatant in case the Chosen One got his hands on Phinneas's book. It was a false clue, meant to set the Chosen One on a potentially fatal trail. The real message, the truth, was more challenging to uncover. It's an old secret code he and I used in our letters," she said. "Once I deciphered the journal using his code, I was able to see what he was really trying to tell us."

Sabine looked from one aunt to the next, but saw no sign of their trying to tease her. "I don't understand," she said. "We risked our lives and wasted time for nothing?"

"I suspect you learned much along the way. Though I do apologize for giving you that first clue. I missed the truth," Agnes said. "Phinneas was trying to tell me, and I only heard what I wanted to hear. We"—she motioned to her sisters—"wanted so badly for you to be selected guardian that when Phinneas told me to give you that vial of elixir, I thought he'd had a vision that you'd be next."

"Everything has centered on you," Lydia said. "That's why Madigan sent you to find the map. And that's why Phinneas instructed Agnes to give you the elixir."

"You and Max," Agnes corrected. "He's played a huge part in all of this."

"And your birthday must play a role," Calliope said.

Her birthday was tomorrow. She looked at each of her aunts in turn. They were speaking so quickly, she could hardly keep up, leaving her feeling as if she'd missed something crucial. "I don't understand. What are you saying? Is Max part of the prophecy? And is the map somehow important, too? Is the map the dove?"

Her aunts exchanged looks heavy with concern.

"No, my dear," Agnes said. "The map isn't the dove. You are."

Her words registered, but Sabine barely understood them. "I . . . I don't understand. The dove is a weapon."

"We assumed the dove was a weapon," Agnes said. "We were wrong. Right here in Phinneas's journal, it says, 'Sabine is the dove, only she can stop him.' That is what Phinneas saw in his vision. Not that you were the next guardian, but that you are the dove."

Her aunts kept talking, but their words flew past. She tried to focus, tried to make sense of what they'd revealed.

She stood and walked away from the bed, going instead to stand by the window. A light drizzle fell from the sky, silently hitting the glass. She was the dove? How was she intended to be a weapon? Time was running out on her figuring everything out. If she didn't stop the Chosen One by her birthday tomorrow, Agnes would be killed.

She turned to find that only Agnes remained.

"I wanted time alone with you," she said. "I hope you don't mind."

"Of course not," Sabine said. She took a deep breath. Shame burned her cheeks. If she couldn't be trusted with a small amount of elixir, how could she possibly be the dove? "Agnes, I lost my vial of elixir. No, that's not precisely true, Max took it from me."

"Come and sit." Agnes patted the chair next to her.

"I still don't understand how I could be the dove," Sabine said, sinking into the chair.

"It is your role in the prophecy," Agnes said. "You were chosen, Sabine."

Sabine shook her head. "None of this makes sense."

"Of course it does, when you look at it from the correct angle. The date of your birth is tied to the prophecy. Your relationship with Max—the one man who was able to locate our map. The final clue of the quest, stating you had to have the right eyes to see what was before you. You said yourself you had to read that clue in the mirror," Agnes said.

"But if the entire quest was built as a distraction for the Chosen One, how would that have worked for him?" Sabine asked.

"It wouldn't. The clue says it all. If you have the right

eyes." Agnes placed a warm hand on Sabine's arm. "Our ancestors set the hunt up to distract the Chosen One, but they must have known it was a possibility that someone else would find the clues."

"But there is no logic to me being the dove," Sabine said. "I have no skills or training that would prepare me to do physical battle with a man. How am I supposed to defeat someone who has already killed military officers and guardians, men far more prepared to defend themselves than I am?"

Agnes merely shook her head, her expression an odd combination of resignation and ruefulness. "I cannot tell you that. All I can say is that you will defeat him. If Phinneas saw it, it will come to fruition."

Sabine knew that Agnes's faith in Phinneas stemmed more from her love of the man than from her belief in him as the Seer. Sabine didn't know if she could find that kind of confidence. "I will have to kill him to stop him." Sabine swallowed hard.

"When the time comes, you will find the strength to do whatever it is you are destined to do. Trust your instincts," Agnes said.

Sabine said nothing. Her mind frantically searched for the answer, for the key to stopping the Chosen One. Nothing came. She hoped Agnes was right, but there was a lot at stake to rely on her instincts.

"There is more than weariness or fear in your eyes, child. I know what the pain from a broken heart looks like," Agnes said.

"He betrayed me," she whispered. "Oh, Agnes, I'm so ashamed. I trusted him; I gave him my body, my heart." She drew in her breath as a wave of pain crashed over her. Damn him.

"Perhaps he had good reasons for taking that vial," Agnes suggested.

"Doubtful."

Agnes said nothing; she simply held on to Sabine's hand, stroking it gently.

"I've been as much a failure as my mother was. When it comes to matters of the heart, we cannot be trusted."

"Sabine, your mother was not a failure," Agnes said.

"She killed herself," Sabine said.

Agnes sighed heavily. "Yes, she was ill. Even so, you are not your mother."

"No, but evidently I'm not any stronger. I fell in love with Max despite my best efforts to avoid it and look what happened. I should have been strong like you and ignored my heart."

Agnes dropped Sabine's hand. "Phinneas and I loved each other from the moment we met, and he never once sacrificed his duty as guardian to follow his heart."

"Strength," Sabine said.

"No, stubbornness," Agnes argued.

"He made a great sacrifice."

"He was a fool, and that sacrifice got him killed. Would any of this have turned out differently had he chosen me?" She shrugged. "Perhaps not. But perhaps it would have. I would have been there. I could have helped him fight off the Chosen One." Her eyes filled with tears.

"And you might have been killed as well," Sabine said.

"But I would have died with my love. Died after having a lifetime of love. Not simply have love trapped inside my heart, but to love every day. We had letters and we saw each other every once and again, but it was so rare."

Tears flowed freely down her cheeks. "I would like

to think that if he had to do it all over again, he might make a different choice. He might choose me instead of duty, then I wouldn't have been available to be selected guardian.

"In the end, his duty killed him and now I am alone. He could have done both, but he wouldn't take the risk." She cupped Sabine's cheek. "Don't make the same mistake we made."

"But our family, our Atlantean heritage, is my destiny," Sabine said.

"No, child," Agnes said. "Max is your destiny."

Chapter Twenty-three

————⋙⋘————

Spencer waited outside the marquess's townhome and watched as Sabine's three aunts climbed into a carriage. A second rig, this one filled with two guards sent to protect them, followed. Then, half an hour later, Max received a summons to report immediately to his club and he left.

He hadn't left Sabine unprotected. There were guards here, too, that Spencer would have to contend with. But Max's absence would give him the opportunity he needed.

It was time, past time really, for him and Sabine to meet.

Sabine tore through another drawer in Max's desk, but still she found no hint of her missing vial of elixir. More than likely, that bastard had it with him. Perhaps he was even now meeting with scientists or a writer from the *Times* intending to finally prove the existence of Atlantis. If that happened, she and her aunts would never have any peace, and her attempts to protect the elixir would never be enough. Not against the whole world.

She dropped the drawer on the floor, not even bothering to replace it in Max's desk. Since he'd departed nearly half an hour before, she'd searched a good portion of his study, but her efforts were proving fruitless.

She turned, and she caught sight of the map. He still hadn't replaced it in its frame, and instead it draped across his desk. She ran a finger lovingly across the illustration. She should take it. Did it not belong to her people? Had he not stolen it from the hiding place they'd selected to keep it protected?

He'd worked long and hard to find it where other men, grown men, had failed. Phinneas's vision had called the finder of the map a "great one." But a Seer could be wrong, couldn't he? Max had only gone after the map to get approval from his family.

He'd never gotten that from them, though. They'd perished before they had the chance to give it.

She traced one of the water rings. She didn't want to love Max, especially now. But damned if she didn't love him. And she'd been right, loving someone else this much hurt.

"Miss Tobias," a man's voice came from the doorway behind her. "We finally meet."

Her blood froze. He was here. The Chosen One. And she was all alone. Slowly she turned to face him, painfully aware that she had nothing of use on her person to inflict any worthy injury.

But she was the dove, she reminded herself. Agnes had told her she had it within herself to destroy him.

The Chosen One was younger than she had expected. Much younger, as he was probably close to her age, but for whatever reason, she'd anticipated an older gentleman. And he was handsome, strikingly so, with pitch-black hair and chilling blue eyes. But knowing how evil he was ruined his attractiveness.

"You know my name," she said carefully. "Perhaps I might know yours as well."

"You've been expecting me?" he asked. He moved farther into the room. It was then that Sabine noticed the pistol in his left hand.

She took a steadying breath. "I knew we would meet one way or another."

"Spencer Cole, special advisor to the queen, at your service." He gave her a mocking bow, but never took his eyes off her.

He worked for Queen Victoria. And he'd murdered her generals right under her nose. "Is that how you've been able to do it?" she asked. "How you've been able to get close to those generals in order to assassinate them?"

His shoulders rose in a shrug. "Working closely with her majesty does have its benefits."

She wanted to keep him talking, partly because she was curious about him, but more to buy herself time. She had no idea how she was going to stop him. Sabine caught sight of Achilles' sword just to her right. "Does she know?" Sabine asked.

"Not yet. Though I suppose before the day is through she will." He shrugged, with the casual air of someone discussing the weather.

"You're younger than I expected." She inched herself so that she was within grabbing distance of the sword.

He smiled with a cruel grin. "My birthday is tomorrow, actually. I'll be—"

"Twenty-five," she guessed. So they shared a birthday— the Chosen One and the dove. What other connection did she have with this man?

"How did you know?" he asked.

"It's mine as well."

For a moment it seemed as if they were strangers meeting for the first time and exchanging pleasantries, but of course, this was much more than that. Lives depended on the outcome of this meeting. Lives quite precious to her.

"The prophecy states nothing about my sharing a birthday with a guardian." He tilted his head with curiosity. "Nor do my grandfather's instructions," he said.

She wrapped her hand around the hilt of the sword. So far he hadn't seemed to notice her standing over the weapon. She did her best to lift the sword, but it would not budge. The heavy gold weapon sat firmly against the wood of Max's desk. She looked up to find him watching her in amusement.

"Even if you could lift that, you can't hurt me," he said.

"I never said I was the guardian." Again she tried to move the sword, but could not leverage it.

"If not the guardian, who else would you be?" He walked slowly toward her, not in a casual manner, but with the slow, steady gait of predator as it circles its prey.

A chill shivered down her back. She wished Phinneas's vision had given her clearer instructions on how to destroy this man.

"Not the guardian." He looked down at his hand, then held it up to show her his ring. "You're telling the truth. Were you the guardian, this would be glowing red. But we obviously have a connection. A shared destiny," he said. "And I know you know who that third guardian must be. One of your aunts, but which one?"

"It would seem my destiny is to destroy you," she said, knowing her words would present no threat.

"You?" He chuckled. "I suppose you fancy yourself the dove, then?" He took several steps toward her, closing the distance. He smiled, but the humor never reached his cold eyes. His right hand snaked around her wrist, holding her in place. "Have you ever really looked at a dove? They're such delicate, defenseless creatures. Fragile, really."

He ran the cold metal of his pistol down her cheek, and she willed herself not to move. She refused to show him the fear surging through her.

"I've always been fascinated with doves," he continued. "I'm sure you understand why, given the prophecy. As a boy I studied them. Put them in cages and simply watched them." His icy eyes bore into her. "There are hundreds of ways to kill a dove once you've caught one. I can crush their bones with a single twist of my hands. I've ripped off their wings, broken their necks—"

She wrenched free of his hold and moved to the other side of the room. He was worse than she'd imagined. She'd expected the Chosen One to be clever, and while certainly a killer, she'd thought he'd be focused on the fulfillment of the prophecy, not a malevolent man who obviously relished torture. Bile churned through her stomach.

He held his arms open and again came toward her. "Do your worst, dove," he said. Then he burst into chilling laughter.

Had she been able to lift that sword, she would have had the perfect opportunity to run him through. But she had nothing. "What happens now?" she asked. "You've killed seven generals, nine people including Madigan and Phinneas. And no doubt I'll be next. After I'm dead," she said, "what will you do?" She had not yet resigned herself to death. But she knew he was skilled and deadly, and that even in extraordinary circumstances, she was at an extreme disadvantage.

He leaned his hip against Max's desk. "I'm truly happy you asked, Sabine," he said. "I've longed to share this with someone. Thanks to the elixir from the other two guardians, I have been able to start feeding it slowly to the new lieutenant-generals"—he pointed the pistol at her—"who, coincidentally, I was able to hand-select."

Sabine listened to his words, but surveyed the room, searching for something, anything that would serve as a weapon. Max was conservative in his decor, and aside from his books and the necessities of the room—chairs, desk, sofa—there wasn't much else. And then she remembered. The spear. It was old, and it was dull, but remarkably, it was also exposed. Max had broken the case and hadn't replaced the glass yet. She knew the spear was behind Spencer, on the other side of Max's desk.

"Having the queen's ear has been key in all of this," Spencer continued, "but it hasn't been easy, I assure you."

He shoved off the desk with a speed she hadn't been prepared for and closed in on her. She, in turn, moved away from him. It was an odd dance of life and death.

"The queen is an old woman now," he said. "But she is not daft and trusts none too easily. I bided my time with her. Waited patiently. Now she trusts me implicitly."

"Why give the officers the elixir?" Sabine asked. She needed to get him around to the other side of the desk with her. But how?

"Do you not know our own history?" He tsked with his tongue. "You ought to be ashamed of yourself." He sighed and rolled his eyes as if having to explain something so basic to her truly tried his patience. "The elixir made our army indestructible. And we were so close; the army had invaded several countries and we'd secured control over their governments. Now my new army will be the same," he said.

"You are Atlantean?" Sabine asked. It made sense, she supposed, but it did surprise her. She'd taken for granted that her people, the ones who had fled the destruction of Atlantis, would have learned from their mistakes. She stepped backward.

His eyes narrowed, and he followed. "Of course. Some of my ancestors fled with yours, on the ships here. One of them reluctantly. But he was smart. Knew that someday one from his line would rise up and complete what had been started. He stole the prophecy from the Seer's book. For generations, those notes were lost to my family, until my grandfather came upon them. He taught me the ways of our people, the true Atlanteans, with bravery and courage, and not weakness and fear.

"The prophecy is my destiny." He touched his chest as he spoke. "I must fulfill it, restore Atlantis to her former glory, and finish the work of our army. And being the sole owner of all three elixirs will give me immortality."

Immortality—it was why the guardians were so carefully selected, why they weren't allowed to be together with other guardians. The temptation to never grow old was too significant. Now she knew where the rumor about the fountain of youth had started. "You do realize that Atlantis can never be restored," she told him. "It sank into the ocean eons ago. There is probably nothing left of it." She felt a pang of sadness at the thought. But she did not want to have anything in common with this man. Again she moved, trying to angle herself in a position to grab the spear.

He frowned. "Not the actual Atlantis; I'm no fool. But rather the ways of the Atlanteans. We were on the brink of domination. So close to having every ruler, every king, every emperor kneel to our own. I will restore that."

"And you intend to do so with England's army?" she asked.

"Yes, I am the Chosen One. Think of it; the elixir fed to an entire army. I will have soldiers who are indestructible. An army under my control that cannot be defeated."

He was mad. Utterly and inexcusably mad. "Do you truly think other nations will allow that?" she asked.

"Other armies won't stand a chance against my own. England already has the strongest military in the world. Now I will make them indestructible."

"Other countries will band together to stop you. You will create a state of permanent war. England will be destroyed," she said.

His lip curled in a sneer. "England matters naught to me. Perhaps I will rule elsewhere. Greece is probably closest to our homeland." He shrugged. "I'll move my army there."

Arrogance was never an attractive quality, but it was even less so when the man in question believed he'd one day rule the world. Her people had planned to do that, and it had literally consumed their continent. Had no one learned from that experience?

"Enough chatter." He held his hand up to silence her. "You know why I've come."

"I told you, I'm not the guardian; I don't have the elixir," she said plainly.

She was very close to the spear. She stood directly behind Max's desk, and the spear was behind her. Not near enough to allow her to grasp it, though. If she made a direct move for it, he would kill her. He would find Agnes eventually, with or without Sabine alive. It would simply be more convenient for him if she cooperated.

"But you know where she is. Your aunt. Which one is it?" He licked his lips. "I saw them leave in a carriage earlier. Did they go to the shop, Sabine? Or perhaps back to their village?"

While he was talking, she took two steps backward toward the spear.

"I will find them. And my ring will reveal to me which one guards the remaining elixir." He smiled—a cruel and heartless grin that chilled her to her bones. "I will kill you if I have to." He meant it. She knew that. "Just as I have done with those who came before you."

"Perhaps you will. But certainly you didn't miss the part of the prophecy that details *your* destruction."

Max had waited patiently in the research library at Solomon's for over an hour. Perhaps patiently was an exaggeration, but at least he hadn't throttled anyone yet. He'd been sent a letter from someone in the club, and Max had assumed it was Marcus. He hadn't wanted to leave Sabine alone, but he'd had enough men guarding the house to know she would be safe.

But Marcus was not to be found, and no one at the club had seen him all day.

Max shoved his hand into his pocket as he paced the library. The glass vial of elixir brushed against his fingertips. He'd brought it along to show Marcus.

The wait gave him a chance to take stock of the current situation. What the hell had he been thinking? Was this foolish quest so important that he would risk hurting Sabine? He'd betrayed her.

The hell with Marcus and his submersible boat. He
stormed from the room and then out the front door of
Solomon's. He had been so damned focused on his own
desires that he might have lost the only woman he'd ever
loved.

"Tell me where the elixir is or I'll kill you. I'll kill
the final guardian eventually, but then perhaps I'll kill the
rest of your aunts simply for my own amusement. Then
I'll come back here for your lover," Spencer threatened.
"Don't test me in this, Sabine. Certainly you've seen what
I'm capable of."

She'd be a liar if she said that his threat didn't give her
pause. The niece in her longed to save her aunts at any
cost, and the woman in her burned to save her lover. But
her aunts weren't at the shop. They'd been packed into a
carriage and sent to the home of a member of Max's club
for protection.

She backed up farther. Only a little more and her fingertips could brush the spear.

"I know it's in this house. I will find it." He came at
her and slammed the back of his hand across her face. His
ring slammed hard into her cheek.

The force of his blow nearly knocked her over. But she
kept her footing.

He cocked his head to the side. "Fitting that my ring
will probably leave a scar on your perfect skin. If you live
long enough for that welt to heal." Momentarily he looked
down at the ring.

This time she was ready and ducked when he came
at her again. He was faster than she was, though, and he
managed to strike her twice more. Her eyes teared up as
the pain of his blows rocked through her.

"I don't enjoy hurting women. You are weaker and less intelligent creatures, bred to rely on men for protection. But I will make an exception for you, since you are the dove. Tell me where the elixir is," he said, his voice softer now, "and perhaps I'll be lenient with you."

He wrapped his hand around her throat and squeezed. Pain spiked through her temples, searing her brain as she lost oxygen. A moment more of this, and she'd be dead. Or ready to tell him everything.

"Or perhaps not. I can search this bloody house, but it will be so much faster if you just tell me," he yelled.

Images of Madigan and then Phinneas settled on her. They had not given up, and they had died horrible, painful deaths. That was what waited for Agnes if Sabine did not stop him. With renewed strength, she twisted away from him. She gasped for air. Her lungs burned as she inhaled a large breath.

Finally close enough, she reached for the spear, but Spencer knocked her out of the way before she could grab it. She stumbled and fell to the ground, but managed to get to her feet before he was upon her again. Her neck ached and her eye was already swelling. She knew blood dripped from her face onto her dress.

She was going to die. The thought surged through her, nearly crippling her with fear.

She loved her aunts, and they had been so wonderful to her when she'd lost her mother. She thought of her people, back in the village, their smiling faces and simple ways. Mostly, though, she thought of Max. Out of all those people, her one regret was not being able to tell Max that she loved him.

Despite his betrayal, she knew that he, above anyone else, needed to hear those words. He needed to know that he mattered to someone. And Agnes needed protection. If Sabine didn't stop this madman, he would single-handedly destroy everyone Sabine had ever loved.

Spencer had pinned her in so that she was caught between him and Max's desk. But she wouldn't run from her destiny, not anymore. She could see things clearly now. Agnes had said that Max was her destiny. But what that meant was that it was her destiny to save him. To save them all.

She charged him, tried to grab his pistol, but of course he was stronger. He captured one of her wrists and held tightly while she continued to fight him with her other arm. She lashed out, making contact with whatever body part she could reach, and desperately tried to inflict some measure of pain. But she knew her blows were nothing but whispers to his stronger flesh.

She threw her body against him, and his balance wavered. Behind Spencer, Sabine could see the spear. Suddenly she knew what she must do. That was her answer. There would be no way for her to escape his clutches to retrieve it herself. But she could force him back into it. It would require all of her weight to pierce his flesh, and she, too, would be impaled. She would die, but she was the dove. This was what she was born to do. To protect Agnes and her other aunts. To protect this country. And to protect Max.

And as if her heart had beckoned him, Max appeared in the doorway.

"Get the hell away from her," Max yelled before he moved in their direction.

Without another thought, she threw her weight into Spencer with renewed strength, pushing him back onto the spear. His arm snaked around her waist and pulled her with him and she felt the blade bite first into the flesh of her abdomen and then come out her back. Her knees nearly buckled from the intense pain.

Spencer's eyed widened with his own pain. "You will die before me," he snarled as he coughed and struggled for breath.

Sabine felt the world around her grow dim. She could vaguely hear Max in the background calling her name. But Spencer's eyes were the last image she saw as her world faded to black.

"Sabine? Can you hear me?" Max cradled her head in his lap and called to her. Fear gripped his heart in a vise so tight he could scarcely breathe.

Her breath was uneven and shallow, her chest barely moving, and the raspy sounds coming from her throat were not promising. He'd ripped his shirt off and pressed the linen firmly against Sabine's wound to try to stanch the bleeding, but his efforts seemed futile.

"Damnation, woman!" he yelled. "What the hell were you thinking? I didn't need saving, and even if I did, my life wasn't worth sacrificing your own." He talked, not caring who was listening.

About five minutes before, her aunts had burst into the room. They now stood in huddled silence as he smoothed Sabine's hair away from her eyes. The lovely brown strands looked just as lustrous even as she lay dying in his lap.

"She's gone," Calliope whispered from behind him.

"No, she's not!" he said. He leaned down and pressed kisses to her forehead and her cheeks. Still she did not move. Then he felt it, the small bottle in his pocket. He quickly withdrew it and uncorked the vial.

He ripped her dress open, then poured the elixir over her gaping wound. The blood dripped down her skin as it mixed with the water.

Nothing.

Max parted her lips and dropped some of the elixir into her mouth. Still he heard no breath.

"No, damn you. Not now. You can't leave me now. Sabine, damn you. Wake up. Don't you know that I love you?" Max leaned over her body, laying his face on her chest. He heard nothing—no pulse, no heartbeat, no breath. His own heart seemed to stop, his breath caught, everything stilled. "I love you," he said again.

He lay there for several minutes, ignoring the cries of her aunts behind him.

Something ruffled his hair.

"I love you, too," a soft whisper said.

He leaned up. "Sabine?"

Her eyes fluttered open, and she coughed several times. Then she winced. "Oh, that hurts," she said.

Max laughed, not caring that he had tears on his cheeks. He looked down at her wound and already the bleeding had stopped. "You scared the hell out of me."

"It was the only way."

"But you heard me?" he asked.

"Of course." She gave him a weak smile. "A woman always hears when a man tells her he loves her. I would have heard that no matter where I was," she said.

"And where were you?" Max asked.

"I was still here. Barely, but still here. You gave me life again."

"No," he said.

"The elixir." She nodded. "I know you took it from me."

"I was a bastard to betray you like that," he said.

"Yes, you were."

"Once I figured that out, I hurried back here." He squeezed her hand.

"So you didn't give it to anyone?"

"I gave it to you." He showed her the empty vial.

"You sacrificed your dream to save me," she said.

"You're my dream." He shook his head. "I was too stupid to realize it, though."

"But what of your lifelong goal? The ultimate proof of Atlantis?"

"You're lying here bleeding all over my expensive rug, and you're going to argue with me?" he said.

She gave him a weak smile. "I just want to make sure you know what you want."

Her steady breathing and strong heartbeat brought new vitality to him. For the first time in years, he felt truly alive. He kissed his way across her face. Blood still oozed from the wound on her cheek, but it was beginning to clot. "There is nothing I want more than for you to be my wife."

"I don't know. You're quite a lot of trouble," she said.

"Says the woman whose destiny involved a world-ending prophecy."

She smiled. "Yes. I would love to be your wife."

"I love you, Sabine."

"You don't know how I've longed to hear you say that," she said. She tried to sit up, but winced from the pain. "I think I might need a few stitches."

Her aunts, who had been standing behind Max crying, began to laugh.

"I'll get the kit," Calliope said.

"I thought you left," Sabine said.

"You were in danger," Agnes said. "I could feel it. So we rushed back."

"What happened to the Chosen One?" Sabine asked. "Is he dead?"

"Yes, you killed him." Max shook his head. "I broke the spear off and pulled it out of both of you."

Calliope came back in with the basket, but Agnes stopped her from moving forward. "Give them a moment," she said.

"It's finally over," he said.

"I love you, Maxwell Barrett." Sabine reached up and cupped his cheek. "I hated the thought of dying without telling you."

"Well, then you'll simply have to make certain I know that every day for the rest of my life," he said.

"I promise."

Prologue

━━━━━━━━━━━━━━━━━◦❧◦❧◦━━━━━━━━━━━━━━━━━

Loch Ness, Scotland, 1881

Thunder crashed, and fat, heavy raindrops pelted Graeme Langford as he plunged the oars into the cold, murky depths of Loch Ness. The muscles in his arms burned from rowing. The storm made the loch choppy and his work more difficult. Still he rowed.

He could see the rocky beach ahead in the distance, and the hills that rose behind the shore. Somewhere in those hills, he'd find the abbey. A foolish, wealthy American had recently purchased the crumbling estate and intended to restore it to its former glory. They were supposed to start construction next week, so Graeme had little time to find what he sought before it was too late.

The small boat rocked against the angry waves, and Graeme fought against the current. His progress was slow and he was damp to his bones. Clearly life in London was making him soft. Eventually he made his way to the beach. He jumped out and pulled the boat onto the shore.

The last ribbons of light hid behind the storm's clouds, limiting visibility, but he'd climbed these hills often enough to do so in limited light. He secured his bag across his body and started up into the hills. The Highlands weren't mountains; he'd seen true mountains in Spain. Still, the rocky hillsides were treacherous, so he minded his steps carefully. The rain slowed and the thunder softened as the storm faded into the distance.

The crisp autumn air filled Graeme's lungs as he climbed up the hill. As raw and untamed as parts of Scotland remained, he loved this land. Loved the history and the rough terrain, loved the people and their lore. Half of him rightfully belonged here, his mother's blood, but it was his father's English blood that ruled his life. Four years earlier, when his father had fallen ill and died, Graeme had taken his place as the Duke of Rothmore. And he did his duty as an English lord, though he longed for time to spend in his beloved Scotland.

It was what drove his quest, his burning desire to find and restore what rightfully belonged to Scotland—the Stone of Destiny, a biblical relic that held mysterious powers. It had belonged to the Scottish monarchy for hundreds of years before it had been stolen by the English, though Graeme had recently come to believe that the stone the English took was a counterfeit. He intended to be the one to locate the original stone. According to his latest research, there was a book he needed to complete his quest. And it lay somewhere within the dilapidated walls of this old, abandoned abbey.

As if his mind had conjured the image, a massive stone structure lay before him, nestled into the next hill. No wonder the monks had left this desolate and secluded location. But Graeme was not alone. The workers were already here, or at least their equipment was, as it littered the hillside. They were early, which meant he just might be too late.

With night falling, it seemed unlikely the men would still be working, so Graeme crept closer. His listened intently for the sound of voices, but heard nothing. Finally he reached the inner sanctum of the abbey. He pulled at the huge arched wooden door and it opened with an echoing creak. Darkness surrounded him. From his bag, he withdrew a simple beeswax candle and lit it. He unfolded a map and glanced at the rendition. The candlelight flickered as he studied the drawing, an illustration of this very structure—or, more precisely, of what lay beneath it.

He stood in what had once been the chapel. Time and thieves had stolen the stained glass from the windows and now they stood as skeletal remains of the once-glorious room. Tools and construction supplies lay up against the wall. He crossed into the next room and there found scaffolding between two pillars.

He moved past the large columns, through the arched doorway, deeper into the ruins. When he'd heard someone had purchased the old building, Graeme had wondered if it was for residential purposes or if someone else sought the treasures that were hidden beneath. So far all the construction efforts looked to be here on the main level.

It had been nearly a hundred years since there had been monks in this abbey, perhaps longer. But legend had it those men of the cloth had once been guardians to many of the church's ancient treasures—lost canons, the Spear of Christ, and the item that Graeme now sought: the *Magi's Book of Wisdom*, an ancient text rumored to contain the most accurate description of the Stone of Destiny.

Hot wax dripped onto Graeme's hand, burning and then congealing on his skin. The hall narrowed, then stopped at a staircase. Graeme wound his way down the spiral stone stairs. He ended up in another hallway that led to several doors. The hidden chamber was another level beneath the abbey, dug deep into the bowels of the hill.

Graeme walked through the sleeping quarters, one room leading to another, twisting and turning through hallways until he came to a dead end. Damnation, he must have made a wrong turn somewhere along the way. He knew he needed to go down, below this level of the abbey, but he hadn't come across any stairs. He pulled out the illustration again and studied the image. His destination was a large room filled with books and treasure, where monks had once guarded the entryway. He'd found this bloody picture in the journal of an old man, a village priest who had a penchant for folklore.

A short burst of wind swirled around him. His candle died. Darkness enclosed him. He dug into his bag to retrieve another, then struck a match on the stone wall beside him. The match flickered to life with a spark. The new candle illuminated the space in front of him, then the flame died, as if someone had blown it out. There was air coming from somewhere.

He leaned against the wall, moving his hands against the cold stone, but found nothing. This entire search could prove futile. He moved his feet against the wall; down by his boot, he noticed something protruding from the wall. He knelt and ran his hand over the protrusion. It was a lever. He pushed it, shoving it against the stone. Something below him shifted. The floor separated and then he was moving. Downward. It was a lift. Evidently the monks had been rather advanced in their technology.

He just hoped this ancient thing worked this well going back up.

The stone chute surrounded him, scraping against his shoulders as he continued to descend, but in the darkness he still could see nothing. Chains creaked and groaned beneath him. Then the platform jerked to a stop. Graeme waited until all the noises ceased before he stepped forward. He relit his candle, and to his right, he found a wall sconce with a tallow-dipped torch. Once lit, it illuminated the area around him. He stood on a dirt floor, and directly in front of him lay a deep chasm, an underground gorge nestled between the hills.

It was far too dark to see what lay beyond the gorge, but if the illustration was correct, across the expanse he would find a chamber. He stepped to the edge of the cliff and stared out into the darkened abyss. How was he to get across? He moved slowly to his left, searching for any sign of a bridge. When his boot scuffed over something, he kicked the dirt out of the way and found a rope stretching out from his feet across the canyon. There was another rope above his head attached firmly to a metal loop anchored to the stone wall. He pulled on it and it slackened, lowering the rope until it was about chest high.

He inhaled slowly. This was not the sort of bridge he'd been hoping for. He hated heights. Having nothing but an aged rope between him and the nothingness below did not evoke confidence. But he was running out of time. If he didn't find that book now, it would likely be lost forever.

It would be impossible to cross the rope bridge while holding the candle, so he pinched the wick between his fingers and dropped the candle into his bag. The torch lit the area behind him, but once he stepped out on the rope, he'd be shrouded in darkness. He checked his bag to make certain it was secure, then put one boot onto the rope. It gave beneath his weight, but held firm to the anchor on the other side.

Without another thought, he took a step with his other foot and grabbed hold of the balance rope. Slowly he began to make his way across, sliding one foot to the left and then following with the other. The rope swayed and moved, jostling him around as he crossed the canyon. What the hell had these monks been thinking? They must have guarded some valuable pieces to go to such lengths to protect them.

His eyes tried to grow accustomed to the blackness around him, but with no light to be found, he still could see nothing. He kept moving. Finally his foot hit against the floor on the other side. He'd made it.

He stepped onto a ledge. Quickly he relit his candle and found a series of torches along the wall. They illuminated a hallway. He crouched as he moved through the space, his height a hindrance in the small area. He lit more torches along the way.

A room opened before him, and he stepped down into it. A large, not-quite-circular space, it was filled with trunks and chests and stone tables covered with a variety of items, from goblets to jewels. Alcoves carved into the stone wall held other, smaller trunks. He began his search, opening the lid of every trunk and rummaging through the contents, going over every surface and examining each item. If the rest of these priceless treasures remained, then certainly that book was here somewhere.

One of the smaller trunks contained every gemstone he could imagine, and another overflowed with gold pieces. If that American did know about these treasures, his wealth would more than double overnight. He pulled a trunk out of one of the wall niches and bats flew at him. He ducked. Dammed vile creatures.

Inside the trunk, he found a map, which he tossed into his bag in case it proved useful. He searched one trunk after another until he finally came to one that was filled with books. He squatted and picked up each book, carefully checking the title as well as glancing at the inside text. He came across two that might be of use to some of his friends at Solomon's and shoved them both into his bag. Then he saw it, a small leather-bound volume encrusted with jewels. Inside he found Hebrew text. The *Magi's Book of Wisdom*.

He extinguished the torches, then took one last look at all the glittering treasure before stepping back onto the rope bridge. He'd found what he'd come for. The rope beneath his feet wobbled. Somewhere to his right, he heard metal scrape against something.

Then the lower rope disappeared. His hands held firmly to the balance rope as he dropped. His shoulders tore at the sudden burden of all his weight, but he would not let go. As quickly as he could, he started moving to his left. One hand moved painstakingly over the other.

He listened as he moved, waiting to hear the sound of fraying rope, but all he could hear was his own heavy breath. His heart pounded. Sweat coated his hands, and he prayed he wouldn't lose his grip. The light to his left grew closer.

Finally he reached the other side. He fell onto the dirt floor and lay there to steady his breathing. He was one step closer to finding the Stone of Destiny.

THE DISH

Where authors give you the inside scoop!

♥ ♥ ♥ ♥ ♥ ♥ ♥ ♥ ♥ ♥ ♥ ♥ ♥ ♥

From the desk of Margaret Mallory

Dear Readers,

Am I unkind? I made Sir James Rayburn wait until the third book in my All the King's Men trilogy to get his own story. First, as a toddler, he watched his mother find love with her KNIGHT OF DESIRE, William FitzAlan. Then, as a young squire, he played a supporting role to his uncle Stephen, the KNIGHT OF PLEASURE, in his quest for true love. And now, when I finally give this brave and honorable knight his own book, I let the girl he loves stomp on his heart in the prologue.

After that unfortunate experience, all Jamie Rayburn wants—or so he says—is a virtuous wife who will keep a quiet, ordered home waiting for him while he is off fighting. Instead, I give him the bold and beautiful Linnet, whose determination to avenge her family is bound to provoke endless tumult and trouble. Worse, this heroine is the very lady who stomped on Jamie's heart in his youth.

Why would I do this to our gallant knight? After he has shown such patience, why not reward him with the sweet, undemanding heroine he requested?

Although that heroine might prove to be a trifle dull, she would be content to gaze raptly at our hero as he told tales of his victories by the hearth.

Truly, I meant to give Jamie a softer, easier woman. But when I tried to write Jamie's story, Linnet decided she *had* to be there. And when Linnet sets her mind to something, believe me, it's best not to stand in her way.

Besides, Linnet was right. Who better to save Jamie from a staid and tedious life? No other woman stirs Jamie's passion as she does. And what passion! If our handsome knight must contend with murderous plots, court intrigues, and a few sword-wielding sorcerers before he can win his heart's desire, then so be it.

I am sure Jamie forgives me. Our KNIGHT OF PASSION knows a happy ending is worth the wait— and it's all the more satisfying if it doesn't come easy.

I hope you enjoy reading Jamie and Linnet's adventurous love story as much as I enjoyed writing it!

Margaret Mallory

www.margaretmallory.com

♥ ♥ ♥ ♥ ♥ ♥ ♥ ♥ ♥ ♥ ♥ ♥ ♥ ♥ ♥

From the desk of Cara Elliott

Dear Readers,

Oh, dear. Just when all the gossip about Lady Sheffield and the Mad, Bad Earl of Hadley (you may read their story in TO SIN WITH A SCOUNDREL)—has died down, the Circle of Sin series is once again in danger of stirring up scandal. This time, it's Lady Sheffield's fellow scholar, the lovely and enigmatic Alessandra della Giamatti, who is caught up in a web of lies and intrigue.

Well, luckily for her, Hadley's good friend, the rakish "Black Jack" Pierson, comes to the rescue in TO SURRENDER TO A ROGUE (available now). A decorated war hero, Jack is also a talented painter . . . not to mention highly skilled in the art of seduction. (Apparently, he is intimately acquainted with all the creative ways a man can use a soft sable brush to . . . er, I really ought to allow you to discover those colorful details for yourself.)

At first blush, archaeology might not seem like a subject that inspires heated passions. However, I chose to plot my story around an excavation of ancient Roman ruins in England because I have always been fascinated by how, throughout history, the idea of buried treasure has resulted in both serious scholarship and serious skullduggery. In Regency times, the "science" of archaeology was in its infancy. Napoleon deserves credit for taking a host of scholars with him to Egypt, along with his invading army, and encouraging them to preserve artifacts of the past for academic study. On the English side, Lord Elgin carefully crated up marbles from the Parthenon in Athens and removed them to London, where they became the nucleus of the British Museum. (Today, there is quite a vociferous debate between Greece and Great Britain about whether the artistic treasures were, in fact, looted from their rightful home—but that is a topic I shall leave to the diplomats to decide.)

In TO SURRENDER TO A ROGUE, things really heat up as the digging begins outside the spa town of Bath, which is, in fact, set on the site of an ancient Roman outpost. Someone is threatening to expose a scandalous secret from Alessandra's past if she doesn't betray all the principles she holds dear. Does she dare confide in Jack? She has good reason not to trust handsome rogues, so it's no wonder that she views him as dangerous. *Oh so dangerous.* But if ever a lady needed a hero to fight for her honor . . .

And speaking of dangerous men, Alessandra's cousin—that unrepentant rake otherwise known as the Conte of Como—is rattling his own sword . . . so to speak. Not content with playing a secondary role in my first two books, Marco saunters into an adventure of his own in TO TEMPT A RAKE (available in winter 2011). As you know, he is a rather arrogant, abrasive fellow, and he is used to having females fall at his feet. So when the free-spirited Kate Woodbridge—the most rebellious member of the Circle of Sin—resists his flirtations at a country-house party, he can't help but be intrigued. Like her fellow "sinners," Kate is both beautiful and brainy—and hiding a dark secret that occurred in her past. When things take a sinister turn at her grandfather's estate, seduction is no longer a game, and she is forced to decide whether a rakehell rascal can be trusted . . .

Please visit me at www.caraelliott.com, where you can sneak a tantalizing peek at all three books in my Circle of Sin series.

Cara Elliott

♥ ♥ ♥ ♥ ♥ ♥ ♥ ♥ ♥ ♥ ♥ ♥ ♥ ♥

From the desk of Robyn DeHart

Dear Readers,

Who out there isn't fascinated by the lost continent of Atlantis? The legend is as compelling as Jack the Ripper and El Dorado, those unsolved mysteries that have been perplexing people for hundreds of years. But it was Atlantis that captured my attention for the second book in my Legend Hunters series, DESIRE ME.

With Atlantis, you have a little bit of everything—Greek mythology, hidden treasures, and utopian societies. I couldn't help but add my own flair to the myth and make my Atlantis home to the fabled fountain of youth. Add in an ancient prophecy, a lost map, and Sabine Tobias, a heroine who is a living, breathing descendant of the Atlanteans—and you've got a recipe for adventure coupled with plenty of trouble.

But what does any damsel in distress need? A good hero. A sexy-as-hell, smart-mouthed hero who is, shall we say, good with his hands. That is, he's handy to have around when you're stuck in an underground chamber or when you need to slip into an old estate without being seen. Enter Maxwell Barrett, legend hunter extraordinaire and expert on all things Atlantis.

With DESIRE ME, I return to my series about Solomon's, the exclusive gentleman's club of legend hunters. This book was, at times, harrowing to write, but not nearly as dangerous for me, the writer, who sat safely at home in my jammies with my faithful kitties to keep me company. Poor Max and Sabine, though, are on a perilous race against time, trying to solve the ancient prophecy before a nasty villain destroys them both. But they find themselves neck-deep in trouble about as often as they find themselves wrapped in each other's arms.

Visit my website, www.RobynDeHart.com, for contests, excerpts, and more.

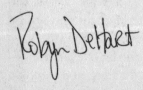

*Want to know more about romances at
Grand Central Publishing and Forever?
Get the scoop online!*

GRAND CENTRAL PUBLISHING'S
ROMANCE HOMEPAGE

Visit us at www.hachettebookgroup.com/romance
for all the latest news, reviews, and chapter excerpts!

NEW AND UPCOMING TITLES

Each month we feature our new titles
and reader favorites.

CONTESTS AND GIVEAWAYS

We give away galleys, autographed copies,
and all kinds of fun stuff.

AUTHOR INFO

You'll find bios, articles, and links to personal
websites for all your favorite authors—and
so much more!

THE BUZZ

Sign up for our monthly romance newsletter,
and be the first to read all about it!